WRITE
MY
WRONGS

DISCLAIMER

This novel is a work of fiction. Any mention of real people, places, companies, and historical events is used fictitiously. The contents of this book serve as a product of the author's imagination, and any resemblance to actual places, persons, or events is entirely coincidental.

Forever dedicated to the ones looking for the strength to right their wrongs.
It's not too late to change the road you're on.

CHAPTER ONE

EREN

"You can do this," I say to the man in front of me. "You can fucking do this."

His hair is cut short and bleached platinum-blonde. Tattoos cover his skin, from the top of his neck to his fingertips. The flickering lights illuminate his deep-brown eyes–eyes longing for the motivation to do what he's about to do.

The man is broken. He always has been and always will be. His tattoos tell his story. It's a story of repeated mistakes and self-destructive patterns.

How is he still alive? Will he ever change?

I reach a hand toward the man, but I can't touch him. My hand is stopped by the mirror between us. The man in the mirror is me, and I spend every day wishing he wasn't.

I shouldn't be here, staring at my reflection in the bathroom of a restaurant in Manhattan. I need to be out there in 10 minutes, but my anxiety keeps me from moving.

Cold water.

I turn on the faucet, and it spews out freezing cold water. Between quick breaths, I splash it against my face.

"You can do this."

I grip the sink to keep myself from grabbing the vial of cocaine in my pocket. I promised myself I'd throw it away earlier today, but I couldn't get myself to. It's not that I'm addicted. I just need it to…

"Get your ass on stage!" a hoarse voice shouts from behind me. The voice belongs to the restaurant owner, who comes trudging into the bathroom. "You don't play, you don't get your fucking money."

"I need that money," I say to the restaurant owner through the reflection.

But I can't perform.

"And I need someone to play music for the restaurant." He pulls his pants up over his gut and lifts his sweaty chin. "Last time I'm gonna tell you, kid."

My eyes flick from his eyes to my own as I stare into my reflection again. "I'll be out in a minute."

The owner rolls his eyes, wipes the sweat off his face, then throws the door open. When he's gone, it's silent.

"I'm asking you to change your ways…" I say to the man in the mirror. "After tonight." I reach into my pocket for the vial of coke.

With every step I take in the direction of the tiny stage, my head grows lighter. I thought the coke would help with my anxiety, but it only made it worse. I can hear my heartbeat in my head. My legs are growing weaker by the second.

The restaurant's music cuts out as I step onto the stage, and the sudden silence forces heads to turn… toward me. How ironic–being an aspiring singer with a case of severe stage fright. This isn't my first time performing, it's just my first time performing in front of people. Behind closed doors, I can sing, write, and strum like I'm serenading a stadium of goddesses. In public, it's a whole different story.

There was a point in my life when I was confident in my singing. I was 10 years old, sitting in the back seat of my mom's car, windows rolled down and music blaring. "Sing it, baby!" she would shout, and I'd watch her smile at me through the rearview mirror. She looked like an angel. But I'm no longer in the car with her, and she's no longer here with me.

Press *Fast Forward* to 18 years later, and here I am on stage without her. Each time I perform, it goes down the same way. First, I get afraid. Then, I'm petrified. Then, I keep thinking I could never live without her by my side.

I wrap the guitar strap over my shoulder, thinking once I hold the guitar, my stage fright will subside. My fingers are slippery along the wooden neck, and the guitar pick shakes in my right hand.

When I turn to face the microphone, I misjudge the distance, and my chin makes contact. A high-pitched ringing sound echoes through the silent restaurant, bringing even more attention to my brewing panic attack.

Dammit.

I grab the mic and bring it close to my lips, saying, "Hi. M-my name is Eren Gratis… and I'm… this is…"

This is fucking embarrassing. That's what this is.

The lighting in the restaurant is dim, but I can still see the cringed-out expressions of the guests. I don't blame them.

"You're hot!" a girl shouts from the back of the restaurant. Muffled laughter follows the comment, and I see that it's coming from a table of four.

I let out a nervous laugh.

Say something. Or play something?

"NEXT!" a man shouts from the same table. More laughter follows the comment as they continue heckling me.

The spotlight suddenly becomes too much to bear. I try to catch my breath, but it escapes me.

You can't do this, I think to myself. *You damn fool. You'll never be able to finish what Mom started. You're an imposter. A fraud. You don't deserve to be on stage after what you've done to her.*

The crowd's whispers bring me back to the present moment. I've been standing here breathing into the mic for who-knows-how-long.

"I'm sorry," I exhale into the microphone. Little do they know, it's not them I'm apologizing to.

I'm sorry, Mom.

I drop my guitar and make a beeline for the exit. When I shove the doors open, I'm embraced by the chilling breeze of the night. I'm overwhelmed by the city sounds–cars beeping, homeless people shouting, herds of people walking in different directions. All of the sounds become one, and I can't find a rhythm.

I shove my hands in my pockets and walk into the alley beside the restaurant. There's nothing but a dumpster and my motor-cycle, which is propped up near the restaurant's back door.

"Dammit!"

I kick the dumpster out of sheer frustration.

BAM!

I'm angry that nothing has changed after all these years. I'm frustrated with myself for submitting to this never-ending cycle…

I book a gig.

I'm called to the stage.

Nothing comes out.

Repeat.

"*Stick to writing songs*," people in the music industry tell me. "*Leave the performing to the professionals.*"

With my back pressed against the brick wall, I lower myself to the ground, burying my face in my palms. It blows my mind how, for the longest time, I've been numb to every feeling but *ashamed*–ashamed for the wrongs I've committed. I'd rather feel nothing at all… because fuck feeling ashamed.

I run my hands over my head and let out a deep breath. It brings me peace, knowing that most musicians are conflicted like me. Maybe that's what makes it okay to indulge in the vices we carry. Being conflicted. Being broken.

I don't know a rockstar who wasn't addicted to drugs, sex, fame, or all the above. And I've got one of those vices at my disposal right now. I pull the coke vial out of my pocket and look at it for a moment.

I already broke my promise to quit today, and I could really use the confidence boost, so I do a bump. I feel the adrenaline rush through me, giving me the will to live until I need the next bump. I pull out a small flask and lean back against the wall.

"Close your eyes, Mom," I whisper toward the heavens. "I'm not getting wasted by myself in an alley again."

Before I can take a sip of my whiskey, a voice sends me into a panic. "I thought I was the only one who talks to myself," the voice says.

I look left and see a silhouette standing at the end of the alley. It takes a few steps closer until it becomes a girl–a stunning girl–standing under the light shining from above the restaurant's back door. She's petite, her black heels making her stand taller than she actually is. Her hands are in the pockets of her pea coat that she tightens around her body.

"I wasn't talking to myself," I exhale.

I was talking to my dead mom, which is probably much more concerning.

"So, I guess *I am* the only one who talks to myself," the girl replies. Her eyes trail to my bike. "Is this your motorcycle?"

"Yeah," I reply dryly.

She nods, taking a couple of steps around the motorcycle to get a better look. Her hair is a beautiful auburn color with strands of gold tied up into a top bun. Her curious eyes flick toward me, and all I see is the color blue–a piercing blue–so blue, they'd make the ocean envious. She looks at me for a moment, pondering what to say. I do the same.

"What're you drinking?" she asks, pointing at the flask in my hand.

While her attention is on the flask, I subtly slip my coke vial back into my pocket. "It's whiskey. You want some?"

The girl scrunches her face, and I can't help but find it cute. "That stuff tastes like gasoline," she mutters.

I smirk. "You don't like the taste of gasoline?"

She giggles, and when she relaxes her shoulders, I catch a glimpse of the diamonds wrapped around her neck. She's wearing $30,000 like it's nothing.

Suddenly, the necklaces disappear behind her coat as she covers them.

Shit. She totally caught me staring.

"Do you usually approach random guys in dark alleys?" I tease, changing the subject.

The girl smiles, then tucks a golden strand of hair behind her ear. "Believe it or not, this is my first time." She takes a long step forward, now standing over me.

The light casts from above, bringing out the details on her face. I don't think I've ever seen a more beautiful girl–the way her freckles decorate the tops of her cheeks. Her full lips look fragile at the touch, naturally parted. Her ocean eyes portray a sense of inno-cence as if she's been protected from the injustices of the world her whole life. She's pure–angelic.

Her voice is soft and a bit raspy as she says, "I wanted to apologize for what my friends were saying back there–okay… my boyfriend was actually one of them–so I guess I'm sorry for my friends and my boyfriend. Look, regardless… they shouldn't have shouted anything at you. So, sorry."

Her voice.

I could fall in love with her voice alone.

"Don't be sorry," I sigh. "I wasn't gonna bring myself to sing anyway."

The girl blinks at me. "What do you mean?"

"I, uh…" My eyes trail down to the flask in my hand. "I have pretty bad stage fright."

She bursts out laughing until she realizes I'm serious. "Oh, shit! Oh my! You weren't joking."

Her state of genuine shock makes me chuckle.

"I'm so sorry. That was rude," she says. "I just–usually singers who perform on stages don't have stage fright because, well, you know… the whole 'performing on stage' thing is all singers do."

"Right," I reply, holding back a laugh. "I'm working on that."

"Maybe you should try picturing people in their underwear. Isn't that supposed to help?"

I wish she didn't say that because now I'm picturing her in her underwear. A black thong to go with her black heels. Or maybe the thong is a dark-reddish color like her hair.

"I'll make sure to try that next time," I say coolly.

Unlike other girls I come across, she effortlessly holds my gaze, which makes me uneasy. I don't know if there's much more she wants to say. She already apologized. At this point, she's lingering like there's something else on her mind.

"Do you sing covers of songs? Or your own songs?" she asks.

"I usually sing my own songs," I reply. "When I'm not having a panic attack like I just did."

The girl grins. I realize that I've forgotten about all the shit that was on my mind earlier. In the brief time she's stood over me, she's brought me peace, but a type of peace that's foreign to me.

"I sort of… kind of… write music myself," she murmurs, avoiding eye contact.

"Really?"

"I do! Is that shocking to you?"

My eyes trail from her slicked top bun down to her diamond-studded neck–her straight-edged pea coat and the black slacks wrapped tightly around her legs. I clear my throat. "Please don't take offense to this, but… you don't really strike me as a songwriter."

The girl closes her eyes and nods her head. "What do I strike you as?"

I study her for a moment. The innocence in her eyes. The thousands of dollars wrapping her hourglass frame. "You strike me as a rich girl who doesn't get out too much," I admit.

She rolls her eyes. "I wish you were wrong. But I swear, I do write songs. It's always been my dream to write songs for singers."

Her words are soft-spoken, but they hit me like a bass drop. Based on her appearance, she's too polished and perfect to be making a couple of grand here and there writing lyrics for singers who wipe their asses with songwriters like myself.

A part of me wants to warn her. I want to tell her how lonely the songwriting part of the music industry can be. Because it's true. I should know. I've wallowed in it for the past 10 years, only to be left wanting more.

"Life is short." I shrug. "If it's your dream to be a songwriter, then *chase it*."

Her eyes narrow, and her head tilts as if she doesn't understand what I said.

"Just *chase it*?" she asks.

I lift myself off the ground. As I stand straight, our eyes lock.

She looks up at me, either in shock at the sudden height difference or because I told her to chase her dream in the simplest way possible.

Was it the wrong thing to say? I only meant to be supportive.

The girl stares into my eyes, and I stare right back into hers. The two of us are fixated on each other, content with this moment we share. Suddenly, my stage fright becomes conquerable. The alcohol and drugs have no hold on me. My world becomes somewhat bearable for once.

"Harlow!" a man shouts from the end of the alley. "How long does it take to say sorry?!"

Harlow.

Her name is music to my ears.

Three silhouettes funnel into the alley. As the silhouettes step toward the light, they become two guys around the same height as me and a girl slightly taller than Harlow. One of the guys drunkenly throws his arm around Harlow as a way of proving they're in a relationship.

He must be the boyfriend.

The other guy and girl are holding hands, remaining a few steps behind.

A large hand makes itself known inches away from my chest. "Jordan," the boyfriend says. I shake Jordan's hand, and his grip tightens while his other hand grips Harlow's shoulder. He glares at me as he mutters, "I'm Harlow's boyfriend."

I force a smile, our hands still locked. "I'm Eren."

"Anything you wanna say?" the other guy asks the girl he's holding hands with.

"I'm Talia," she says with a smile. The guy nudges her shoulder. Talia rolls her eyes. "Okay, okay. I'm sorry for calling you hot while you were on stage." As if her words have been rehearsed, she adds, "I don't actually think you're hot. I am in a happy relationship with my boyfriend, Spud."

Her boyfriend offers his hand and introduces himself. "I'm Spud."

There's an awkward silence between the five of us until Jordan says, "Whelp! The apologies have been issued. Good luck with your little music career, Eren. Here's some advice. If you're gonna get on stage to sing, it might help to actually sing."

Harlow opens her mouth to speak, but Jordan pulls her toward the end of the alley before she can say anything. Spud and Talia follow, and I'm left with my lonely self.

When Harlow disappears around the corner, my problems make themselves known again. I embarrassed myself tonight in front of Harlow. I'm never going to get over my fear of performing. Not to mention, I'm running low on cash.

I take a sip of whiskey, feeling it burn my throat. Chills run down my arms, and I feel a buzz coming on quicker than I usually do. I picture the whiskey mixing with the adrenaline rush Harlow gave me. Her presence alone made me feel something I've never felt before—a feeling worth writing about.

I take another sip of whiskey and pull my leather notebook out of my backpack. I lower myself against the brick wall and begin writing.

I'm afraid to fly,
I'm afraid to fall,
I'm afraid of love,
But for you, I think I might try this,

I'm afraid of the truth,
I'm afraid to be hurt,
I'm afraid of you,
But for you, I think I might try this,

I can't fake it, love's calling,
When I face you, I'm all in,
Now I'm frightened, I'm falling,

When you walked my way,
When I saw your face,
Then I felt a change,
Now for you, I think I might try this,

Then I heard your name,
You're the song I'll replay,
For the nights and days,
For you, I think I might try this.

I title the song, "*Love is Calling*," then slide my notebook into my backpack.

It's been a couple of months since I was paid for the last song I wrote. While I've always written decent lyrics, the lyrics I've written never resonated with me because the songs are for other artists. The songs are never about my life, my experiences, *me*.

I have lyrics in my notebook that make up another song, though. A song to be sung by me and only me. Maybe if I ever get over my nerves, I'll be able to share these words with the people willing to listen. Until then, I take another shot of whiskey, and I ride.

My motorcycle roars under my legs as I swerve through the city traffic, left then right. The smoky aftertaste of the whiskey lingers on my lips as I claim the road ahead. My eyes are focused on the gaps I seize between cars, but my mind is fixated on the thought of Harlow—her voice, her eyes, her lips, her presence—and that worries me.

This shouldn't be happening.

I fight off the thought of her, remembering I can't afford to get attached. A connection like the one I just shared with Harlow is bad news for a guy like me. Since I was 10 years old, I've lived by my golden rule: *Don't get attached.*

It's simple. Attachments lead to love and love leads to heartbreak. And my heart can't be broken if I never give it to anybody. I learned my lesson the hard way when I was 10, and I prefer to learn my lessons once.

This is why I ride.

Thankfully, my songwriting career allows me to bounce from one town to the next. The record label covers all of my living expenses. They ship my motorcycle wherever I end up, which is all I really need besides the clothes on my back and my notebook. Depending on the project I'm writing–whether it's a song or a full album–the record label will even convert the place I'm staying at into my own studio.

There's only one problem. There is hardly any leftover cash when I finish each project. Don't get me wrong, I choose passion over a paycheck any day. Moving from one town to the next gives me the freedom I live for.

If I sit still for too long, I'm afraid what's chasing me will finally catch up. So I continue to throw myself into life's constant current. There's no telling what tomorrow will bring, which gives me hope that one day… I'll be able to right my wrongs.

♫ ♫ ♫

"Wake up," a voice demands.

I struggle to open my eyes. It takes a while for my vision to adjust. I don't know how long I've been asleep. All I know is that it was a deep sleep and now the hangover is kicking in.

"Wake up." The voice is harsh and low-pitched. "You're on my shit-list, Eren."

The world suddenly goes black as a shirt is thrown over my face. I recognize the voice as Blake's, my manager–well, friend and manager. He became my songwriting manager 10 years ago. Since then, we've become pretty good friends. Good enough for me to have passed out on his couch last night.

I lift the shirt off my face and sit up on the couch. "My head hurts," I groan.

"Good," Blake snaps. He's standing in front of me, pointing out the trail of clothes leading from the front door of his apartment to the couch I'm sitting on. "Are you kidding me with this?"

I do a neck roll and stretch out my arms. "They're just clothes! I'll pick 'em up right now."

"Not the clothes. *This*." Blake holds up my coke vial, which I could've sworn was in my pocket. It was in my pocket… of my jeans… that are on the floor… in the middle of the living room. "You can't leave this shit around my floor. I have a one-year-old who can walk now, and he walks everywhere. God forbid he thinks your cocaine is Fun Dip."

I reach for the vial, but he pulls it away. "You said you were gonna quit it with this 'rockstar' bullshit."

"I'm troubled," I reply, successfully snatching the vial from his hand this time.

Blake rolls his eyes. "We're all troubled, Eren."

"I'll get rid of it," I lie. "Don't worry about me."

"You make it hard not to," Blake sighs, then heads for the refrigerator and pulls out a tray of eggs.

I pull my pants on, slip the vial back into my pocket, and sink back into the couch. "What time is it?"

"Almost 10." He tosses me an Advil bottle. "Where were you last night?"

Before I consider telling him the truth, I hold my tongue. Blake doesn't know I'm trying to get into the performing side of the music business. I'd rather keep it that way, considering he signed me exclusively as a songwriter, not a singer. I'm the best writer he represents, so I don't want him to fear losing the best he's got.

"I went on a date. Some Italian restaurant in the Lower East Side."

"Was it Angelo's?" he asks while scrambling the eggs.

How the hell does he know the name of the restaurant I was at?

"Y-yeah," I stutter. "How'd you know that?"

"My kid-sister is always over there with her little college friends."

I fill a glass of water and take three Advil, then another for good measure. A pitter-patter sound comes from the hall across the living room, and out comes Blake's one-year-old son, Charlie.

With a smile on my face, I say, "Hi, Charlie!"

All I see is Charlie's big head and googly eyes peeking out from behind the kitchen table. His eyes are a bright blue, and his hair is an auburn color—a spitting image of Blake. Charlie smiles, and his cheeks are so chubby he can't even keep his eyes open when he laughs.

I crouch a few feet away from Charlie and spread my arms. After taking a few wobbly steps, he hugs me. My heart melts… every… time. It's not often a guy like me gets this kind of attention from people, especially kids. A 28-year-old man covered in tattoos from the neck down with an array of ear piercings, the encounters usually happen the same way. People get scared and turn away, or they stare at me like I'm some sort of zoo exhibit.

I don't blame them, though. Society has embedded the idea in people's minds that guys who look like me are criminals. Society hasn't corrupted Charlie yet, which is why he treats me as an equal.

"Any word on new projects?" I ask. "I feel bad staying here as long as I have."

"You're fine. It's only been a week," Blake replies while setting the table. "I'll check when I go into the office tomorrow. It's been nice having you around to watch Charlie during the days I go in anyway. I'm saving a fortune by not hiring a nanny."

"Maybe I should start charging you," I tease.

I sit in my usual seat and feel a pit in my stomach when I see the three place settings at a four-person table. Blake lifts Charlie and squeezes him into the high chair across from me, then claims the seat at the table's edge between us. To my left is the empty chair.

Blake catches me looking at it. There's a brief moment of silence before he says, "I'm doing better. In a couple of weeks, it'll be a year since she… you know."

I nod. "Time is the best healer," I say hollowly.

If I believed that were true, I wouldn't be carrying around a flask and a vial of cocaine everywhere I go. Blake picks up on my discomfort and begins scooping eggs into his mouth. Charlie flings his arms around. Occasionally, one of his blueberries manages to make it between his lips.

"How're you doing on cash?" Blake asks without looking up from his plate.

"Running low," I sigh, then smile. "Nothing new."

Blake laughs under his breath. "I'm headed up to my parents' place today. I'll stop by the bank on my way back."

I watch him run a hand back through his hair, which is usually thick and wavy, but it's slicked because it's Sunday, and Sundays are when Blake visits his parents for their weekly "Sunday brunch" up in the Hamptons. He dresses the part in his pastel-blue sweater, cropped khaki slacks, and boat shoes. I've never been up to the Hamptons, but if everyone up there looks like the Ken Doll sitting next to me right now, I'll probably keep my distance.

Blake is always rolling his eyes about visiting his parents. He says these brunches are more like business meetings than they are family gatherings. I couldn't imagine being a part of a family that's compared to a business, but Blake does a great job painting the picture for me.

It's not like I have much to refer to anyway. I've been alone since I was a kid. Blake and Charlie would be the closest thing I have to a family, but I have to keep them at arm's length because of my golden rule that seems to keep me going: *Don't get attached.*

CHAPTER TWO

HARLOW

Eren's words play in my mind like a broken record… *"If it's your dream to be a songwriter, then chase it."*

I can't get the words out of my head.

Hardly anybody knows that it's my childhood dream to be a songwriter. Since I can remember, that dream has been lingering in the back of my mind, waiting to be pursued. I've always stuck to what I know because I'm good with what I know. And I don't know songwriting. I just know that I love to write songs.

"Can you turn up the music?" I call out to Francis, our personal driver.

"Yes, Ms. Harlow," Francis replies.

He presses a few buttons on the screen, and *"Can't Stop"* by Red Hot Chili Peppers plays on the radio. As he turns up the music, Talia and I roll down the windows. The ocean breeze fills the car as we make our way up the coast to my parents' estate.

Jordan and Spud roll their eyes as Talia and I shout the lyrics: *"THE WORLD I LOVE, THE TEARS I DROP, TO BE PART OF, THE WAVE CAN'T STOP, EVER WONDER IF IT'S ALL FOR YOU…"*

"Babe, we're having a conversation!" Jordan shouts before telling Francis to lower the music. Francis lowers the music along with our spirits. The drive from Manhattan to the Hamptons is a couple hours, but it feels like an eternity when all we talk about is work.

"Oh, come on, babe," I pout. "Save the work talk for work."

Jordan habitually lifts my leg onto his lap. His strong hands work wonders as he massages my foot, so much so that I let him keep talking about investments with Spud. He knows me too well.

I've always admired Jordan's ambition, but it's his ambition that sometimes bores the hell out of me. I'd be fine with him talking about work any other day, but work is all my father talks about at Sunday brunch as it is.

"I think I see a gray hair on your head, Spud," Talia teases. "I think all this business talk is starting to age you."

Spud blinks at Talia. "This 'business talk' bought you that new Birkin bag you were pestering me about for months."

Talia pretend-zips her mouth shut.

"The shareholder meeting is coming up," Jordan says to me as his hands work their way up my calf. "Do you have your speech prepped?"

"The legal team is reviewing it this weekend, so I'll run through it tomorrow."

Jordan blows a strand of dark-brown hair out of his face. His green eyes light up when he says, "This is a big year for us. If we can get the shareholders on our side, we'll have a shit-ton more freedom to invest as a firm."

Jordan and I have been together for five years now, and I still never get tired of the confidence behind those green eyes—confidence in our relationship and the future we've planned together.

He's always been the "man on a mission" ever since we met back in college. He was my first for a lot of things. I guess you could say he's my *only* for a lot of things. I've always been the "woman on a mission," which I suppose makes us all the more compatible. Together, we're the Dream Team.

I graduated high school with straight A's and applied for one school and one school only… Cornell University. It's where Father went, and I grew up knowing Cornell would prepare me for the real world like it prepared him. I busted my ass and graduated top of my class with a degree in finance. While all of my friends traveled after graduation, I went straight into working at Beck Holdings, the largest firm on Wall Street. It also just so happens to be Father's firm.

Mother and Father have groomed me to play my role in the company. I intend to do exactly that, as I have for the past two years. I stick to what I know because I'm good at it.

I'm in complete control of my destiny.

It's nice having Jordan work for my father, too. Working on Wall Street typically drives couples apart, but I like to think that it brought us closer over the years.

My phone vibrates, and I look down to see a text from my older brother.

BLAKE: I'm not going in until you do
HARLOW: Almost there

Francis opens my door, and a warm breeze pulls at the white linen I'm wearing as I step out of the Cadillac. I adjust the baby blue bandana tied around my neck, my Cartier jewelry binding my wrists like a clingy mother's grip on her newborn.

I take a deep breath, then exhale. The bottoms of my white Gucci slippers clack against the gravel driveway that wraps around the front of the estate. I can't contain my giddiness when I catch sight of my brother, Blake, holding my nephew, Charlie.

"Look, Charlie! It's Aunt Harlow!" Blake shouts as he gets out of his car.

Charlie's entire face becomes a smile as he wobble-runs to me. They're too cute, both wearing pastel-blue sweaters and khaki pants.

I do a little dance before Charlie lifts his hands for me to pick him up. "Hi, cutie!" I chirp.

Charlie says something in his foreign baby-language.

I pretend to understand him. "I missed you, too, my little prince."

He smiles so hard, his chubby cheeks force his eyes shut.

"Hey, winner," I mutter to Blake.

He smirks. "Hey, loser."

I roll my eyes. Our video game rivalry as kids became so serious that now we identify each other based on the outcome of our latest game results. In case it wasn't obvious, I'm currently the loser until the next time we play.

"You like our uniforms?" Blake teases, pointing out their matching outfits.

"You both look very handsome," I say as I bounce Charlie in my arms.

"When do you think he'll grow into his head?" Jordan teases, offering Charlie one of his fingers.

Charlie stares up at Jordan, eyes wide open.

Blake forces a laugh. "You know what they say… 'the bigger the head, the bigger the star.'"

As soon as Spud and Talia join the group, a sharp voice shouts from above. "Feel free to come in whenever you'd like!"

We look up to see Mother standing straight as an arrow. She's been watching us from the top of the stone staircase. Her blonde hair glistens, slicked back into a top bun. The diamonds on her neck and wrists dance in the sunlight. Her pastel-blue blazer and cropped slacks complement the colorful flowers hanging over the luxurious balustrade she stands next to.

"Hheelllloo, Mmootthheerr," Blake and I say in unison.

We make our way up the steps, and she extends her arms. "Come here, sweets!" She grabs Charlie from my arms, ignoring the rest of the group. *Nothing new.*

Charlie giggles as Mother tickles him. Her eyes suddenly dart in my direction. "Is your phone broken? I've been texting you all week. I gave you life, didn't I? The least you can do is let your mother be a part of it."

It's only been seven days since I saw her last.

"Sorry, Mother."

She smiles down at Charlie, studying his little face. "His head is huge," she mutters. "At least he looks like *you*, Blake."

Everyone's eyes widen at Mother's remark, which could easily be considered a jab at Blake's deceased wife's looks.

"Alright, Mother," Blake snaps, prying Charlie from her cold hands.

"Well, welcome, all!" Mother twirls and heads through the front door. "William is finishing up a business call. Come! Come!" We slowly follow her inside, and she disappears around the corner.

"I should probably listen in on that call," Jordan says. He presses a warm kiss to my cheek and walks up the hall.

Spud and Talia follow Jordan while Blake and I stop to look at the family portrait hanging on one of the walls. It overwhelms me to this day–Blake, Mother, Father, and me… in matching outfits… straight-faced. I'm only a child in the portrait, while Blake looks like one of those preppy schoolboys who picks on the poor kids. The older I get, the more ridiculous the portrait seems, especially when it's the first thing you see upon entering the house.

"We need to update this or something," I whisper to Blake.

He steps up next to me. "Or we burn it."

"Jameson!" Mother shouts from the living room. "Jameson! Champagne to the backyard terrace at once!"

The sound of light footsteps fills one of the halls. They keep a slow and steady rhythm. I recognize the sound of those footsteps, and I can't help but smile when Jameson turns the corner.

"Hello, Ms. Harlow," Jameson greets with a smile.

His bulky dress shoes click against the floor as he spreads his arms for a hug. Without hesitating, I leap into his arms. Jameson was hired as our butler when Blake was born, though, over the years, he's become a part of the family.

Growing up, Mother and Father were always traveling for work, so Jameson was there to give us the attention we needed while they were gone. It was the encouraging winks and nods he'd give us from the corner of the room that made life in this house liveable.

When our parents told us how to live our lives, Jameson reminded us that our life decisions were ours to make. When our parents told us things were impossible, Jameson reminded us that anything is possible as long as we believe it to be.

Jameson pulls back and gently squeezes my shoulders. There's a tear in his eye as he looks at me like it's been years since we've seen each other.

"Are you crying again, Jameson?"

Jameson dabs his cheeks with a handkerchief he keeps on hand. "You're growing up all too quickly, Ms. Harlow."

"You say that every time I walk through these doors."

"And you grow a little more every time you do." He looks back over his shoulder to see if anyone's around, then whispers, "How's the songwriting coming along?"

"It's coming," I lie.

He gives my hands a light squeeze. The wrinkles beside his eyes show as he smiles from cheek to cheek.

One of my earliest memories was sitting on the floor of the kitchen. My parents started fighting in the living room, their voices growing louder. To drown out the noise, I started singing under my breath. The louder they shouted, the louder I sang. There was a point where they turned to me, cursing at me to get out.

"Shut your damn mouth, Harlow… fuck!" I remember my father shouting.

Jameson insisted on escorting me up to my room. I remember trembling, sitting at the edge of my bed. I had never seen my father so upset. Jameson grabbed a piece of paper and told me to write down my thoughts–how the world was making me feel in that moment. It turned into the first song I ever wrote.

As I grew older, Jameson would check up on me…

"Have you been writing new songs, Ms. Harlow?"

"Keep writing, Ms. Harlow… through the highs and lows."

"Don't listen to the world, Ms. Harlow. Listen to your heart."

A part of me feels like a fraud when I have to lie to Jameson about my songwriting every week. The truth is that my heart is in writing songs, but the world I was born into can't sustain what my heart wants. I've been meaning to talk to Blake about it, considering he went against our parents' wishes to be in the music industry. But there's no chance I'll get to talk to him about music with Mother and Father around.

Jameson turns to Blake and Charlie. "Mr. Blake and Mr. Charlie."

"Jameson!" Mother shouts from across the house. "Champagne to the backyard terrace!" She quickly turns the corner and throws her hands up. "Yes, Jameson. The kids are here, as you knew they would be. As they are every Sunday. Do you mind if I spend time with them, too?!"

"My apologies, Mrs. Beck. I will have that champagne to the terrace immediately."

"Come, children. Your father is off his call." Mother opens up her stance and gestures for us to walk up the hall.

As we walk deeper into the house, it still doesn't feel like anything more than a house. I like to think when adults come back to the houses they grew up in, they're overwhelmed with nostalgia. Not me. Not here.

Besides the scary family portrait near the front door, there aren't many other remnants of Blake and me downstairs. It's just one expensive art piece after another. The house looks like one of those model homes you see in magazines. It's nice but too nice for anyone to actually live in.

A million smells become known as we walk through the kitchen. Private chefs are preparing an array of our favorite brunch foods. I flash a smile, and the chefs check to see that Mother isn't looking before they smile back.

We step onto the backyard terrace that's decorated with plush white couches and a few dining tables. Just below the terrace is the pool. Behind the pool is a perfectly-mowed grass lawn and then the ocean beyond. Despite Mother's cold introduction, the weather is warm. There's not a cloud in the sky, and the sand looks whiter than usual just before the shore meets the water.

Father is sitting on one of the couches next to Jordan. He lifts his chin to greet us. "Good afternoon, children." He smiles without getting up. *Once again, nothing new.*

It's surprising how every time I see Father, I think he'll show some sort of affection. Then every time I see him, I'm disappointed that it's never shown. *Maybe next time.*

I hardly get alone time with Father at work, given how high he is in the company ranks. William Beck, the founder and C.E.O. of Beck Holdings, doesn't work on Wall Street. William Beck *is* Wall Street, which means he is never alone. When he's at work, he's followed by his legal and P.R. teams. When he's at home, my mother and Jameson are waiting on him, or he's on a work call.

He catches sight of Charlie and extends his arm. "There he is." Blake reluctantly hands Charlie to Father. Charlie doesn't smile.

He just looks at Father with his googly eyes, absorbing every milli-meter of his intimidating face. "Big head," Father adds.

After sitting Charlie on his lap, Father commands us to sit. I cuddle up next to Jordan while Blake, Spud, and Talia sit on the couch across from my mother. Naturally, we form a half-circle around the coffee table, where Jameson sets a tray of filled cham-pagne glasses.

Father's eyes pan around the group, and he addresses us like this is a business meeting. "My apologies for keeping you waiting. I'm organizing my address for the shareholder meeting this Thurs-day."

"How is it sounding?" Jordan asks eagerly.

My father lets out a posh laugh. "Our shareholders are gonna come themselves when they see how good our earnings were last quarter."

"Very nice," Blake replies, trying to relate. "So, business is going well?"

Father's smile fades. He knows Blake has no idea what a shareholder meeting is or how they work. "Sure, Blake," Father says condescendingly. "I suppose you could say business is going 'well.'"

Father, Jordan, and Spud snicker. The tension across the ta-ble is so obvious, you can almost taste it. Father doesn't care, though. Ever since Blake chose to pursue music over a career at Beck, Father has fed on Blake's lack of knowledge in all things business.

"How's your little music stuff going?" Father patronizes.

Music stuff.

Jordan and Spud lower their heads, struggling to hide their laughter. I nudge Jordan to stop.

Blake forces a smile. "Good!"

"Good?" Father snaps back.

"Good."

Father stares at Blake with a sheer look of disappointment.

I admire Blake for chasing his dream. He and I have always shared a passion for music behind closed doors. Blake just had the courage to go against our parents, which made room for me to become the trophy child.

Being the trophy child has its perks—a penthouse apartment and a reputation on Wall Street—but there are moments that make me want to drop it all to chase my passion instead of a paycheck.

There was that moment last night with Eren.

There was that moment just now with Jameson.

How many more moments is it going to take for me to finally do what I love?

Our five-course meal is served in the main dining room. Father runs the show, sharing his opinion on politics, economics, and anything worth debating. Mother chimes in with her two cents. Jordan and Spud blindly agree with every word pouring out of my father's mouth. Talia's eyes are glued to her phone as she edits selfies she just took in the backyard. Then Blake, Charlie, and I sit silently and inject occasional hollow comments to remind the group that we still exist. Times like these make me think our parents only invite us over to force their worldviews down our throats. For the most part, it works.

As the day turns to dusk, the group naturally disperses around the backyard. A series of lights illuminate the different levels, from the elevated terrace to the grass lawn leading to the shore.

I find Blake alone on the terrace. He's sitting on one of the couches with Charlie asleep in his arms. His eyes are fixated on the ocean until I step into his peripherals.

I greet him with a respectful nod. "Winner," I whisper playfully.

He nods back. "Loser."

We both laugh as I cuddle up next to Charlie. If you get close enough, you can hear his little high-pitched snore. My heart melts… every… time.

"Don't let him grow up," I whisper to Blake. "It's a trap."

Blake smiles down at Charlie, then continues staring at the ocean, the sound of waves crashing in the distance.

"How're you doing?" I ask.

"Good."

"Blake… how're you doing?"

He lets out a long exhale. Blake is notorious for keeping his struggles to himself. It's been almost a year since his wife, Miranda, passed away from cancer. Since then, he's become more reserved. More distant.

We used to be closer back when we were kids, teaming up against our parents. The two of us kept each other motivated. But when I made the decision to work at Beck two years ago, it felt like we were no longer on the same team. Then Miranda's passing practically made us strangers.

"Our parents suck," Blake murmurs. "I'm well into my career, and it still stings not having them support what I do. It stings even more now that Miranda isn't around to have my back when they patronize me." He takes another deep breath, then continues. "They seem to love Jordan, though."

"Come on, Blake. They love us. They just don't show it the way other parents do."

Blake flicks his eyes toward me. "What about you?" he asks. "How are you doing?"

I cock my head back, Blake's question catching me by surprise. I was planning on bringing up songwriting soon, but not this soon. *Is now the time?*

"I, uh–"

"Are you happy working at Beck?"

I bite my lip, contemplating an answer. The right answer.

The honest answer.

I hope the right and honest answers are the same.

"No," I confess. "I'm not happy. To be honest, I envy you."

Blake laughs. "I wouldn't envy me. I grow less financially stable by the day."

"But you're doing what you love. You're living life. Sure, working at Beck has its perks, but I'm afraid that I'll be 30 or 40 years old… wishing I took the leap–wishing I chased my dream like you did."

"Well, Harlow, life is short and mostly unfair, so I don't see the use in letting it pass you by while you're unhappy. Representing artists is what I do for a living, and while Mother and Father may think it's a joke, I don't. What I'm saying is… you're my little sister, and if it's your dream to be a songwriter, I'll help you chase it. But you have to be all in. You have to be serious about it."

My eyes widen, his words getting stuck in my head along with Eren's words... *"Life is short. If it's your dream to be a song-writer, then chase it."*

I let out a sigh and sink deeper into the couch.

If only dreams could simply be chased.

"I don't know if I'm ready," I mutter.

Blake shrugs and then looks out over the horizon. "If you don't know, then you're not ready, Harlow."

CHAPTER THREE

EREN

There's not a cloud in the sky over Central Park. Just blue, all blue, *Harlow*-blue. The last time I saw a blue this pure was in her eyes a few nights ago in that alley.

"Harlow." I whisper her name under my breath because it's all I can do.

I never got her number, so I can't call her. I never got her last name, so I can't look her up online. What I have is her name, a vivid memory of her, and lyrics describing the way she made me feel. She's like a thorn in my side, pricking at me, testing my ability to follow my golden rule.

"Don't get attached," I remind myself. "Don't get attached."

Charlie mumbles sounds in his little made-up baby-language while I push him around the park. I occasionally reply as if I understand what he's saying.

"Interesting thought, Charlie. I'll make sure to mention it to Blake later."

"I disagree, Charlie. You'll be a phenomenal musician one day."

"I'm hungry, too, Charlie."

I stop by a fruit cart to buy Charlie a bowl of berries and a smoothie for myself, then we make ourselves comfortable on a bench in front of a street musician. There's some serious talent in the city. It's a damn shame that some of these city artists will never make it in the industry.

Charlie and I quietly watch the street performer in front of us. She's strumming her acoustic guitar, her soothing voice riding the melody. I subconsciously feel for the coke vial in my pocket, its presence calling for me to take a quick bump. I know I told Blake I would get rid of it, but it's hard to when you rely on it as much as I do.

"Bobo," Charlie says. His googly eyes are fixated on the street performer as he shoves berries into his mouth.

I nod in agreement, letting go of the vial. "You're right, Charlie. She is pretty good."

A woman stops to compliment Charlie. "Oh my goodness. His eyes!"

Charlie giggles and replies, "Blahhhba."

I flash a smile at the woman. "He says, 'Thank you!'"

"So cute!" The woman continues on her way.

I turn to Charlie, who is focused on his berries. "You might be the best wingman I've ever had."

In the short life Charlie has lived so far, he's been a people-magnet. It might be weird to describe a baby as charismatic, but that's exactly what Charlie is. It's as if he has his own little personality. He's too young to realize it, but the kid is born to be a star. Not just because he's got a big head but because he lifts the spirits of the people around him without even trying.

The world is brighter when Charlie is around. People don't get intimidated by my presence when they see that I'm with him. They're probably thinking, *If the baby is safe around this guy, I'll probably be safe around him, too.*

Charlie and I spend the afternoon strolling around the park, stopping to listen to every street performer we find. A man banging on a bunch of buckets here, an acapella group there. I can't fathom being one of the people passing by these performers without stopping to listen. They only make a couple bucks an hour while performing in the beating sun or freezing cold.

I grew up witnessing the blood, sweat, and tears that go into making music. I watched my mom perform in the tiniest bars and restaurants. She had the voice of an angel, yet there were only five or six people clapping for her after each song she played.

She poured her life mistakes, regrets, and heartbreak into the songs she performed. I watched my mom pursue fame for the first 10 years of my life, and after each performance, we hit the road so fast, it was like something was chasing after us. Eventually, the something that was chasing us finally caught up, and it took my mom with it.

Charlie is mumbling random sounds when I feel my pocket vibrate. "Excuse me for a moment, Charlie."

My heart drops when I see two missed calls and texts from Blake.

BLAKE: GET TO MY APARTMENT NOW.
BLAKE: URGENT.

"Shit," I gasp. "Charlie, we need to go."

I fasten Charlie into the stroller and haul through the park in the direction of Blake's apartment. I weave through pedestrians and cut in front of street performers like I'm the only one in all of Central Park. People shout…

"Watch it, buddy!"

"The fuck?!"

"Jerk!"

Their words hardly register. When I reach the crosswalk, I

slap the *Walk* button repeatedly as if it'll help us cross sooner. I've tried calling Blake twice. He hasn't picked up.

My phone vibrates some more.

BLAKE: CAN'T TALK ON PHONE. EREN HURRY.
BLAKE: AND DON'T FORGET MY KID.

I bolt across the street and into the crowded sidewalk. I can hear Charlie laughing in the stroller, which probably feels like a rollercoaster.

My mind is racing as I approach the lobby.

Is someone hurt?

Is Blake in some kind of trouble?

Am I in trouble?

I kick the lobby door open. Within seconds, we're in the elevator. Charlie looks up at me. He's beginning to pick up on my panic, so I flash him a smile and tickle his stomach.

PING!

The elevator door opens, and I push the stroller up the hall in a sprint. As I get closer to Blake's door, I hear music playing from inside.

What is going on?

I get the key into the keyhole, twist the knob, and shove the door open.

Blake pops a bottle of champagne, sending Charlie and me into a panic. "Eren! Just the man I wanted to see!" He begins filling champagne glasses.

I do a quick scan of the room. No sight of anybody. But Blake is celebrating like we just won a Grammy.

"What's going on?!" I ask.

Blake hands me a champagne glass and clinks his own glass against it. "We got a new project!"

My eyes widen, not because I'm shocked I got a new project. I'm shocked at Blake's enthusiasm toward the news.

Did he think I'd never get hired again? Because he's celebrating like it.

"I've gotten projects in the past, and you've never brought out the champagne like this," I say, competing with the sound of the music.

Blake takes a sip, sets the glass on the table, and picks up Charlie. "That's because I know how much we're getting paid to write this thing."

I lean forward, urging him to continue as he dances around the living room.

"How much?!" I ask.

Blake grabs the T.V. remote and pauses the music. "Try to guess!"

"$10,000."

"More."

"$20,000?"

"Way more."

My jaw drops. "$40,000?!"

"Still not even close!"

Blake bounces Charlie excitedly while waiting for me to reply.

"$100,000?!" I shout, lifting my hands in the air.

Blake stops bouncing Charlie. His tone is stern as he states, "We're making *$800,000* off this project."

My heart drops into my stomach. My legs feel light. My eyes widen. Blake and I start jumping around the living room, punching air and shouting until our vocal cords give out. I've never had more than a couple thousand dollars in my bank account. I can't even fathom receiving my share of $800,000. Songwriters like me never make this kind of money off of a single project.

I sit on the couch, trying to catch my breath. "$800,000…? Blake, please tell me you're not messing around."

"I swear to you." Blake sets Charlie down and sits on the coffee table, facing me. "$800,000 for you to write an eight-song album."

I suck in a quick breath. "They're paying me $800,000 to only write eight songs? I've written a lot more for a lot less. Who is this album even for?"

Blake stands and rubs his hands together to build suspense. "So, it's for a male rockstar who was huge in the 80's and 90's. He wants to make his big comeback into the industry with a whole new sound."

I lift my chin, waiting for him to continue. "Aanndd?"

"Aanndd, that's all the info we have right now. When I spoke to the artist's manager over the phone, he said the artist would like to remain anonymous until you meet in person. He's considering a new artist name and rebrand."

Blake seems to pick up on my disbelief. He quickly claps his hands and runs to the kitchen table. "I know you still don't believe this is real. Just take a look for yourself. I highlighted the terms in the contract summary on the front page."

He hands me a packet, and my eyes hover over the highlighted phrases.

TO THE ATTENTION OF: EREN GRATIS'S MANAGEMENT

PROJECT OVERVIEW: 8 SONGS TO FORM A FULL ALBUM

PROJECT DURATION: 2 MONTHS

TOTAL PAY: $800,000 AT COMPLETION OF THE PROJECT

"Shit," I mutter under my breath. "You weren't kidding. Of all the writers out there, why me? And why this much?"

Blake sits next to me. "Listen, this doesn't make any sense to me either. But sense is beside the point because this is real, and this is happening. The offer landed on my desk today. They want to have a call with both of us tomorrow at three. That is, if you're willing to take on this project."

I cross my arms and lay back on the couch. My vision blurs as I stare at the ceiling, wondering how the hell I went from being broke an hour ago to making $800,000 for only writing eight songs.

I've been in this industry long enough to know the most important question any artist like me can ask: *"What's the catch?"*

The sad truth about the music industry is that there is always a catch. Easy money doesn't just fall on your lap. You get what you pay for, and this artist is paying me much more than I'm worth.

What do they really want from me? Because it sure as hell isn't just gonna be an easy eight songs. Not for $800,000. No way.

I let out a long exhale. *I guess I'll find out tomorrow on the call. Until then, we celebrate.*

My eyes meet Blake's as he stares at me, anxiously awaiting my response. I extend my arm in his direction. He glances at it, then back at me.

"I'm in," I say with a smirk.

He grabs my hand and gives it a firm shake. "Yes! Okay, amazing. I'll respond to the artist's manager right now and tell them we're in for the 3p.m. call tomorrow."

I reach for my champagne, gulping the rest of it. And just like that, I'm on top of my career again. With my line of work being as inconsistent as it is, it feels good to finally have some stability–to finally have enough money to better my life in some way.

Life on the road has been a wild ride, to say the least. And I'm starting to feel like I can't outrace what's chasing me for much longer. I can feel it not too far behind, picking up speed. Whatever it is, it's coming for me, but this project can be my saving grace. In a way, it's already giving me hope.

There's still time to change the road I'm on.

♫ ♫ ♫

As dusk approaches, I'm zipping through the rush hour traffic. One of the beauties of riding a motorcycle is that I can lane split, which means I can cut between cars I'm faster than.

My white T-shirt and blue jeans flail in the wind as I hit 50 miles per hour–now 51… now 52. I'm pretty sure the speed limit within Manhattan city limits is 45, but it's not like the cops can keep up with me on this jam-packed road.

The breeze is cool against my arms and neck while I listen to the song playing in my AirPods. I nod my head to the beat as I swerve from the right side of the road to the left. I've been on a high today after hearing about the new project, so tonight calls for some celebrating.

Blake told me about this speakeasy lounge down in Tribeca called "RAW." It's known for booking the best underground musicians in the country. According to Blake, some of the greatest artists of all time performed at RAW, and while the lounge only fits up to 40 people, the people consist of closeted millionaires, agents, and managers… all involved in the music industry.

Eventually, the road begins to narrow, and the buildings around me shrink in size. As I slow down, the monstrous modern buildings making up Upper Manhattan turn into aged apartment buildings lined side by side. There are fewer cars on the roads down here, and I notice more families scattered around the parks and side streets.

The G.P.S. calls out through my AirPods. "Montana's Barbershop is on the right."

I've never been to a speakeasy before, but supposedly these restaurants, bars, and lounges are hidden pretty well here in New

York.

"Go to Montana's Barbershop," Blake had instructed. *"Park your bike out front. There is a dumpster in the back alley with a homeless man sitting next to it. Walk up to the homeless man and offer him a nickel. Nothing more, nothing less. He's not a real homeless man. He's the doorman. The nickel is your ticket in. My sister and I used to go to this place all the time. You're gonna love it."*

It all sounds pretty out-of-pocket, but when you've been almost all over the country like I have, you learn to question less. There's some pretty weird shit out there.

I hang my helmet on the handlebar of my motorcycle and fix my hair in the side-view mirror. My brown roots are starting to show under my bleached hair. I'll need to shave my head or dye it back to brown soon. It's a good thing I got this new project. For me, a new project means a new town which means a new look. The real question is… where is this new town gonna be?

The question is immediately answered when I see the large green sign that reads, "MONTANA'S BARBERSHOP," right above me. The words are written over an image of pine trees and mountains.

Montana.

I smile at the thought of me riding through the trees making up the lush green. I consider it a sign both literally and figuratively. I've never been to Montana, and I know nothing about it, which gives me all the more reason to write this next project there. A whole new world to explore while writing new music.

I feel for the nickel in my pocket as I walk up to the barbershop. A cheap *CLOSED* sign is hanging on the door.

I look left. There's nobody in sight.

I look right. Still nobody in sight.

It's a bit eerie, standing out here all alone. A thought pops into my head. Blake could totally be kidding about this lounge even existing. I can't even look up RAW because phones aren't allowed in the lounge. Not a single trace of it on the internet.

I pull out my phone to text Blake.

EREN: You sure about this place? Montana's is closed.
BLAKE: Dumpster

My sneakers are silent against the sidewalk as I make my way around the barbershop. I get nervous when I see a long alley. It's near pitch-black despite the fluorescent light shining down over a dumpster at the very end.

I let out a quivering exhale, and a cold sweat comes over me. It pains me to realize I left my vial in my duffle bag at Blake's apartment. I could sure use a dose of courage right now.

I step deeper into the silent alley until I'm swallowed by the darkness. As I near the dumpster, I notice a ball of blankets to the right of it. The ball of blankets suddenly shifts, and I realize it's a man sitting against the wall.

My hands feel my pockets for anything I can use as a weapon in the event that this encounter goes south. Nothing but my phone, wallet, flask, a nickel, and motorcycle key.

I step out into the light and pause just a few feet away from the homeless man. He doesn't move a muscle. I can see his scraggly beard poking out from under his hood. He's holding a blanket around his back to keep himself warm, and I instantly feel bad for the guy. I reach into my back pocket for my wallet, but before I pull out a five-dollar bill, I remember Blake's words… *"Walk up to the homeless man and offer him a nickel. Nothing more, nothing less."*

The homeless man slowly lifts his chin. His eyes meet mine as he asks, "Got any spare change?"

I slide my wallet back into my pocket and pull out a nickel. "This is all I got."

The man lets out a disappointed sigh. "That's all you got? What the hell am I supposed to do with a nickel?"

Dammit. Blake was totally messing with me.

I take a look at the nickel in my palm and decide to give it one more shot. "The nickel is all I can give you," I say softly.

The man slouches forward and lifts his palm toward me. I place the nickel in his palm and wait for some sort of response. He flicks the nickel into a nearby cup and knocks on the dumpster three times. A low hum comes from under the dumpster, and my jaw drops when it separates down the middle.

"Woah." I take a step back and peek into the gap between the dumpster halves. "Do I… go inside the dumpster?"

The homeless man says nothing. I take a nervous step toward the opening.

What better way to celebrate a new project than getting swallowed up by a dumpster?

I head through the opening and down an illuminated staircase leading into a dimly-lit lobby. A host is standing behind a podium next to a bouncer who is easily twice the size of me.

"Good evening," the host says. "Would you mind handing me your phone?"

The host is wearing a black turtleneck and black slacks, his hair dyed bright red. The bouncer has blue dreadlocks, his jaw sharper than glass. I reluctantly hand the host my phone, and he slips it onto a numbered shelf behind him.

"Last name?" he asks.

"Gratis."

"Spread your legs."

My eyes widen. "I'm sorry, wha–"

The bouncer lifts my arms and begins patting up and down my torso.

"What're y–"

He runs his rugged hands from my waist down to my feet and then back up again, finding nothing suspicious until he gropes my ass.

"HEY!" I jump. "You're gonna have to take me out to dinner first, my guy." The bouncer shifts around me, so we're standing face to face. He looks down at me and sticks out his palm, gesturing for me to hand him something. "What?" I ask.

He wiggles his massive fingers. I roll my eyes and hand him the flask in my back pocket. "That's good whiskey," I mutter. "Don't let it go to waste."

So much for celebrating tonight.

Just before I'm convinced that the bouncer is mute, he says, "Cool tats." He steps aside and slides a door open.

"Thanks," I reply dryly. "But the compliment doesn't make up for you stealing my only flask."

"Down the hall to the right," the bouncer says, ignoring my statement.

I step through the door, the red carpet muting my footsteps. The walls are decorated with signed pictures of history's most famous musicians. The hairs on the back of my neck stand when I see a signed portrait of *Fai* among other legendary artists. Fai was my mother's favorite musician, so we were always singing his songs while on the road.

As I continue down the hall, the sound of live music grows louder. I make a right, and a red sign shines above the archway, which reads, "ON THE AIR." I tiptoe through the archway, and my jaw drops at the sight of the venue.

I'm standing behind a small crowd of around 30 people scattered across plush leather chairs and tables made up of dark wood. It's an intimate setting where someone could easily point out the details of each and every person's face in the room. The ceilings are high, made of dark wood lined with velvet, and the walls are covered in music records and plaques.

The crowd is entranced by the woman playing piano on the opposite side of the room. She's on a stage elevated just high enough for her to be the center of attention without demanding it. Still, the crowd responds as if the attention is, in fact, demanded.

I quietly order a whiskey neat at the bar lining the back of the room, then stand against the back wall. The performer's voice is magnetic–so perfect, it pains me to imagine never hearing something so beautiful. Her voice cracks when she hits specific notes, but it's intentional, adding an emotional flare to the lyrics she sings.

When she finishes, the crowd claps. It's somewhat of a neutral clap. Not one of amusement, which serves as a reminder that there is always a better singer out there. It's yet another one of the sad realities of the industry, and the people in this crowd have been around long enough to know it.

As the performer prepares to sing her next song, my eyes hover over the faces in the crowd. Adults, both young and old, sip their drinks and puff their cigarettes and cigars.

I take a sip of my whiskey and nearly spit it out when I spot a familiar face. The face belongs to a stunning girl who is sitting alone, patiently waiting for the performer to play the next song. I instantly recognize her as the girl I met in that alley the other night.

The freckles on her cheeks.

Those piercing blue eyes.

Her auburn hair tied up into a top bun.

Harlow.

My brain tells me to keep my distance, but my heart has other plans.

CHAPTER FOUR

HARLOW

I tap my nails against my champagne glass, anxiously waiting to hear the next song. RAW has always been known for booking amazing talent, but this lady is among the best I've ever heard, the way her voice molds to the piano keys.

Her eyes are closed the entire time she sings, and I wonder if it's because it helps her play the song better than she would if her eyes were open. As she begins playing her next song, I close my eyes, too. I want to see what she sees, hear what she hears, feel what she feels.

Oh. My. Lord.

It's as if cutting off my sight elevated my hearing. I find myself slowly nodding my head to the song she plays, and I couldn't stop if I tried to. The song becomes four-dimensional, and I sink into a state of comfort I never could have fathomed. I might as well be alone in this room because nothing around me matters but the music itself until…

"Hey," a voice whispers.

My eyes flick open. Across the tiny circular table is a guy covered in tattoos from the neck down. His bleached hair is so bright that it stands out even in the dimmed lighting. His elbow is comfortably resting on the table as if we came here together and he's looking at me like he knows me and I can't help but think maybe we…

EREN.

He smirks and then whispers, "I thought I recognized you."

Before I can even respond, someone taps Eren's shoulder and shushes him.

"Sorry," he mouths back to the person. His eyes meet mine again before dropping down to the notebook lying next to my champagne glass.

His eyebrows raise as he points at my notebook and pen. If he thinks he's going to get a peek inside my songbook, he can think again. I've never shown anybody my songs. Not Blake. Not Jordan. Not Talia. Not anybody.

Instead of passing him the book, I silently rip out a blank page. Eren hasn't taken his eyes off of me, watching every move I make like I'm the main event. I'd usually feel pretty creeped out, but he already knows I have a boyfriend. While keeping my eyes on the performer, I slide Eren the piece of paper and pen.

After a moment, he slides it back, and the conversation begins.

> EREN: Do you remember me? From the other night.
> HARLOW: I do.
> EREN: What's my name?
> HARLOW: Eren. The guy who drinks gasoline.

He smirks upon reading my response, then slides the paper back to me.

> EREN: It's whiskey… I have some here if you want to try it.

HARLOW: Champagne is my drink.
EREN: Fine, more gasoline for me. How'd you find
      this place?
HARLOW: I've been coming here for years. What
      about you?
EREN: My manager told me about it. Wanna grab a
      drink after this?
HARLOW: You know I have a boyfriend.
EREN: He can come, too.

I look up from the page to see Eren smiling at me. I roll my
eyes because he can see I'm out alone tonight. I didn't have much
of a choice. Jordan doesn't care for live music, and Talia is at trivia
night with Spud. I'd rather come here alone anyway. It's one of the
main places I find inspiration for the songs I write.

I look at Eren, who's patiently waiting for my response. He's
leaning back in his seat, chin resting on his fist, watching me with a
grin on his face. I slide him the paper.

HARLOW: One drink. And we're only going to talk
      about music.
EREN: One drink? In that case, where can we get
      the BIGGEST drinks?
HARLOW: I'll show you after this next song.

Eren folds the paper and puts it in his pocket. We both turn
back to the performer. I find it hard to focus until I turn back to Eren
and see that his eyes are closed the same way mine were. His head
sways to the rhythm as he takes in each and every note played. I hold
back a smile, appreciating the way he's appreciating the music. I
close my eyes and find the rhythm easier than ever before.

"Just one drink?" Eren asks as we step out into the alley.

"Just one."

He nods politely as we reach the end of the alley. "Should I call us an Uber? It probably won't be too expensive if we–"

I lift my arm. Within seconds, a matte-black Cadillac swerves out of its parking spot and pulls up right in front of us. Eren suddenly grabs me by the arm to pull me back from the car. I let out a laugh. *He's trying to protect me from my own driver.*

Eren shakes his head, confused. "Is this your ride?" he asks. "Or do pretty girls always get rides this quick?"

"Both," I reply with a smirk.

Francis steps around the car and opens the door leading to the back seat. As we approach the open door, Francis offers a courteous head nod. "Good evening, Ms. H–"

"No rich talk, Francis," I whisper. "He's just an old friend."

Francis lifts his chin. "What's up, Harlow?" His words sound nowhere near as smooth as he probably thinks.

Francis has been my driver for years now. He used to drive my parents, but when I moved out for college, he became my personal driver and has been ever since. He's one of the few people I trust won't report my daily habits back to my parents. Like Jameson, Francis understands both the world I was born into and the world I wish I was a part of. *I wish the two were one and the same.*

"The pub on Chambers and Broadway, please," I whisper to Francis.

Eren crawls into the back of the S.U.V. like it's a foreign spacecraft. His eyes pan up to the ceiling that's studded with lights resembling stars, then to the built-in cooler between us. The backs of my family's S.U.V.'s are converted, so four plush leather seats are facing each other–two seats facing the front and two facing the back. Eren sits with his back to the passenger's seat while I sit directly across from him.

"You didn't tell me you're the President," Eren teases.

I smirk. "The President actually reports to me."

We silently hold each other's gaze for a moment like we did the other night in the alley. It's as if we're learning more about each other with our eyes, nothing needing to be said.

One drink, I think to myself. *Just one drink.*

Eren points to the notebook sitting on my lap. "Is that what you write your songs in?"

He remembered I write songs.

My grip tightens around the book. Nobody has ever asked about this book or what's in it, and I don't see myself willing to open it up for anybody any time soon. I usually shy away from conversations that have to do with my songs, but there is something about Eren's presence that makes me feel slightly more comfortable about it.

My grip loosens on my notebook. "There's nothing like–"

"Writing on paper," he replies smoothly, finishing my sentence for me.

"Exactly."

There's a moment of silence, but it's not awkward by any means. Eren is just taking in his surroundings–taking *me* in every time he looks my way. I want to look down at the tattoos on his arms, but I'd rather not make a statement out of it. He leans forward, resting his elbows on his knees. It makes it easier for me to look at his arms, but I refrain.

"So you wander into alleys alone. You go to underground bars alone." Eren flashes a grin. "Either you're extremely confident or simply curious."

"Maybe I'm both," I reply. "Do you want some champagne? I'd offer you whiskey, but unfortunately, we keep the gasoline in the gas tank and not in the cooler."

Eren's eyes follow my hand, which opens the leather cooler built into the floor. "Does the glass of champagne count as my 'one drink?'" he asks.

"Not if you tell me what you were doing at RAW." I slowly lift the champagne bottle out of the cooler.

"What do you mean?"

"I mean, everyone in that room is affiliated with someone in the music industry. Are you?"

"My manager told me about the place, but I guess, yes. I'm in the music industry myself," Eren explains. I pour our champagne as he continues. "This is gonna sound crazy. But you know how you told me it's always been your dream to be a songwriter? That's actually what I do for a living. I've written songs for artists for the past 10 years."

I pinch my eyebrows together after handing him a glass. "You're kidding. You've been a songwriter for 10 years, and you have stage fright?"

"Woah, woah, woah," Eren lifts his palms. "Writing and singing are two completely different things!"

"Okay, true." I take a sip. "I'm a horrendous singer."

"Well, you have a very nice voice."

"Thank you."

I immediately blush. I want to tell him that he has a nice voice, too.

Would that be considered flirting?

If I say it, I wouldn't mean it in a flirtatious way, per se. Regardless, I decide against it. No mixed signals here.

"Do you usually go out alone?" I ask.

Eren looks at the star-studded ceiling, pondering an answer to a question I thought would be a simple one.

"I guess you could say so," his voice softens. "I'm staying with my manager–I mean, I guess he's more of a friend, and I'm only in town for a bit, so I… I don't wanna say I'm always alone? I'm just always on the road, so…" Eren lets out a laugh, realizing he's saying too much and too little at the same time. "Look, I don't have too many friends," he sighs. "I guess my only 'friend' couldn't come out tonight because he's with his kid."

Eren's eyes look defeated under his straight brows. I couldn't imagine only having one friend who is also the person I work with. He seems like a sweet guy who is nice enough to have many friends. The fact that he is handsome also makes me question whether or not he has a girlfriend, but that may be a question for another time.

The car comes to a stop, and Francis opens the door. When Eren climbs out of the car, I'm quick to remove my jewelry. I get a bit self-conscious about the luxuries I carry with me when I'm not around my usual crowd. So, I slip every visible piece of jewelry into my cup holder.

As we step out onto the sidewalk, Eren leans toward me and whispers, "Should we invite your driver in with us?"

I let out a laugh, well-knowing that Francis just heard what Eren said. Before I can get around to inviting Francis, he smiles and politely steps back toward the car. "I shall await your return, Ms. H–"

"No rich talk," I mouth.

Francis nods. "I'll wait outside."

Eren opens the pub's entrance door and appears shocked at what's inside. It's a laid-back Irish pub, with nothing special about it, besides the fact that it's authentic. Various accents fill the room as people share animated conversations. The floor is coated with a thin layer of sawdust to soak up spilled beer, and the wall behind the bar is lined with mugs made up of different designs.

We find two seats at the end of the bar, and within seconds, the bartender approaches us, asking for our orders. Eren flashes me a smirk. "You said one drink?"

"One drink," I reply, holding back a smile.

Eren looks back at the bartender. "I'll take the biggest drink on the menu."

The bartender's eyes flick to mine, and I politely shake my head. He turns away, leaving me with a confused Eren.

"You're not getting anything?" Eren asks.

"I'm not a big fan of the menu," I reply without trying to sound posh.

Eren laughs. "Then why'd you take me here?"

With both hands, the bartender slams a colossal beer stein in front of Eren. Some of the foam pours over the side, soaking the bar top.

"Woah!" Eren blurts out.

"The deal is one drink." I shrug. "And this pub is known for having the biggest."

The truth is, I picked this bar for three reasons. The first is that none of my friends would be caught dead in a bar like this, which is good because they'd instantly get the wrong idea about Eren and me. The second is that there's no way a guy like Eren would be comfortable in the bougie restaurants I go to with my boyfriend and friends. The third is that it makes me feel far away from home… far away from the work, drama, and all the noise that comes with city life. Their drinks just so happen to also be pretty big.

I remember the late nights I would share with Blake here. We'd listen to artists perform at RAW, and then Francis would drive us here so we could reflect on the talent and vent about Mother, Father, and the cushioned world we were born into.

"Tell me what it's like… living a life where you get to write music every day." I try to appear neutral about the topic, though I'm dying to hear what it's like for somebody to live my dream.

Eren sets down his massive bowl of beer. "I have my highs and lows like anybody else would." He lifts his hand to play with one of his earrings. "Sometimes I have singers and musicians lined up to have me write for them, and other times I have no work at all. I actually came out tonight to celebrate a new project I landed today."

My eyes widen. "That's exciting! What kind of project?"

"It's an eight-song album for a Rock & Roll singer who was big in the 90's. I guess he wants to make some sort of comeback."

What Eren is saying doesn't even sound real to me. It sounds like child's play, but I don't mean it in a demeaning way. I mean it in the best way possible. I remember what I wanted to be before the world told me what I needed to be. As a kid, I wrote songs, and I loved doing it. But as I got older, the world around me began to bury what I loved to do under the things it considered necessary. Things like getting a job, finding my person, and letting go of my imagination. It seems like Eren never lost sight of his inner-kid.

"An eight-song album for a Rock singer?!" I ask. "That's amazing. What's his name?"

Eren takes a gulp of his beer, then says, "That's the weird part. I don't really know yet. Supposedly, he wants to remain anonymous until we meet in person. I'll know more after our call tomorrow."

"Yeah, that's kind of weird."

Eren places his elbow on the bar top, his eyes narrowing in on mine. There is something so unique about the way he looks at me. It's like he's looking through me, as if he sees what's in the back of my head. It doesn't feel like he's flirting. It just feels like he genuinely wants to understand what I'm about.

"So, I know what you want to do," Eren says. "Tell me about what you do now."

I tap my bottom lip with my finger.

How do I make what I do sound exciting?

I'm not happy with my career, but I can at least try to make it seem like I'm happy. After about 30 seconds of trying to come up with something, I simply speak the truth.

"I'm President of Domestic Operations for Beck Holdings."

Eren almost spits out his beer. "Come again?"

I laugh under my breath. "I basically help make decisions and manage the company on the day-to-day."

"That's…" Eren clears his throat of whatever beer is stuck in there. "That's really impressive. I mean, I don't know what that means, but it sounds impressive."

"I'll be honest," I sigh. "I make good money. But I have this lingering fear that someday in the future… I'll wake up and realize I should've chased what I love instead of wasting time chasing what I've been told to chase."

I cringe at myself.

Was that an overshare? Did I just kill the mood?

I nervously tap the empty bar top in front of me. There's nothing I want more right now than to down a glass of champagne. I hate talking about my life. I'm great at what I do, but it's not like I deserve my career, my apartment, and my life. I was raised into it while my heart pulls me in a completely different direction.

Eren can sense my discomfort. His face softens as he says, "I'll tell you what. I'm gonna order a big plate of fries, and then we're gonna talk about surface-level things. How does that sound?"

I let out a deep breath. "That sounds amazing."

Eren orders the large plate of fries, and when it's slid in front of us, I completely disregard the fact that I've been on a strict diet. I can't pass them up. Not now. Not here, talking to this guy about all-things music.

I rarely ever get the chance to talk to people about music. Jordan only talks about work and golf. Talia only talks about reality T.V. The only person I talk to about music is Blake, but it hasn't been much since I started working for Father. Since then, we just FaceTime occasionally and see each other at Mother and Father's on

Sundays.

When there is finally a pause in our conversation, I take a moment to use the bathroom. As soon as I get back, Eren stands. "You ready?" His question catches me by surprise. I don't even know how much time has passed since we started talking. "I should be getting back to the apartment. I don't want to risk waking up my friend's kid."

"Yeah! Yeah, sounds good." I check my phone to see that a couple of hours had flown by. Eren's beer really did the trick, considering there is still a bit left. As I grab my coat, I notice the to-go box in Eren's hand. "You got more fries?!"

"They were that good," he replies with a smirk.

Eren opens the door for me, and we step out onto the sidewalk. Francis greets us, and the second we crawl into the back of the car, I subtly scoop the jewelry out of my cup holder. Eren sits in the same seat as before, then knocks on the tinted window separating Francis from the back of the car.

"Hey, man. Thanks for waiting for us. I got you fries. They're incredible."

Francis is shocked by the gesture. I can see his face through the rearview mirror as he reluctantly accepts the fries. It's almost as if Francis thinks receiving acts of kindness is breaking the driver code.

"Th-thank… thank you," Francis stutters.

I haven't known Eren for very long, but he seems to be a living paradox. His outward appearance is harsh and intimidating–his many ear piercings and ink-covered body–but he's just so… kind.

Eren has sparked my curiosity, but not in a way that would threaten my relationship with Jordan. In the few hours I've gotten to know him, he's shown me that life is simply about living. I forgot how music and fries in a hole-in-the-wall pub could make for such a great night.

When we arrive in front of RAW, Francis opens the door closest to Eren. "I'm glad you took me up on the drink offer," Eren says softly.

"I'm glad I did, too. Those fries were amazing."

Eren smirks. My head feels light as we remain fixated on each other. He's undeniably attractive, but it's the world he comes from that excites me the most. Nothing has ever excited me this way. I'd never cheat on Jordan. I love Jordan. I just wish Eren would get out of this damn car before my curiosity gets me into trouble.

"I know it's not my place…" Eren takes a deep breath.

Please don't ask for my number.

He exhales before continuing. "But I think you should do what you love. I hear the way you talk about music. I watched the way you listened to that performer tonight. I said it before, and I'll say it again… if it's your dream to be a songwriter, then *chase it*."

I smile. I love and hate that he said it again. I love it because this is the support I've been looking for my entire life. I hate it because deep down, I'm scared that if I chase my dream, I may never reach it.

"Goodnight, Harlow."

We smile at each other one last time.

"Goodnight, Eren."

It brings me a sense of comfort seeing Eren as someone just passing through. Someone sent to motivate me. And that's that.

Francis shuts the door behind Eren. I watch Eren head for his motorcycle, then take one last look at the car.

Francis gets into the driver's seat. "You said that was an old friend of yours, Ms. Harlow?"

"Yes. His name is Eren," I reply, holding back my smile.

I already know what he's going to say.

"I like Eren," Francis says as he takes a bite out of a french fry. "I like Eren a lot."

♫ ♫ ♫

It's a beautiful morning...
to fuck...
shit...
up.

I repeat the same phrase first-thing every morning.

Jordan and I have our morning routine. Wake up at 4a.m. for our home workout, drink our green smoothies while dissecting the Wall Street Journal, take a cold shower to boost blood flow, get ready, and then Francis is here to take us to work.

With my headphones on, I bump my head to *"Everlong"* by Foo Fighters, hyping myself up for the day as we drive down the bustling city streets. Our company's annual shareholder meeting is tomorrow, and it's the first time I'm speaking directly to the public.

I'm not nervous. How could I be nervous? I was raised on Wall Street with the wolves. Not to mention, my last name is literally the stock's ticker symbol: *BECK*.

I place my headphones on the seat as Francis opens the door for Jordan and me. "Thank you, Francis," I say as I step out onto the sidewalk.

"My pleasure, Ms. Harlow."

I adjust my white Alexander McQueen single-breasted blazer and pants. My fit has been perfectly tailored to my liking, my hair pulled up into my signature top bun.

"You smell that, babe?" Jordan adjusts his suit lapel as we make our way up the polished granite staircase. "Smells like filthy fucking money." I flash him a cunning grin, and he places a gentle hand on the small of my back. "Dream Team, baby."

With Wall Street's public eye on my father and me, there is no room for public displays of affection. At least not until Jordan is my husband. So, until then, we keep our poker faces on. Being a member of the family that owns a public company means even the slightest fuck-up can send the stock price plummeting. So, you best believe I'll get them hot and show them what I've got because they can't read my poker face.

As my heels click against the lobby's marble floors, heads turn from all around.

"Good morning, Ms. Beck."

"Hello, Ms. Beck."

The morning is my favorite time of day because I'm alert, and the rest of the day holds endless potential. It's also when I have the most energy, thanks to my…

"Iced coffee with a shot of espresso and low-fat organic oat milk. Just the way you like it, Ms. Beck," Penny says the same way she does *every* morning.

"You're a saint, Penny."

I take the coffee off her hands as Jordan, Penny, and I step into the elevator the same way we do *every* morning.

"Hi, Penny," Jordan says to Penny the same way he does *every* morning.

"Good morning, Jordan," Penny blushes.

Well, that's a first.

Penny never blushes.

She presses the *45th Floor* button and begins running through today's agenda as any assistant would. "Ms. Beck, you have a shareholder 'prep' meeting in the executive suite in 10 minutes. I pushed back your 11a.m. call, so you have enough time after the meeting to get situated for the day. The Forbes *30 Under 30* journalists will be here at 1p.m. to interview you for your magazine feature."

I blink at Penny. "I'm sorry, wait. What shareholder 'prep' meeting?"

The three of us step out of the elevator and walk between neatly aligned cubicles and window-facing offices.

Penny struggles to keep up. "Your father–I mean… Mr. Beck… called it first thing this morning."

I roll my eyes because I know exactly what this is about. Father read the speech I plan on giving at the shareholder meeting tomorrow. And he doesn't like it.

"Interesting," I sigh, my eyes locked onto the executive suite–Father's office.

The wall of Father's office is made up entirely of glass, separating my father from his corporate minions. On the other side of his office is a wall made up of windows overlooking all of Wall Street. I push open the glass doors to see my father sitting at his desk while his legal and P.R. teams are scattered across the couches and chairs.

"Good morning, Harlow," Father smiles. "I'm glad you got my meeting notice in time."

"Me, too," I reply coolly. "I thought we were already prepped for the meeting tomorrow. Why do we need to have another 'prep' meeting?"

Father glances at the few men and women sitting around the room. "I read your speech." He leans back in his chair and tilts his head. His slicked white hair reflects the light seeping in through the wall of windows.

"And?" I cross my arms.

"And I'm scrapping it from the agenda."

The room grows painfully still. Everyone looks in a different direction.

"Scrapping my speech?" I hiss. "Why?!"

"It's sappy," Father blurts out. He stands over his desk. "There's too much fluff. Too much emotion."

I pinch my eyebrows together.

Sappy? Fluff? Too much emotion?

My speech explained how our investments are made to better the world we live in–to put quality of life before money. Regardless, he told me I could write my own speech, and I spent a month writing it to find out it's now scrapped?

Father steps around his lavish desk, then leans back against it. "Harlow, don't be naive." His cold blue eyes fixate on mine. "Do you know why the media refers to us as 'wolves?'" I bite my lip in an attempt to hide my frustration as he gives me one of his infamous lectures, showcasing his dominance. "It's because we're hungry… ruthless…" He shifts his weight forward, straightening his stance. The people in the room flinch, but I stand still. "We're territorial, and we show no mercy to those who keep us from the money. We're killers."

I see one of the men taking notes in my peripherals. It's amazing how having an executive office can make people fear and respect you.

"What does this have to do with my speech?" I ask.

"Your speech makes us sound like… *puppy dogs*," Father snaps. "Wolves, Harlow. We're wolves! This is the real fucking world, not some fictional fairy tale. Your creativity has no place here, especially in your speeches. Our shareholders only care about how much money is in their pockets. Not this 'quality of life' bullshit." He takes a deep breath and crosses his arms. "I'd like for you to make my introduction at the meeting. That'll be all."

I clench my fist as Father turns his back to me. I work my ass off every damn day in this office, playing with the cards I've been dealt. I do everything Father tells me to, and I've never complained. Now the one chance I get to express myself through my writing, he has to take it away from me. It's bad enough I never got his support with my songwriting, but now this?

I flex my jaw. "So, that will be all?"

"That will be all, Harlow," Father says before addressing the group. Penny opens the door for me to walk out of. As I leave, I hear Father say, "Jordan! Stay a moment, will you?"

"Yes, sir," I hear Jordan reply.

I'm fuming by the time I get to my office. My wall is also made of glass, so I can see directly into the executive suite until I lower my blinds.

"9-1-1, Penny. I need a cigarette or a shot of something," I mutter, aimlessly rummaging through my drawers. "Send someone to get me a cigarette."

"But, Ms. Beck… you don't smoke."

I pause.

"Just…" I sit in my chair and bury my face in my palms. "When is my next call?"

"A little over two hours," Penny replies.

I smile at her for a moment, and she lifts her chin, awaiting my command. I wonder what it's like to be in her shoes. To wear her glasses and be the petite little corporate errand girl that she is. I wonder if she's happy being my assistant. I wonder if she has a shitty father or mother or if her dreams were referred to as a "waste of time" like my parents would refer to mine.

I have to hand it to her, though. Penny has been my assistant since I started working here, and she's the most loyal any assistant could be. In a way, I feel sorry for her. I can't help but hope she makes a name for herself one day, the way I'm trying to myself.

"I need a moment, Penny," I say softly.

"Certainly. I'll be right outside, Ms. Beck."

I follow her to the door and then lock it behind her. With a pen in hand, I pull out a piece of blank paper and pour my thoughts onto the page.

I feel the weight of my world,
And it keeps pulling me down,

How can I be enough,
When it keeps pulling me down,

I've got this thought in my head,
A dream to chase, but it's fast,
I'm trying to catch up to it,
But they keep holding me back,

I met a man in the dark,
But in him, I saw the light,
He's from a world not too far,
A world that I want to find.

When I finish writing, I feel a weight lifted off my shoulders. Call it a gift or a coping mechanism. Regardless, writing songs will always turn my lowest of lows into my highest of highs. Despite the few things I genuinely care about, it's safe to say that music trumps them all.

The rest of the day goes smoothly, despite the rocky morning. After a couple calls, some meetings, and an interview, I'm back in my office drinking my 4p.m. green smoothie.

I let out a sigh of relief, sinking into my couch which faces my view of Wall Street. With one leg crossed over the other, I scroll through my missed texts, pausing on a couple of messages from Blake.

BLAKE: Hey loser

BLAKE: I've got the opportunity of a lifetime for you

BLAKE: Meet at Angelo's tomorrow. 12pm. Bring your songbook

CHAPTER FIVE

EREN

I think I'm going to be sick when I walk into Angelo's. It's only been five days since I had my panic attack on stage here. It was also the night I met Harlow, who–no matter how hard I've tried–I can't get out of my head.

Sitting across from her in the car two nights ago. Munching on fries at the bar and talking about music. The night feels like a dream… a really, really good dream. I savor it because I don't have good dreams too often. Instead, I have these episodes I consider worse than nightmares. If I don't drink myself to sleep, my mind will literally replay my darkest memories. I don't know why or how it happens, but whiskey seems to get me through the nights.

My memory of Harlow has etched itself into my mind like a tattoo. Locking onto those eyes. Hearing the slight rasp in her voice that I can't get enough of. She could scream at me, and still, her voice would bring me peace.

But no… no. I told myself then, and I'll tell myself now…

Don't get attached.

How can I break the only rule I live by?

When I catch myself thinking about her, it helps to remind

myself that she's in a happy relationship. I don't think that I'll see her again, but I can't deny that we shared a moment that will last till the end.

It's around lunchtime, and a guitarist is playing on the tiny stage in the corner of the restaurant. I do my best to keep a low profile, considering I ran off that same stage, leaving the owner with nobody to perform that night. I can't afford him recognizing me in front of Blake. Blake finding out that I'm trying to focus less on writing and more on singing–especially after our call about this new project–would be bad news.

"I still can't believe it," Blake says as he squeezes Charlie into his high chair. "$100,000 per song. An eight-song album about *your* life and whatever inspires you. You have complete creative freedom!"

"It still doesn't feel real," I reply, keeping my head down.

I'm wearing a cuffed black beanie and a long-sleeve shirt to cover most of my tattoos, so the owner doesn't notice me. So far, so good.

"You think you'll be able to meet the artist's deadline?" Blake asks. "Eight songs in two months doesn't sound too bad. You've written a lot more in a lot less time."

I shrug. "Should be pretty easy."

The call with the artist's manager went well, but I still can't fully wrap my head around it all. I've written a lot more songs only to be paid a lot less, and I've written a lot more in a lot less time. It's like this contract is a "gimme," some kind of handout. With my experience writing songs, this project will be a breeze.

Blake orders four drinks for the table–a whiskey for me, a beer for him, a cranberry juice for Charlie, and a champagne for…

"Who is the champagne for?" I ask when the waitress walks away.

Blake holds his breath for a moment, itching the side of his head. "So, I sort of need a favor," he exhales, nervously twiddling his thumbs. "My kid-sister always dreamed of becoming a professional songwriter. And I thought, you know… with this new project and all… it could be an opportunity for her to work with–"

"No," I snap. "Blake, we agreed years ago. No more interns. Especially after what happened last time."

"That was different!" Blake says. "Neither of us knew that girl, and it's your fault she fell in love with you and turned out to be badshit crazy."

I shiver. "Badshit crazy is an understatement."

"Right. This is different, though. I know my sister. She's not crazy. Plus, she's in a happy relationship. Unfortunately, it's with a douchebag, but she's still happy. You're also not her type at all. This is purely professional, Eren."

"I don't know, man," I sigh. "You know I work better alone."

"You do everything alone. I get that." Blake lifts his hands. "Listen... I know you hate to hear stuff like this, but you're like family to me…"

Please stop.

"You're like the brother I never had…"

I cringe.

"So, I'm not asking as your friend or your manager. I'm asking as a brother–"

"Alright, alright!" I shout. "Your sister can help me with the album, but there are gonna be some conditions."

Blake smirks, crossing his arms. "List them."

I lean forward and start counting them off. "She can visit me *once* at the place I decide to write the album from. We only communicate through text. And when she flies out to wherever I am, all of her travel expenses are covered by you."

"Have you put some thought into where you wanna write the album?"

"Montana."

Blake blinks at me. "Why Montana?"

I remember seeing the green sign above Montana's Barbershop. "I dunno." I shrug. "Haven't been there yet."

Blake laughs under his breath. "Got it. So my sister can visit you once in Montana, you communicate through text, and all of her travel expenses are covered by me. Those are all your conditions?"

I nod. "That's all of 'em."

"Done deal. She'll be here any second."

We shake hands as the waitress sets our drinks down.

"Rara," Charlie says from across the table.

"That's right, Charlie," I reply. "Your dad does owe me one."

Blake flashes a smirk. "Something amazing is gonna come of this. I can feel it."

I roll my eyes. He says that about every project we get, and still, nothing amazing comes of them. It's always onto the next, like the people and places in my life.

I've got to hand it to Blake, though. He's managed to stick around the longest without me pushing him away. Maybe it's because I have a soft spot for Charlie. I know how tough it is to be raised by a single parent, and I wouldn't wish it upon any kid, so I'll help out when I can.

Other than Charlie and Miranda, I really don't know anything about Blake's family. I just know he doesn't get along with his parents. He says they never supported him when it came to getting into the music industry. He also says if he didn't have Charlie, he wouldn't even go through the hassle of visiting his parents on Sundays.

As Charlie beats his kids menu with a crayon and Blake scrolls through his phone, I take a moment to imagine what Blake's little sister looks like. I imagine her having bright blue eyes like Blake. Maybe she's shy at first, like he is. Maybe she has reddish hair like him. Freckles? Thin lips? Full lips?

God forbid she calls me out for my bad habits like Blake does. If having two Blakes in my life means giving up my vices, rip the contract. I'm sure as hell not ready to give them up. Not until I finally make it as a singer.

I reach into my pocket and roll my coke vial between my fingertips, feeling the urge to take a quick bump in the bathroom before Blake's sister gets here… until my attention is pulled toward the front entrance.

I let go of the vial when I see the girl enter the restaurant. Her charisma radiates like she's somebody—not just anybody. I can tell she's beautiful, even as she tries to keep a low profile. Her hair is tied back into a low bun, and though we're indoors, she keeps her sunglasses on under her baseball cap. She clutches a leather note-book against her black designer trench coat.

I've seen that book before.

I follow the rhythm of her footsteps like a song stuck on repeat—the song you never get tired of—a timeless classic. I can't look away. Nowadays, I hardly ever pray. But I pray she turns away before my infatuation with her becomes an obsession. Because even the songs we're obsessed with eventually make their way to the bottom of the playlist.

"Hey, loser!" Blake shouts.

Did Blake just call this random girl a loser?

"Loser!" he shouts again.

I lean across the corner of the table. "Blake, what're you doing?!"

Blake ignores me, and before he can call the girl a loser again, she storms in our direction, keeping her head down.

Shit. He just pissed her off.

My chair makes a screeching sound as I stand. I lift my palms, preparing to apologize on behalf of Blake. Before I can, her white teeth show between her full lips. She kisses the top of Charlie's head, and Charlie beams in her direction, clapping his hands.

"Hey, winner," the girl says to Blake.

The subtle rasp in her voice.

When she takes off her sunglasses, my heart skips a beat because I know those freckles under her piercing blue eyes.

No

fucking

way.

When her eyes meet mine, I can hardly breathe. My eyes tear up, not because I'm happy or sad, but because what are the odds? Fuck chance. This is fate, and I may need to fight fate to the death to keep myself from getting attached to this girl.

Blake and Charlie's heads swivel left and right between the two of us.

"Eren, this is Harlow, my little sister," Blake says, suspecting nothing.

Harlow and I don't break eye contact. My hand slowly hovers over the table, and I hate that I melt inside when her trembling hand meets mine. It's the first time we touch.

Is she nervous?

Am I nervous?

I don't think Harlow told Blake about me, considering he introduced us like we're strangers meeting for the first time.

Did she know Blake is my manager?

Will she still want to work together knowing she'll be working with me?

She introduces herself calmly, despite her trembling hand. "Harlow."

"I'm Eren."

We both sit, and she quickly removes her hat and smooths out her hair. She has a polished look, her hair slicked back and a white dress shirt peeking out between her trench coat.

"Why are you dressed like an F.B.I. agent?" Blake asks Harlow between bites of complimentary bread.

Harlow takes a sip of champagne to calm her nerves. I take a sip of whiskey to do the same. "The shareholder meeting is going on right now," she says.

"You skipped the biggest meeting of the year?!" Blake snaps.

"Shh!" Harlow looks around. "I did the introduction and then snuck out the back."

I can't look at her without smiling. I also can't look away. She has to be as shocked as I am, and I'd do anything to be inside of her mind right now–to know why her hand was shaking in mine just a moment ago.

"You said it was an opportunity of a lifetime," Harlow adds. "So, I'm here."

"It is." Blake butters a piece of bread and hands it to Charlie. "Eren is one of my songwriters, and he just got hired to write an eight-song album. He agreed to let you co-write it."

She cocks her head back. "I…"

Harlow's eyes nervously flick in my direction. I continue smiling. To Blake, my smile is expected. But to Harlow, I'm insinuating that this wouldn't be just any songwriting opportunity. It would be the opportunity I urged her to pursue the few times we've spoken. She knows that *I know* being a songwriter is her dream. While I've felt the typical urge to distance myself from Harlow, I'm suddenly swayed by this urge to help her chase that dream.

"I… I don't… I've never written songs professionally," she stutters.

"There's a first for everything," I reply.

"Exactly," Blake adds. "Harlow, since we were kids, I've known that music is where your heart is. The other day, you said you don't know if you're ready. I'm telling you now that this is your shot."

Harlow lowers her head and lets out a sigh. "I can't just skip out on work." Her apologetic eyes meet mine. "Eren, I'm grateful, really–"

"Are you?" I interrupt her, my tone coming across as more aggressive than intended. Blake, Harlow, and Charlie look at me. "Blake said writing songs has always been your dream."

"It is–was. It's not my dream anymore." Harlow bites her lip, catching herself in a lie.

I tap my finger against the tabletop. "Can I ask you something?"

Harlow reluctantly nods. I lean forward, my voice low as I ask, "Do you ever think to yourself, '*What if someday in the future… I wake up and realize I should've chased what I love instead of wasting time chasing what I've been told to chase?*'"

I narrow my eyes, waiting for her to catch on–waiting for her to realize I just threw her lingering fear out in the open. She confided in me a few nights ago, and I'm throwing it back at her with no remorse.

I know you want this, Harlow. Stop holding yourself back.
It's time for you to take the leap–to do what you love.

As she processes my question, I feel the thorn in my side. It reminds me that spending time writing with Harlow could lead to me getting attached to her. But for the first time, I'm willing to risk breaking my rule if it means getting Harlow to take the leap.

With Harlow involved, this project can be about so much more than the music we write. When I'm around Harlow, my vices have less of a hold on me. It's one thing for her to walk away from an opportunity to chase her dream. It's another for me to let her walk away when I feel life's current pulling me in her direction.

She might be able to save me from myself.

"Okay," Harlow finally says. "What are the details?"

I find myself smiling again, but this time, smiling like a fool.

"Thatta girl!" Blake gives Harlow an appreciative nudge. "You have two months to write eight songs together. Eren wants to write this project in Montana, so I'm gonna have the record label set up his living situation. Harlow, you decide when you want to meet him out there. Eren is making me pay for your travel expenses."

Harlow giggles. "Very thoughtful of you to make Blake pay for my travels, Eren."

I lift my whiskey and nod. It was thoughtful until I realized Blake's sister is Harlow Beck, and Harlow Beck sitting first-class would be considered a downgrade. Judging from what she wears and what she does for a living, I wouldn't be surprised if she has her own jet.

It starts to dawn on me how good and bad this is. Staring at Harlow from across the table is like an alcoholic staring at a wall of liquor behind a bar. I'm tempted to get to know more about her, but can I afford to? My heart was shattered into a million pieces when I was only 10. Now I'm 18-years sober of attachments. I can't afford to relapse.

But I can't resist life's current. And as much as I don't want it to, I feel the current pulling me toward her now.

♫ ♫ ♫

It's around 6p.m. when Harlow texts me.

HARLOW: We need to talk
EREN: On the phone?

Harlow's text doesn't really catch me by surprise. Lunch today was a lot for both of us. It's not often you run into the same person three times in a single week, only to find out you'll be working together for two whole months.

I've spent the entire afternoon watching paint dry… literally. I spray-painted my motorcycle matte black in Blake's apartment building's garage. In a couple days, I'll have a new place in Montana, a different-colored bike, and a new look. It's all a part of my creative process, minus my new co-writer, who is currently blowing up my phone.

> **HARLOW:** Talking in person would be better
> **HARLOW:** Alone
> **HARLOW:** Meet me by the carousel at Central Park
> **HARLOW:** Don't tell Blake
> **EREN:** Sounds good

It's only been half a day, and Harlow already has me breaking one of my conditions: *Only communicating through text.*

After checking to see that the paint on my bike is dry, I'm on my way to Central Park. Rush-hour traffic has died down, so I take my time, absorbing the sunlight reflecting off the building windows. The sky is painted with rows of pink and orange clouds, giving the atmosphere a dream-like feel. Everything about this evening is peaceful until Harlow's nail stabs me in the chest.

"Are you fucking following me?!" A fire burns in her eyes as her finger rises toward my face. "Have you known who I am this whole time?!"

"Following you? What?!" I step back and raise my palms. "How was I supposed to know you're Blake's little sister?"

"I don't know. Maybe ask? You're literally living with the guy, and you don't know his sister's name?"

I roll my eyes. "I don't see what the big deal is. You've always wanted to be a songwriter, and now–"

"You don't get it!" Harlow turns her back to me for a second, then faces me again. "My life. My routine. My work. My future. I've had it all under control until *you* started popping up in all these stupid alleys!"

"*All under control until me…?*" I shake my head. "Am I making you lose control of something?"

Harlow sits on a nearby bench and drags her hands down her face. She seems like a bit of a hot mess right now, so I keep my distance.

After a loud exhale, Harlow continues. "Yes, songwriting has always been my dream. But it's just a dream. That's all it should be."

Her tone is softer now, so I use it as a cue to sit next to her.

"Sure, it's a dream," I say. "But this is a chance to make it a reality. If you don't want to do this, you don't have to."

"It's not that I don't want to," she mutters. "It's that I *do* want to. I'm scared, is all."

"Scared?"

"I've never written with a professional like you. I've also never been to Montana. Why the hell did you even choose Montana? What's in Montana?!"

I laugh and lean back. "Montana is on the list of places I've never been to. I don't know. It seems nice."

Harlow raises a curious brow. "You see, that's crazy to me. You choose to go to a place because you know nothing about it. I choose to go to places I know like the back of my hand."

"What's the fun in that?" I ask, scrunching my face.

Harlow leans back next to me. We both look ahead, sitting shoulder to shoulder. "What am I supposed to tell my boyfriend? '*Hey, Jordan. I'll be in Montana with some random guy writing an album you won't care about. It's fine, though, because this random guy is friends with my brother.*'"

"Sounds good to me," I say casually.

Harlow exhales. After a brief pause, she faces me. "Do you

really think I can do this?”

"Not alone," I reply. "That's why I'm here."

"Alright, Eren. I trust you."

CHAPTER SIX

HARLOW

Jordan steps out of the shower and wraps a towel around his waist. "You need a vacation because you're stressed over work?" He runs his hands back through his hair. "You're never stressed."

This is the first time I've lied to Jordan. I mean, technically, it's not a lie. I'm stressed, just not over work. For once in my life, I can't predict what the future will bring because I know nothing about pursuing what I love. *That* is stressing me out.

But I can't be honest about this. I know Jordan wouldn't be happy to hear that I'll be across the country with Eren. Never mind this being an opportunity for me to make my way into the music industry. If Jordan knew I'd be working alone with Eren, his jealousy would get the best of him. Eren and I could be putting together the cure for cancer, and Jordan would still want to beat the shit out of Eren for being alone in a room with me.

Over the years, I've avoided situations that could make Jordan jealous. His temper is no joke, and while I've never triggered it myself, I've seen it triggered by almost everybody else.

When we first met, he was honest about how he struggles with his temper, and I respected him for taking ownership of it. I'll never change Jordan, and I don't want to anyway. We've grown together, and I've grown to love him more by the day–his flaws included.

"I just feel like I've been bottling in everything at work," I sigh. "I thought I'd feel better after the shareholder meeting, but I think I just need a little vacation–a change of scenery."

"Just make Penny do more of your work," Jordan insists. "Assistants are supposed to relieve this kind of stress."

"I don't want to overwork the poor girl."

I watch Jordan through the bathroom mirror. He tilts his head as he presses his waist against me from behind. "Is everything alright with you?" He catches my eye in our reflection. "You know you can talk to me about anything." His lips are warm against my shoulder, sending chills down my body.

"Jordan…" I turn to face him, my lower back now leaning against our marble sink. "I won't be gone for long. Just a week. I need a reset."

Jordan places his hands on the sink–one on each side of me. Heat radiates from his body, and I can still smell the bodywash on his muscular chest–eucalyptus mint.

"Hmm." He bites his lip, then narrows his eyes.

Jordan has every right to question my behavior. He knows I don't like to travel, period. The two of us get off on having our routine. Being consistent–borderline automatic.

"I'll go with you," he states. "I'll have to move around some things at work, but I can squeeze in a trip. Especially if you're stressed."

My heart drops.

What am I supposed to say now?

I force a smile. "That would be amazing! But–"

"But…?" A line shows between Jordan's eyebrows. His voice is harsh as he says, "Harlow, what kind of trip is this?"

Think, Harlow…

Going alone sounds too suspicious.

Going with Talia sounds even more suspicious.

Going with Blake sounds…

PERFECT.

"But I already told my brother I would go with him." The words pour out of my mouth like a leaky faucet. No confidence whatsoever. In a last-ditch effort to avoid suspicion, I let out a sigh and say, "With it being a year since Miranda died, I told him we'd treat the trip as some sort of 'retreat.' To help him get his mind off of losing her. I didn't want to make this a big deal because I don't want you to worry about him, too."

"Ah." Jordan straightens his stance and itches the hair on his pecs. "Blake is still hung up on that, huh?"

I roll my eyes. "Really, Jordan? '*Hung up on that*?'"

Jordan has always spoken his mind without a filter. It's nice because I always know what he's thinking, but it also sucks because I always know what he's thinking. Even when he's being insensitive.

Jordan lets out a quick exhale and lowers his head. "I'm sorry. You know I didn't mean it like that, babe." Long brown strands of hair hang over his face until I run my fingers back through it. "When are you two leaving?"

"Not sure. I think in a couple days," I reply. I let out a squeak when he lifts me onto the edge of the marble sink.

"In the five years we've been together, we've never spent time apart, you know."

"We'll make up for time lost when I'm back." I bite my lip, looking up at him.

Jordan smirks, then slowly spreads my legs. "So, I can't convince you to stay?"

I press my back against the mirror, which grows foggier by the second. "I'm going, Jordan. But you can still try to convince me for the hell of it," I tease.

Jordan gently unwraps my towel, then kisses me from just below my breasts, to my stomach, to my–*oh*.

I'm still going to Montana, but I'll sure as hell miss this.

♫ ♫ ♫

"I can't believe you," Blake snarls from the seat facing me. "Using my life problems to justify you lying to your tool-boyfriend. You're becoming more like Father by the day."

"Look, I'm sorry. What else was I supposed to tell him?!"

"Maybe the truth?" he hisses. "That you've been asked to co-write an album?"

Before I can reply, the flight attendant steps in to refill our champagne glasses. Blake holds up his hand. "I'm good, thanks."

"Oogooba," Charlie says from the couch lining the wall of our jet.

"You see? Charlie understands," I tease. "Now that you're coming, I'm not really lying to Jordan, you and Charlie get to go on a vacation, and I don't have to worry about Eren being some serial-killer-psychopath."

"Is that what this is about?" Blake asks. "You don't want to be alone with Eren?"

I shake my head, although he's right. I don't know Eren well enough to be alone with him in a cabin across the country. Having Blake come also makes me feel a little less guilty about lying to Jordan.

"I've just been told we will be preparing for landing," the flight attendant says.

Charlie crawls onto Blake's lap. I stare out the window, seeing nothing but green below us–an entire ocean of pine trees despite some snow on the mountaintops. I don't think I've ever seen this much green in my life.

"Are we gonna be, like… in the dirt?" I ask.

Blake bounces Charlie on top of his knee. "Well, the house is in the woods, so I'd assume there's some dirt."

Shit. Shit. Shit.

I didn't pack clothes for "dirt."

We touch down at an airport with only one runway. There's no sight of a building within miles–just more green.

"So, why did Eren pick this place again?" I ask from the top of the jet's foldout staircase.

"Because he's never been here before."

My eyes pan to the airport in the distance, then the plain beyond. A world of nothingness.

"I wonder why he's never been here before," I mutter sarcastically.

There are no people.

There are no buildings.

There is literally nothing out here except for… nature.

Within five minutes, we leave the tiny airport in our rental car. I haven't been in a car this small since–actually, I've never been in a car this small. I keep my hands in my lap because I'll vomit if I touch one of the many food and drink stains.

Blake looks in the rearview mirror. "Charlie, please stop licking the seat belt."

"Babada."

"I don't care if it tastes good, buddy."

Blake syncs his phone to the car speakers and starts playing songs we sing along to. As we drive farther from the airport, the green plains become walls of pine trees on both sides of the road. I remember when I first moved to the city, my neck would be sore from all the time I spent looking up at the buildings. Now here I am, doing the same, trying to see the tops of these pine trees.

Every couple of miles, I spot a house. There is this fascination behind seeing how much untouched land there is out here. I'm just so used to bumping shoulders with strangers every day on the sidewalk. Montana feels like a world away.

After about an hour of driving, Blake turns onto a dirt road. The atmosphere darkens under the shade of the pines, and the car shifts left and right over the rocky dirt road. In the distance, I see a modern house made of wood. The corners of the house are sharp, and the design is sleek, with lots of large windows. When I step out of the car, I catch a whiff of something citrusy—or is it smokey?

"What's that smell?" I ask.

"Nature," Blake teases as he lets Charlie out of the car. "Charlie, slow down!" Charlie makes a beeline for the front door. "Harlow, you should go inside and let Eren know we're here."

I jam my hands into my coat pockets and follow Charlie to the front door. I slowly push it open and knock a few times. "Eren?" There's no point in calling for Eren because of the blaring music coming from the other side of the wall.

Charlie sits by the door and begins taking off his shoes while I follow the music. It grows louder, pulling me to a room that's been converted into a studio. There's a random guy sitting in a chair with his back to me—his short hair brown against his tan skin. There are angel wings tattooed on the back of his neck. Besides that, he's in a white long-sleeve shirt and gray sweatpants. I look around for Eren. No sight of him.

Whoever this guy is, he's not a part of our world. Instead, he's entirely in his own. The music is loud enough to literally be felt, and the guy feels it as if he's one with the music. Nothing matters except for the melody playing from the speakers as he tweaks the random sounds. I'm witnessing him become one with his own craft, and I can't help but want to sit back and admire him admiring his own work.

"Hey!" I shout. The guy doesn't hear me. He nods his head to the beat, adjusting the sounds playing from all the different speakers. "Heelllloo…"

I'm inching forward because I don't want to scare him, but I might have to. The music is so loud the walls are shaking. He has no idea what's going on in the world around him at this very moment—that strangers are in his house in the middle of the woods.

I take a deep breath, extending my hand out. *If I poke his shoulder lightly enough, maybe I won't scare him.*

I gently tap his shoulder. Without turning, he itches the spot where I tapped. I gently–gently–place my hand on his shoulder. The guy quickly turns, and before I'm able to say a word…

"AHH!" It's a shriek that came from his gut, up his throat, and out of his mouth. The only reason I can hear him is because he threw himself onto his keyboard in a panic, unintentionally pausing the music. "WHAT... WHO... HOW DID YOU…?"

I cover my mouth while watching him suck in heaps of air. "I'm sorry!" I shout from behind my palm. I'm holding back a laugh when I realize this "*random guy*" is Eren. "Eren?!"

Eren's face is painted with disgust as he looks at me. His ink-covered hand is resting over his racing heart. He takes heavy breaths until he realizes it's me. His facial expression softens, and I feel so bad I sort of want to hug him.

"You scared me," he whispers as if I didn't just watch him shriek for his life. He shakes his head. "Okay, wow. You're in the house now. Okay." He runs two fingers over his eyelids as his breath steadies.

I laugh harder than I probably should. "I'm so sorry."

The look on Eren's face softens even more. He smirks, and despite his hair being dyed brown, I finally recognize him.

"I totally thought you were someone else," I say, regaining

my composure. "You look different."

He stands straight and fixes his shirt. "I suppose dying my hair will make me look different."

Charlie mumbles something as he waddles across the room. He lifts his hands to be picked up by Eren.

"I missed you, too, Charlie!" Eren says as he picks him up.

"You speak Charlie's secret baby-language," I murmur.

"I'm fluent," Eren replies with a smirk.

Blake slams his bags on the ground in the doorway. "Ah, new place, new look?"

Eren shrugs while bouncing Charlie in his arms. "Back to brown."

"Love it," Blake replies while undoing a few shirt buttons. "I'm gonna go nap on the first couch I find." He disappears down the hall.

Charlie squirms until Eren sets him down to catch up with Blake. "Can I get you something to drink or eat?" Eren asks. "I bought champagne because I figured… you know. That's all I've seen you drink."

"Maybe in a bit," I reply while looking around the room. I'm nervous, and I can't tell if it's because it's the first time I'm in a room alone with Eren or because it's the first time I've left New York.

Eren smirks. "Okay, well, you've already shown yourself the studio. I'll show you the rest of the place."

We walk through a small hall that opens up into the kitchen and living room. On the opposite side of the living room, there is a tall sliding glass door. Eren and I cross the kitchen, and he opens a bedroom door for me to enter.

Wow.

The walls are stone. The furniture pieces are made up of autumn colors. The ceiling and floor consist of light-colored wood panels–each plank long enough to stretch from one end of the room to the other.

I step toward the glass lining the back wall. "This is my room?"

Eren shrugs. "I know you have pretty high standards, so I had the label pick a nice place."

I smile, eyes fixated on the breathtaking view from my room. The house is sitting on an acre of grass slanting down toward an ocean of dark-green pine trees. The sky is a baby-blue color painted with streaks of thin white clouds.

Eren is now standing next to me. The sunlight illuminates his side profile as he looks out the window. His eyes pan over the grass.

"Where's *your* room?" I ask.

"You already saw it." He turns to the door. "I sleep in the studio."

Is he doing that because I'm here?

Before I can tell him that he deserves this room, he's halfway out the door. "Once you get settled, meet me in the studio. And bring your notebook."

My notebook?

I cringe at the thought of showing a professional my songs.

After unpacking my things, I take a shower and put on my finest sweats. Before I know it, I'm sitting on my bed, flipping through my songs.

What if Eren doesn't like them?

What if he hates them?

I could tell him I forgot the book. Then he wouldn't have the chance to hate what I'd already written.

No. Harlow, you're good enough. You can do this. Be proud of your work. It's time to fucking do this.

When I walk into the studio, Eren is scrolling through his phone, leaning against a speaker. When he sees me, he gestures to the open seat next to him. "You ready to show me what you have?"

I take a deep breath and sit next to him.

"Sort of," I say.

Not at all, I think.

"Blake told me you've been writing your whole life."

"Y-yeah," I stutter. "Since I was a kid."

Eren extends an open palm.

He wants me to give him my notebook.

I don't want to give him my notebook.

"You don't want to give me the notebook," Eren says as if he can read my mind. "Do me a favor and hand me the notebook behind you."

I look over my right shoulder to see a black leather notebook on the shelf. His notebook. I grab it delicately, like I'm holding a newborn baby.

"Thanks," Eren says as I hand him his baby. "This is one of my songbooks. I've got a few. This one's full of songs I wrote for other artists. It's okay if you don't wanna show me what's in yours because your writing is personal to you. If it's for your eyes only, it's for your eyes only." He opens his notebook to a blank page. "We can start from scratch."

I feel myself growing more comfortable with Eren by the second. I can tell he just wants to make me feel comfortable with my writing, and it's working. I gently squeeze my notebook against my chest. Eren smiles, grabs a pen, and begins writing.

The only sound in the room is his pen gliding over the page. He's biting his lip, focused on each and every letter he writes. A couple words written, a couple words erased. A smile, then a frown. Then more words written, more smiles smiled.

I'm looking at the sparrow tattooed on his neck when his deep-brown eyes meet mine. "What do you think?"

I lean over the page to read what he wrote.

All I have is time to share with you,
Because this house just isn't big enough for us two,
Still, Imma share it with you cuz I feel it's right,
We could make this work, unlike the other times,
I couldn't care less if the world's on our side,
It's only 'bout the time we share alone tonight,

Yes, it feels foreign, but you'll know me,
If we work toward it, then soon you'll see,
That this is worth it, that I've got your back,
If you're for this, we'll start from scratch.

My heart flutters as I read it over–every word.
It's about this moment. This exact moment.
We're starting from scratch.
"This is…" I lean back in my chair. "This is really good."
"I exaggerate a little with some of the wording," Eren re-plies. "I know it can come across as if we're 'together,' but heightening emotions in the lyrics will evoke emotions from the listener. You get where I'm going with the overall idea."
I'm reading back over the lyrics when I feel a spark of inspiration. "Can I?"
Eren hands me the notebook. "Go for it."
I begin writing.

All I want is time to share with you,
To me, this house is perfect for just us two,
Promise me it's worth it, staying all these nights,
We could make this work, and I'm ready to try,
I couldn't care less about the world outside,
It's only 'bout the time we share alone tonight,

Yes, it feels foreign, but you'll know me,
Can we work toward it, so soon I'll see,
That this is worth it, I've got your back,
I'm all for this, we'll start from scratch.

I slowly hand Eren the notebook. I wait for his response, but he remains silent.

"I mean, it's just a thought," I say in case he thinks it's stupid. "I know it looks like I just reworded your verse, but that's kind of what I was going for… like a duet. If you had two people singing to each other, then it'd make sense. I hope that makes sense. Does that make sense?"

I'm babbling. Shut up, Harlow.

Eren finally breaks the silence, quoting one of the lines I wrote. "*We could make this work, and I'm ready to try*." He gives me a nudge. "You're ready to try, huh? Harlow, this is perfect."

I feel a wave of calm come over me, followed by a rush of excitement.

I can do this. *We* can do this.

♫ ♫ ♫

As the sun sets, Eren is in the kitchen cooking pasta. The glass door making up the back of the living room is slid open, where Blake is watching Charlie run around the grass. "Charlie, please don't eat that!" he shouts.

"So, tell me. Have you always known how to cook?" I ask between sips of champagne. "Or did you recently learn?"

Before Eren can answer, a flame erupts over the stovetop. He panics, setting his whiskey glass on the table before he dumps a glass of water over one of the pans.

"Dammit!" He turns the stone off and runs back to his phone. "The recipe said, *'ten minutes!*' It's only been eight."

I hold back a laugh.

Eren sighs. "Well, if me ruining dinner doesn't make the answer obvious, I never learned how to cook."

Was he making dinner without knowing how to make dinner?

I still can't get over the irony Eren embodies. The blend of tattoos. The piercings. He has a rugged and irresponsible look about him, but his actions make him appear considerate.

"Well…" Eren sighs as he dumps the burnt food into the trash. I hide my smile behind my glass when Eren holds up his phone and asks, "Do you like pizza?"

I nod, letting him see my smile.

He places an order for enough pizza to last us a week. With the house being as close as it is to a small town, the pizza gets here quick. It's nothing special and it's not on my diet plan, but it's so damn good.

The living room is filled with laughter as Blake and I share stories about how outrageous our childhood was.

"Tell Eren the story about the bunk bed!" I shout.

Blake shakes his head. "I hate that story."

"I wonder why," I reply with a mouthful of pizza. "Fine, I'll tell it!" I set my pizza slice down and stand over the coffee table for dramatic effect. "So, we went out on our yacht back when we were teenagers. Blake and all of his friends snuck alcohol into our room, and they thought it'd be a good idea to feed me shots of jäger–"

"Which you handled well," Blake interjects. "At first."

"At first," I repeat. "I kept telling the older kids that alcohol doesn't get me drunk, so they kept feeding me shots. We were all in the hot tub, and before I knew it, I was blacked-out drunk. They put me to bed on the top bunk in our room, and in the middle of the night…" I burst out in laughter as Blake lowers his head, embarrassed. "In the middle of the night, I threw up over the side of the top bunk, and it landed all over Blake's face because his head was hanging over the side of the bottom bunk."

"No!" Eren shouts, joining in on the laughter. Charlie giggles, feeding on our enthusiasm.

Blake shakes his head, then mutters, "Some of it landed in my mouth."

"Who puts the drunkest person on the top bunk?!" I laugh.

Eren points at Charlie. "Don't get any ideas," he teases. Charlie giggles some more.

As the laughter dies down, my eyes land on Eren. "Do you have any funny childhood stories?"

Eren folds his lips between his teeth as he and Blake look in different directions.

"Funny stories?" Eren asks, breaking the awkward silence. "Let me think." His eyes trail up to the ceiling as he ponders an answer.

I refine my question, thinking it'll help jog his memory. "Do you have *any* childhood stories?"

Eren just lets out a laugh to buy himself time to answer.

"What time do you guys plan on writing tomorrow?" Blake interrupts. At first, it seems rude to me, but I realize he's doing it to save Eren from answering my question.

Eren puckers his lips and flicks his eyes to mine. "What time do you usually wake up?"

"Four," I reply.

"A.M.?!" Eren and Blake reply in unison.

"Is that bad?" I ask innocently.

I suppose it sounds a little intense, but it's my routine. I can't change my routine just because I'm in a new place. If I tweak it even the slightest, then my entire day will be thrown off.

Eren stands. "Well, I'll be up when I wake up. We can start writing after breakfast."

"I have a call with the artist's manager in a couple days," Blake says while placing Charlie in his lap. "Hopefully, I'll get more details about who this guy even is."

"Sounds good," Eren replies. His tone is gentle as he says, "Goodnight, everybody."

When he disappears into the studio, I lean toward Blake and whisper, "Did I say something wrong?"

Blake shakes his head. "Eren doesn't really like to talk about his past."

CHAPTER SEVEN

EREN

I shut the studio door and sprawl myself onto the couch. The fact that I'm so calm right now is making me anxious. I don't feel my usual urge to drink myself to sleep.

What's different about tonight compared to every other night?

I hear Harlow's laugh coming from the living room, and that's when it becomes clear.

I'm not alone.

For the first time, I feel like I'm sharing life with somebody other than myself. I close my eyes, and I see Harlow. I see Blake. I see Charlie. I can't help but smile. I fall asleep happy, and still, the nightmare begins…

"PULL OVER!" the police officer shouts. "PULL… OVER!"

I crank the throttle of my motorcycle, thrusting myself for-
ward.

I can't go back, *I think to myself.* Faster. Ride faster.

Blue and red lights flood my peripherals as I weave through the highway traffic. My eyes frantically scan the road ahead, looking for a way to lose the two cop cars that are gaining on me.

There's no point in surrendering now. I have two pounds of drugs shoved into the backpack strapped to my chest. I'm only 16, but there's no doubt that I'll get arrested for the amount of drugs I have on me here in Nevada... or am I in Arizona?

All I can think is, There's no way in hell I can go back to juvie.

Up ahead, I spot another cop car merging onto the highway. I'm so jacked up on adrenaline right now I can't even be upset with my foster parents for using me to do their dirty work for them.

The two cop cars are gaining on me, and the merging cop car pulls up to my right. I turn to see the officer speaking through her radio. "SIR. PULL OVER. IMMEDIATELY."

I don't listen. I pick up speed.

I can't go back.

My front wheel pulls ahead of the cop car, putting all three of them behind me now. If I get arrested, I'll have to start all over again. They'll take me back to the orphanage. They'll pin me with a new foster family. At this point, I'm running out of second chances.

I can't go back.

The traffic ahead of me is clearing up. My heart drops as I spot the police barricade—a wall of blue and red flashing lights. A helicopter hovers above them, and I prepare to cut my losses.

"No, no, no," I repeat under my breath, but I can't slow down. I look left, then right. No way out. I'm finished.

The distance between the barricade and me becomes less by the second. My eyes fixate on the cement barriers blocking the road ahead. If I hit the barriers hard enough, I won't have to go back because I'll be dead.

I see the police officers clearing out from behind the barriers.

"IT'S A SUICIDE!" one of them screams to the other.

"Fuck," I whisper.

Just before I decide to meet Death, I slam the brakes. I'm within a hundred feet of the barriers when I jerk the bike and it skids out from under me. Sparks fly as I fall back onto the asphalt, but the motorcycle keeps sliding until...

I wake up in a puddle of my own sweat. My chest rises and falls with every heavy breath that leaves my trembling body.

"It already happened," I whisper to myself the same way I do every time this happens. "It's over. It already happened, and now it's over."

It takes me a second to realize I'm lying on the couch in the studio.

I'm in Montana. I'm safe.

I look around the dark room. Moonlight seeps through the window above me, casting shadows across the guitars mounted on the walls.

I sit up on the couch and itch the stubble on my face. I find it disappointing how, no matter where I go, my past finds a way to reach me through my nightmares. I wish I could tell myself it's only a nightmare, but it actually happened. It's one of the terrible memories I'm forced to relive when I fall asleep.

I don't always have these weird *memory-nightmares*. They only come when I go to sleep sober. It's as if my past lives on, pulling me back from my future.

I pull out a joint to smoke myself back to sleep with, but my eyes land on Harlow's notebook lying next to mine. I imagine her sleeping peacefully in the other room while Blake and Charlie sleep in the living room. I would never read Harlow's notebook without her consent, but the mere presence of it puts my mind at ease. Before I know it, I'm back asleep.

♫ ♫ ♫

I wake up to a moist sensation between my lips.

Mmmm.

I inhale the aroma, and I instantly crave it. *Bacon.*

I'm staring at the wood panels above me while caressing Harlow's notebook against my chest. "Shit!" I quietly set her notebook next to mine, exactly where I found it last night.

The morning light shines in streaks through the blinds until I raise them. Light pours into the room, and it takes a second for my eyes to adjust. I spot the joint on the floor next to the couch, realizing I didn't have to smoke it to fall back asleep. I turn back to Harlow's notebook.

Did sleeping with Harlow's notebook keep me from having my usual nightmares?

Suddenly, a second aroma sweeps my nose. *Waffles.*

I check my phone to see that it's just past eight. It's the earliest I've woken up in months. I shift my upper body, hearing a couple cracks as I reach the door. I open it as quietly as I can, just enough to peek through the narrow opening.

Harlow is dancing around the kitchen. A song is playing from the T.V. speakers, and she's singing the lyrics under her breath. The room is a blend of beautiful music and unhealthy breakfast foods. There is a high chance I died in my sleep last night because I like to think this is what heaven looks like.

I remember Harlow scaring me yesterday. Her back is to me, making this my chance to get even. I tiptoe into the kitchen. I'm nearly a foot away, looking down at her when I raise my hands and shout, "HARLOW!"

Harlow is mid-bacon-flip when her shoulders tense. "OH MY!" She throws her arms up in the air, and a piece of bacon flies in my direction. I catch the piece of bacon and smile at her. Until I hear a sizzling sound coming from my hand.

"AH! FUCK!" I'm frantically scanning the kitchen for a place to put the bacon strip when my eyes meet Harlow's.

"Why are you holding on to it?!" she shouts. "Drop it, Eren!"

I drop the sizzling piece of bacon onto the floor. "Ow, ow, ow."

Harlow takes on the form of Super Woman, flying to the freezer to pull out an ice pack. She lightly dabs it over my hand as my shock dissolves and the pain sets in. Her shoulders start shaking up and down, and I lower my head to get a look at her face. She dodges my glance. "Are you laughing?!" I ask, holding back my own laughter. "You're laughing!"

I finally hear her giggle. "I'm sorry, but you just tried to get even after I scared you yesterday. And now your hand…"

Our laughter is cut off as Blake groans from the couch. "Some of us are still sleeping over here."

Charlie's big head pops up between some blankets, and he flashes a little smile.

"I made bacon and waffles!" Harlow shouts. "Time to get up."

"How long have you been up for?" I ask, taking a seat at the table.

She sets the table and sits on the kitchen counter. "Since before sunrise. I did my home workout, made a green smoothie, read the Wall Street Journal, and took my cold shower. I even had more than enough time to make you kids breakfast."

Harlow's words come out so fast that I have to wait for them to register before responding. "I don't know how you managed to do all that."

"It's her daily routine," Blake mutters as he claims the seat next to me. "Pretty *psychopathy* if you ask me."

Harlow rolls her eyes. "The most successful people in the world have morning routines."

"I think you mean… most successful *psychopaths*," Blake replies.

Harlow ignores Blake's jab. "Eren, you don't have a morning routine?"

Blake laughs because he already knows the answer. I stuff my mouth with a bacon strip and nudge his shoulder. "I brush my teeth when I wake up. That's about it."

"And when do you usually wake up?" Harlow asks.

"Whenever my brain wants me to."

Judging by the repulsed look on her face, I can tell that Harlow doesn't have a spontaneous bone in her body. She probably knows what tomorrow will look like. And the day after that, and the day after that. But that's just not me. I go wherever life's current takes me.

"Is there a plan for today?" Harlow asks.

I swallow a piece of waffle. "We're just gonna write songs till our hands fall off."

"Amazing," she whispers. "Blake, are you and Charlie gonna spend the day with us in the studio?"

"Nah, we're going on a little walk today, right Charlie?" We turn to Charlie, who is nibbling on a bacon strip bigger than his head.

"Sounds great," Harlow says. "We'll touch base after that." She winces at her own words.

"*Touch base*?" Blake cringes. "You sound like Father."

"I know," Harlow snaps back before standing. "I need mouthwash. That left a horrid taste in my mouth."

After changing my clothes and brushing my teeth, Harlow and I meet in the studio.

Harlow is flipping through songs I've written for about 10

minutes before she mutters, "No offense, but these are depressing. They're really good. They're just… sad."

"Which one?" I ask from the couch. I watch her bun move from side to side as she reads over the lyrics like she's going to be quizzed at some point.

She reads some of the lines aloud. *"I've been broken down, my heart's been torn right out, my love life is my hell, she's still on my mind."* She flips a page. "These lyrics make me sad. Some of these songs were on the radio?"

"Yep." I shrug. "People are broken, and for some reason, they like to be reminded through the music they listen to."

She swivels her chair toward me, her curious eyes meeting mine. "So, you write for people instead of yourself."

"I write for whoever pays me."

Harlow studies me, then says, "Eren, they're great songs. They just don't seem like they're written by you."

Her words sting a bit, but I'm not too offended. It only stings because I've thought the same. Maybe it's because I write songs for other people to sing. Maybe it's because I've spent all these years writing for artists singing about their own toxic lives instead of *my own* toxic life.

Harlow's eyes pan around the studio–the guitars hanging on the walls, the stacked speakers and equipment.

"I write music for other people," I explain. "The songs aren't supposed to sound like they're written by me. That's the point of me writing them for other artists."

"Have you ever written for you?" She holds my gaze, and the hairs on the back of my neck stand. Harlow is asking some intense questions for somebody who has never written songs professionally.

"Have I ever written for me?" I glance at my notebook lying on her lap. "Sort of."

The truth is that I have, the most recent song being based on the night I met Harlow. She walked into that alley, and when she left, the lyrics just poured right onto the page.

"You and Blake said this artist wants the songs to be about your life, not his." Harlow flashes a smirk. "So, that's exactly what we're gonna do. We're gonna write about your life." She grabs a pen. "Come here. Sit."

I do what she says. But when I sit, I have no idea where to start. The blank page mocks me as I sit there in silence.

"Not feeling too inspired, huh?" Harlow asks, now standing over my shoulder.

I usually put myself in the mind of the artist I'm writing for. But having spent every second of my entire life in my mind, you would think that writing about what's on my mind would be easy. It's not. Not when I've distanced myself from my emotions most of my life.

I glance around the room until I spot the sea of trees outside the window. If I'm going to get inspired, I'll have to stick to what I know works, which is throwing myself into the unknown–submitting myself to life itself.

"We're going on a hike," I say, making my way to the door.

"A hike?! What?! Why?!"

I start slipping on my boots. "To find some inspiration."

"But we don't even know what's out there."

I smirk. "Exactly. Meet me on the back deck in five minutes."

In a few minutes, I'm standing on the deck overlooking the grass stretching out to the pines. The crisp air tickles my face as I jam my hands into my jeans pockets. It's warm, and the clouds are airbrushed delicately across the blue sky.

I hear the sound of the back door shut. "Don't laugh," Harlow says.

I turn around and instantly laugh. It couldn't be more obvious that Harlow has never hiked.

Harlow shakes her head. She's wearing a white hoodie, white jeans, and white sneakers–her notebook in hand. "I didn't pack anything for hiking," she mutters.

"Right. I can see that. But you've been hiking before, right?" Harlow avoids eye contact. "Harlow…"

With her chin lowered, she looks up at me, pinching her lips together.

I sigh while tightening my backpack straps. "Well, there's a first for everything. Just know that those white shoes are about to get dirty."

I hop down the wooden steps and begin trudging across the grass plain. "Those green things out there in the distance? Those are called 'trees.' They're like buildings, but not like buildings at all."

Harlow smiles, taking my jabs like a champ. "I can't believe you're actually getting me to do this."

The two of us are swallowed by the towering pine trees, and the world around us darkens. I stay a step behind Harlow so I can admire her admiring her surroundings. The dark shades of green. The crunch of twigs below our shoes. The sunlight poking through the treetops. The whispering wind.

Sunlight coats the side of Harlow's face as the corner of her lips curls up. "I don't get out as often as I should."

"Have you lived in one place your whole life?"

"Blake and I grew up in the Hamptons." Harlow shrugs. "I know what you're thinking. A couple of rich kids who have never experienced… well… any of this. Our parents kept us close, so I suppose you could say I've lived a pretty cushioned lifestyle."

"Nothing wrong with that. It's not like we choose where we grow up."

"True. But there's something wrong with choosing to never *leave* where you've grown up. I grew up in the Hamptons, and after graduating high school, I moved an entire hour-and-a-half away to Manhattan, where I met Jordan."

"Jordan, the boyfriend?"

"Boyfriend of five years." Harlow smiles at the ground as we continue walking.

I'm shocked by her response. Five years seems like an eternity to somebody like myself, who has never even been in a relationship.

"Jordan reminded me of home," Harlow adds.

"Is that good or bad?"

"Both," she replies. "Sometimes I ask myself–do I love him for who he is or because he's all I know?" She suddenly stiffens. "I can't believe I just said that. How did you just get me to say that?"

I chuckle, lifting a hand in surrender. "Hey, I'm just listening."

While a part of me is happy to find out that Harlow isn't completely satisfied with her relationship, it also worries me. I'm scared to imagine what I would feel if she were single. Right now, Harlow having a boyfriend and Blake staying with us might be the only two things keeping me from getting attached in some romantic way.

Harlow hops up onto a log, and we're almost at eye level when she lifts her chin. Her eyes narrow in on mine. "Where did you grow up?"

I shake my head. "No, no. We're out here looking for song-writing inspiration. This isn't a therapy session."

"Oh, hush."

"Nope."

"Eren…" Harlow's voice is concrete. She places her hand on my shoulder to keep herself from falling. "Your past is a part of your life, you know. And your past is something you can pull inspiration from.”

Her words make themselves at home in my mind. I’ve never used my past as inspiration. Instead, I ran from it. I lock onto Harlow’s curious eyes and instantly feel one of my many walls come crashing down.

“I grew up everywhere,” I admit. “My dad left my mom when he found out she was pregnant with me. The first 10 years of my life were spent on the road with her, and I’d watch her sing at bars and restaurants all around the country. She was an aspiring singer. She had a manager and all that. When I was 10, she…”

I look down. My throat tickles as if my words are turning to sand before they leave my mouth. When my eyes meet Harlow’s again, she nods, encouraging me to continue like it’s necessary for me to.

It’s emotionally draining for me to say what I’ve kept to myself all my life. I let out a quivering breath and continue with the remaining energy left in me. “When I was 10, my mom committed suicide. I remember her getting off the phone with her manager the night before I found her body. I don’t know what they talked about, but she cried most of that night. The next morning, I woke up next to her like I did every morning. But this time, she never woke up. I was only 10, so at first, I thought she was kidding. After a while, I got scared, and I saw some of her pills spilled on the floor by her nightstand. I thought she wasn’t waking up because she didn’t take her medicine. Little did I know, she took too much of it.”

I’m holding back tears like a dam on the verge of overflowing. Harlow doesn’t move a muscle, but I watch tears fall from her eyes.

I exhale another quivering breath. “At the funeral reception, I overheard her manager saying it’s my fault. That I’m the reason my mom could never fully pursue her dream of becoming a singer.

Giving birth to me killed her chances of making it, and she gave up on herself because I wasn't enough. It's like she gave life to what led her to take her own."

I force back tears until they're no longer waiting to make their way into the world. "After that, I bounced between foster homes until I was 18. It was one terrible family after another. When I turned 18, I felt life pulling me into the music industry. I started with songwriting, but it wasn't till recently that I realized I wanted to start singing like she did. I have this feeling that if I can make it as a singer, then maybe she didn't end her life for nothing."

I look up at hints of blue poking between the treetops, then close my eyes. I feel lighter, as if the blame weighs less than it did before. When I look back down at Harlow, she lifts her notebook. It's turned to a blank page with a pen lying in the middle of it. She hands it to me, the smooth leather cool against my open palms. I sit on the log Harlow is standing on and begin writing.

I've been over it, over it,
The life I need won't wait,
I'm the man I don't wanna be,
But I made it that way,

I've been trapped in my mind,
Got a whole lot of time for games,
I'm the man I don't wanna be,
And I'm trapped in my ways,

Now all these thoughts won't leave me alone,
I don't know if I could ever let go,

I don't need your sympathy,
Just tell me that you're listening,

Tell me how I'm alive somehow,
Tell me what I need,
I've got all these thoughts inside of me,

Because of all my flaws, I'm building up walls,
Believing that drugs keep me sane,
Sometimes I'll sit right down at the doorstep,
And I'll shake it off,
Everybody's gotta walk by,
And they stare like I'm insane,
I've got anxiety,
That I bury deep right inside of me,
Bottoms up keeps them down,
That's how I solve the pain,

Mama, are you watching? Are you looking down?
No one ever listens, and I miss having you around.

A teardrop lands on the page. Then another. And another.

I read the words back. Again. And again.

It takes me a couple minutes of rereading the lyrics before I realize Harlow's arm is around me. She smiles at me as tears trickle down her freckled cheeks.

"This." Harlow takes a deep breath. "*This* is written by you… for you."

I lock eyes with her, and though I'm smiling, tears just keep falling, and I let them. I don't know what to say, nor do I know what to do other than be grateful for what Harlow just did for me.

I wipe one of my tears with my sleeve. "I think you might've just changed my life," I say.

Harlow wipes a final tear just above her smile.

We don't say anything because we don't have to.

The moment itself is enough.

I knew Harlow was different from the moment I met her in that alley. And now, she's showing me how. Here she is, bringing out a side of my songwriting I never knew existed. She's just shown me that something beautiful can grow from the ash, like land turns to life. I can't help but feel every one of my walls come crashing down.

CHAPTER EIGHT

HARLOW

For the first time in years, I wake up to sunlight instead of my morning alarm.

For the first time in years, I sleep in.

For the first time in years, I'm–*I'm behind.*

I sit up in my bed, clutching the bedsheet against my chest.

I overslept.

I was supposed to be up at 4a.m. for my workout. I need my smoothie. The rest of the world is already well into their day. I feel like a mess. A slob. An underachiever.

My phone is littered with notifications. Emails from work, a couple of texts from Talia, and three missed calls from Jordan. Above the notifications is the time: *9:03AM.*

"Dammit."

I only have three hours left of my morning until it's noon. The wolves of the world have already started hunting for the day while my lazy puppy-dog ass is still naked in bed.

Wait a second.

I look around the room, taking in the smoky aroma of pine trees flowing through the opening of my bedroom window. I scoot myself to the edge of the bed and press the bottom of my feet against the wood floor. With the sheet wrapped around me, I approach the window to see a cloudless sky. Endless blue stretches over the frosted mountaintops standing tall over the sea of pines.

I'm not in the city.

I don't need to clock in to Beck.

And I'm actually rested.

For once, I catch a glimpse of what life is like without a routine. A part of me hates how much I like this feeling–the feeling of not knowing what today will bring besides getting to write songs. I still can't believe this is Eren's life, every day.

I slept like a baby after our hike yesterday. Eren's story left me dumbstruck to the point where I must have forgotten to set my alarm for this morning. I couldn't think about anything or anyone besides him after he confided in me the way he did.

It hurts to know that a guy like Eren hurts the way he does. No child deserves to go through what he went through, finding his own mother the morning after she commits suicide, then hearing he's the reason for it. I can't fathom carrying that kind of weight, and I respect Eren for being able to carry it all these years.

My phone vibrates, and I see that it's Jordan calling.

I answer. "Hi, babe."

"Harlow, are you alright?!" Jordan gasps. "It's been 24 hours, and I haven't heard a damn word from you."

"Sorry, I went on a hike yesterday and I was so tired when we got back that I just passed out."

"Hiking?" Jordan scoffs. "*You* went hiking? With Blake?"

I pinch my lips together, realizing Jordan still thinks I'm on this trip with Blake and only Blake. "Yeah! It was actually really nice. We–"

"You never hike," Jordan says skeptically.

"You know, there's a first for everything," I reply with less confidence than I might've hoped for.

"A first for everything, huh?" There's a moment of silence until Jordan says, "When are you coming home?"

"The plan is to stay out here with Blake for the week, so I think we'll fly back on Sunday."

Whispering voices exchange words on the other side of the line.

"Are you at the office?" I ask.

"Yeah, sorry. Penny just needed me to sign off on something. Listen, I called you because, as of this morning, Beck is a leading sponsor for a charity gala taking place tomorrow night. Your father says we need to be there… together."

"But I'm with Blake until–"

"Right, we get that you need to be there for your brother," Jordan's voice turns to a whisper. "But you know how important this charity shit is for Beck's image. Babe, we need you here. I wouldn't be bothering you if I didn't think this was important."

I lower my head. It's like Father senses me out here chasing my dream, so he finds a way to mess it up for me. And he's using my boyfriend to do it for him.

Jordan's tone softens. "I understand that Blake thinks he needs you right now, but your father needs you. Beck needs you. *I* need you. I was asked to give a speech, and I want you by my side when I give it. After all, we're the Dream Team."

"Okay, okay," I exhale. "I'll fly back tomorrow afternoon."

"*Tomorrow afternoon*," Jordan repeats. "Perfect. Text me before you take off so I know when to send Francis to pick you up. Okay?"

"Okay."

"Don't forget," he adds. "Text me before you take off. I love you."

"Love you, too."

The call ends, and I'm suddenly alone in this room that's way too big for one person. After one more silent stretch, I head to the bathroom to get ready. For the first time in years, I don't shower. I brush my teeth and spit my toothpaste into the sink. When I look up, I smirk at the fact that my hair has a mind of its own. Instead of it being tied into my usual top bun, it's parted down the middle, my wavy locks falling well-past my shoulders and stopping just above my waist.

Growing up, Mother was always the first to remind me that my natural hair should be tied back because of how wild it is. When I moved in with Jordan, he continued reminding me the same. But neither of them are here.

I slip on my pajama pants and a white crop top. When I open the door, I immediately regret not tying my hair up.

"Harlow?!" Blake gasps from the kitchen counter.

When Eren's eyes meet mine, he spits a mouthful of coffee at Charlie, who is sitting in his high chair.

"Dude!" Blake shouts at Eren. "Did you just spit coffee at my kid?!" Blake picks up a crying and confused Charlie.

I hold Eren's gaze. "Holy shit," he whispers, completely unaware of what he just did to Charlie.

Blake bounces Charlie in his arms to calm him down. I grab a roll of paper towels and start dabbing Charlie's coffee-stained forehead.

"I'm so sorry," Eren says. "I just… I wasn't expecting–"

"Wasn't expecting what?" I smirk while taking Charlie from Blake's arms. "Shh, shh, it's okay, Charlie. Your favorite aunt is here."

Eren struggles to hide his grin. "I wasn't expecting you. I wasn't expecting you, is all."

Blake sits on the stool and leans over his laptop. "You can tell her you think she's pretty without spitting coffee at my kid, you know," Blake teases. "Harlow, I forgot how long your hair is."

"Is it too much?" I ask. "I can always tie it back up."

"No, I think it looks great," Blake replies. "Plus, Mother and Father don't like your hair this way, which means I love it."

Eren blinks at Blake. "I'm sorry, wait. Your parents *don't* like you looking like this?!"

I shrug, then set Charlie down. "It's a bit on the wilder side."

"Well, I love the wilder side," Eren snaps back with a smirk.

"Easy there, buddy. That's my sister," Blake replies without looking up from his laptop.

Eren and I laugh. As I reach for a coffee mug, Eren cuts me off. "Allow me," he says. "You made breakfast yesterday, so the least I can do is pour you coffee." He begins pouring. "I would cook for you, but after the other night, I should probably stay far away from pots and pans."

I smile. "Coffee is perfect."

"I was thinking we can all go into town tomorrow night," Eren says. "It's a small town, but I'm sure we can find something fun to do."

"That'd be great." I take a seat at the counter next to Blake. "But Beck Holdings is sponsoring a gala, and they sort of want me to make an appearance." Blake stops typing. He continues staring at the laptop screen, waiting for me to continue. "I told Jordan I would fly in tomorrow."

Eren's eyebrows draw apart after he hands me my coffee. "So, you're leaving tomorrow?"

I caress the warm coffee mug between my palms. Eren is disheartened, like a kid who just found out the tooth fairy isn't real.

"But you've only been here a couple days," Eren adds.

"He found a way to get to you, huh?" Blake mutters.

"What do you mean?"

"Father found a way to reel you back in." Blake clenches his jaw, his frustration growing more by the second. He's always been soft-spoken, but the tension in the room suggests otherwise. "Even when he thinks you're out here with me because I'm 'grieving' over Miranda, he thinks it's more important for you to be in the office." He shakes his head.

Eren picks up on the tension. "It's alright," he chimes in. "It's fine. Go tomorrow and take care of business. You can always fly back out here and we'll keep writing."

Blake continues typing. I glance back at Eren. He flashes a half-hearted smile and nods as if understanding my situation. Here I am, enjoying Eren's world to the fullest, chasing my dream. And yet, my world finds a way to suck me right back into it. I feel spineless, now a victim of the routine lifestyle I no longer want to live.

♫ ♫ ♫

Eren and I spend the entire day writing one song after another. The songs are decent, but nothing worth celebrating. At this point, I've found myself becoming more comfortable writing with Eren.

"Some days will be slower than others," Eren says while strumming one of his guitars. "Regardless, we just need to keep writing. Something will eventually click."

I lean back in my chair with my feet up on the table. I could list the things Jordan would complain about right now, from my hair being down to my feet being up on the table, yet Eren accepts me as I am. I can't help but feel a sense of freedom when I'm around him. I'm free to look however I want while I do whatever I want.

I watch Eren on the couch with the guitar on his lap. He plucks a melody with his fingers that makes me feel like I'm floating. He's not even trying right now, and still, I could listen to him play all day. I feel gutted when he suddenly stops.

The corner of his lips curls up. "Let's go into town tonight."

"Tonight?"

"Tonight. Come on! We can find a bar or something and meet some of the locals."

He stands, ignoring my pondering expression. I suck in a quick breath when he pulls me up from my chair.

"Blake!" Eren shouts while prancing into the kitchen. "We're hitting the town to–"

Blake presses a finger to his lips for us to be quiet. "Charlie is napping," he whispers. "You guys go ahead. I'll be hopping on that call with the artist's manager soon."

"Are you sure?" Eren whispers, leaning against the kitchen counter. "Do you want us to stick around for the call?"

Blake waves us off. "I'll just let you know what they say later." He glances past Eren's shoulder where I'm standing. "You two go. It'll be nice for Harlow to check out the local spots before we fly back tomorrow."

"You're going, too?" Eren sighs.

Blake nods. "It's probably best for me to get back to the office. I'll catch up with you when the artist asks to meet with us."

Eren slouches against the countertop. His saddened expression turns into a forced smile when he looks my way. "Meet me out back at sunset," he says before walking back to the studio.

♫ ♫ ♫

As the sun sets, I'm digging through my bags for an outfit that makes me look hot, but not too hot–something that says, *"I want you to think I look hot but don't even think about making a move."*

I pull out a plaid jacket, wondering how to make it look less bougie. I pull the jacket over a black bandeau and squeeze into some black jeans that make my ass look bigger than it usually looks. As I fix my hair in the mirror, I see a cream-colored cowboy hat hanging on the wall behind me.

Do I dare wear the cowboy hat?

I've never been outside of New York, so I don't even know if it's socially acceptable to wear a cowboy hat here in Montana. Then again, it's on the wall, and it works with the jacket I'm wearing.

I step out into the living room, bracing myself for Eren and Blake's disses.

Blake looks up from his phone. "Good God," he whispers from the couch. "I want to make fun of you right now, but I also want you to have a great time tonight."

"Well, thank you, partner," I say in my best cowboy-voice.

I tip my cowboy hat like I see them do in the movies. Blake cringes, then says, "That's *winner* to you, partner. I think Eren is out back somewhere."

"Much obliged, winner."

I peek out the glass door lining the back of the living room. My eyes pan left to right–slowly–taking in the view I may never get tired of. It's beautiful, only, there is a difference this time around. I spot Eren's back as he sits on the edge of the deck.

I make sure the back door doesn't make a sound when I open it. Not because I want to sneak up on him, but because I see him playing one of the acoustic guitars from the studio.

My heart takes flight when I hear his voice suddenly become one with his strumming. It enhances the world around us, making it seem like the world smooths over. Oxygen suddenly becomes easier to breathe. The colors of the setting sun and the shades of green in the distance become a painted picture. This moment is anything but real.

The melody Eren sings makes its way through my body as I bring myself closer to him. It feels like medicine curing an illness I never even knew I had. Hearing his voice makes me feel so good, the thought of becoming addicted to the sound doesn't even phase me.

I could overdose on his voice, and anyone who hears him sing will understand why I made the decision to.

He stops when the wood creaks under my shoe.

No, don't stop.

Eren turns, wide-eyed. "How long have you been standing there for?!"

"So, you *can* sing," I say, ignoring his question.

Eren looks like a whole different person from the one I met back in the alley. His bleached hair, the defeated look on his face back then. Now, here he is, with an entirely different look and calming presence created by the sound of his voice.

Is this the same voice he was afraid of showing the restaurant that night?

When I sit next to him, I catch a whiff of cologne–a combination of lavender and orange blossom. He sets the guitar down, and his eyes shoot above my forehead. "Is that your cowboy hat?"

I feel my face flush. "I, uh… found it." I take the hat off and cover it in my lap. "It was a joke."

Eren smirks. "It's cute."

I don't want his comment to make me blush, but it does. I look down to hide my reaction. Being around Eren is starting to make me feel guilty. My curiosity is gradually becoming more than mere curiosity, which isn't something that should be happening when the love of my life is on the other side of the country. But then again, it's my last night in Montana. Tomorrow I'll be reunited with Jordan, and I can go back to what I know, which is loving him like I always have and always will.

My eyes land on Eren's notebook between his feet. The page is lined with lyrics.

"Did you write this right now?" I ask.

"Yep."

"Is this what you were singing?"

"It is." He picks up the book and hands it to me.
I read the page out loud.

I've got you in my head,
Thoughts about that night when,
You gave me a reason to change,

You're all I've been thinking about,
I can't believe it,
You gave me a reason to live,

Now I'm somehow standing still,
For you, I know I will,

So don't stop, tell me now,
You won't stop breakin' down my walls,
I'll open up for you,

Ink may cover my scars,
But you gave me a new start,
Reminded me that I have a heart,

My world isn't too far,
So, please don't make this too hard,
I'll give you a reason to stay.

A cold sweat comes over me.
Are these lyrics about me? No, no, no.
The book trembles in my hands as I hand it back to Eren.
"Are you okay?" he asks.
I want to say no. Eren's words shouldn't give me the butter-
flies I currently feel and I shouldn't have come out here because this

is all becoming less about me chasing my dream and more about me wanting to learn more about Eren and I can feel myself suddenly not wanting to leave tomorrow and this is becoming absolutely fucked.

"Harlow?" Eren's voice pulls me from my trance.

I hug my knees, looking over the ocean of trees. A sliver of sun is left for us to see over the mountaintops. I clear my throat before saying, "I have to ask. Is this song about me?" I prepare to let him down easy.

"Hypothetically speaking, what if I say yes?" Eren's eyes lock onto mine.

"Then, hypothetically speaking, I'd say I have a boyfriend."

Eren chuckles under his breath. "Well, hypothetically speaking, it doesn't matter if you have a boyfriend. It doesn't matter how you feel about me. It doesn't matter if you even know me. You can inspire a song by simply existing." He stands and offers to help me up with his ink-covered hand. "And you inspired this one. Don't overthink it."

Don't overthink it?! He just did one of the most thoughtful things someone could do.

I've only known Eren for a couple weeks, and not only is he helping me chase my dream, but he's introducing me to a whole new world. Maybe it's a good thing that I'm flying home tomorrow. I'm afraid of what will happen if I stay another day in this house with this man.

Eren guides me to the front of the house. "As much as I love the cowboy hat, I have something else for you to wear."

The wind sweeps the trees above as I follow Eren to the garage. Day has become dusk, and it's getting cold out—cold enough to see my own breath. I'm buttoning up my jacket when Eren unlocks the garage door. My eyes widen the second he opens it. I take a small step back. It's what my instincts tell me to do at the sight of danger.

"I can't ride that," I blurt out.

I've never even been on a motorcycle.

"You don't have to," Eren says as he hands me a motorcycle helmet. "*I'm* gonna ride it, and you're gonna hold on to me while I do."

I shake my head. My parents aren't even here right now, but I can hear them scolding me. I'm 23 and living on my own, but I feel like they'll ground me if they catch me riding this thing. I've never known anyone with a motorcycle. It's not common in the Hamptons or in Manhattan. It's not common because you'd be stupid to ride one. Or at least that's what I've been raised to believe.

"Where's *your* helmet?" I ask before putting the helmet on.

Eren rolls his eyes as he sits on the motorcycle. The bike looks vintage, most likely from the 90's.

"The town is less than four miles away." Eren suddenly jerks his body, and the engine roars. It might be the most attractive thing I've ever seen, and the engine's purr is making me feel a rush in all the right places before I even…

"Get on," he says with a smirk.

My body glides toward him before my mind decides whether or not I should. Something in me obeys the urge before I do. I'm led to believe it's curiosity, which I'm realizing may be a symptom of living the sheltered life I've lived.

I tighten my arms around Eren's torso. He's wearing a denim jacket, but I can feel his muscles tighten through the layers. I feel vulnerable, trusting Eren with my life while on the back of this motorcycle. As we jolt forward, I begin to whimper, but the thrill follows… the thrill of submitting myself to the unknown.

CHAPTER NINE

EREN

I get butterflies when her arms tighten around me. I'm careful in the way I ride over the dirt road. It's one thing to ride a motorcycle by yourself. It's another to have someone trust you enough to ride with you. It becomes a surreal moment, weaving through the pine trees reaching for the dark-blue sky above.

"How you doin' back there?!" I shout over the roaring engine.

"Amazing!" Harlow shouts back.

Her grip tightens more than I thought it could, and I like the feeling of it more than I thought I would. We reach the main road, two wide lanes that extend in either direction forever. Not a car in sight, which means the open road is ours. I make a left onto the asphalt and look up at the sky as we pick up speed. The dark-green trees are becoming black silhouettes against the sky as it turns to its darkest shade of blue the higher up you look.

I wonder if Harlow has ever been on the back of a motorcycle. I still remember the first time I rode one. I was 15, living with a foster family in Colorado… or was it Wyoming? At the time, a motorcycle was cheaper than a car. It was the quickest way to get me back on the road.

When I was a kid, I didn't understand why my mom lived life on the road. Losing her made me realize that if I live life on the road, moving from one place to the next, I would ensure that I never lose another loved one again.

Life on the road means no responsibility, no drama, no heartbreak. I craved this lifestyle so much as a teenager that I broke laws to live it. I craved life on the road so intensely, and for so long, I can sense when somebody else craves it. I can feel it like arms wrapped around my body. I can feel it in the way I feel Harlow right now. She wants this life, and I want to give it to her.

The more I pick up speed, the tighter Harlow holds me, so I pick up speed as often as I can. I find her lack of experience attractive. It gives me an opportunity to provide for her in a way she would never expect. She makes me feel like I can be desired.

Gaps appear between the walls of trees on both sides of us. Illuminated signs that couldn't be more straightforward: *BAR, RESTAURANT, MOTEL, LIQUOR, LIQUOR, LIQUOR, BAR, LIQUOR.*

Harlow points over my shoulder at a neon-blue sign. It's on the side of the road, reading "*BAR.*" I pull over into a dirt lot to see a litter of Harley Davidson motorcycles, some beat-up cars, and a couple R.V.'s.

Even under the blue light, I can see Harlow beaming when she takes off the helmet. "THAT WAS SO FUN!" she shouts, her voice even raspier from the spike of adrenaline.

She shakes her hair out, and it lays messily past her shoulders. Just when I thought Harlow couldn't be any more stunning, she let her hair down. Ever since she walked into the kitchen this morning, taking my eyes off of her feels like an injustice.

She lifts her hands, bouncing on her tiptoes. "The wind! The trees! The road! The road just keeps going! Does it ever end?!"

"I think it ends when you hit the ocean," I tease, leaning back against my bike. "Was that your first time riding a motorcycle?"

Harlow ignores my question as she twirls around the lot. "The stars! You can actually see the stars out here. How tall do you think the trees are? Do you think if we just kept riding, the woods would turn into the desert? What is even out there? Is this what life on the road is like?!"

I cross my arms, taking in Harlow's fascination with my world. I could stare at her forever, just watching the way she lives her life. I'll watch her from the front row for as long as she lets me.

It's never been more obvious that Harlow has lived her entire life in a box. It may be a nice box, but it's still a box. We didn't even drive four miles, and this is her response. I wonder how she would respond to my life if she lived it with me. We could cover hundreds of miles a month.

Harlow's constant outpour of thoughts and questions becomes a trickle. Her eyes land on the blue sign.

"Bar," she whispers. "What do you think is inside?"

"It's probably a pet shop," I tease, lifting myself off the bike. "I've always wanted a Husky. Maybe I'll adopt one tonight."

Harlow laughs. "Huskies shed, you know."

"Perfect." I open the front door for her. "I shed, too."

The bar is simple but crowded for a weeknight. The town is so small, its entire population could very well be in here right now, but chances are these are all people who live life on the road. *My fellow detachers.*

The bar is long and narrow. The bar top lines the left wall, while booths line the right, and a stage is built against the back wall. Nostalgia creeps into my mind when I look at the stage. I've been here before. But then again, this bar looks like it'd be straight out of a Western movie. *That's it. I've probably seen it in a movie.*

We find two leather barstools between a biker gang and

random couples smoking cigarettes. It's dark but not dark enough to miss the crooked smile on the bartender's face. Her teeth are yellow, her hair ratty. She makes us smile in an instant.

"Hello, beautiful people." She has a smoker's voice, hoarse and low. "What can I grab you?"

"Do you have a drink menu?" Harlow chirps from her stool.

There is no way in hell this bar has a menu. I would be surprised if they have toilet paper in their bathrooms.

The bartender laughs. It's genuine, not one intended to mock Harlow. "The menu is on the wall, hun." She raises her arms, and we look at the wall of scattered bottles.

Harlow blinks at the wall, not knowing which drink is what, so I say, "We'll do two whiskeys… neat."

The bartender nods and starts on the drinks. I spin myself around, so my back is pressed against the bar top.

"Two whiskeys?!" Harlow glares at me. "I'm not drinking your gasoline-drink."

I get comfortable, spreading my arms along the edge of the bar top. "You also thought you weren't gonna ride on the back of my bike." I smirk. "But you did, and you liked it."

Harlow rolls her eyes. She silently takes in her surroundings, absorbing every millimeter of the place and the people in it. One of the biker gang members accidentally presses up against my seat as he scoffs at somebody in his group. I don't address it, considering they're all massive and already hammered-drunk.

The bartender sets our glasses on the bar top, and Harlow eyes her glass of whiskey like it's a dead rat.

I lift one of the glasses, locking eyes with Harlow. "To life on the road."

She reluctantly clinks her glass against mine, then forces a sip while I down half my glass with ease. When I see the burning whiskey taste finally leave her tongue, I say, "Tell me more about your boyfriend."

"We met at Cornell University. I was only 18, and he was 22 at the time… a 'senior.'" She adds air quotes to the word. "We met at one of my first sorority parties. He was bugging me all night, asking me to go on a date with him. I thought he was super cute, but I heard stories about these frat parties and how the older guys go for the freshman girls, so I kept my distance."

I raise a brow. "Kept your distance until…"

"Until the following Monday. Nothing happened between us at the party besides him getting into a fistfight with his friend over something stupid."

"Woah, a fistfight?"

"Jordan has a bit of a temper," Harlow says casually. "Anyway, I'm studying with my roommate in the library on Monday afternoon. He comes in, pulls up a chair, stands on the chair, and not only apologizes for being drunk when asking me out, but he asks me out in front of the entire library."

"And that worked?!"

Harlow shakes her head. "Nope. I said no, but he wasn't finished. One of his friends came in and placed a rose on my desk. Then another friend came with another rose. Then another, and another. They just kept coming! Jordan said he'll keep giving me roses until I agree to go on at least one date with him."

"So, you said yes."

Harlow takes a deep breath. "I was a freshman. Of course I said yes. I mean, here is Jordan, the popular frat-boy stud who makes this outrageous public display of affection toward me–*me*, of all people! I couldn't refuse."

I cock my head back, shocked at her statement. "What do you mean, '*me of all people*?' You're a catch."

She smiles. "On that first date, Jordan told me his plan… Wall Street. Investment banking. A penthouse in the Upper East Side.

I found it really attractive that he had a plan for himself and he was determined to make it happen."

I swallow the rest of my whiskey. "What about *your* plan?" I ask. "Did you have a plan for yourself at the time?"

Harlow takes a sip of her whiskey and coughs. "My plan just-so-happened to be the same as his. With my father being *the* William Beck of Beck Holdings on Wall Street, it only made sense for me to walk in his footsteps–Wall Street, investment banking, and everything that comes with it. For my entire life, my parents injected this lifestyle into my veins like I'm their lab rat. And it worked. My heart was always in music like Blake, though. I just let my parents make my decisions for me. Now, here I am."

Harlow looks down at the near-empty glass in front of her. The conversation is quickly turning into one about our mommy-and-daddy issues, which is probably why she swallows the rest of her glass. This time, she doesn't wince at the taste.

She exhales. "My father and Jordan really hit it off. I think it's because they're a lot alike. They're both money-hungry and tough-loving."

The biker gang cheers at something going on in their circle, so I scoot closer to Harlow. "Do you love him?" I ask.

Harlow's eyes narrow. "Do I love Jordan? Of course," she snaps. "I've been with Jordan for five years. You can't not love someone you've been with for that long."

The bartender sets two new whiskey glasses on the bar top. I look at mine for a second, then at Harlow.

"What does love feel like?" I ask softly. I immediately cringe. I'm 28, asking what love feels like. But I can't help it. I've never known.

Harlow laughs, then sees that I'm being serious. She straightens her posture, pondering an answer. "*What does love feel like?*" she repeats.

I regret asking the question. It sounds even more ridiculous when I hear it leave Harlow's lips.

How do you even explain what love feels like?

And how could I not learn it for myself at this point?

"HEY, BUDDY!" a hoarse voice shouts from over my shoulder.

I turn to face one of the bikers. My eyes widen when I see the entire gang staring at me. I'm pretty tall but still the shortest out of everyone in the gang. They might be twice my height and three times my width. Or at least the whiskey is starting to make it seem that way.

I tighten my grip around my glass, ready to use it as a weapon if one of them disrespects Harlow. The biker farthest from us splits the group and stops in front of me. I'm looking up at him when I feel something shoved into my chest. I look down, and a cold sweat comes over me when I see it. It's a notepad. The title on the page reads, "*KARAOKE SIGN-UPS.*"

"Why me?" I exhale.

I look up at the man glaring down at me. His gray handlebar mustache is soaked in liquor. I get a secondhand buzz when he says, "WINSTON SAYS HE'LL SING FOR US. BUT HE DOESN'T WANNA GO FIRST."

"Who is Winston?" I ask.

The man opens up his stance, and one of the other bikers gives me an intimidating nod.

That must be Winston.

I don't want to mess with Winston. Winston is wearing sunglasses indoors.

"WE WANT WINSTON TO SING!" one of the biker-ladies shouts.

I feel a tiny hand on my shoulder. "He'll sing!" Harlow shouts from behind me.

"What?! No!" I retort. "I can't sing!"

"He can sing," Harlow says. "He's damn good at it, too."

There's more force pushing from behind the notepad now digging into my chest. The man grabs my shoulder with a hand bigger than life.

Is this how I die? Smashed against a bar top for refusing to sing karaoke?

"What's your name, kid?" the man asks.

My voice quivers. "Eren."

He glares at me while slowly lifting a pen between us. He clicks it and begins writing on the notepad. I look down at what I think should be my name, though it's written, *"Airin."*

He lifts the notepad in the air. "HEY, EVERYONE SHUT UP! SHUT UP!" The bar is dead silent at his command. "AIRIN IS GONNA SING A SONG FIRST!"

Nobody claps. Nobody says anything.

I look back at Harlow and shake my head. She mouths, "Sorry," just before I'm shoved away from my stool.

With every step I take in the direction of the stage, my head grows lighter. I habitually feel my pocket for my coke vial but realize I left it back at the house. I can hear my heartbeat in my head. My legs are growing weaker by the second.

Eventually, I reach the stage. It's hardly a stage. It's two wood pallets stacked on a sheet of cardboard. Two purple lights shine weakly from above, and upon blinking, I'm facing the crowd with the microphone just inches from my lips.

The purple spotlights suddenly become too much to bear. I try to catch my breath, but it escapes me.

Like every time I've stood on stage before, I think to myself, *You can't do this. You damn fool. You'll never be able to finish what Mom started. You're an imposter. A fraud. You don't deserve to be on stage after what you've done to Mom.*

The crowd's whispers bring me back to the present moment. I've been standing here breathing into the mic for who-knows-how-long, but when my eyes meet Harlow's, it doesn't even matter. Our eyes lock, and I feel the anxiety, the stage fright, and my demons all loosen their grip on me. In the same way light dissolves darkness, Harlow dissolves everything holding me back.

"What song?" the bartender asks from behind the counter.

What song? What am I supposed to sing at a biker bar in Montana? If I sing something everyone knows the words to, maybe this will be less awkward.

I clear my throat. "'*Mr. Brightside*' by The Killers," I say softly.

I'll take my chances with this one.

The wood pallet creaks under me as I stand at the mic. I shield my eyes from the purple spotlights to read the room. The mountainous biker gang is silently watching, most of them with their arms crossed. Harlow is covering her mouth, and I can't tell if she's laughing or genuinely scared for me. The rest of the people are silhouettes, but the room is packed.

You know those moments in life where you think to yourself, "*How the hell did I get here?*" The moments that don't feel real, even when they couldn't be more real, unraveling right before your very own eyes. You almost have to laugh at the fact that every decision you've ever made got you there. In my case, it's *here*. And I might as well make the most of it.

"This one goes out to Winston," I say into the mic. There's some laughter from the crowd. The guitar riff from "*Mr. Brightside*" begins, and there is a slight shift in the room.

I sing the first line: "*COMING OUT OF MY CAGE AND I'VE BEEN DOING JUST FINE…*"

I notice bodies standing from the booths when they hear my voice. They make their way to the middle of the bar, standing just below me.

I'm gripping the mic: "*GOTTA, GOTTA BE DOWN, BE-CAUSE I WANT IT ALL. IT STARTED OUT WITH A KISS, HOW DID IT END UP LIKE THIS? IT WAS ONLY A KISS…*"

The bar erupts, singing the next line with me: "*IT WAS ONLY A KISS…*"

I instantly get chills. The crowd continues singing with me, and a surge of energy courses through my body. The chorus of the song is approaching, and the room is buzzing. I hold out the microphone, and at my command, they sing the lyrics: "*BUT SHE'S TOUCHING HIS CHEST NOW, HE TAKES OFF HER DRESS NOW, LET ME GO…*"

I feel on top of the world as I bring the mic back to my lips. Gripping it with both hands, I sing out: "*I JUST CAN'T LOOK, IT'S KILLING ME, AND TAKING CONTROL…*"

Is this what fame feels like? The rush. The cheers. The smiles.

All

eyes

on

me.

The more energy I put into the words I sing, the more energy the crowd puts into their shouts. The bikers are now in the middle of the bar, shaking the entire building as they jump to the beat of the song. Harlow is standing on her seat, laughing–smiling.

I point to her when I sing the next line: "*DESTINY IS CALLING ME… OPEN UP MY EAGER EYES… 'CAUSE I'M MR. BRIGHTSIDE…*"

As the guitar solo plays, a heavy arm wraps around my shoulder. I turn to see Winston in his sunglasses and bandana. We headbang to the rest of the song, switching off singing each line. Lights flash in our direction. Phones are out, recording the moment.

Recording *me*.

The song ends, and I step off the stage into a sea of appreciation and applause. I make my way back to Harlow, trudging through compliments and pats on the back.

"E-Man put you two on his tab for the night," the bartender says when I reach Harlow.

"Who is *E-Man*?" Harlow asks.

The bartender points between us into the crowd. We turn to see the man with the handlebar mustache, the one who pressured me into singing. *E-Man*. From the middle of the crowd, E-Man lifts his chin and holds up a drink in our direction. Harlow and I smile.

"Incredible!" Harlow shouts as we step onto the dirt lot. "Simply incredible."

"I'm still shaking," I admit. "I can't believe you told them I'd sing."

"Could you imagine if you *didn't* sing?! Eren, you just breathed life into that place! That was amazing! You're amazing! You're like a *real* rockstar! That's what I'm gonna call you from now on. Okay, rockstar?"

I lean against my bike, processing Harlow's words. People have always appreciated my writing, but they've never appreciated me.

I remember sitting in the back seat of my mom's car, the windows rolled down. I see her dark-brown hair blowing in the wind. She sings to the music. It blasts in and around the car as we claim the open road ahead. I look at the trees stretching over us as I sing the words with her. I'm only 10 years old. She looks in the rearview mirror and shouts, "Sing it, baby! Sing it!" I sang like Mom said to, and I could see her loving me for it. I see the same look in Harlow's eyes as she recounts what just happened.

I turn to face the blue *BAR* sign, and it hits me. A tear falls when I realize where we are. The nostalgia I felt back inside the bar strangles me, and I want to drop to my knees because I've been here before and I remember when.

Harlow freezes. "What's wrong?"

I look at the dirt below my boots, my vision blurred by tears ready to befriend the ground. "She sang at this bar," I say softly, feeling a pit in my stomach. "At this exact bar on the stage I just stood on."

I crouch down with my elbows on my knees. Mom was here. She parked in this parking lot. I held her hand while we walked through that entrance door 18 years ago. It was one of the last stops she ever made to sing one of the last songs she ever sang.

"Eren," Harlow crouches beside me. "You're doing it. You sang in front of a ton of people without breaking down like before. Your mom would be so proud of you."

Harlow is so close to me that she could catch one of my tears. Between sniffles, I say, "It was just karaoke."

"No way. Those people were going crazy for you. Don't tell me that was just karaoke. That was the real deal."

I look up in an attempt to keep more tears from falling. All this time, I've done everything I can to help Harlow chase her dream. I never even realized she was doing the same for me. I wouldn't be able to do any of this without her, which makes me fear the thought of not having her by my side.

Harlow's hand caresses my shoulder. As my tears subside, her face becomes all I see. It's all I want to see. She looks back at me as if she comes to the same realization. We slowly rise to our feet, facing each other with our heartbeats finally in sync.

This isn't supposed to happen.

I'm not supposed to fall for Harlow. I'm not supposed to fall for anybody. Since I was 10, I've been alone. And since then, I grew to love being alone. But for once, I'm not alone. And in this very moment, I like not being alone.

Harlow and I stare into each other's eyes with the same intensity. The yearning in her gaze is like a fire craving something to burn, and I want all the smoke. I take a silent step forward. She lifts her chin, and her lips part, waiting for me to make my move.

Right now, I don't care about her boyfriend. I don't care that I'm broken. I don't care about my stupid rule. I don't care about the world around me. I care about expressing how grateful I am for Harlow.

I tuck her hair behind her ear, leaving my palm on the side of her face. She leans into it and makes a soft moaning sound.

In a perfect world, Harlow's lips meet mine for the first time. In a perfect world, the distance between us becomes naught. In a perfect world, I never have to ride alone again. But this isn't a perfect world, and I'm reminded of that as she places her hands on my chest, stopping me from kissing her.

She lowers her head. My heart drops right into my stomach. I don't know if I'm embarrassed or bummed or both.

"I can't," she says to the ground. "I need to–*we* need to leave… right now."

Harlow steps around me and picks up her–*my* helmet.

"Harlow," I say. "Did I read the moment wrong?"

Her hands are shaking as she tries to unbuckle the helmet strap.

"I–"

"You didn't read the moment wrong, Eren. The thing is, I *want* to kiss you." Harlow gives up on the helmet strap. "Which is exactly why I need to leave."

CHAPTER TEN

HARLOW

When we pull into the garage, I let go of Eren.

"Harlow," he says. "I'm sorry."

I hand Eren the helmet and continue out of the garage. I can't look at him right now. I can hardly look at myself. I allowed us to spend too much time together. I let my curiosity get the best of me, and now it's toying with my heart. I'm not upset with Eren for wanting to kiss me. I'm upset with myself for wanting to kiss him back.

I stop and take a deep breath. "It's not you."

The dimmed lighting in the garage casts a shadow across Eren's face. With the house being in the middle of the woods, it's silent besides the exaggerated breaths of two people who both want what they can't have.

"I went in for the kiss. It's my fault." Eren takes two cautious steps toward me. "I think I'm just overwhelmed with how good all of this has turned out to be. I don't think you get it."

"Stop." Eren cocks his head back, surprised by my abruptness. "I don't think *you* get it. I'm in a relationship with Jordan, but you make me forget that I'm even in a relationship at all."

Eren blinks at me. I take a step back into the garage, my

finger pointed at his chest. "You make me feel beautiful. You make me feel heard. You make me feel like my life is mine to do whatever I want with…"

"Because it is!" Eren snaps. "It's yours to do whatever you want with, but all you do is let other people make decisions for you! Your parents, your boyfriend–"

"You see, that's it!" I snap back. "I'm not used to making my own decisions. I'm not used to doing what I think is best for me. I'm not used to songwriting, motorcycles, and guys like you. And the more I spend time with you, the more I learn that you might be what I want. But I don't trust myself to make that decision."

Eren closes the gap between us. I'm overcome by his scent. "If I'm what you want, then choose me. Make the damn decision for yourself," he says sternly. "I didn't plan to develop these feelings for you. Or to let you in, but it happened anyway." He takes a shaky breath. "I hear the way you talk about your boyfriend, and I respect that you're loyal to him. But he's holding you back! And if I make you forget you're in a relationship–like you say I do–then maybe you should rethink your relationship."

His words pierce my heart. I hate how right he is. Eren is making me rethink my relationship, which is why I need to see Jordan. I need to feel how real our relationship is, and I need to be reminded of why I've been with him for this long. I need to know that Jordan is the one and that this is all just a test–a test I refuse to fail.

Eren is the one thing in my life that I don't know, and that could be why I'm having these thoughts. His entire world is my unknown. And while it's been a fun ride, it's time for me to get back to what I know.

"I'm leaving first in the morning," I say, crossing my arms.

Eren lowers his head, so I can't see the disappointment lurking in those deep-brown eyes. "Good," he mutters. "It's probably best for the both of us anyway."

I storm off, holding back tears until I reach my bedroom. I force the door shut behind me and slide myself down to the wood floor, where I let my tears land.

I don't know what scares me more…

The thought of giving up on Jordan or the thought of giving up on Eren.

♫ ♫ ♫

"So much for letting your hair down," Blake teases the next morning.

I adjust my top bun. "It was a one-time thing."

"That's sad to hear. It suited you."

The jet is just now taking off, and we haven't spoken a word to each other until now. I look out the window, watching the color green fade. The flight attendant sets a beer in front of Blake and champagne in front of me.

It feels like last night was a dream—anything but real. It just kept getting better and better. From listening to Eren sing on the back deck to the bikers cheering for him at the bar. The laughs and tears shared over the past three days are embedded in my head, stored away with the other memories. The studio, the trees, the motorcycle.

Being on the back of Eren's bike felt better than it should have. Riding it felt so good, the ride alone made me feel like I wasn't being faithful to Jordan. I finally let loose. I finally let go of what people think of me. I rode with the wind. I was free.

The entire night has been weighing on me, making me too tired to even sleep. Nothing happened between Eren and me, but I still feel this unwavering guilt as if I cheated on Jordan. I eye the champagne glass. I can't tell if I want to chug it or not touch it at all.

It's one or the other.

"How did last night go?"

Blake's question sends me into a panic.

Did he hear us talking in the garage?

Did he talk to Eren before we left this morning?

"Good," I reply casually. "We went to a bar."

Blake picks up on the guilt seeping through my pores. "I heard the motorcycle. Did you ride with him?"

"Yeah. It was cool." My tone is neutral to keep him from knowing it was the best feeling I think I've ever felt.

"That's it? It was just… cool?" Blake's eyes narrow. "Harlow, I know you well enough to assume you were either thrilled or scared shitless. I'm sure it wasn't just 'cool.'"

I bite my lip. When he smiles, I finally break.

With my head lowered, I mutter, "It was the most fun I think I've ever had. The wind, the trees. We were going so fast, it was all a rush."

Blake nods while taking a sip of his beer. "I knew this would be good for you," he says. "For you to get out of that box you've been so comfortable in. You got a taste of what's out there."

I let out a laugh. When my eyes meet Blake's, I see a side of him I haven't seen in a while–a supportive look in his eye. I haven't seen this look since before I chose to work at Beck.

We're on the same side again.

"Do you think you'll keep working on the album with Eren?" he asks.

I can't help but think about the feelings that were developing between Eren and me. It's not fair for me to keep working with Eren unless I'm honest with Jordan about the album. Once I'm reminded of how strong my connection is with Jordan, then maybe I can be around Eren with some newly-set boundaries.

"I want to," I reply confidently.

"Just be careful with Father," Blake says softly. "I think he picked up on you detaching yourself from the company. He's good at recognizing when he's losing control of us. Father came at me full-force when I talked about moving out and working in the music industry. He found ways to keep me around for months until I was finally able to pull myself away. Just be aware of him. That's all I'm saying."

"Trust me, I know how Father can be," I assure him. "I'll be fine."

When we land, Blake calls us an Uber. Before we know it, we're on our way through the Lincoln Tunnel and up Manhattan to my apartment.

"Babo," Charlie says as I step out of the car.

"I'll miss you, too, my little prince." I blow him a kiss before turning to Blake. "Thanks for coming on this trip with me, winner. I'm sorry for putting you in that position."

"Anytime, loser." We hug, and Blake keeps his hand on my shoulder as he says, "Listen, I know I'm the only one in your life helping you pursue music. I think you should at least tell Jordan that you're giving music a shot. If he's the right guy, he'll support you no matter what, the same way Miranda did with me."

"Thank you." I hug him again, tighter this time. "Are you coming to the gala tonight?" I ask, slinging my bag over my shoulder.

"Father didn't invite me," he murmurs.

"Oh, shut up. You know you can always–"

Blake lifts a hand, signalling for me to stop. I want him there, but I understand how difficult his relationship is with Father. Resentment is a silent relationship killer, and his resentment toward Father has been growing inside of him for a decade now.

I make my way up to my penthouse, more exhausted than ever. I think a hot shower and a nap are all I need before seeing everyone tonight. A part of me is happy that Jordan doesn't know I'm coming home as early as I am. I forgot to text him when we took off, which works out because I'll need time alone to get acclimated to my world after living in Eren's world the past few days.

When I approach the front door, a banging sound comes from inside. "Jordan?" I call out, anxiously digging through my purse for the keys. At this hour, Jordan should still be at work.

I find the key and silently open the door. To my surprise, I walk in on our cleaning crew aggressively cleaning the apartment. My schedule has been thrown off while in Montana, so I completely forgot that it's Friday, which is when the cleaners usually come.

Isabella, one of the cleaning staff members I've become friends with over the years, appears shocked to see me. "Ms. Harlow!" she gasps. Isabella's tone suggests that she wasn't expecting me, which is fair, considering I'm usually at work during this time on Fridays.

"Don't mind me," I say while carrying in my bag.

Isabella sets her dish rag on the kitchen counter. "Ms. Harlow, I'm sorry if we startled you."

I make my way toward the bedroom. "Oh, no. You didn't startle me. I just forgot it's Friday."

"Ms. Harlow, it's *Thursday*," she says to my back.

I stop in my tracks, realizing my lack of sleep is getting to me. I slowly look over my shoulder to see Isabella standing utterly still.

"Why are you all here on a Thursday?" I blush, assuming Jordan must have wanted the place to be spotless when I arrived.

"Ms. Harlow, I need to show you something," Isabella whispers. She leads me into my bedroom closet, where she pulls out my navy blue lace bra. Isabella hands my bra to me like it's been contaminated.

"Jordan asked for us to come clean the apartment before you

got home. I found the bra under the bed an hour ago. Forgive me, Ms. Harlow. I mean no offense, but I've been doing your laundry long enough to know that this bra isn't your size. Does it belong to you?"

Her question stuns me. *"Does it belong to me?"*

I draw a shaky breath and cover my mouth with my palm.

I don't own a navy blue lace bra.

I shiver when I imagine all the nights I've slept next to a man I thought I knew–a man I've opened myself up to in exchange for betrayal.

I feel my world crack right down the middle. It shakes, then folds over itself, and I no longer recognize it. From the plans Jordan and I made for our lives to the foundation our relationship is built on, I'm forced to question it all.

"I will dispose of it immediately," Isabella says, reaching for the bra.

"No. I'll need it for when I confront him."

She nods. "Please be careful, Ms. Harlow. Jordan's temper. I don't want to be the reason–"

"I won't say a word about you," I say sternly. "That'll be all, Isabella." My voice is cold, though my blood boils.

Isabella nods and leaves the room. In less than a minute, the entire crew is packed up and out of the apartment. I sit on the edge of the bed, staring at the bra in my lap. In the five years I've been with Jordan, I never had a single reservation about him.

As much as I don't want to, I imagine how my father would react to the situation. I feel naive. Stupid. Weak. Wolves don't get played like this. Puppy dogs do, and I'm not a puppy dog.

I'm a fucking wolf.

I take a deep breath to calm myself. As terrible as this looks, maybe I don't have to jump to conclusions. If my parents find out about this, I'll appear even weaker than I do now, and I can't afford to give them more ammunition.

I want to find out who this bra belongs to so I can deal with her myself. I can make an example of her and prove that I'm the wolf my father raised me to be. Jordan and I spend almost every moment of every day together, so it'd be impossible for him to be seeing someone behind my back.

So, who the fuck slept with my boyfriend?

I look down at the tag on the bra and make a mental note…

32B.

I'm shocked, angry, confused, and hurt all at the same time. To keep my hands from shaking, I grab a pen. To keep my mind from racing, I grab my notebook. And I write.

Can't help but see you different in the light,
When you let all the dark into my life,
I thought that I knew you, we were fine,
Now I sit here, I'm broken down tonight,

You were all I know, all I would feel,
Falling for your heart, but was it real?
When I gave you everything, your love's the deal,
I gave my everything, and still, you steal,

So don't break my fall,
I gave my all,
Now my world is burning,
My world is burning down,

Little did I know, you would surprise,
I'd never believe, I've realized,
When I gave you everything, you don't wanna try,
I gave my everything, you let it die.

After putting my notebook away, I somehow manage to shower and get ready for the charity gala. When I finish getting ready, I sip champagne while anxiously tapping my nails against the kitchen countertop.

I know I need to confront Jordan about the bra. I just don't know how I'm going to do it yet. I've never raised my voice at someone before, though he deserves to be yelled at. I've never suspected Jordan would cheat, though I'm fondling a stranger's bra. It's funny how the ones who claim to love us the most are the same ones capable of the harshest betrayals. I've known Eren for a short time, but still long enough to know that he would never betray me like this.

It's nearly six when I watch the front door open. Jordan steps out from behind, and his eyes widen the moment he sees me. "Jesus!" He lets out a shriek, nearly dropping the bouquet of roses in his hand. "When did you get home?!"

"I've been home all afternoon." I clench my jaw.

"I told you to text me," Jordan says while scanning the living room and kitchen. He steps toward me, raising the bouquet between us. "Well, welcome home, baby." His veneers show between his lips.

A small part of me softens when I see the bouquet of roses. It's been years since Jordan bought me roses, but I'm forced to consider why he got them for me *now* of all times.

Being on your best behavior might as well be a symptom of guilt.

I tighten my grip around the bra under the countertop. After taking a sip of champagne, I force a smile.

Jordan's breath is warm against my neck as he says, "I know you were only gone three days, but that was three days too long." He presses a warm kiss against my neck and then another just below my ear. "I missed you like crazy."

I get chills, feeling my body crave his affection like a bad habit. "I missed you, too," I hear myself say.

The bra.

I let out an exhale, preparing to show Jordan the bra. "Jordan, I–"

KNOCK! KNOCK! KNOCK!

Our eyes are pulled to the front door. Talia's head appears through the opening.

"She came early," Jordan sighs back to Talia before facing me again. "We were gonna surprise you."

Oh, I got my surprise. I'm holding it under the kitchen counter.

Talia enters the room a few steps ahead of Spud. Her black hair is pulled back into a long straight ponytail. A diamond barrette is clipped above her left ear, complementing the diamond choker around her neck. Her dress is a dark red and made of velvet, perfectly matching Spud's red tie. Talia sprints to me as fast as her heels will let her as I slip the bra between me and the seat cushion.

"She's here!" Talia shouts. "I haven't seen my bestie in like a week! Where the hell have you been?!"

Talia leaps into my arms, forcing me to shelve my conversation with Jordan for when we're alone. Rumors spread like wildfire in the Hamptons, and Talia loves rumors. Plus, breaking up is one thing, but we'd be the laughingstock of Wall Street if it became known that William Beck's daughter was cheated on by another Beck employee. I refuse to be Beck's sign of weakness.

"I was in Montana!" I reply with forced enthusiasm. "I was there with Blake."

"Is that in California?" Talia asks. "Where is Montana?"

"Montana is in Montana, honey," Spud chimes in. "It's a state."

"Sounds fun!" Talia squeaks.

Jordan heads for the bar in the corner of the living room. "I invited Spud and Talia over to pregame for the gala. Hope you don't mind that, babe." He fills two glasses of Cognac and hands one to Spud.

"I'd be upset if you didn't!" I lie, tightening my arms around Talia.

Talia pulls back and places a hand on my shoulder. "How is your brother doing? It must be so tough with it being a year since Miranda died."

"Better," I reply. "Thank you for asking."

"Of course. Blake is family." She rolls her eyes. "I told Jordan to let you stay the full week. I mean, there will always be another charity event."

"Harlow is *literally* here for a good cause." Jordan wraps an arm around my shoulder and tops off my glass. "Plus, I missed my beautiful girlfriend."

I want to cringe when I hear him say he missed me. I would find it pretty hard to miss the person you're cheating on.

"So, why Montana?" Spud pinches his eyebrows together.

I flash a smirk, remembering Eren's response when I asked him the same question. "Because we had never been to Montana," I say to Spud. "It seemed nice. And it was."

"I'm surprised there's life outside of New York," Spud says smugly.

"After visiting, I'm not surprised at all."

The group doesn't react much to my response. Instead, they tend to their usual work talk and Hamptons gossip. While they brush off what I said, this is the first time I've stood by an opinion my friends might not agree with. And it feels good to have my own opinion for once. Come to think of it, I prefer they never go to Montana.

They would never last.

♫ ♫ ♫

We step out of the S.U.V. to flashing lights and paparazzi standing behind stanchions.

"Harlow, over here!"

"Love the white dress, Harlow!"

The event is being held at Madison Square Garden. The colossal "BECK" banner hanging over the entrance makes the building appear even bigger than it usually looks.

Talia, Spud, Jordan, and I smile and strike occasional poses for the paparazzi before heading inside. With his palm against the small of my back, Jordan guides me into the lobby.

The thought of Jordan cheating is lingering over my head like a storm cloud. Lightning can strike at any moment, though I would rather it strike in the privacy of our apartment. Not while we're surrounded by the most influential people on Wall Street.

Jordan and I bounce from one conversation to the next, where I hear the same thing over and over again. Something along the lines of, "We'd love to do work with Beck Holdings. Can you help us get a meeting with your father?" I do my best to keep from rolling my eyes, but it's becoming difficult after hearing it for an hour straight.

Heads turn toward the entrance, and the crowd applauds as the great William Beck walks into the lobby with Mother at his side. Every few seconds, their faces flash white from the various photographers orbiting their entourage.

For the first time tonight, Jordan's hand leaves my back to meet my father's hand. "Good evening, William." He hugs Mother. "How are you, Claire?"

"Jordan!" Father greets with a smirk. In an instant, his chilling blue eyes flick to mine. "Nice of you to show, Harlow." He gives me a cold peck on the cheek for the photo op, then pulls away to greet Talia and Spud.

He doesn't even bother asking how Blake is doing. As far as he knows, my trip to Montana was to help Blake get his mind off of Miranda's passing, but he couldn't care less.

When the entrance spectacle dies down, Father addresses Jordan. "Are you rehearsed?" he asks.

"Y-yes," Jordan stutters. "I am."

Father frowns. "You don't sound too confident."

"I'm rehearsed," Jordan says confidently.

"Rehearsed?" I turn to Jordan. "What's your speech about?"

"You'll see," he whispers with a reassuring grin.

When doors to the banquet hall open, people funnel inside. Conversations fill the room, which is decorated in white and lavender. A wide stage dominates the front of the venue, where purple lights illuminate massive letters that spell out, "GIVING BECK," Beck Holdings's charity initiative.

"Welcome back, Ms. Beck!" a familiar voice greets from behind me. I turn to see a young woman in a dark-green dress. Her petite frame straightens, her hair curled and falling elegantly past her shoulders. Before I can ask if I know her, she says, "It's Penny!"

My jaw drops because she looks nothing like the corporate errand girl I know her to be.

"Penny! Wow, hi! You look so… pretty. My goodness." I give her a tight hug, then do a double-take.

She lets out a nervous laugh. "Thank you, Ms. Beck."

"Please, *call me Harlow*. We're not in the office."

Penny beams at me. "Thank you, Harlow."

I feel a hand graze my hip, and I look up to see Jordan finishing a conversation with Spud. "Harlow, I need you to…" He freezes when he notices Penny. "I–"

"Hi, Jordan," Penny says.

Jordan dodges Penny's glance, and an awkward tension

makes itself known between the three of us. He finally gives her a cold nod.

What the hell is going on here?

"I need Harlow for a moment," Jordan says, turning us toward our table.

A cold sweat comes over me before we reach our table. I didn't think for a second that the woman he slept with could be Penny until I saw how stunning she looks tonight—a side of her I've never seen. The same side Jordan couldn't resist.

Maybe I'm overanalyzing, but I can't find any other reason for them to be this awkward around each other. With everything in me, I fight the urge to find Penny and ask if she's a size *32B*.

"Penny looks stunning," I whisper to Jordan, monitoring his response. "I hardly recognized her at first."

"Really? Yeah, no—I mean, I guess." Jordan avoids eye contact. The beauty of being with somebody for this long is being able to tell when they're hiding something, and that's exactly what Jordan is doing. "Listen, I need you up on stage with me when I give my speech," he adds.

"Do you really need me for your speech?"

"Yes." Jordan's hand tightens around mine. "We're the Dream Team. Just come up on stage with me when it's time."

I catch Father's eye across the table. Jordan pulls my chair out for me to sit between him and Talia while Father, Mother, and Spud make small talk on the opposite side of the table. The M.C. begins his opening speech, claiming the attention of the entire room.

"Are you okay, Harlow?" Talia whispers. "You look bothered."

"I'm fine," I lie while fixing my dress.

I feel a wave of heat under my skin when I spot Penny in my direct line of sight, sitting a few tables away. She can't avoid looking at me, considering our table is just below the stage.

As fucked up as this sounds, I need to find out what bra size my assistant is.

When I see Jordan whispering to Father across the table, I lean toward Talia. "I need you to spill champagne on me."

Talia's head swivels. "What? Like, right now?"

"Right now. I'll explain later," I whisper. "Talia, please."

Talia waits a moment, then picks up her glass and stands. She pretend-trips and lets out a gasp as she pours her champagne all over my chest.

Perfect.

I suck in a breath. "Talia!"

She reaches for a napkin. "Shit, Harlow. I'm so sorry. Here, let me–"

"Talia, are you serious right now?" Spud snarls from the seat to her left.

"Woah! Looks like the night has officially begun!" the M.C. teases to the crowd.

Father watches me, straight-faced, while Mother uses her hand to mask her embarrassment. The surrounding tables exchange whispers among one another.

Jordan extends a napkin in my direction. "Here."

"It's fine," I whisper. "I'm gonna dry off in the bathroom."

Before Jordan can object, I stand and head to the back of the room. Penny watches my every step as the distance between us becomes less.

As I pass her, I whisper, "9-1-1, Penny. I need you right now."

In one swift motion, Penny tosses her napkin on the table, stands, and walks alongside me. "I can have a new dress delivered within fifteen minutes," she whispers sternly. "How bad is the spill?"

We burst into the bathroom, and I check to see if anyone else is inside. We're alone.

I look at my reflection, pretending to be infuriated that my dress and bra are soaked. "I can't wait fifteen minutes. Jordan needs me on stage for his speech any second now." I raise my hands over my eyes and take quick breaths. "Dammit, dammit, dammit."

Penny watches me pace from one end of the bathroom to the other. She folds her lips between her teeth, looking at my dress and then her own.

"We can swap dresses if you think you can fit in mine!" Penny finally says. "Not that I think you're too big to fit in my dress. I just mean… we might be different sizes, so if–"

"Yes!" I throw my hands up. "How did I not think of that?! Penny, you're saving my ass here. Thank you so, so much."

Penny lets out a nervous laugh. She unzips the back of my dress, and I sigh when I look down at my soaked bra.

"Damn, it's my bra, too. If I'm on stage and people see my bra soaking through the dress, I'm screwed."

"Here, take mine if it will fit," Penny insists as she undoes her shoulder straps. "What size are you?"

My heartbeat doubles over. "I'm a *34A*," I reply. "What are you?"

Penny shimmies out of her dress, and my fists tighten when I see the lace bra she is wearing underneath. It's a black lace bra, the same exact one Isabella found in my apartment, just in a different color.

"I'm a *32B*," she states.

I freeze, my dress in hand.

"Oh, Penny," I sigh. "Please don't tell me you have the same bra in navy blue."

"I do! Or at least, I did. I haven't been able to…" Penny is about to undo her bra when she picks up on my disappointed tone. Her eyes flick up to mine. "How did you…?" Her eyes widen. "Harlow, I–"

"Please, *call me Ms. Beck.*"

Penny's eyebrows part, and she raises a hand to cover her mouth. "Ms. Beck, I'm so sorry. Jordan made it seem like you two were fighting and that you ran off to Montana and–"

I raise my hand to silence her. "Did you sleep with him?" I ask dryly.

"Harlow, I–"

"Ms. Beck," I correct her. "And it's a simple… fucking… question." I flex my jaw. For once in my life, I feel the sick thrill of dominating another. I begin to feel what my father feels every day. "Did you sleep with him?"

Penny winces at my question, then lowers her head. "Yes, Ms. Beck." She sniffles as I pull my dress back on. "I'm so sorry."

"Will you please zip me up?" I ask politely, my soft tone catching her off guard.

With my back turned to her, I see the two of us in the mirror. She slowly zips up the back of my dress. I fill my chest with air, staring into my reflection. I reach up and undo my top bun, letting my wavy locks fall down my back.

When I exhale, I recognize the woman in the mirror–her wild eyes, her untamed hair. She is the part of me begging to be set free. I've met her once before, on the back of a motorcycle somewhere in Montana. I don't know her well just yet, but I love her already.

"You won't last in this business, Penny. I can promise you that," I mutter while heading for the door. "Get out while you can."

I make my way to the lobby exit, my heels echoing against the tile floor. I imagine how Blake will react to Jordan cheating. He's always had his reservations about Jordan. He may not be surprised at all.

I imagine how Eren would react. The past few days have affected me in so many ways, all for the better, and instead of embracing it, I chose to neglect it for Jordan. I remember looking up at Eren last night outside of that bar. Helping him break through everything holding him back was not only inspiring, but it's something I want to keep doing. In the short time I've known him, he's revealed this part of me I never knew existed. And I want him to reveal even more.

"Harlow," a stern voice calls from behind. As much as I want to ignore the voice, I acknowledge it out of habit. I turn to face Jordan as he asks, "Are you leaving?" His eyes scan me from head to toe. "What's up with your hair?"

I feel a fire within me, waiting to be released. I take a step in his direction, staring right through his guilt.

"We've been together for five years," I say. "Together every day for five years."

"That's right." Jordan pinches his eyebrows together. "I don't understand."

"The Dream Team," I mutter.

"That's right," he replies with a crooked smile, reaching for my hands.

I pull away from him. "Don't touch me as if you haven't been fucking my assistant."

Jordan flinches at my words. He closes his eyes, then whispers, "Harlow, can we please, *please* talk about this later?"

"You want to talk?!" The higher I raise my voice, the more it trembles. Because this isn't me.

I've never confronted anybody like this before, let alone my disloyal boyfriend. "Okay, Jordan. Let's talk. Let's talk about how you left Penny's bra under our fucking bed!"

Jordan purses his lips together and clenches a fist. He takes a step toward me, but before he can speak, Father's voice sweeps the lobby like thunder.

"HARLOW!" Father shouts. His shoes click against the floor as he walks toward us. The sound echoes off the walls, breaking me down more with each step. He lifts his chin. "Stop acting like a fucking child."

A breath escapes me.

Me? A child? The one time I'm standing up for myself, he calls me a child.

I grind my teeth together. "Tell him what you did," I snarl at Jordan.

Jordan lowers his head with no emotion, a few brown strands of hair hanging over his forehead.

"I know what he did because you just shouted it across the lobby," Father says. "And he is a fucking moron for doing it, but all boys are fucking morons." His eyes dart between the two of us. "And the sooner you learn that, the better."

Father takes a step, standing between Jordan and me. I instantly feel smaller, less in control of my emotions and thoughts the more he speaks. "You would be naive to think that you won't be tested in life the way Jordan was tested. And you would be a fool to think that you won't fail tests the way Jordan has failed *this* test."

My head grows light with every word my father says.

He's wrong. I was tested with Eren, and I passed. I was loyal to Jordan. Now here Father stands, taking Jordan's side even after Jordan cheated on his own daughter.

"Harlow, I fucked up," Jordan whispers, still clenching a fist at his side. "That's all it was. A fuck-up."

"And it won't be the last time you fuck up because you're human," Father adds. His eyes flick to mine. "I've been working him harder than ever at Beck, so he was bound to do something idiotic. Don't throw five years away because Jordan thought with the wrong head one time."

My hands are trembling. I want to stand up for myself, but the words won't form. I want to scream, but my voice is bottled up in my chest. The hairs on the back of my neck stand as Father places a hand on my shoulder.

"You two will make up after the gala," he says, facing me. "Now tie your hair back up and meet us inside. Jordan, I'm having the M.C. take your speech off of the agenda."

Jordan raises his chin, and I notice a vein throbbing along the side of his forehead, his disappointment turning to anger. I sense it brewing inside of him, and I want nothing more than to see him erupt at my father for scrapping his speech the way my father scrapped mine last week. Just before Jordan erupts, my father puts his arm around him, holding my gaze until their backs are to me.

My jaw drops. I'm left in silence as their silhouettes fade behind the banquet hall doors. I look back over my shoulder at the lobby exit. I crave that exit with everything in me. An exit from the world I came from, the same world that still consumes me.

The only thing keeping me from breaking down right now is the thought of seeing Eren again–escaping this sick reality where I am enslaved to the thoughts I was raised to think.

In a perfect world, Eren is waiting right outside for me on his motorcycle. In a perfect world, we ride west until my world no longer has a hold on me. In a perfect world, I'm free to chase my dream and the life I want to live. But this isn't a perfect world, and I'm reminded of that as I walk back into the banquet hall with my hair tied up to win the approval of my own father.

What Father says… goes.

But for how much longer?

CHAPTER ELEVEN

EREN

I haven't written a single word since Harlow left this morning. I haven't strummed a single chord on my guitar. I haven't eaten a single bite of the Hot Pocket sitting beside me. This is the first time I've *really* lacked inspiration.

Clouds overwhelm the sky as if Harlow took the sunlight with her. I don't blame her for not saying goodbye this morning. I'm an asshole for thinking she would kiss me when she has a boyfriend.

I'm not sorry for expressing how grateful I am for her, though. I felt what I felt, and I acted on it. If she ever gave me the chance to kiss her again, I'd take it in a heartbeat. I was starting to believe I didn't even have a heart until I met Harlow in that alley. I didn't think there was a person in this world who could get me to break my golden rule.

"*No attachments,*" I would say.

And yet, here I am, attached.

I sit down at the edge of the back deck. I look down at the sea of pine trees, all swaying in a single direction with the wind. A setting like this would always bring me peace. But right now, I feel anxious.

Since Harlow, Blake, and Charlie left, it's been painfully silent. I feel alone. I'm beginning to think that *being alone* is one thing while *feeling alone* is another. After last night, Harlow has made me realize that I don't care for either.

It's a shitty thing, having scared off the one person I've opened up to. If I didn't try to kiss her, I wonder if I could have talked her into staying. Maybe she'd give me a chance if I took things slower.

I feel a raindrop land on the back of my neck. I bury my face in my palms. Could today get any worse? I'm alone. I have no desire to write. Now, I'm cold and wet.

I walk back inside to find the one thing that can pull me out of this slump. Whiskey.

I've kept my drinking to a minimum and haven't touched coke once since Harlow came around. But Harlow's no longer here, so I can hear my vices calling.

CLINK!

I set a glass on the kitchen counter, pour myself a shot, and down it goes.

CLINK!

I set the glass on the kitchen counter, pour myself another shot, and down it goes.

Before taking my third shot, I play music from the T.V. speakers. The music sweeps the living room, and already, I don't feel so alone. If anything, I just feel buzzed.

CLINK!

I set the kitchen counter on the glass, pour myself another shot, and goes it down.

A loud exhale follows. My body loosens. The beauty of alcohol is that it numbs the mind. But it also makes any emotion that pops up harder to control. I nod my head to the music, singing the lyrics to keep me from feeling lonely. At this point, I should start calling myself *Mr. Lonely* because I have nobody for my own. No family. No friends.

CLINK!

"Shit." To my demise, the whiskey bottle is empty. "More whiskey," I slur under my breath.

The town is only four miles away. I'm pretty drunk, but I can probably make it. That "probably" can become a "definitely" with the help of some…

"There you are," I whisper, pulling my coke vial out of my backpack. My eyes trail around the studio that I somehow stumbled into. I drop to a knee in front of the computer screen, spilling the remainder of the vial next to the keyboard.

I mean to do a bump, but the bump becomes a line. I feel a rush of adrenaline course through me. Without thinking, I slam my fist against the keyboard. The computer screen suddenly flashes white, and I see the blank document I was staring at for the first half of today.

My breathing grows heavy, eyes narrowing in on the blank document. I take the happiness, sadness, and everything in between, then write.

When we're not in touch, I'm in my head,
Being in love is what I dread,
I do drugs, I know that's bad,
But it's better than being dead,

I'm scared to come down, because I'll be fucked,
If you're not there,
I'm scared to come down, you're the one,
Now I'm aware,
So, now I'm high and alone,
Inside some house, not a home,

I need you here for my own,
So, I get high now to cope,
And I'm scared to come down,
I'm scared to come down,

Hung up on the way I've lived,
Drowning in a sea of sins,
Blame is all I'm breathing in,
Pain is all I see, it's thick,
I'm begging for a way out, how am I still living?
I'm begging for a way out, till then,
I'll keep my distance.

My breath is the heaviest it could possibly be when I finish the song. I don't even read it back.

I want my whiskey.

I smoke a joint to calm my nerves. Before I feel sadness leaking into the holes in my heart, I decide to drive into town. I slip my boots on and stumble around the front of the house. I slap my face a couple of times to keep from seeing double. It's pouring rain now, and the cloudy sky casts a shaded tint over the shaky world around me.

It's only four miles.

I lift the garage door to see two motorcycles propped up–wait… I rub my eyes to see only *one* motorcycle propped up. I blink, and suddenly I'm on the motorcycle. I blink again, and now it's roaring under me.

It's only four miles.

I crank the throttle, thrusting myself onto the dirt road. The raindrops stick to my face as I zigzag through the trees. My bike skids left, then right, the wheels unable to grip the muddy terrain.

It's only four miles.

My eyelids are growing heavy until I see a car up ahead. I squint my eyes to get a better look.

I know that car.

"Mom!"

Mom's car slides over the mud less than fifty yards away. Now forty yards. Now thirty. I crank the throttle, picking up speed.

"Stop!" I scream like a madman.

Mom speeds up like a madman is chasing her.

A tree suddenly appears between us. I swerve around it before it claims my life. I catch air over a slope, gaining on Mom's car. I'm nearing the left side of it and I see Mom's silhouette in the driver's seat.

"Mom, it's Eren!" I shout, waving a hand. "Stop the car! Pull over please Mom please pull over stop!"

She looks at me with apologetic eyes and opens her mouth to speak. I merge onto the dirt road, extending my hand for her to grab through the window.

"Eren," she says, her voice coming from inside my head.

Before she says another word, my bike slams into a tree stump. I fly through the air, unable to process what's happening until I'm rolling through bushes and forest debris. My head slams against the ground, and sounds of pain escape me until I'm lying still.

"Mom," I whisper between quick breaths. "What're you running from?"

My vision blurs, head consumed by a pounding so painful I'm convinced it might kill me. There is a deafening ringing in my ears as I stare at the gray sky between the treetops. I blink, and when I open my eyes, the sky is black. I have no idea how much time has gone by.

I have to be dead.

I feel my body for cuts, bruises, and broken bones but find

nothing.

How am I not dead?

I sit up, having no idea where I am at first. I slowly stand to my feet and groan because of my raging migraine. I'm more sober than I was before I landed, and it's gradually starting to dawn on me how lucky I am to be alive.

I slowly walk through the path my crash-landing made until I reach what remains of my bike. It's mangled, a pile of warped metal. I drop to my knees and place a hand on the dented fender.

My eyes land on a broken fragment of my side-view mirror. I lift the glass, and in the reflection, I see a man. The man is broken. He always has been, but maybe he doesn't have to be. His tattoos tell his story. It's a story of repeated mistakes and self-destructive patterns. But the patterns end here and now.

A tear runs down my cheek. The things I thought were keeping me alive almost led to the death of me. The drugs. The alcohol. My vices were chasing me all along. And for some reason, I've been given another chance.

"I'll change my ways," I whisper to the man in the broken mirror. "I'll change my ways."

♫ ♫ ♫

I'm on the couch listening to music when Blake FaceTimes me.

His face pops up on my screen. "Eren! What's up?"

"Just chillin'." I check the time on my phone. "Isn't it midnight over there?"

"Yeah, it's past my bedtime." He shrugs. "I wanted to talk to you about something."

My heart drops when I realize Harlow might've talked to Blake about what happened. Different moments play out in my head.

The one where I tried to kiss Harlow and the one where I sang at the karaoke bar. I'd rather Blake not know about either.

"What's going on?" I pause the music and sit up.

"It's about my sister."

Fuck.

I stay silent as Blake takes a deep breath.

"She's never gonna quit her job," he sighs. "And I know she wants to. Even *she* knows she wants to. I saw a side of Harlow in Montana that I never knew existed. She was happy, like truly happy."

Until I fucked it all up.

Blake continues. "Our father and her boyfriend are toxic for her, and I think they're gonna try to take her away from this project. But writing this album is helping her finally find herself. I just think…" He pauses, squinting his eyes at me through the screen. "Wait." His eyes widen. "You're letting me confide in you."

My jaw drops at his realization. I've never had the desire to get to know anybody on a deeper level, which Blake has always known.

"Holy shit," Blake mutters with a grin. "Harlow got through to you."

I let out a laugh, covering my face with my hand.

"Blake, I–"

"Was I playing matchmaker without even realizing it? How did I not pick up on this?"

"Blake–"

"Damn, I don't really know how to feel about this because, well… you know. She's my sister and you're my friend and–"

"BLAKE!" I shout, leaning forward. I bite my lip to keep from shuddering at the sudden headache I get from shouting. "It wasn't my plan to have feelings for your sister. We met in an alley outside of Angelo's one night, and then I ran into her again at RAW the night we found out about this project. You introduced us after all that. I didn't want it to be weird if you found out we already knew each other. If this is all ridiculous, I can let it go."

Blake pinches his lips together, processing everything I said. After a long exhale, he says, "Eren, I don't know." I feel a pit in my stomach, picking up on the reluctance in Blake's tone. "You're a good guy, and you're exactly what Harlow needs when it comes to music. As your friend, you know I support you. But as Harlow's brother, I have one reservation."

I lower my head. It's not what I wanted to hear, but I can accept it. "What's the reservation?" I ask.

"The 'rockstar' bullshit–the drugs and the excessive drinking–I don't want that anywhere near my sister."

"For what my word is worth, I dropped it all," I say softly. "I respect Harlow, and I respect you, Blake. If you want me to give her space, I'll give her space. But she's changing me for the better. And I like to think I'm doing the same for her."

"I know she is. And I know you are." Blake's eyes soften. "She's my sister, but she's also an adult who can make her own decisions. I appreciate you opening up to me about Harlow. As your friend and as her brother, you have my blessing if you promise you're done with the drug stuff like you say you are."

I lift a hand, placing it over my heart. "I promise."

"Alright."

"So, we're good?"

"We're good," Blake replies. "She likes you, you know."

"What makes you say that?"

"Harlow *never* lets her hair down. I knew the moment she walked into the kitchen yesterday that you were really getting through to her. Regardless, you two need to finish what you started with this album."

I nod. While I agree, it's going to be tough for me to be alone in a room with Harlow. I've never had feelings like this before. This is all foreign to me. I won't know how to gauge it, and I could slip up like I did last night.

"We left sort of abruptly this morning, so I didn't get a chance to tell you about my call with the artist's manager. The artist is ready to meet you as early as this weekend. I'll make arrangements with his manager. I just wanted to give you a heads up to make sure you're ready."

"I'm ready." I nod. "Let's meet this guy."

My shoulders relax. It feels good to think about writing with an artist again. Having this new artist in the mix will give me a chance to come down from this high Harlow has me on. It's time to come back down to Earth.

It's time to get my ass back on the road.

CHAPTER TWELVE

HARLOW

"I'm starting to think you're actually in the F.B.I.," Blake teases.

I force a smile under my sunglasses and baseball cap. He scoots to one side of the park bench, offering me the other. The last time I sat on this exact bench was with Eren before we left for Montana.

I look down at my phone to see a handful of missed texts from Jordan.

JORDAN: Can we talk? Anytime today or tonight
JORDAN: Hope you have an amazing day Harlow
JORDAN: You're not coming to the meeting?

"I'm skipping a meeting to be here, so I don't want to risk running into anybody from the office," I mutter. "Where is Charlie?"

"With the nanny. Is everything alright? Your text seemed pretty urgent."

I suck in a deep breath to keep from crying. Up until yesterday, there were no hiccups in my relationship with Jordan. No doubts. No insecurities. Just plans for our lives together. Plans ruined by *32B*.

Blake leans forward, trying to read the expression under my sunglasses.

"Harlow, what's wrong?"

"Jordan cheated on me." I let out a quiet laugh, followed by a sniffle.

Blake's posture shifts in my peripherals. "I'm—wait, he what?"

"Jordan slept with my assistant while we were in Montana. One of our housekeepers found her bra in our room yesterday. I confronted her at the gala last night and then Jordan owned up to it."

"You're fucking kidding." Blake stands over me. "You know I always thought he was a tool, but I didn't think he had it in him to be an actual scumbag." His head swivels left and then right, his fists clenched. "Where is he?"

I tug at his arm. "Blake, sit."

"No." Blake yanks his arm away. "He flat-out disrespected you."

"I know. And Jordan knows," I snap back. "You don't need to talk to him. I can talk to him myself."

Blake unclenches his fists. "Oh, Harlow," he says softly as he crouches in front of me. "Don't tell me you're actually gonna hear him out."

Father's words echo through my mind until I say them out loud. "It was one fuck-up, Blake. And it won't be the last time he fucks up because he's human."

"Yeah, a shitty human who doesn't deserve you." Blake shakes his head. "He cheated on you. He slept with someone else in your bed."

I wince at the thought of Jordan and Penny in *my* apartment having sex in *my* room in *my* bed.

Blake places a hand on my shoulder. "He's at the office, isn't he?" He jumps back up to his feet.

"Blake!" I shout, but it's already too late. He's trudging up the walkway, keeping a few feet ahead of me as I try to stop him. "Blake, stop." He raises his hand for a taxi, but I force it back down.

"Stop?! I'm sick and tired of seeing you like this. You're a puppet, doing whatever Jordan and Father tell you to. You do whatever the hell they want you to do, and you're miserable. You tell yourself you're happy, but you won't know happiness until you make your own goddamn decision for once. I saw you in Montana. I see the way you light up when you talk about music. If you stay with Jordan… if you keep working for Father…" Blake sucks in a breath. "I swear to you, Harlow. You will wake up one day wishing you took a chance while you had it–writing the album, seeing the world, and choosing the right guy."

"Choosing the right guy?" I repeat.

Blake bites his lip, realizing he might have overshared. He sighs. "Eren told me he has feelings for you. We're adults now, Harlow. You can make your own decisions. But for what my opinion is worth, Eren is bringing out a side of you that is worth exploring more of. I know you see it, too."

Blake is right. Eren has had a tiny place in my heart since we met, and I've denied its existence out of respect for Jordan. Now that I no longer have respect for Jordan, I'm even more enticed at the thought of seeing Eren again.

"Did you go home with Jordan last night?" Blake asks, his tone fragile.

I shake my head. "I'm staying at Talia's till I get my head on straight."

"Good. I know he has a temper. Just please don't be anywhere near him until this blows over."

"I know, I know."

I've seen Jordan snap on everyone but me. It frightens me to imagine what might happen if Jordan doesn't get his way while we're alone.

After a moment of silence between the two of us, Blake sighs, then says, "You should see him."

I blink at him. "I thought you said not to be anywhere near him until—"

"Not Jordan. You should see *Eren*."

I can't hide the smile that suddenly spreads across my face. The thought of dropping everything to fly across the country for Eren right now fills me with warmth.

"But, Harlow…" Blake adds cautiously. "Eren is a conflicted guy with a loaded past that he's still getting over. If you're gonna pursue each other, be aware of that."

Blake's words go right over my head. It's hard to be present when my mind is pulling me toward Montana, and my heart is pulling me toward Eren.

♬ ♬ ♬

"Where to, Ms. Harlow?" Francis asks as he opens the car door for me.

"The apartment, please. Then to the airport."

I crawl into the back of the S.U.V. When Francis sits in the driver's seat, his eyes meet mine through the rearview mirror. "Will you not be returning to Beck Holdings today?"

"An important matter has come up," I reply.

Francis nods, starts the car, and merges onto the busy street. I'm struggling to hold back my smile. I never fathomed being spontaneous enough to fly across the country on a whim.

I get chills at the thought of seeing the sea of pine trees outside the jet window. Driving through the lush green forest until my shoes meet the dirt. Walking up to the front door. Seeing Eren's face when he sees me. And the rest–I'll leave the rest up to life itself for once. No more plans. No more knowing what happens next. I'm craving the feeling of standing face to face with the unknown. I'll welcome it with open arms.

"I'll be down in 10 minutes!" I shout to Francis when we reach my apartment building.

"I'll be patiently waiting, Ms. Harlow."

I bolt through the lobby, heels in hand. Within seconds, I'm on my way up to my apartment. My reflection beams at me through the elevator mirror as I undo my hair, letting it fall down to my waist. I haven't even left yet, and already, I feel more comfortable in my own skin.

"This can be you," I say to the woman in my reflection. "For as long as you want it to be."

When the elevator opens, I glide down the hall, my bare feet tapping against the cool marble. With Jordan still at work, I'll be able to take my time packing.

I slam one of my Chanel duffle bags onto the bed and stuff it with clothes. I pack the clothes I care the least about, considering I now know what to expect.

The dirt. The road.

Two things I can't wait to get back to.

"Where you goin'?" a familiar voice asks.

I almost leap out of my body, spewing random curse words. "AHH! SHIT… dammit… fuck ass." I turn to see Jordan standing at the doorway. He stares calmly at the open duffle bag on our bed. "What're you doing here?" I ask, catching my breath.

Jordan's green eyes flick from the duffle bag to me. They're so disheartened, a mere glance could serve as an apology. But I still won't accept it.

"I like your hair down." His compliment bounces off me like

a ball against a brick wall. I know it's a lie. He's always been the first to tell me to tie it up. "I didn't see you at work," he continues. "I fired Penny. She's gone. Harlow, it was a stupid mistake."

I grind my teeth. Jordan thinks we can pick up where we left off just because the girl he cheated on me with is no longer doing my coffee runs. I clench a fist, and Jordan lifts his hands apologetically.

"I know I'm an asshole," he takes a step into the room. "I'm a shitty person who made a shitty mistake, but that's all it was. A stupid mistake. And I–"

ZZZZIP!

I zip my duffle bag shut. Hearing Jordan speak is beginning to make me sick because the words he says don't register the same anymore. I recognize his voice, but the words coming out of his mouth don't hold any weight. He broke my trust, so now his words are just words. Nothing more.

"Stop talking," I say, partially because I assume it's bullshit. And partially because I'm afraid he could somehow convince me to stay. Spending five years falling in love with somebody can make un-forgivable mistakes seem forgivable. But I can't afford to forgive this somebody right now.

I have a flight to catch.

"Harlow," Jordan exhales, taking another step in my direc-tion. "Don't run away from this. I'll explain what happened."

My legs habitually grow weak when he gets closer. I can smell his cologne, a familiar scent I'm conditioned to submit myself to.

His scent is home to me.

His voice is home to me.

His touch is home to me.

My breath is shaky as his jacket leaves his shoulders. He says, "Baby, you know me. I did a bad thing, but I'm not a bad per-son." He's using the same tone he uses when he makes love to me.

I despise that he's using everything he can to keep me here. I hate that… hate that…

He gets even closer. If I don't look up at his eyes, I'm staring directly into his chest, a chest I know almost better than I know my own. A chest I've slept on. A chest that holds the heart I've grown to love. I try to step around him, but his hand grips my shoulder.

"Let go."

His lips hover near my ear. "I just want to talk," he whispers smoothly. "We can't talk?"

His thumb is grazing my shoulder and it could be so easy for us to just sit and work this out and maybe this whole Montana thing is all just a cry for help and…

"Sorry to interrupt, Ms. Harlow," a voice says calmly. I peek my head around Jordan to see Francis now standing at the doorway. "You mentioned we would depart in 10 minutes. It has been 12. I wanted to make sure that you don't miss your 'important matter.'"

"Important matter?" Jordan blinks at me, then lets go of my arm.

I fold my lips between my teeth to keep from smiling. Jordan lets out a defeated sigh as he opens his stance to let me pass.

"Thank you," I whisper to Francis as he opens the front door for me. Francis nods, well-aware that he went from being my driver to being my guardian angel.

It takes Francis an hour to drive us to Newark Liberty International Airport. It's just past 3p.m., which means it's just past 1p.m. in Montana. By the time I land, Eren and I will still have enough time to enjoy the sunset, to explore, to do whatever we want because we can.

Francis pulls up in front of the terminal. Before he gets out, I reach over the front seat and place my hand on his shoulder. "Thank you for what you did back there," I say softly.

A warm smile spreads across Francis's face. "My pleasure, Ms. Harlow. Have a safe flight."

I open the door before he's able to, then sprint into the private jet terminal with my duffle bag in hand. I'm in and out of security within minutes, and before I know it, I'm blasting music in my headphones as an S.U.V. escorts me to my jet.

Imagining Eren's reaction to me randomly showing up puts a smile on my face. I'm excited, not because of what I expect to happen, but because of what I *don't* expect. I have no idea how he'll feel about me coming back. I have no idea how *I'll* feel about me coming back. And I love that–not knowing what happens next.

I bury my phone in my bag, so nobody can reach me. I want to dive headfirst into Eren's world again, this time without worrying about a single piece of my own world. No thoughts of work, no thoughts of toxic people. Just music, nature, and Eren.

"Anything to drink, Ms. Harlow?" the flight attendant asks.

"Do we have any whiskey?"

The flight attendant blinks at me. "We, unfortunately, do not. But I can bring you champagne!"

"That's alright." I flash a smile. "I can wait until I land."

My excitement makes the five hours feel like forever, and I get chills when I look out the window. We descend over a sea of green, and it baffles me how I thought so little of it the last time I flew in.

The jet's staircase folds out, and I've never been so excited to receive the keys to a beat-up rental car. Broken air conditioner. Stained seats. Fine by me.

I roll down the windows, turn up the music, and claim the open road ahead. It's not hard to find my way to Eren. Most of the drive is a single highway until I recognize the dirt road that'll take me directly to him.

The pine trees swallow me as my tires mold to the rises and

dips of the dirt road. In the distance, I can see the house that gradually becomes larger the closer I get. My heart is racing as butterflies make themselves known in my stomach. The road crunches under my tires as I pull up to the garage door.

I silently grab my bag and tiptoe to the front door. I want to scare him like I did last time. I quietly open the front door and peek my head through. Silence. The house is still–not a single beat. I take a few silent steps and see that the studio is empty. Eren's bag is lying open by the couch, but there is no sight of Eren.

I creep into the kitchen. No sight of Eren.

I creep into the living room. No sight of Eren.

My eyes pan to the back door, which is slid open. There, standing at the edge of the back deck staring out over the sea of trees, is Eren.

"Hey, rockstar," I say.

He looks over his shoulder at me, and his eyes widen in disbelief. He fully turns, and I realize he's not wearing a shirt.

It's the first time I've seen him shirtless. He really is covered in tattoos from the neck down, and when I say covered, I mean *covered*. Ink coats him like paint on a canvas. It'd be an injustice to take my eyes off of his body because he's taken on the form of a priceless art piece... a one-of-one.

The dim lighting accentuates the sharpness of his flexed jaw. He's surprised to see me, and I don't blame him. The last we spoke, I pushed him away, and now here I am, ready to close the gap between us.

Our eyes fixate on each other, but this time is different from any other.

This time, there is no trace of guilt.

This time, we're alone.

This time, there's nothing holding me back.

CHAPTER THIRTEEN

EREN

My heart drops when I see Harlow step on to the back deck. Her presence pulls at me like gravity. Inescapable. Inevitable.

This is impossible.

The drugs should be out of my system by now.

"Am I hallucinating?" I ask.

Harlow shakes her head, then takes a step closer.

"Am I dead?"

Harlow shakes her head again, then takes a step closer.

"This is *really* happening?"

She nods. We stand chest to chest. We don't say a word, and I'm glad we don't because I want to take this moment to silently appreciate her beauty. The way her blue eyes are timid and wild at the same time. The way her lips naturally part, ready to overwhelm me with their touch. Her scent is temptation. Her beauty is bliss.

I step forward, my eyes locked on her lips. "I want to…"

"You should."

The distance between us dissolves as I caress her lips with mine. *They're softer than I thought they would be.*

My fingers meet the small of her back, palms pressed against the curve of her waist as I guide her inside. The only time my lips leave hers is when I need to breathe. *Damn oxygen.*

I've never felt this kind of connection, so I pull her in like my life depends on her touch. Every time our lips meet, my addiction to her is fed but never met. I can't get any closer to her, but I try to get closer anyway. With every beat her heart forces against mine, my heartache subsides.

Just before we reach the bedroom, I pick her up. Her legs wrap around my torso, and I feel a warm sensation drop to my waist. The warmth settles between my legs, and Harlow pulls back a moment to see the look in my eyes–to see how in tune we've become.

She moans when I bury my lips in her neck–biting, kissing, sucking. I want to taste her any way I can. She keeps her legs wrapped around me as I stand at the foot of the bed, and she removes her shirt like it's on fire.

"Put me down," she whispers between heavy breaths.

I obey, and she quickly undoes her bra and pants. They join her shirt on the floor, and that's when I come to the sudden realization…

I'm not gonna last.

I pick her up, feeling her warm skin against mine, but it's not for long. I drop her onto the bed, and she looks me up and down with eager eyes. As much as I want to stand back to appreciate her physical beauty with my eyes, I drop my sweatpants and crawl onto the bed.

"For a second, I thought *every* part of you was tattooed," Harlow teases.

I smirk. "Not *every* part of me."

Her hand is warm against the only part of me not covered in ink. Her jaw drops as she exhales an exhilarated breath against my lips. I place my hand along the side of her face, guiding the back of her head deeper into the bed. For 18 years, I lived without feeling, which means I have 18 years of feeling to make up for. And I plan to start now.

I rub against her while my left arm props me up and my right palm remains on her cheek. I outline her jaw with my fingers as she explores my lower abdomen with hers.

"Can I?" I ask, now grazing the trim of her thong.

She bites her lip and smirks. I lower myself, gently removing it as I move back to the foot of the bed. My lips meet her ankle, her calf, her inner thigh, her…

"Mm," Harlow whines.

My lips continue introducing themselves to her stomach, her breasts, the vee at the bottom of her neck.

She suddenly places her palm against my chest. "Eren…" She lets out a quick breath. "I've only been with one person."

I smile at her innocence–her lack of experience.

"I don't care where you've been," I whisper against her lips. "The only thing that matters is that you're *here*."

I guide the length of me inside her, and our bodies mold to-gether, heartbeats in sync. Every pleasure-filled sound that leaves her mouth is the sweetest sound, sweeter than any song ever sung. I pour everything I am into physical touch.

My tongue sweeps her lip, which she uses as a cue to slide her nails down my back. She moans, which I use as a cue to slide deeper into *her*.

It's not long before warmth flows between the two of us, her body trembling against the flexing of my every muscle. Our worlds become one, and after a few deep breaths, Harlow giggles, covering her face with her palms. "Was it obvious how much I liked that?" she asks.

I smirk against her lips. "I'll make sure you love it next time, and every time after that."

Harlow's eyes dart left and right between mine. I give her

one long passionate kiss before I roll on to my back and she cuddles up next to me, her head resting on my shoulder. Her long wavy locks spread themselves along the pillows, sheets, and my chest. Auburn looks good on me.

I glance at Harlow to see her admiring my neck and chest.

So, this is what it feels like to be desired.

For once, my golden rule has lost its shine. For Harlow, I'll risk having my heart broken. I'll risk it all for this girl because she's saving me from myself.

"Tell me about your tattoos." Her voice gives me chills. "Starting with the bird." Her nail runs gently over the side of my neck.

"What's more free than a bird?" The corner of her lip curls up as I continue. "I've lived almost my entire life without attachments. In a way, it helped me feel free. And I'm happiest when I feel free."

Harlow's finger moves to the back of my neck. "And the wings on the back of your neck? Why the wings?"

I avert my eyes from hers. While my tattoos are on display for everyone to see, I've actually never been asked about them, so I tread carefully.

"They're angel wings," I reply softly. "My mom's angel wings. I like to think that she always has my back."

Sadness looms in Harlow's eyes as they find my lips. She kisses me, and I taste empathy. I don't open up to people the way I've opened up to Harlow. I don't even know if I'm doing it right. Regardless, I couldn't be more grateful that she's willing to listen.

Her nail trails down from my neck to my chest. "And the tattoos on your chest?"

"My lyrics," I reply. "From songs I wrote, interwoven with music notes and symbols." I lift a brow, then tease, "Because I write songs sometimes."

Harlow playfully slaps my chest. "Really? I didn't know that."

The two of us laugh until I gently tuck her hair behind her ear. I sigh before asking, "Why did you come back?"

She pulls my hand to her chest. She holds it there for a moment before saying, "I told you I wanted to kiss you that night. I just didn't think it was fair to Jordan."

I blink at her, looking our naked bodies up and down. "But making love like we just did *is* fair to Jordan?"

Harlow's eyes flick up to the ceiling. "Well, I'm no longer with Jordan."

"You're no longer with Jordan…"

"He cheated on me with my assistant."

My jaw drops. "What?! When?"

"While I was here," she murmurs.

"Harlow, I'm so sorry." I sit up, my back now resting against the headboard. "Are you okay?"

Harlow lets out a shaky laugh. "I'm fine. Either way, it shouldn't have taken Jordan cheating to make me acknowledge the feelings I have for you. And now I know what my heart was trying to tell me that night outside of the bar… that you're the one."

I wrap her hand with mine. It's hard for me to dwell on the possibility that I'm Harlow's second option when I'm too busy being grateful for her presence. It's a chance at a fresh start, to correct the way I've perceived relationships for most of my life.

"I'm sorry that Jordan is all you've ever known," I say softly.

"He's not all I know *anymore*."

Harlow smiles, and I don't wait another second to kiss her. Our lips caress one another until we fall asleep in each other's arms.

♫ ♫ ♫

My eyes open and I'm staring at the ceiling. I'm lying in the middle of the bed, naked between white linen sheets. I quickly lift myself onto my elbows. I rub my eyes and open them, praying that I see Harlow next to me. But I don't.

Please don't let last night be a dream.

I frantically look around the room for anything she might have left, any remnants of her presence. I fall back against my pillow, forcing the base of my palms into my eyes.

"Fuck me, it was a dream," I mutter under my breath. "I'm having serious Harlow withdrawals."

Before I consider checking into Harlow-holics Anonymous, I smell bacon and waffles.

BACON AND WAFFLES.

I leap out of bed and hop across the room while pulling my sweatpants on. I swing the door open and see Harlow making breakfast. She's wearing one of my T-shirts that fit her like a dress, her hair falling down to her lower back. The back door is slid open, letting in a cool breeze as music plays from the T.V. speakers. I silently watch her dance while she cooks, smiling cheek to cheek.

I want to smother her with kisses, but I also don't want to disturb her. She dumps a mountain of bacon onto a plate, then catches me admiring her.

She smiles. "You spying on me, rockstar?"

"Just admiring."

Harlow flashes a cheeky grin before biting into a bacon strip. "You just gonna stand there and admire, or you gonna come here and eat?"

I walk toward her, slowly shaking my head. I cup the side of her face and kiss her forehead. "What do you want to do today?"

"Anything."

The two of us lean against the kitchen counter, picking apart pieces of bacon and waffles.

"We have a world to explore and an album to write," I say while leaning into her shoulder.

Harlow's eyes light up. "Let's explore first! Then we can come back and write!"

I chuckle at her enthusiasm. Seeing her excited excites me. I'd do anything she says she wants to do. If Harlow wanted to jump off a cliff, I'd probably do that, too. *Damn, I'm falling quick.*

After breakfast, we change and head out across the grass plain and into the woods. The sun is shining from directly above, casting rays of light through the openings between the treetops.

"Does Blake know you're here?" I ask.

Harlow pokes the ground we walk over with a stick. "He actually convinced me to come."

"Blake? Really?"

"Really." She smiles. "He said you're bringing out a side of me that's worth exploring more of."

Since I met Harlow, I've watched her become more comfortable in her own skin, from her songwriting to the way she embraces the unknown. This side of her is undeniably worth exploring more of. I want to explore it, too.

"Why are you smiling?" Harlow asks.

I glance at her as we walk side by side. "When I met you, it seemed like you had this desire to be set free. I'm just happy to see that you found it."

Harlow's eyes fall to my hand, which she holds without hesitation—a perfect fit.

"Have you and Blake always been close?" I ask.

There is a moment of silence as Harlow ponders. "I would say so. We were really close as kids. As teenagers, too. It wasn't until I started working for my father that we became pretty distant."

"Why distant?"

Harlow tosses her stick to the side. "We shared a passion for music behind closed doors. When he chose to pursue it and I chose to stick with the family business, we spoke less." Harlow takes a deep breath, then exhales. "Then, when Miranda died, he sort of became this shell of a person. He became passive–numb."

"Is he still passive?" I ask.

Now that Harlow mentions it, Blake has become more reserved over the years. I feel a sliver of guilt. I've known him for 10 years and haven't made a single effort to see if he's doing alright. Mourning his deceased wife, being a single father, not getting along with his parents, and working with broken artists like me.

"He's coming around more," Harlow says confidently. "You actually sort of brought us back together in a way."

I smile. It warms my heart knowing that even though I might not have my own family situation, I'm making someone else's a bit better.

"Look!" I stop in my tracks, yanking Harlow to my side.

"What?!"

I pull her off the path and down a slope until we reach a small cliff overlooking a river.

"Hell no," Harlow blurts out when I reach for a rope hanging from a nearby tree. "No chance, Eren."

The current pulls the river water in a single direction, and I get chills at the thought of submitting myself to it.

"Oh, come on!" I tug at the rope. The branch it hangs from doesn't budge. "You don't trust me?"

"I trust you." Harlow sighs. "I don't trust that rope."

"Have you ever done something like this before?"

"I've jumped into a pool."

"Okay, but have you ever *thrown yourself* into a pool?"

I begin kicking off my boots.

"Eren, please don't!" Harlow pleads. "This just seems dangerous."

I grip the rope and hold it up between us. "Take the leap," I whisper.

Harlow reluctantly looks down at the rope. I can see her taking my words to heart, hearing them in more ways than one. She can take the leap physically, throwing herself into the water without being guaranteed a safe landing. But more importantly, she can take the leap figuratively, submitting herself to something she can't control: *Life's constant current.*

Her eyes meet mine and her bottom lip folds out. "Please don't," she pleads softly.

I pinch my lips together, looking down at the river, then at the rope in my palm.

Don't look into those puppy-dog eyes, Eren. You'll lose this battle.

I instantly cave when she pulls at my arm. "Please don't jump."

I drop the rope, and Harlow throws her arms around me. As we head back in the direction of the house, I kiss the top of her head and whisper, "One of these days, I'm gonna get you to take the leap."

CHAPTER FOURTEEN

HARLOW

I've never done drugs before. But I imagine Eren's kisses have the same effect. I hear people do drugs because drugs can make the world around us seem more colorful. They can heighten our senses. They can give us an absurd amount of confidence. They can make life *seem better*. So, yeah. I've never done drugs and will never have to because Eren's kisses do all of those things. It's as simple as that.

I didn't plan to come back to Montana. I didn't plan to develop feelings for Eren. I didn't plan to enjoy sex with Eren as much as I did, and I didn't expect to crave it as much as I do now. But all of these things are happening, and I couldn't be happier about it.

"I love it," Eren says from over my shoulder. He reads my lyrics aloud, *"I'm chasing highs, till I feel like you're by my side, even when I'm alone."*

"It's just a thought," I mutter with my pen hovering over my notebook. "I'm gonna change it."

Eren lays back on the couch. "Why would you change it?"

"It could be better."

"Well, let me ask you…" Eren laces his fingers behind his head while crossing one leg over the other. "Are you chasing highs?"

"In a way, yeah."

"What kind of highs?"

I bury my hands in my lap. When I swivel my chair to face Eren, I notice him studying me with attentive eyes.

"I guess the high is this thrill of not knowing what happens next," I confess. Eren slowly nods his head, instantly validating my lyrics.

"And who are you writing to when you write, *'Till I feel like you're by my side, even when I'm alone?'*"

"You."

"If you're being true to how you feel, I wouldn't change a thing." A smile slowly spreads across Eren's face. "Especially if you're feeling that way about me," he teases.

I raise a brow and try to keep from blushing. I look back at my notebook and continue writing. I hear the couch cushions shift, then feel Eren standing over my shoulder again.

Eren places his hands on my shoulders. His palms are warm against my skin as he strokes my shoulder blade with his thumb. I get chills when his lips press against my ear. He whispers, "Can I?" The smoothness in his voice makes me want to say yes to absolutely anything.

I see the words and symbols on his arms as he reaches over me and begins writing below my lyrics. The warmth of his body envelops me as he presses against my back. I read the words he writes just below mine, "*Fuck lonely nights, I need you here, I'll be your ride, we'll claim the road.*"

"*Fuck lonely nights, I need you here,*" I whisper under my breath. I quietly stand to my feet and face him. "Who are you writing to when you write, *'I'll be your ride, we'll claim the road?'*"

The corner of Eren's lips curls up. "You."

I hold his gaze while placing my palm firmly against his chest. I'm gentle but stern in the way that I guide him down onto the couch. I don't let go of his gaze as I straddle him, wrapping my arms loosely around his ink-covered neck, grazing over his cheekbone with my thumb.

Never in a million years would I think a man could have this effect on me with his words alone. I grew up pouring my emotions into my writing. I never imagined being the reason somebody pours their emotions into their own writing. It's as if Eren and I are developing a secret language, one spoken through the lyrics we write.

Eren's smirk softens and brows straighten. "Can I ask you something?"

"Anything."

"Do I intimidate you?" There is a subtle tremble in his voice.

I blink at him. "Do you intimidate me? No, why would you ask that?"

"I don't know. I guess with the way I look–the tattoos and all–people are quick to look away. Or they stare at me like I'm some kind of zoo animal." Eren's voice quivers. "I feel like, over the years, I've let strangers' opinions of me define who I am. I've grown to believe the only person who can love me is me."

My hands slide from the back of Eren's neck to the sides of his face. It's not fair that Eren is judged by his appearance. If only people heard his voice. If they could see what's inside, people would line up to simply breathe the same air as him.

"You're not intimidating," I say with conviction. "If someone is judging you by the way you look, what should their opinion matter anyway? No one knows you better than *you*, so you can't let strangers define who you are." I drag my eyes down his chest. "For what it's worth… to me, you're living art."

Eren's lips are suddenly caressing mine. I whimper because there is something behind this kiss different from each one before. I taste gratitude. I feel passion. And I'm obsessed. My hands drop from the sides of his face because I'm so invested in this kiss, I don't even know what to do with them.

Eren's tongue brushes against mine again and again. The rhythm of our kisses picks up in accordance with the beating of my heart, which doubles when I feel him grow hard between my legs. I move my hips back-and-forth as a way of showing him where I want him.

Our lips depart from each other, so I can pull my shirt off. The shirt meets the floor. I continue rubbing myself over him, my hands dragging down his chest. He reads my mind, feeding the fire within me as he lowers his sweatpants and kicks them across the room.

Before I get up to remove my thong, he stops me. As if he can't wait another second, I feel his hand move my thong to the side. I raise myself onto my knees, and with one hand gripping his jaw, I guide the length of him into me with the other.

I whine. We've barely started making love, and I already want to make love again and again after that. Eren pulls me in, so his lips can explore my neck, adding a surreal sensation to the list of sensations I'm feeling right now. His lips are soft against my skin like the sweet sound of a violin, but he rocks me like a hurricane, making love to more than just my body. I can tell by the way I feel him deep in my mind and heart. It's the song I never want to end.

Eren dips his forehead to mine. "I want you to feel me."

I suck in a breath. "Trust me, I do."

"No," he whispers against my lips. "I want you to feel me, *even when you're alone.*"

The low frequencies in his voice instantly make my body tremble until every part of me is shaking. I throw my arms around him, pulling his face into my neck as my body tightens around him. I pull back, my eyes wide open.

Eren smirks. "I know," he whispers, knowing exactly what he's done to me.

I place my hands on his shoulders, then narrow my eyes on his. "Look at me," I whisper sternly. "Don't you look away."

He obeys.

I roll my hips back-and-forth, our eyes fixated on each other. It's in this fixation that I feel Eren the most–in the way we get lost in each other's eyes. It all started the night we laid eyes on each other in the alley, and I can't believe I'm lucky enough to look into his eyes the same way now.

His jaw drops when my body roll becomes a gyrate. My jaw drops the same length as his. I can feel him feeling me. It brings me pleasure knowing that even though Eren has been around the country, he's still never experienced anything like me. I see it in the way he looks at me. I feel it in the way he comes here and now.

I smirk. "I know," I whisper, knowing exactly what I've done to him.

Eren smiles from cheek to cheek. We adjust ourselves so that we're lying chest to chest on the couch.

Eren exhales. "I've been almost everywhere. And still, nothing compares to being with you."

"What if I went everywhere *with* you?" I rest my chin on his chest. "Then you won't have to compare at all."

"I'll have to buy you a helmet."

I get chills at the thought of being on the road with Eren. Living a life without knowing what tomorrow will bring. The change of scenery. The new faces. The memories we'll make. The stories we'll tell. The songs we'll write.

"Can we ride into town?" I ask.

I feel Eren stiffen. "Right now?"

"Right now."

Eren bites his lip, and I can feel something is off about him. His body is tense, and he fixates on the ceiling in deep thought.

"Is something wrong?" I ask.

"I need to tell you something." He takes a deep breath, then says, "I sort of crashed my bike a couple days ago."

"What?" I sit up. "You got in an accident? Are you okay? Are you hurt? You don't seem hurt."

"I'm fine," Eren says calmly. "But there's a bit more to it." We sit straight up on the couch. "I don't know what Blake might have told you already, but I've developed some bad habits over the years."

"Bad habits?"

"I've sort of relied on drugs and drinking as a way to keep me going–to keep me from falling off the edge. When you came into the picture, I started cleaning up my act. But when you left, I completely lost control. The motorcycle accident a few days ago was my breaking point, and it made me realize that I need to let go of my vices if I'm gonna one day be good enough for you."

The tone in Eren's voice is fragile, his eyes sincere. It's no surprise that he comes from a world of recklessness and instability, but he doesn't deserve to wallow in that world forever, the same way I don't deserve to wallow in mine.

"Promise me you'll never lose control again," I say.

Eren nods, and the corner of his lip curls up as he whispers, "I promise."

"This 'accident.' Was it bad?"

"My motorcycle is ruined," he exhales. "It was raining, and I ran into a log."

"And you didn't get hurt?"

"Somehow, no. I get pretty bad headaches here and there, but overall, I'm fine."

"Where is the motorcycle?"

"Buried it."

Guilt creeps into the back of my mind when I picture the accident happening the day after I left him. A part of me feels like I'm to blame for his spiral. God forbid he died in that accident. I would be living the rest of my life knowing I'm responsible for his death. The guilt of knowing I killed someone I care about would kill me, and I feel for Eren even more now that I realize this is how he feels about losing his mom.

I take a deep breath and run my hands through his hair. "I'm glad you're okay."

"Me, too," he replies. "I'd hate myself if you came all the way back and I wasn't here to see you."

I lean in and plant a gentle kiss on Eren's forehead. My phone rings from the table, and I stand to see that Blake is FaceTiming me.

"It's Blake," I say. "As much as I hate to say this, we should probably put our clothes back on."

We put our clothes on before I pick up the call.

"Hey, loser," Blake greets as his face fills my phone screen.

I roll my eyes. "Hello, winner."

"Wait a minute. I know that ceiling." Blake grins. "You're there! In Montana!"

I immediately blush. Eren pops his head out from over my shoulder and waves. A grin slowly spreads across Blake's face, as if he comes to the realization that not only are Eren and I together, but we're *happy* together. Instead of addressing it, Blake raises his phone to reveal Charlie's head poking out of a baby-carrying vest strapped to his chest.

"Check this out. I took the day off work to walk around Central Park with Charlie. I never realized how good of a wingman my kid is."

"Foffee," Charlie says before trying to lick Blake's phone.

"Eren, I tried calling you earlier," Blake continues. "Harlow, this will be good news for you, too. The artist asked Eren and me to meet him at his house in Miami tomorrow. I know it's sudden, but the guy is paying us, so we work on *his* time. We're finally gonna meet this mysterious artist."

"Can Harlow come, too?" Eren asks. I feel his hand graze the small of my back.

"It's probably best that we show up just us two when we meet him. That way, we can see what he's all about. We don't wanna risk overwhelming him. After all, he doesn't know we brought Harlow in to help write the album."

"Makes sense," I chime in. "I'm sure I can stay at Talia's until it's okay for me to fly out."

"You can stay at my place," Blake says. "You and Charlie can do some auntie-nephew bonding until the artist invites you down to Miami."

Charlie makes a high-pitched sound, and I smile at him through the phone. "You hear that, Charlie?! You get to hang out with your favorite aunt!" Charlie smiles, his chubby cheeks forcing his eyes shut.

"One last thing," Blake says with far less enthusiasm. "Mother and Father want to throw me a party for my 30th birthday."

I let out a sigh. "Please tell me you said no."

"They wouldn't let me," Blake mutters. "We'll talk about it with them at Sunday brunch."

"Fine," I groan.

"Alright, I'll let you two get back to writing." Blake lifts the phone up to his face. "Bye, loser. Bye, Eren."

"Bye, winner."

I feel Eren's hand glide around my waist. The second I hang up, Eren lifts me and covers me in kisses. I wrap my legs around him and ask, "Are you ready to meet this artist tomorrow?"

"What artist?"

"The artist we're writing this whole album for…"

"We're writing an album?" he teases.

I roll my eyes. "Don't tell me I'm distracting you."

"You're no distraction, Harlow." Eren smirks. "You're my *inspiration*."

CHAPTER FIFTEEN

EREN

"A birthday party at your parents' house?" I ask. "Is there gonna be a bounce house?"

"Shut up," Blake replies. His eyes are fixated on the road as we pass under a row of palm trees.

"I'm joking, I'm joking," I reply. "Of course I'll be there. 30 years old?! You're an old geezer now."

Blake laughs under his breath. "Alright, good. This is a bit off-topic, but I wanted to talk about you and Harlow."

The smile on my face fades as I prepare myself for the unexpected.

Blake exhales. "Your relationship with my sister is really none of my business. Like I said before, if you're done with the drug stuff, you have my blessing," he says. "When I saw you together over FaceTime, I realized… you're good for each other. She needs to let loose and you need to tighten up. You sort of bring the best out of each other. Just respect her and respect yourself. That's all I'll say about that. If you want to talk music, then I'm all ears. Otherwise, no need to elaborate on whatever you two got going on."

He subtly lifts his hand for me to shake. I shake it with a

smile on my face. "So, this is all good?"

"All good," he says while glancing at the G.P.S. "But from here on out, refer to me as 'Cupid.'"

"Done deal, Cupid."

For so long, I've kept Blake at arm's length because of my stupid rule. I thought not getting attached was keeping me alive. Instead, not getting attached was making my life worse.

"You've arrived at your destination," says the G.P.S.

My eyes pan from the marker on the map to the mansion outside my window. I roll it down, and the humidity floods the car.

Over the past 10 years, Blake and I have worked with some very successful artists, so a mansion this big doesn't really phase us. It's what is inside that sparks my curiosity. A nameless musician who is overpaying me to write his album. I'm forced to ask myself the question I asked myself the day I got the contract: *What's the catch?*

Blake drives up to the keypad built into a stone column. After a few beeps, the gate opens, and we pull onto the driveway. It's long and wide without a single car parked on it.

Blake leans over the steering wheel to get a better look at the entrance. "His manager said we don't need to knock. We just walk through the front door, I guess."

We make our way to a front door so big, you would think a giant lives here. It doesn't even make sense to have a door this big. *Maybe this guy really is a giant.*

We open the door, and sunlight pours inside, illuminating the white walls and tile floors. The sound of music plays from a distant room, echoing through the long halls.

"Did his manager say where to go?" I ask.

"He just said, 'come on in,'" Blake replies as he walks deeper into the house. "I guess we follow the music."

The music gets louder as we walk straight through the main hall leading to the back of the house. The walls are decorated with

Grammy and American Music Awards from the 80's and 90's.

Above one of the plaques is a picture of a young man in his early twenties performing in front of a stadium of people. His cherry red guitar reflects the array of spotlights, all pointed toward him at center stage, his long brown hair hanging over his face. I freeze when I read the name of the musician the plaque is awarded to: *FAI.*

My jaw drops to the floor.

Fai?! There's no way I'm writing for Fai.

I know the words to almost all of his songs after having grown up singing them in the car with my mom. His C.D.'s have been burned into the back of my mind since I could walk.

There's just no way.

"Found him," Blake whispers from the end of the hall. His back is to me, and when I step up next to him, I see a man playing the piano in a living room overlooking the bay.

The man's voice is deep, with just the right amount of rasp. He plays every key with intent. His emotions seep through his lyrics. Blake and I stand still. It would be an offense to interrupt such talent.

A beam of sunlight casts across the man's face, revealing wrinkles beside his closed eyes. He must be in his fifties. His narrow body frame is covered in sporadic tattoos that look randomly stamped onto his body. Dark-gray hair hangs over the sides of his face as he plays the final notes. He holds a high note until the sound of the piano fades.

The house is suddenly still. Blake and I glance at each other and simultaneously begin to slow-clap.

"Woah!" the man shouts. "You guys scared me!" He slides a pair of glasses on and walks toward us. The glasses have a tint to them, but the lenses are clear enough to see the deep-brown eyes behind them.

"Sorry, we probably should have knocked," Blake says. "But your manager said to come in."

The man laughs while stroking his goatee. "I should know. I'm the manager!"

"You're the manager?" I ask, genuinely surprised.

It's six in the afternoon, and it looks like this guy just woke up. But even with the little effort he put into his appearance, his charisma radiates.

"You sing pretty damn well for a manager," I add.

The man smirks and puffs out his tattooed chest. "I appreciate that, kid." He's a couple inches taller than me and almost a foot taller than Blake.

Blake offers his hand. "I'm Blake, Eren's manager." They exchange a firm handshake before facing me.

"So, that must make you Eren," the man states. He scans me from head to toe. "You're writing my album, huh?"

I blink at him. "I thought you said you were the manager."

He smiles. "I manage *myself*. I'm Fai." Our tattoos form a work of art when we shake hands.

"You manage yourself?" Blake asks.

"Yep," Fai replies. "Who knows me better than me?" He smirks. "You guys hungry?"

Fai casually turns and struts toward the backyard.

Blake lifts a finger in my direction, then whispers, "Don't get any ideas. You need a manager."

I pat Blake on the back. "You're right. Who else is gonna drive me places?"

"Very funny."

We follow Fai down a set of steps and onto a wide dock with a barbecue on it. Fai faces the grill. "Do you guys cook at all?" He lifts the aluminum foil off a large plate of steaks and vegetables, then places them neatly on the grill.

"I cook whenever I can," Blake replies.

"Good man," Fai says. He raises a brow at me. "What about

you, Eren? You cook?"

"I'm terrible at it," I admit. "But I try to sometimes."

The steaks begin to sizzle after Fai flips a few pieces. "You got a girlfriend?" he asks coolly.

"I don't," I reply.

"Because you can't cook?" He hides his smirk behind a sip of his sparkling water.

Blake laughs and nudges me. "That's probably one of the reasons."

I've known Fai for 10 minutes, and he's already poking fun at me like we've known each other for years. He's smooth with his words, making it tough to tell whether he's being serious or sarcastic. Either way, he's overpaying me to write his album, so he can poke all the fun he wants.

"I'm just messin' with you," Fai adds. He flips a couple pieces of vegetables. "Tell me about you guys. Where you from?"

"I'm from the Hamptons," Blake replies. "But now in Manhattan with my kid."

Fai itches his goatee, perplexed. "You came down to Miami without your kid?!"

Blake shrugs. "A man has got to make a living. And I was looking forward to meeting you."

"I respect you for thinking that, but a man should spend time with his family."

Blake opens his mouth to speak but says nothing. We've never worked with an artist who puts family first. So, this is unchartered territory for us.

Fai flips open the grill and starts loading food on a plate. "Well, go on! Have your record label add your flight to my expenses, and I'll cover it. First-class. Go spend time with your kid."

Blake hesitates. "Are you… are you sure?"

"Take it from a guy who has everything but a family," Fai

replies. "Go spend time with yours. Next time you come down, feel free to bring your kid."

Blake turns to me with confusion in his eyes. "You alright with me leaving? I guess you guys don't really need me around at this point."

A part of me is excited to be working with a rockstar I've idolized since I was a kid, but another part of me is nervous. I've worked with enough artists to know that crazy shit happens behind closed doors, so I'm forced to consider what crazy shit Fai might be into. Then again, he's paying me more than I'm worth.

I nod. "Yeah, I'm alright with it. You go spend time with Charlie."

Blake claps his hands. "Alright, sounds good! I'll fly back out sometime next week to check on you guys." He gives us each a pat on the shoulder and heads back into the house.

In most cases, I would feel weird about staying in a stranger's home the first night I meet them. But there is something calming about Fai's presence–something that makes me trust him without a second thought. I've met enough strangers in my life to recognize someone's intentions upon meeting them. Fai's intentions appear to be pretty good so far.

"Time to eat!" Fai shouts.

I follow him across the backyard, which seems to keep expanding the farther we walk. Exotic fruits hang from trees of all different shapes and sizes. A fountain here, a statue there. The entire place seems way too big for one person to live in.

"Do you live alone?" I say to his back.

Without turning, he says, "Lived alone my whole life."

"Same. Well, for most of my life."

We reach the top of a stone staircase, where a table is set overlooking the bay. On the table, there are three place settings already laid out.

"Most of your life, huh?" Fai sits at the edge of the table to my right, so we're both facing the sunset. "How long have you been doin' life?"

"I'm 28. So, I guess I've been doin' life for 28 years."

"Ah, what I would do to be 28 again." Fai sets a piece of steak and a handful of veggies on his plate. "Help yourself."

I load my plate. My knife glides through the steak like it's butter. The aroma is so alluring my mouth waters before the steak even reaches my lips. "This is really g–"

I fall silent at the sight of Fai praying. His elbows rest on the table, his chin on top of his interlocked fingers. I quickly swallow my bite and bow my head, pretending I've been praying with him this whole time.

He whispers, "Amen," and kisses one of the many rings on his fingers. He cuts a piece of steak, and before lifting it to his mouth, he says, "So, your manager is from the Hamptons. Where are *you* from?"

I usually don't do well with this question. Besides Blake and Harlow, nobody understands my lifestyle–my home being myself rather than my home being a place. A life of no responsibilities. No attachments. Bouncing from one place to the next just doing me. I decide to lie, picking the first place that comes to mind.

"I'm from Montana."

"What city in Montana?" Fai snaps back.

Shit. Why can't I remember what city I was just in?

I was literally just there.

Fai notices me looking for an answer. He swallows a bite of asparagus and leans toward me. "I don't gamble anymore. But if I did, I would bet on you not being from Montana."

I let out a defeated sigh. "You would win that bet. I'll be honest with you. My earliest memories are on the road. I don't really even know where I'm from."

Fai's eyebrows part, and his expression softens–a look of sympathy.

"It's not a bad thing," I murmur in an attempt to cover up my little sob story. "When I turned 18, I chose to continue living life on the road."

"It's not a terrible way to live," Fai says. "I lived it when I was your age. My advice to you would be to keep in touch with the ones you love. Fame and life on the road blinded me from seeing the importance of my relationships."

Upon hearing Fai's words, faces flash through my mind.

I see Harlow.

I see Blake.

I see Charlie.

"Where do you live now?" Fai asks.

The sun sinks below the Miami skyline in the distance. Lights hanging around the backyard turn on, casting a dim light over us.

"Shit," I whisper, burying my face in my palms.

"What happened?"

"My plan was to stay at a local motel until my record label set up my living situation. But I just realized my bag is in the rental car Blake took back to the airport. It's got my bathroom stuff, note-book, wallet…"

"A motel?!" Fai scrunches his face. "No way. I've got five guest bedrooms in this place. Take the one detached from the house."

"Fai, I… I could never. That's too much to–"

"Nobody lives here but me, Eren. You'll be doing me a favor by using the room. Plus, it's actually more of a house itself. It has its own kitchen, shower, and all that." He leans back in his chair and crosses his arms. "My room is on the complete opposite side of the house, so you'll have all the space you need. Text Blake tomorrow, and we can figure out the bag situation. In the meantime, just borrow some of my clothes."

I lower my head. "Thanks, Fai. I really appreciate it."

When I look up, I catch Fai studying me. "No need to thank me. Just write me the best album you've ever written, and we'll call it even."

He extends an open palm toward me. I slap my hand against his, followed by a fist bump.

"Deal."

When we finish dinner, Fai brings me a handful of clothes from upstairs. "These should fit you," he says, handing me some oversized T-shirts and shorts. "Go out the back door, make a right down the stone steps, and follow the path till you see the guest house on your left. There's all kinds of bathroom stuff in there that you can use. Help yourself to whatever."

"Thanks again, Fai. For everything."

"Stop thanking me." Fai smirks. "Goodnight, kid."

"Goodnight."

I head out the back door, make a right down the stone steps, and look for the guest house. I follow a narrow cobblestone walkway sandwiched between tropical wildlife. It curves left until I spot a tiny cream-colored house. The house is designed identically to the main house, just smaller in size.

I open the front door and can't see a thing. I spot a green light against the wall next to me and feel around for a button. Upon pressing it, dim lights fill the room. It's a spacious room with a large bed pressed against the back wall. A kitchen lines the wall to my right, and the bathroom is to my left.

The room is chilled, which feels refreshing after being out in the humidity. I set Fai's clothes next to the bathroom sink and begin going through drawers. Brand-new toothbrushes and grooming products fill the drawers, and the shower is stocked with shampoo, conditioner, and an array of bodywashes.

I can't remember the last time I stayed somewhere this nice. A part of me feels like I don't even deserve to stay in a place this nice. Not yet anyway.

I open one of the bottom drawers and pull one of the hair clippers out. I set it on the bathroom counter. With my hands pressed against each side of the clipper, I look at my reflection. My hair has grown a bit since I dyed it dark, and my stubble is taking on the form of a beard.

"You know the drill," I say to the man in the mirror. "New place, new look."

Without hesitation, I run the clipper's edge up the sides and back of my head. The hair on the top of my head now curls over the shaved sides. I glide the clipper's edge up my cheekbones, giving my beard a clean line-up along the sides of my face.

I watch the pieces of me fall to the floor, and when I look up, I feel brand new again. *Maybe this version of myself deserves to stay in a place like this.*

I shower, brush my teeth, and crawl into bed. My heart flutters when I see Harlow's text light up my phone screen.

> **HARLOW:** Hey rockstar:) You meet this mysterious
> artist yet?
> **EREN:** It's FAI... crazy... I used to listen to his music
> as a kid and now I'm staying in his guest house
> lol.. You're gonna love him

I get the urge to tell Harlow that I miss her. It's hardly been over a day since I saw her last.

Am I supposed to miss somebody this soon?

Is it wrong for me to admit it?

Think of something else. Anything else.

But I can't.

I want to know what she's up to. I want to know how her day was. I want to hear the slight rasp in her voice. I want to kiss her–hold her. I want to dive deeper into her mind, heart, and soul until I know her better than I know myself. With only Harlow on my mind, I fall asleep happy, and still, the nightmare begins…

Smoke fills the basement. It's thick–so thick I can hardly see the kids sitting around the crooked fold-out table. I'm in Kentucky… or is it Arkansas? Either way, I've only lived here for a couple weeks, and it's the first time my foster brother is letting me hang out with his friends.

"Kyle should be here any minute," my foster brother says. He sits directly across from me, his eyes the darkest shade of red. He's so high he can hardly keep them open.

The kid to my right is rolling a third joint with the other two neatly displayed in front of him. I don't know why he's rolling a third. We're already high off our asses, and there's no more room for smoke in this basement. When he finishes rolling it, he places it a foot away from the other two joints.

"Is that the one?" my foster brother asks the kid.

"Yeah."

They both snicker, exchanging devious looks.

"Is that one different from the others or something?" I ask.

"Don't worry about it," the kid hisses.

"Just tell him," my foster brother says. "Pa will beat the shit out of me if Eren accidentally smokes it."

The kid rolls his eyes. "This joint is laced. It's got cocaine in it."

My eyes widen. I'm only 14. I smoke weed, but I couldn't fathom smoking something with cocaine in it. "You're gonna smoke that?" I whisper.

"Hell no," my foster brother snaps. "Kyle is gonna smoke it."

"Why would he smoke that?" I ask.

"We're gonna tell him it's weed."

I itch the side of my head. "Why would you do that?"

"Kyle has been talkin' shit on us around school…" My foster brother leans forward, the red in his eyes turning black under the dim light. "But he doesn't know that we know. We told him to come hang with us, so we're gonna play a little prank on him… to get even. To show kids like Kyle why they shouldn't say bad things about kids like us."

I slide my sweaty palms against my jeans when I realize we're about to drug a kid for talking shit on us.

KNOCK! KNOCK!

A sliver of light sweeps the basement as Kyle steps in. My foster brother and the other kids hide their smirks and snickers as Kyle reaches the bottom of the creaky staircase. He waddles toward the table, and the light hanging over us brings out the roundness of his face. From the looks of Kyle, there isn't a shit-talking bone in his body.

"H-hey, guys," Kyle stutters, his tone timid.

"What's up, Kyle?" my foster brother hisses. "Come light up."

"Are you smoking cigarettes?" Kyle asks innocently, his forehead sweating.

"Nah," the kid to my right chimes in. "It's weed. Here, you can smoke this joint I just rolled."

Kyle's eyebrows draw apart when he sees the joint. "Oh, no thanks. I've never smoked weed before," he says softly. I can see the sweat glistening over his plump cheeks. "I just came to hang out with you guys."

"There's a first for everything," my foster brother urges. He

grabs the joint and forces it into Kyle's hand. Kyle looks at him, then nervously places the joint between his lips.

I feel a profound urge to intervene–to tell Kyle not to smoke the laced joint. I want to pull it from his lips and stomp it out. I want to tell him to get out of here before my foster brother and his friends try to ruin his life for something so trivial. But it's too late. My foster brother lights the laced joint, and Kyle inhales the first hit like it's fresh air.

My foster brother smirks. "You've got to hit these types of joints two or three times straight to really feel good." He lifts his hands toward Kyle's face. "Go on."

Kyle takes another drag, then another, and another. The other kids watch from the shadows with their malicious grins. They hide their snickering as Kyle begins to sway.

WHAM!

Kyle's back hits the floor, his arms sprawled at his sides. The other kids laugh hysterically over Kyle's unconscious body, making jokes about his weight. I stay seated.

I feel the darkness consuming the basement and everything in it. The kids suddenly go silent when we hear a cough. Everyone steps back as Kyle's body begins shaking on the floor. I manage to catch a glimpse from between two kids, and panic overwhelms me when I see Kyle foaming at the mouth.

"What the fuck?!" one of the kids shouts. "Is he having a seizure?"

"Shit, shit, shit," another mutters.

"Somebody do something!" I scream, now standing over Kyle.

My foster brother steps in. "Don't touch him! You'll only make it worse."

Kyle's body suddenly goes limp. His eyes are open, strained from his final moments struggling to survive. Kids begin sprinting up the stairs, separating themselves from the soon-to-be crime scene. I'm frozen, standing over Kyle's lifeless body.

"Holy shit, holy shit. We just fucking killed this kid," a kid whispers to my foster brother. "What do we do?!"

"We?" my foster brother snaps back. "It's your joint."

"It was your idea!"

The two pause before slowly turning back to me. My eyes lock onto the dead body of an innocent kid lying between us.

"Eren has only been here for a couple weeks," the kid whispers to my foster brother. "He doesn't have a case if we pin it on him."

My foster brother takes one last glance at Kyle's body, then his red eyes meet mine. "What was in that joint you gave Kyle tonight, Eren?" he asks. "You just killed the poor kid."

I freeze. "What?" I reply. "I didn't... that wasn't mine... that was yours! You guys drugged him!"

My foster brother tosses the laced joint against my chest. It rolls down onto my palm. Reality quickly sets in. I have nobody to defend me. It's my word against the word of all the other kids. I knew what was happening, and I chose to sit by and watch this innocent kid die. I'll lose this battle, without a doubt. I drop the joint, and as if in slow motion, it falls to the floor until...

I wake up in a puddle of my own sweat. My chest rises and falls with every heavy breath that leaves my trembling body.

"It already happened," I whisper to myself. "It's over. It already happened, and now it's over."

It takes me a second to realize I'm lying in bed.

I'm in Miami. I'm safe.

I look around the dark room. It's been almost a week since my last nightmare, and I realize why. With Harlow around, I don't have my usual nightmares. Like my vices, my tainted past has no hold on me when Harlow is around. I pull out my phone and text Harlow without hesitation.

EREN: Miss you

♫ ♫ ♫

It's just past 9a.m. when I shut the door behind me. It's a short walk from the guest house to Fai's back door. His tattooed back is to me as he cooks something over the stove in the kitchen. I open the door, and my mouth waters when I smell breakfast being made.

"That smells incredible," I say.

"Hopefully it tastes as good as it smells!"

Fai is wearing the same sweatpants he wore yesterday. No shirt. He flicks eggs and vegetables around with one hand while reaching for the toaster. "You mind grabbing the toast?"

I step around the kitchen counter and unload the toast onto a plate. Fai glances at me. "I know you said you can't cook. You think you can manage to butter the toast?" He flashes a smirk under his tinted glasses.

"Very funny," I chuckle while buttering the toast.

Fai lifts the smoking pan over the plates and starts serving omelettes. "Good form," he teases.

We take our loaded plates to a table in the backyard. Pitchers of chilled water and orange juice stand in the middle of the table that's been set with utensils. This time, I wait for Fai to finish praying before I start eating.

"How was your first night?" Fai asks between bites. "I see you gave yourself a haircut."

I shrug to buy myself time to swallow my food. "I hope you don't mind. I usually switch up my look when I move to a new place. It's a little tradition I have."

"Trust me, I've been there."

"Fai, listen." I clear my throat. "I couldn't help but notice that you're overpaying me for this album. I have to ask, why so much?"

Fai smirks, stabbing eggs with his fork. "You don't think you're worth that much? I think I'm paying you the right amount."

"It just seems like a lot of money for my level of talent."

Fai lowers his chin, his eyes peeking at me from over his glasses. "If you're questioning your worth, then you won't ever be worth much," he says softly. "If you think I'm overpaying you, push yourself enough to be okay with accepting what I'm paying you. I'm not gonna pay you any less."

I give an appreciative nod. "Thank you," I say. Fai smiles, remaining silent as I look around the backyard. "So, tell me about you," I add. "You're not in a relationship or married or anything like that?"

Fai takes a long sip of orange juice, then leans back in his seat, looking out over the water. The warm breeze sweeps strands of hair across his face. After stroking his goatee, he says, "I didn't have much time for relationships while on the road." He spreads his arms and looks around the backyard. "It might be tough to see, but life on the road bit me in the ass. I ended up alone."

"Are you kidding?" I ask with a mouthful of toast. "No responsibility. No attachments. Tons of cash. You're living my dream. All I need is my motorcycle, my notebook, and the clothes on my back. I'd have my bike with me now if I…" I stop myself before mentioning my accident back in Montana. "I plan on getting a new bike soon," I add.

"So, you ride a motorcycle?" Fai lifts his chin. "I hate to rain on your parade, kid. But I would trade in all of my music success on the road to start my own family. Life on the road is nice, but eventually, you'll run out of gas, and you won't have anyone left in your life willing to give you a ride."

It's difficult to take Fai's words to heart, partially because I'll always want to live life on the road and partially because I feel a raging migraine coming on. I can't help but think the pounding in my head is because Fai is challenging a lifestyle I have come to love living.

I want his life… being on stage… performing my songs for thousands of people at a time. It's what Mom wanted. And now it's what I want.

When I feel my migraine finally fade, I say, "You don't seem too old, and it's never too late to start a family."

"You would be surprised." Fai is still looking at me, but his mind is somewhere else. "You start to realize how important certain things are when they're no longer in reach." After a brief moment of silence, Fai snaps out of his trance. "Alright, writer. Tell me what you need to get your writing session started today."

"You got a studio?" I ask.

"Indeed, I do."

"That's all we really need besides my partner."

Fai tilts his head. "Your partner?"

I nod. "I hope you don't mind. I brought somebody on to work with me. She's helped me a lot so far. She's amazing. You'll really like her."

"By all means…" Fai lifts his hands. "You're writing my songs here. It's about *your* process. Not mine."

"I appreciate it." A grin spreads across my face. "Harlow will, too."

"Harlow?" Fai blinks at me. "Is that her name?"

"Yeah."

"Wow." He raises a brow. "That's a beautiful name."

I try to hide my smile as I text Harlow.

EREN: When's the soonest you can fly out?:)

CHAPTER SIXTEEN

HARLOW

I'm beaming at my phone screen when I wake up to Eren's texts. My heart nearly skips a beat when I read that he misses me, then it drops when I see him ask how soon I can fly down to Miami. I don't give myself a second to think of a response.

HARLOW: I miss you too:)
HARLOW: I'll fly out FIRST thing tomorrow

I let out a squeak while stretching in bed. I'm alone in Blake's bed because he wouldn't let me sleep on the couch. I prance into the living room to see Blake pouring coffee.

It brings me joy to see Blake and Charlie content in such a tiny apartment. Mother and Father scoffed at Blake's lifestyle when he started doing his own thing. I remember visiting Blake all the time while I was in college–all the times he would give me relationship advice, take me to concerts, and let me vent to him about Mother and Father when they got on my nerves.

It's nice to have a brother again.

"Happy Sunday, loser," Blake says, handing me a filled cup

of coffee. "What's got you smiling this early?"

I blush. "Oh, nothing."

I've had Eren on my mind since we parted ways a couple days ago, and now that I know when I'm seeing him next, I feel on top of the world. I kiss Charlie's forehead and sit next to him at the kitchen table. "We're gonna need to game again soon. I'm getting pretty tired of being called 'loser.'"

"Maybe today after brunch, loser," Blake teases. He slides a bowl of berries in front of Charlie, then sets a breakfast sandwich down in front of me.

This week has felt like the longest week of my life but also the quickest. From the highs with Eren to the lows with Jordan, I feel myself sandwiched in the middle as I mentally prepare myself for our weekly brunch.

"So, tell me more about Fai." I lean forward, ignoring my breakfast. "What is he like? Were you nervous? Do you and Eren feel good about working with him?"

Blake smirks. "Someone is excited." He takes a sip of his coffee. "Fai seems like a great guy. Really relaxed and super nice. He's the first artist to stress putting family first, too, which is cool."

"Did you guys show him any of the songs we've written so far?"

"Not yet. It was more of an introduction."

I slouch in my seat and cross my arms, wondering if Eren is proud of our songs.

Has he mentioned me to Fai?

Is Fai even okay with me co-writing his album?

"Has Eren reached out to you about flying down?" Blake asks.

"I'm flying out first thing tomorrow morning."

"Good!" he shouts, playfully nudging me. "That's great, Harlow."

I smile until a chilling thought crosses my mind–the thought of seeing Father today. He's going to ask why I skipped out on work this week. He'll want to know where I've been.

"Brooba," Charlie says from the head of the table.

"Good observation, Charlie. Aunt Harlow *does* look like she's gonna be sick." Blake's eyes flick to mine. "You're thinking about brunch today, aren't you?"

I nervously twiddle my thumbs. "What am I supposed to tell them? That I flew out to Montana because I'm writing an album for Fai?"

"Sounds great to me," Blake says coolly. "What's Father gonna do? Fire you?"

I nod, staring blankly at the tabletop. "He will probably do exactly that."

"Okay, he fires you. So, what? If you're fired from Beck, you'll be forced to pursue your dream." Blake takes a long sip of coffee. "That might be the best-case scenario for you."

I roll my eyes because I hate how right he is. It's not like I actually have the courage to quit my job to pursue songwriting. My father literally chose Jordan's side the night of the gala, and he hasn't followed up with me since.

"Do you think Jordan will be there today?" I ask.

"He would be an idiot to show up."

While I agree with Blake's statement, Jordan was also an idiot for cheating on me. So, I wouldn't put it past him to show up at my parents' estate. My phone vibrates, and I look down to see a text from Talia.

TALIA: Are you going to your parents' today?
 I wanted to check on you. I'll come alone if I have to
HARLOW: Ya I'll be there.. come alone please

I clear my throat. "Last thing…"

Blake tilts his head.

"Should I mention Eren?"

"I wouldn't," he replies. "Not yet."

Blake and I take turns getting ready. My hair pulls at my scalp when I tie it into my top bun as if it's upset with me for going back to my old ways. As I finish tying it up, I feel a tug at the bottom of my trousers.

"Gooba," Charlie says.

"Hello, my little prince."

Charlie's eyes are fixated on my bun as I wrap him in my arms. He looks adorable, per usual, wearing his tiny green polo and khaki shorts. I lightly bounce to make him smile, his googly eyes just inches from mine.

SNAP!

I shudder upon feeling a pinch at the top of my head. "Ow! Charlie, what did you–"

My hair gracefully parts in the middle, falling elegantly past my shoulders. My eyes lock with the woman in my reflection. Charlie drops my hair tie and places his chubby palms over my cheeks, his eyes flicking between mine. I want to cry because even my one-year-old nephew can see the better side of me while I continue ignoring its existence.

"*This is you*," I want to tell the woman in the mirror, but she already knows.

"Harlow, you ready?" Blake calls from his room. "Francis is downstairs waiting for us. Charlie, where are you, buddy?"

He freezes at the bathroom door, picking up on the intensity of the moment. I look at him, then confidently say, "We're ready."

♫ ♫ ♫

Blake and I sing to songs blaring throughout the S.U.V. as Francis drives us through the Hamptons. Charlie flails his arms around, making sounds as if he's singing with us.

"I had no idea this song is by Fai," I blurt out.

Blake shrugs, then says, "I'm telling you, Fai was a big deal back in the day."

I let out a nervous exhale. It's already a wild thought for me to write an album, but to write an album for an award-winning rockstar like Fai? I would have never thought it was possible.

"Do you think Mother and Father know who Fai is?" I ask. "I mean, he's an artist from their generation."

Blake looks out the window at the luxurious estates we pass. "Fai was on the top charts back then, and our parents weren't living under a rock. So, they've probably heard of him." He leans forward and taps my knee with the back of his hand. "I still wouldn't bring up the album. Not yet."

I shake my head, eyes wide open. "No chance I tell Mother and Father."

"They're gonna ask where you've been since the gala," Blake replies.

"I'll tell them I went out of town for a bit to get my mind off of Jordan."

"Mother and Father know that you don't 'go out of town' alone. I'm just saying, you better have a solid alibi, or they're gonna find a way to get in your head."

"I'll be fine. Mother and Father don't need to keep tabs on me."

Blake laughs. "Took you 23 years to realize that."

As we pull up to the front of the estate, Talia is sitting alone at the bottom of the stone staircase. She springs to her feet when I step out of the car. "Your hair!" she shouts in awe. "Harlow, you look wild. But, like, wild in the best way."

"Thanks." I flash a subtle smile which she uses as a cue to hug me.

Blake and Charlie step out of the S.U.V. in their matching outfits, and the four of us make our way up to the house.

"Has Jordan reached out to you since?" Talia whispers when we reach the top of the staircase. "Spud is golfing with him right now."

"He texts me almost every day."

"I still can't believe he could do such a thing." Talia shivers. "What a fucking douchebag."

"Easy, Talia. I don't want my kid's first word to be 'douche-bag,'" Blake says from a few steps behind. "But it's true. I've been saying this for years."

We knock on the massive door and brace ourselves for Mother's typical dramatic greeting. Almost a minute passes before Jameson opens the door with a welcoming smile spread across his face.

"Good afternoon, children," he greets with a nod.

Talia, Blake, and Charlie are the first to enter, making their way down the hall. Just before I step inside, Jameson says, "I love the new hairstyle, Ms. Harlow. How are you doing?"

"Good!" I reply hollowly.

Jameson places a gentle hand on my shoulder. I can feel it shaking from years of putting this entire family on his back. "How are you doing, Ms. Harlow?" he asks again.

I begin forcing back tears behind my hollow smile. Jameson knows something happened between Jordan and me. And even if he doesn't know, he knows something is wrong.

I can feel everything I've dealt with over the past week boiling to the surface. Thoughts of maintaining a version of myself that pleases my parents. Thoughts of seeing a part of me I never knew existed. Thoughts of giving up my old life for one that actually makes me happy.

I see what I had with Jordan, *what I know*.

I see what I could have with Eren, *the unknown*.

And I feel the pressure of it all.

Jameson can always sense when something is wrong, even if I can't sense it myself. I lower my chin. Before a tear can fall to the floor, Jameson flicks out a handkerchief and thumbs my cheeks with it. I thought I could keep it together today, but now I want to run. I want to scream.

"I'm under so much pressure, Jameson," I whisper.

Jameson wraps his arms around me and pats my back. "There, there, Ms. Harlow," he whispers. He pulls back, looking me in the eyes. "Do you know what pressure makes?"

I shake my head.

Jameson lifts a shaky hand, tapping my diamond necklace. "Pressure makes *diamonds*, the most precious stone there is. Can you believe it?" The corners of his eyes wrinkle as he lets out a laugh. "The most precious, most beautiful thing is created from the stress, the heat, the pressure. When you come out of whatever you are going through right now—and I know you will—you will be shining brighter than any diamond you own."

Jameson gently grazes his thumb under my eyes once more. I sniffle, cry, and laugh all at the same time.

"Thank you, Jameson."

"No need to thank me, Ms. Harlow," he replies softly. "You'll make the right decision. And if you don't, then you'll learn until you do make the right decision."

Jameson offers me his arm and escorts me through the halls. When we reach the backyard terrace, I see Mother sitting across from Talia, bouncing Charlie on her knee. In the distance, Father is smoking a cigar with Blake down by the pool.

"I was beginning to think you disappeared!" Mother teases. Her eyes are hidden behind her designer sunglasses and above her posh smirk. "Come sit, Harlow."

I obey like the puppy dog she makes me out to be. "Sorry about that. I was speaking to Jameson," I say while sitting on the couch next to Talia.

"Oh." Mother's face flattens. "You know, I'm starting to think Jameson needs to be reminded that he is an employee and not a member of the family."

I clench my jaw, infuriated that she takes Jameson for granted. She has no idea that Jameson is the only reason Blake and I haven't lost our minds in this house.

"Well, I consider Jameson to be a part of the family." My head grows light. It's the first time I've said something my mother doesn't agree with. I grab one of the champagne glasses from the tabletop and take a sip.

Mother stops bouncing Charlie and tilts her head. In a conde-scending tone, she mutters, "Oh my God… your hair."

"Doesn't it look good, Ms. Beck?" Talia chirps. "It's so long! I had no idea."

Mother ignores Talia, her eyes burning a hole through her own sunglasses. "You look homeless," she hisses at me. "Talia, will you take Charlie inside for a moment so I can catch up with my daughter?"

Talia doesn't waste a second. She picks up Charlie and carries him down the steps to the pool. My mother carefully folds her sunglasses on her lap. Her piercing blue eyes flick up to mine.

"What are we doing wrong, Harlow?" she asks softly. "You just keep disappearing on us. You've been distant. You're changing your look. Is this about Jordan?"

I remain silent for a moment, wondering if now is the time to be honest… if now is the time to tell her that I'm frustrated about Father siding with Jordan. That I'm ready to finally pursue my dream, and I'm tired of being told how to live my life. But I'm forced to consider that I've never stood up for myself and my parents won't change their ways any time soon.

I exhale a shaky breath.

Don't you cry, Harlow. Wolves don't cry. Puppy dogs cry.

"I'm just going through a lot right now, Mother."

It's the truth, just not all of it.

There is a stillness in the air as Mother's gaze softens. She nervously taps her thigh, then, for the first time in my life, she pulls me in for a hug. Her embrace feels foreign to me, and I want someone to take a picture so I can stare at it until it permanently etches itself into my memory.

My mother is hugging me.

Before I can fully take in this moment, Mother pulls herself back. The flustered look on her face makes it evident that she is just as shocked as me. Before either of us says anything, she quickly stands to her feet and makes her way to the kitchen.

I stare at the space she was just sitting in, doing the best I can to absorb every detail of what just happened. A mother hugging her daughter is the bare minimum a mother can do, but my mother's hug serves as so much more.

Mother is on my side.

"Is something wrong with your mother?" Father asks as he steps onto the terrace with Blake.

He's wearing a white polo and navy blue shorts, his slicked white hair and Rolex reflecting the afternoon sun. Blake is slightly taller than him, but his reserved demeanor around Father makes him appear smaller.

"I think she went inside to check on the chefs," I say in an attempt to keep this moment to myself. I would rather it not be tainted by Father.

"You haven't been at work. Not even a notice that you would be gone." Father's eyes narrow. "You *do* realize people report to you, right?"

I bite my lip to keep from saying what I want to say, but it comes out. "You *do* realize that one of those people had sex with my boyfriend, right?"

Blake's eyes widen. "I'm gonna go check on the food," he blurts out before scurrying into the house.

Father's lips curl up. "Your assistant disrespects you, so you flee the state?"

"I didn't 'flee the state,'" I snap back. "I took time off to get my head on straight."

Father glares at me. "*Took time off,*" he mutters. "So, when life fucks with you, you take time off?"

I wince at his words, feeling myself shrink.

How could he be so insensitive?

How could he not feel for me after Jordan cheated on his own daughter?

Father straightens his stance. "One day, you will finally stop letting the world walk all over you. Or you will let it swallow you."

His words land like a 20-pound mic drop before he struts inside the house, leaving me alone to wallow in my broken world.

♫ ♫ ♫

Forks clink against fine china until Mother finally says, "Blake, your father and I have started sending out invites for your birthday weekend."

Blake almost spits his mimosa across the dining room table. "Wait, birthday weekend?! You mean birthday *party*. And who are you inviting to my birthday?!"

"We've invited some colleagues from the firm and the country club as well," Father chimes in. "We plan on opening up the guest rooms for special guests to stay in both Friday and Saturday night. We'll program Saturday with your birthday festivities."

Mother places her hand over her heart. "Blake, we are celebrating you. The more guests, the merrier!"

Blake rolls his eyes. "Nice of you to invite people I don't know to my own birthday. Can we just do a dinner on Friday night?"

"Nonsense!" Father snarls. "Turning 30 is a big deal, so we intend to celebrate it the way we want."

"Who would you like to come?" Mother asks Blake between bites of quiche. "Anyone. Name it, and we'll make room."

Talia and I turn to face Blake.

Eren. Please say Eren.

"Talia and Spud can come." Blake taps the edge of his fork against his bottom lip. "And I want to invite my friend, Eren."

"Who is Eren?" Mother asks.

"A good friend of mine." He pauses a second before adding, "And a good friend of Harlow's."

Everyone turns to me. To keep from raising suspicion, I take a long sip of champagne.

Mother blinks at Blake. "Why haven't we met Eren before?"

"He's not about all of this bougie stuff," Blake says dismissively.

"Interesting." Father's face turns to stone. "Well, I look forward to meeting Eren."

Jameson clears his throat while standing at the doorway. There is a trace of reluctance in his voice as he says, "Pardon me. Mr. Beck, your guests have arrived. They are waiting at the front terrace." His eyes land on mine, and he gives an apologetic nod.

"Ah, perfect timing," Father says, standing to his feet. "Harlow, come with me to greet our guests."

Mother, Blake, and Talia exchange looks of confusion. I set my napkin on the tabletop, just as confused as everyone else. Jameson makes room for my Father to pass through the doorway and averts his eyes from me as I follow closely behind.

Something isn't right.

"I didn't know other people were coming," I say to my father's back as we reach the front door.

Father slowly opens the door, and I step up beside him. A cold sweat comes over me when I see the men standing at the bottom of the stairs.

"Don't let five years go to waste," Father whispers to me, his eyes fixated on one of the two men standing below. I feel Father's chilling stare against my right cheek. "In order for you to grow, you need to make mistakes." He turns to face the men. "Jordan has learned from his mistake, and he will grow from this. I advise you to hear him out."

Jordan looks up at me from the foot of the stairs while Spud stands behind him. My heart habitually softens at the sight of Jordan, and I hate that I didn't give it to Eren when I had the chance. Because now I'm standing between the two men I'm the most familiar with. The same two men I have repeatedly sold myself to in exchange for their love and approval–my father and Jordan.

My legs make their way to the head of the stairs before I even decide to give Jordan a chance to explain himself. My father's words have left me vulnerable to Jordan's presence. My heart is telling me to hear him out, but my mind is telling me to run.

Don't let five years go to waste.

I'm halfway down the stairs when I stop, giving myself one last chance to turn back, but there's no point. This is Father's plan, and if I want to be successful in life, I need to stick to Father's plan.

"I know I don't deserve you right now," Jordan says softly. "But if you give me a chance to explain myself, maybe we won't have to throw it all away."

I cross my arms, feeling the lump in my throat. I've grown with this man and he's grown with me. The Dream Team. Every amazing team has suffered a loss–a setback of some sort–and every amazing team came out victorious.

Jordan's eyes hover over my shoulder as Blake comes trudging out the front door.

"YOU FUCKING PRICK!" Blake screams, running down the steps. "I'm actually glad you have the balls to show up, so I can kick your ass myself!"

Spud quickly intercepts Blake. "Easy there, bud," he says while holding Blake back.

"Don't call me 'bud,'" Blake snarls while squirming in Spud's arms.

Jordan's eyes don't leave mine. "Please," he mouths.

"Blake," I take a step down the staircase. "Blake, stop." I place my hand on his shoulder.

Blake's eyes narrow. "Harlow, you can't! After everything–"

"I got this," I say softly. "I appreciate you defending me, but I'm not a kid anymore. I can make my own decisions."

Blake's eyebrows draw apart. "You can't be serious."

"Spud?!" Talia calls out. "You've got to be fucking kidding me. What're you doing here?!"

Spud lets go of Blake. "It's fine. Mr. Beck told us to come."

"William, is this true?" Mother asks from the front door. "Why would you do this?!"

"Everyone back inside!" Father demands. "No need for a show. Let the two adults talk their shit out."

Designer shoes tap against the stone floor as everyone makes their way inside. While still in my line of sight, Blake flashes me a look of skepticism. "Be careful, Harlow," he whispers before walking away.

I step down the remaining few stairs and walk past Jordan, who struggles to catch up. The gravel crunches under our footsteps as we cross the driveway onto a grass lawn with scattered oak trees.

Jordan's hand gently grazes my arm.

"Let me start," I say sternly. Jordan purses his lips out of frustration, my sternness challenging his ego. "For five years, we were inseparable. Five years of working on ourselves, working on each other, working on 'us.' I don't understand how you could throw that all away for a night with some girl we work with. What were you thinking? Like, honestly, what was going through your damn mind?"

Jordan sighs, adjusting the sleeves of his white collared shirt. "I don't understand either." He jams his hands into his pockets. "I truly don't understand how I could be so insensitive. So selfish. Harlow, I wasn't thinking at all. That's why I did it. We had never spent time apart in the five years we'd been together, and I just panicked. I failed you miserably."

Jordan's words catch me by surprise. I expected to hear some elaborate excuse that would justify what he did, but instead, he's taking responsibility. Cheating is undeniably wrong and fucked up and something I'd never play down. But I didn't expect Jordan to take full ownership of his mistake like he is.

"You know what the most messed up part is?" Jordan runs a hand back through his hair and lets out a nervous exhale. He reaches into his pocket, and the world stops when he pulls out a diamond ring.

I gasp, cupping my palm over my mouth. Chills cover my body from the neck down, and I want to cry, not because I'm happy or frustrated that he would think to propose now of all times. I think I want to cry because I'm just genuinely shocked.

"Jordan, don't."

"Don't worry, I'm not," Jordan sighs. "I was going to,

though. I've had it for months. This is the most messed up part, Harlow. I think my decision to spend the rest of my life with you also led me to make the mistake I made." He lowers his head. "I needed to know for sure that there was nobody but you. My mistake taught me the most valuable lesson I could learn. It taught me that five years ago, I found my person, and I'll never look at anybody else the way I look at you. I'll never *feel* for anybody else the way I feel for you."

I can't speak. My heart is about to burst. I'm staring at the ring in his open palm, but I don't see a ring anymore. I see the good times we've had, the consistent growth, the talks of our future. We're invested in each other. And I'm beginning to think that we have enough good times in the bank to afford one mistake.

Jordan wraps his fingers around the ring. "I'll never let go of this ring," he says softly. His eyes meet mine. "I'll carry it with me until it's on your finger. That's where it belongs. Harlow, I'm not asking you to get back together with me. I'm just asking for the chance. Don't cut me out of your life. I'll prove to you that I'm the one. We're the Dream Team. We can grow from this."

Tears begin to blur my vision. I take a few deep breaths to suppress the adrenaline.

Jordan was going to propose.

After seeing the ring with my own eyes, Jordan's mistake may not need to be the end-all of our entire relationship. I feel my disappointment begin to subside, and guilt gradually makes itself known.

"I slept with somebody." I regret saying the words before I even finish speaking them into existence.

A line shows between Jordan's brows. "You what?"

I don't want to say it again, but the words escape me once more—an attempt to come clean, so everything is out in the open. "I slept with somebody after I found out you cheated on me."

Jordan's fist tightens over the ring, so much so that the veins on his forearm make themselves known. With his teeth grinding together, he whispers, "Who is he?"

I nervously fold my lips between my teeth.

"Harlow," Jordan growls. "Who… is… he…?"

"His name is Eren."

I place my hand over his fist in an attempt to calm him down. "What you did really set us back. I was done with you. This was over."

A few strands of hair hang over Jordan's straight brows as he lowers his chin. He releases a shaky breath, then mutters, "I can accept the consequences of my actions." His eyes meet mine. There is conviction in his words as he says, "But I'm not going anywhere. What we have is too strong."

While I agree with him, I don't intend to give up what I have with Eren.

"I need time to think," I exhale. "To process all of this."

Jordan exhales, then reluctantly says, "Take all the time you need."

I was hoping this conversation would clear things up for me–maybe give me some closure. Instead, I'm more confused than ever, and mad as hell at myself for telling Jordan something he has no business knowing.

But Jordan is right. For five years, I poured my heart into this man. For five years, he poured his heart into me. It doesn't seem fair to burn everything over a minor setback. He loves me. He knows me. He's a part of my family and we've planned our lives together. But then again, I've gotten a taste of what it's like to live without a plan… with Eren.

I'm torn.

Trying to decide between the two…

Jordan and Eren.

The known and *the unknown*.

CHAPTER SEVENTEEN

EREN

I've been waiting for Harlow on the steps in front of Fai's house for 30 minutes now. The sun is starting to cook my shoulders. It's been years since I've been in a place this humid, and I think that's the reason I've been getting pretty bad headaches every couple of hours. I don't mind the heat and headaches, though. All that matters is that I'm the first to greet Harlow when she arrives.

I'm hoping I've written enough with Harlow for her to not be nervous when we write with Fai. She doesn't need to be nervous. I'm honored to write with her and Fai should be honored, too. Her presence alone has inspired me to become a better writer, and I have no doubt that she'll have the same effect on Fai.

I nervously tap my phone against my thigh before reading over her last text.

HARLOW: Just landed:) be there soon

I told her to pack enough clothes for the week, although I haven't asked Fai if she can stay at his house just yet. He mentioned having more than enough room. At this point, I decided that I'm sharing a room with her, whether it's in Fai's guest house or at the nearest hotel. I'll be the last person she sees before she sleeps and the first she sees when she wakes.

A smile spreads across my face when I see a black S.U.V. turn onto the driveway. I stand to my feet and dust off the back of my shorts as the car comes to a halt. Harlow steps out, and I couldn't look away if I tried. I'd be insulting God by neglecting the perfection He created–the perfection standing before me now.

"Hey, rockstar," Harlow says, looking up at me with a couple of bags in one hand and her notebook in the other. "I brought your bag."

"Thank you," I say. "You look incredible."

She's wearing a white linen romper that stops halfway down her thighs. Her skin is glistening as if she rubbed lotion into her arms and legs right before getting out of the car. I feel honored to have kissed those legs, that chest, that neck, those lips. I make that honor known in the way I kiss her now, but there's something different in the way the kiss feels. I know I don't have experience when it comes to relationships, but something feels off. It's as if Harlow is slightly more distant with me now than she was the last I saw her.

Maybe I'm just overthinking it.

"Wait." Harlow's eyes widen. "Did you cut your hair?! You look different again."

I smirk while taking our bags off her hands. "New place, new look."

"I like it," Harlow says. "But I have to ask because this isn't the first time I've heard you say, 'New place, new look.' Why do you change your look every time you move to a new place?"

I raise a brow, pondering an answer. It seems too early in the day to get into a topic this deep. She might not expect a deep answer at all, but I decide to give her one anyway because that answer is also the truth.

"As a teen, I'd hop from one foster family to the next. I began to think maybe my look had something to do with it. Changing my look made it easier for me to mold to whichever family or town I was a part of. I thought maybe that version of me would be the version of me worth keeping."

"Eren…" Harlow places a warm hand on my cheek. "I only see one version of you and trust me. It's worth keeping."

Before I can reply, she wraps her arm around mine, making it known that I don't need to reply at all. She just needs me to believe what she said to be true, and though I find it hard at first, I *do* believe it to be true.

After guiding her up the walkway, I open the towering door, and Harlow takes in every inch of the entry hall. "This place is huge!" she whispers. "Does Fai live alone?"

"Surprisingly, yeah." I set our bags by the door. "Are you ready to meet him?"

"I'm nervous."

"Don't be," I say calmly. "Fai is the nicest guy. You're gonna love him."

We make our way down the hall, and I watch Harlow's gaze fixate on the trophies and plaques lining the walls. She bites her lip, clutching her notebook against her chest. Her uneasiness grows with every step, so I slip my hand into hers to remind her that we're in this together.

I guide her left, down another long hall. The moment we turn into the hall, we can hear music coming from one of the rooms. The music grows louder, and Harlow's grip on my hand tightens just before we turn into the studio.

CHAPTER EIGHTEEN

HARLOW

Eren and I step into a studio nicer than any I have ever seen. The walls are painted a dark red, lined with blue L.E.D. strips. Speakers are built into the walls between the strips, and I watch them vibrate as the sound attaches itself to my heart, mind, and soul.

There's a man sitting in a chair with his back to me—his dark hair hanging over the sides of his head. It's too dark for me to make out the tattoos on his neck. Besides that, he's in a black shirt and black sweatpants. I look around for Eren, who's standing behind me. He flashes a smirk and nods his head to the music.

I turn back to the man, who isn't a part of our world. Instead, he's entirely in his own. The music is loud enough to literally be felt, and the man feels it as if he's one with the music. Nothing matters except for the melody playing from the speakers as he tweaks the random sounds. I'm witnessing him become one with his own craft, and I can't help but want to sit back and admire Fai admiring his own work.

The sight seems oddly familiar. It must be from the hundreds of pictures I scrolled through when I Googled Fai on the way here. The music suddenly cuts out, and in an instant, you can hear a pin drop. Fai turns his swivel chair to face Eren and me. He smiles.

"How did you know we were in the room?" I ask.

Fai points at a mirror that's been attached to the side of his computer screen. "It's like a rearview mirror! Someone snuck up on me once, and I bought it the next day."

"I know the feeling," Eren teases from behind me.

I let out a laugh, remembering how bad I scared him back in Montana.

"I'm Harlow!" I step forward, offering my hand as he takes his tinted glasses off. I notice his many tattoos, like Eren, but he doesn't have anywhere near as many. My eyes are pulled from his tattoos to his deep-brown eyes. Fai's smile introduces a dimple on each cheek as he stands over me.

"Eren has told me a lot about you," Fai says warmly while shaking my hand. "He says he's helping you write my album." He flashes Eren a cheeky smirk.

"Well, Eren has been a big help." I wink at Eren, who shakes his head while making himself comfortable on a leather couch lining the back of the studio.

Fai slips his glasses back on, sits, and pats the swivel chair next to his. "Please sit! Tell me about you, Harlow."

I glance at Eren as if he knows what my response should be.

Do I start with where I was born?

Do I tell him what I studied in college?

How are people in the music industry supposed to answer this question?

Eren calmly looks down at the notebook in my hand and then back up at me.

Tell him about your writing.

I look at Fai, his smile inviting and assuring, stripped of all judgment.

"I write songs," I say softly.

"I sure hope you do!" Fai teases as he leans back in his chair. He crosses one leg over the other and rests his chin on top of his palm. "How long have you been writing songs for?"

"My whole life." I sit in the seat next to him. "But I've never written professionally."

Fai lets out a laugh. "There is no such thing as being a professional when it comes to music," he says softly. "Especially when it comes to *writing* music. Writing music is just communicating what you're feeling in a way that's true to you. Writers don't get 'better' at writing. Instead, writers write in ways that are truer to the feelings they wanna express. It's the industry critics who try to rank songs as if one is better than another." Fai rolls his eyes. "That's all a load of bull. Just be… you."

I absorb every word that comes out of his mouth like it's divine wisdom. For the longest time, I've held out on sharing my songs because I never thought they were good enough. I've known Fai for five minutes, and he's already taught me that it's not a matter of being good at writing songs. It's a matter of being me.

"That was beautiful," I say. "I've never thought of it like that."

"Not a lot of writers do." Fai shrugs. "Which is why a lot of writers aren't happy with their writing."

I glance back at Eren, who has been silently watching me. His head is tilted to the side, and his gaze is one of genuine fascination. I've never met somebody who looks at me the way he does. It's as if he's fascinated by me simply existing.

Fai claps his hands. "Why don't I show you what Eren and I have been working on?" He spins his chair to face the computer. Eren and I exchange a flirty gaze before I turn back to Fai as he presses *Play*.

The mood shifts as the sound of a piano fills the studio. It's an emotional melody with soothing chords. A voice makes itself known over the piano keys. It sounds four-dimensional and filled with passion. Within seconds, I deem the song perfect.

I notice Fai and Eren's eyes are closed as they listen. I smile at the sight, then close mine and become one with the song.

> I'll say the same thing every time,
> So you know I mean it,
> And when we're grown old, you and I,
> I'll love you like I mean it,
>
> Until LORD says that it's time,
> And that we've both lived out our lives,
> At least I know I've done it right,
> Because I'm next to you,
>
> And I wouldn't change anything, oh you,
> I wouldn't change anything, oh you,
>
> Because I'm in love with the way you move,
> So move with me till the ground might give in,
> I'm in love with the way you move,
> So move with me till our final minutes.

When the song ends, I open my eyes to see Fai grinning back at me.

"Damn," I whisper. "You wrote that?"

Fai points to Eren. "He did."

I quickly rotate my chair to face Eren, smiling cheek to cheek. "Who are you writing to when you write, '*I'm in love with the way you move, so move with me till the ground might give in?*'"

The corner of Eren's lips curls up. "Somebody I met in an alley a couple weeks ago."

A part of me melts. It's one thing to listen to a beautiful song, and it's another for that beautiful song to be about you.

"Whelp!" Fai stands. "I don't want to interrupt your process. Harlow, will you be joining us for dinner?"

Eren suddenly stands and says, "Fai, I was actually gonna ask if–"

"Yes." Fai smiles. "Harlow can stay for dinner. She can stay as long as she likes. You're both welcome in my home, which is already way too big for me alone."

The door shuts behind Fai, leaving Eren and me alone in the dimly-lit studio.

"So, what do you think?" Eren asks.

I lean back in my chair and run a finger along my jaw. "There is something about him that seems so… familiar."

"I mean, the guy is a celebrity."

"True." I shrug. "Regardless, Fai is amazing. His take on writing is so inspiring. And his voice… his voice is incredible."

Eren sits in Fai's chair and places a warm hand on my thigh. "I have a good feeling about this."

"About what?"

"About Fai. About the album." His hand tightens around my thigh. "About *you*." There's a gleam in his eye. He taps on my notebook. "So, we put these feelings into words."

I scoot my chair closer to him. I want so much more than his touch, but our arms touching will have to do for now. From his touch alone, I become overwhelmed with passion and emotion. After writing, erasing, and rearranging lyrics together, we write a song inspired by the way we feel in this very moment.

Be the one I can show off and love,
The one I dream of,
Only one I want to wake up next to,

You don't know how many times I've realized,
I wanna make up another way,
To keep you interested,
It's all you I invest in,
All of my hard work and what's left of my heart,

Show you around, no doubt you'll light up the city,
And I'll show you how to be loved,
When you're with me,
I've never been the one to brag,
But you're another story,
I'll be the best you ever had,
If you could make time for me.

When we finish writing, I walk around the studio while Eren reads over the lyrics. The shelves are lined with Fai's awards and photos of him with celebrities.

"What a life," I say in admiration. "Have you asked Fai what it's like to be a singer?" I pick up a photo of Fai performing. "Or about life on world tours and performing in stadiums?"

Eren stops writing. He lifts his chin and ponders my question. "Not really," he says. "I guess I just assumed it's amazing. How could it not be amazing?"

I set the photo back on the shelf and wander across the room to the wall of guitars. "Does he know you sing?"

Eren is quick to shake his head. "No, no, no," he laughs. "I would never tell him I sing."

"Why not?"

"I was hired to write his album, not sing it. If I tell artists I write for that I also sing, they'll think I'm trying to plug myself as an artist rather than someone they hired to write. I don't know. I guess it just doesn't seem very professional."

"There's no such thing as being a professional when it comes to music," I quote Fai with a smirk.

"Wow." Eren lets out a laugh. "You're a good listener."

My phone pings from the table behind Eren, but we ignore it.

"And you're a good singer," I say.

I pull one of the acoustic guitars off the wall and hand it to him. I lay back on the couch, propping myself up with my elbow. "Let's hear it, rockstar."

Eren bites his lip, undressing me with his eyes. I can't help but want to kiss him… to feel the full weight of him force me deeper into this couch… to feel his lips on every part of me like I did back in Montana. I want to feel the warmth of his breath and the heat of his body against mine. But he doesn't give me what I want. Instead, he gives me what I need.

Erens glances back at the lyrics in the notebook and begins picking at the guitar strings. One after another, the strings mold together to form a sound so sweet that I can taste it. The lyrics leaving his lips are so deep, I feel them.

His deep-brown eyes meet mine as he continues singing, and suddenly I care less about the world around me. I care less about what's outside of this room. I care less about myself, so I can care more about him… about this guy I met in an alley… about this guy I haven't known for long at all. But it doesn't matter that I haven't.

His voice is soft, and yet, it breaks me down to the core in the best way. Until my phone rings from next to the computer screen.

Dammit.

Eren stops playing. "Do you need to get that? It rang a few times."

"No, no. Please don't stop playing."

"It's all good! You should at least see who's calling in case it's an emergency."

Eren swivels the chair so that his back is to me. "It's…" He slouches forward. "It's Jordan," he sighs.

DAMMIT.

Eren lets out a defeated sigh. I quickly jump to my feet, pick up my phone, and force it into my pocket. "It doesn't matter."

"Looks like it does." Eren faces me. "Judging from the text he sent you."

I slowly pull my phone out of my pocket, bracing myself for what I'm about to see on the screen. My heart plummets when I see the notifications. A missed call and an unread text from Jordan.

JORDAN: Thank you for giving us another chance.. I won't let you down

"I thought he cheated on you," Eren mutters.

"He did."

"So, you're giving him another chance?" he asks, his eyes fixated on the lyrics we just wrote.

"It's not like before."

He looks up at me, his gaze now skeptical. "What's it like then?"

I take a cautious step toward Eren and place a hand on his shoulder. I want to speak, but I'm so hung up on how the hell I let it come to this. I can't find the right words to say.

"Harlow," Eren groans. "What's it like between you two now?"

I sink into the chair next to Eren. His chest rises and falls as he reads me. He's trying to decide whether or not he made a mistake by opening up to me, and I don't blame him.

It's the disappointed look he gives me that suddenly makes me realize what my father has done. He's using Jordan to get in my head, to sabotage me chasing my dream, to keep controlling me like he always has. And it's working.

Eren stands, mounts the guitar back on the wall, and paces around the studio. "I don't get it, Harlow. You told me back in Montana… you said I was the one–that it shouldn't have taken Jordan cheating on you to make you acknowledge the feelings you have for me!" His voice rises out of frustration. "You got me to open up to you about my past. I'm out here confiding in you. And I have no idea what I'm doing, but I'm trying to figure it out for you because I think you're more than worth it! All while you're working things out with somebody who doesn't deserve you at all."

My vision blurs behind tears as I lower my head, ashamed. Eren has every right to feel the way he does. He's done nothing wrong. He's been there for me since the beginning, and here I am, leading him on, giving half of my heart to him and the other half to Jordan because I'm simply more familiar with him.

Eren crouches down in front of me. "I'm gonna make this very clear for you. The real world isn't just New York, your nine-to-five job, and Jordan. That's just *your* world. You can't choose the world you came from, but I promise you, Harlow. There is so much more out there. You've seen just a small piece of it in Montana. I watched the way you took it all in. I see the way the unknown makes you feel."

He places his hand on mine, his eyes narrow as he continues. "I don't want you to miss out on the world just because you're not familiar with it. I want to show you the world myself, if you'll let me." He tightens his grip as if begging for me to understand the words leaving his lips.

I hold Eren's gaze, and in that gaze, I see the world I want to live in.

I see Eren.

The two of us riding west.

Writing music.

I see an undiscovered world ready for me to discover.

And here is Eren, offering it all, more than willing to make me a better version of myself.

"I'm not gonna force you to be with me." Eren stands, his hand still holding mine. "I'm gonna show you what you've shown me. And you'll see that I'm the one."

I wipe the remaining tears from my eyes as I ask, "You're gonna show me what I've shown you?"

"Yes," Eren replies. "Harlow, you've shown me a part of me I never knew existed. I didn't know there was a side of me with a heart until you revealed it to me. So, I'm gonna reveal the part of you that you never knew existed."

CHAPTER NINETEEN

EREN

I stare at the man in the bathroom mirror. It's the same man I always see when I look in the mirror, but there's something different about him this time.

He's a fool.

I flush the toilet, even though I didn't use it. I stepped out of the studio for a bit to clear my head after reading that text Harlow got from Jordan.

Am I a fool for opening up to her?

For breaking my golden rule?

For getting attached?

It blows my mind how a girl like Harlow could settle for a guy like Jordan. This guy just wants to keep her locked inside of a box while I know she needs to be set free. She needs to follow her heart, and I'm witnessing Jordan and Harlow's father keeping her from doing that. As my feelings for Harlow develop, so does my hatred of Jordan. I feel the hatred creeping into my heart ever so quietly, just waiting to be tapped into.

Jordan knows exactly what he's doing, toying with her heartstrings the same way her father does. I refuse to let them manipulate her. I pray that I don't run into them anytime soon… for their own sake.

I turn on the faucet, rinse my hands, and give my cheeks a few light slaps. I've done the best I can to make my feelings for Harlow known. Maybe what I've done for her just isn't enough yet.

I remember Fai teasing me about not knowing how to cook, then suggesting that might be why I don't have a girlfriend. I know he was only teasing, but there has to be some truth to what he said. I want to find out if he's right.

I Google "beginner recipes" and find a simple one for making rosemary chicken.

"Fai?" I call down the hall, but no response. "Fai!" I call out louder this time. I call for him in the kitchen. I call for him in the living room. I call for him in the backyard, the front yard, every yard, then in each of his guest rooms. No sight of Fai.

I walk up one of the two grand staircases toward Fai's bedroom. After a few steps, my mind goes completely blank.

What did I come up here for again?

I look aimlessly around the hall until I'm suddenly reminded by the pictures lining the walls.

Fai! That's right. I'm looking for Fai.

Harlow and I have been in the studio for hours. I have no idea where Fai could've gone since he left us alone. His bedroom door is closed, so I knock before quietly pushing it open. "Fai?"

Guitars are scattered around the room between posters and framed pictures that haven't been put up. Or maybe they've been taken down. It looks like he's packing them up for some kind of trip. His bed is massive, but my eyes are drawn past it to a machine in the corner of the room. Next to the machine is a recliner chair and table topped with bottles of prescription pills–tons of them.

VROOM! VROOM!

I panic when I hear a roaring sound coming from the garage

below. The sound grows louder, shaking the floor beneath me until it suddenly stops. I shut the bedroom door and run downstairs. I walk outside and spot Fai on the driveway.

"Don't come over here!" Fai shouts, shooing me away. He frantically presses a button on his phone, and the garage door closes behind him. "Don't look!" He jogs across the driveway and places a hand on my back.

"Sorry," he says, guiding me back through the front door. "I have something in there I don't want anyone to see just yet."

"All good," I reply. "Quick question. Would it be okay if I make dinner tonight?"

Fai raises a curious brow. "You wanna cook? What happened to you 'being terrible at it?'"

I nervously twiddle my thumbs. "I just thought, maybe I could give it a go."

"I'm messing with you," Fai shakes his head, then places a comforting hand on my shoulder. "No need to explain. Just tell me what you need."

"Well, I was wondering if you could help me out with it," I admit.

Fai slowly nods, grinning cheek to cheek. His gaze locks onto mine through his tinted glasses. It starts to make me feel uncomfortable, his silent stare without saying anything.

I slowly lift my phone between us. "So, I–um–I have a recipe I want to–"

"Right!" Fai snaps out of his trance and claps his hands together. "Right. Why don't you text me the recipe, and I'll go grab the ingredients."

"If I can borrow one of your cars, I can just go myself. I feel bad making you go."

"It's no problem at all. There's a store right up the street. I'll be back in 20."

"Awesome! Thanks, Fai."

"No problem." Fai's eyes soften. We stand silently for a beat, awkwardly smiling at each other. "Okay, so recipe."

"Recipe," I repeat. "Thanks again."

The bottoms of Fai's boots squeak against the tile as he stutter-steps out the front door.

♫ ♫ ♫

"I still can't believe this is happening," Harlow says from the other side of the kitchen counter. "Fai, you should have seen Eren make pasta back in Montana." She giggles. "Is that the right word for what you were doing, Eren? Cooking?"

I laugh while chopping slices of zucchini. "Hey, it's not my fault. It's the pasta's fault for catching on fire."

I make light of the fact that I'm cooking right now, when in reality, I'm breaking a sweat. I've watched enough of Fai cooking over the past couple of days to be confident that I won't set anything on fire. But the night is young and anything can happen.

"Ah, yes. It's the pasta's fault." Harlow turns to Fai. "So, Fai, tell me. What made you want to ask Eren to write your album?"

Fai smiles. "Honestly, his name caught my attention. I was skimming through writer profiles on record label websites. Eren was my father's name, so I felt the urge to check him out. And I'm glad I did because I love his work."

I try to hide the fact that what he said makes me blush. "I really appreciate that, Fai. I'm happy to be here."

"Aww." Harlow places her elbows on the table. "Fai, you seem like you would be quite the catch…"

"I know where this is going," Fai mutters before sipping his sparkling water.

Harlow throws her hands up. "I mean, how could you not

be married?! Handsome, talented, a kind soul. I mean, you're letting Eren, a complete stranger, live in your home! You have a big heart, but nobody to share it with? Nonsense."

Fai lifts his chin, twirling the ice in his glass. "The woman I love is… *out of town*," he says.

I stop chopping.

This is the first I've heard of a woman being in his life.

"Is she traveling?" Harlow's eyes twinkle with interest. "When will she be back?"

I set my knife down on the counter to give Fai my undivided attention.

He looks down at his glass. With a smirk, he says, "She's not coming back any time soon. So, I'll be the one traveling to her in a couple months."

Before Harlow can ask another question, Fai points at the stove behind me. "I would check on that chicken if I were you, kid."

Shit!

I quickly turn. Thankfully, nothing is on fire… yet. The chicken is perfectly cooked, ready to be pulled off the stove. "Good call," I say, placing the pieces of chicken on plates. "Time to eat."

When we walk outside, Fai claps at the sight of the table I set while he was gone. I set it the exact way I've seen him set the table. I didn't think he would appreciate it as much as he does right now.

"Great stuff, kid!" Fai shouts as he takes a seat.

I sit across from Harlow while Fai sits at the table's edge between us. The sun has set, and streaks of blue and orange decorate the sky just over the horizon. Before Harlow takes a bite of her chicken, I place a gentle hand on hers. She pauses at the sight of Fai bowing his head. We bow our heads, and when he finishes praying, we start eating.

Time stops and flies at the same time. Fai tells stories about life in the limelight. Harlow tells stories about life in the Hamptons.

I tell stories about life on the road. Our stories overlap one another, making it seem as though our different lives become one and the same.

"You're lying!" Fai shouts when Harlow tells him she's never been in the ocean at night.

"It's too cold!" Harlow whines.

"Then this must be your first time in South Florida because *nothing* is cold down here. Especially the water."

Harlow averts her eyes away from the table.

I lean over my empty plate. "Wait. This is your first time in Florida, isn't it?"

She looks up and shrugs. The hanging lights bring out Harlow's striking features, which I'll never get tired of. Her piercing blue eyes. The streaks of gold that weave through her auburn hair. The freckles around her nose. Her pearly white teeth that show between her full lips as she laughs.

"It's my first time in Florida," she murmurs.

"It was your first time in Montana and now it's your first time in Florida," I say. "You don't travel much, huh?"

Harlow's smile flattens. "I was always busy with school, then I became busy with work, so I never made time for traveling."

Fai crosses his arms. "Do you ever feel like you're missing out on seeing the world because of how busy you are?"

"I did until I met Eren." Harlow subtly smirks in my direction. "He's shown me a lot over the past few weeks."

"Ah, I see." Fai nods. "How did you two meet anyway?"

I stab at my chicken, waiting for Harlow to answer first. I look up to see her doing the same.

"It was in an alley outside of a restaurant in Manhattan." I stop myself, thinking of a way to tell this story without admitting that I was trying to perform on stage that night. My eyes land on Harlow's. She nods for me to speak the truth, so I continue truthfully. "I was performing at the restaurant. Well, I was… I mean–I was *trying* to perform.”

Fai blinks at me.

My voice trembles when I say, “I’m trying to sing more, but I have really bad stage fright. So, I ran off stage, and I was just drinking in the alley until Harlow came out and started talking to me.”

“In Eren’s defense…” Harlow chimes in. “My friends were being immature, heckling him a bit. So it made sense for Eren to not want to perform.”

Fai adjusts himself in his seat. He lowers his chin, eyeing me from over his glasses. “You have stage fright?”

I slouch a bit, avoiding eye contact. “A little bit.”

“He shouldn’t,” Harlow blurts out. “You should’ve seen him sing back in Montana. It was incredible. He brought the entire bar to life!”

“It was just karaoke.” I shrug. “It wasn’t even one of my own songs, so I don’t think it counts.”

Fai leans forward so quickly, his chair screeches against the floor. “Hey, if you’re singing, you’re singing! It doesn’t matter what you sing! I used to have stage fright, you know.”

Harlow and I glance at each other. “Really?” we say in unison.

“Oh, absolutely!” Fai rolls his eyes. “Until my pops gave me the best advice I ever got.” We lean forward, eager to hear. His tone softens as he says, “The best way to get over your fear of performing is to forget you’re even performing at all.”

I squint at Fai. “What do you mean?”

“The songs you sing. Don’t sing them for the crowd’s approval. Sing them because you believe in the lyrics you’re singing. It shouldn’t matter whether you sing alone, in front of 10 people, or in front of thousands. You sing because you believe in the words you wrote.”

I feel Harlow's foot rub against my leg under the table. Fai's words make such an impact on me, I feel like I could perform in front of a stadium crowd in this very moment. I've never had a father figure in my life, and Fai is slowly becoming the closest thing to it, based on his advice. It makes me both grateful for Fai and angry at my real father for being absent my whole life.

"You're right," I say. "You're so right."

Fai slowly raises a finger and wags it in my direction. "I want to hear you sing soon, kid. Unfortunately, it's getting close to my bedtime, so I'll let you two have a lil' date night to yourselves. Harlow, I'm glad you're here." While gathering our empty plates, he says, "There are towels in the shed near the dock."

I let out a laugh.

Harlow's jaw drops. "*Towels in the*–are you kidding? I'm not going in that water!"

Fai shrugs. "You don't have to. You two can do whatever you want! I'm just saying, should you decide to go in, the towels are in the shed by the dock." He lowers his chin and winks. "Goodnight, kids."

Fai strolls into the house. When I face Harlow, she's blushing. "He's amazing," she whispers.

"Almost too amazing," I whisper back, then sigh. "I wonder what the catch is."

"*The catch*?"

"Yeah." I place my elbow on the table. "I've been in the industry long enough to know there's always a catch–something somebody secretly wants. Or some hidden problem. Fai is paying me way too much money to write his album. And he's letting me stay in his house. It's all just too good to be true."

Harlow grabs my hand under the table. "Eren, there isn't always a catch. It's okay to be happy. I know you've had some bad times, but the same way there are bad times, there are good. At least love yourself enough to let the good in."

I nod my head and tighten my hand around hers.

Harlow lifts her chin. "Is the water really that warm down here?"

"Only one way to find out," I say with a smirk.

I look out at the bay. I can still see the ocean surface, despite it being dark out. I notice it moving in one direction. Every drop. All in unison, creating the current.

"I'll dip my feet in," Harlow mutters.

"I thought you were gonna surprise me for a sec," I admit, standing to my feet.

"Surprise you?"

"I thought you were gonna jump in. And I would've been surprised if you did."

Harlow crosses her arms and squints up at me. "I see what you're doing. And it's not gonna work."

I shrug, then open my stance for her to lead the way. We walk onto the dock. The city skyline is miles across the water, giving us the freedom to swim as far out as we want.

My heart flutters when I catch sight of the rope hanging from a nearby tree. The tree is long and narrow, curving out over the water. "Um, Harlow…"

"You've got to be kidding me."

I turn back to her, cupping her cheeks in my palms. "You remember when we found that rope swing back in Montana? When I told you I'd get you to take the leap?"

Harlow's breath becomes unsteady as her eyes flick between me and the rope. "Eren…"

"No," I snap. "I won't let you talk yourself out of this." I grab her hand and pull her toward the rope. "You can do this. Stop thinking!"

When we get to the tree, I reach over the edge and pull the

rope in.

"But, the current!" Harlow whines. "Eren, I'm sure you know this by now, but I'm small. I'll get swept out to sea."

"I won't let it take you. Don't be afraid of the current, Harlow. Don't be afraid of throwing yourself into the unknown." I offer her the rope, but she turns away. "Harlow, listen to me. *Listen.* That current out there is life passing you by while you just watch it from the shore. You have to jump. You have to take the leap!"

Harlow's eyebrows draw apart.

"You took a risk by being here with me because you trust me. Now it's time for you to trust something bigger than yourself. Trust that whatever happens will happen. Trust the *current.*"

Harlow clenches her fists. "Eren, stop."

But I don't stop. Instead, I raise my voice. "You're full of all this potential, and you let Jordan and your parents convince you otherwise! You let them keep you trapped in this tiny box, and I know you want out! I know you want to jump. You want to be free, but you're stuck because you choose to be. You can't even jump into the wa–"

In one swift motion, Harlow pulls off her clothes and yanks the rope from me. She sprints to the edge of the dock. And she leaps. She leaps higher and farther than I thought she could–an angel taking flight under the moonlight. Her hands let go of the rope, and she gracefully lands in the water.

I can't think for a second longer. I take off my clothes and throw myself headfirst into the water next to her. I feel the warmth consume me. The sounds of the bubbles underwater become sounds of Harlow's heavy breathing when I breach the surface.

I'm face to face with her, and… *wow.* There's not another place in her world, my world, or our world that I would rather be. There's not another moment in this life I would rather live in. There's not another memory in my mind I'd rather remember. This is it. Letting life pull me wherever it pleases with Harlow by my side. This is true freedom.

Harlow and I are staying afloat only a few feet from each other. A light trail of mascara drips down her cheeks as her chest rises and falls. Her hair is darker when wet, bringing out the blue in her eyes as it reflects the moonlight. Her lips are parted, and I desperately want for them to meet mine like every time before. I notice tears glide down the trails of mascara.

"What's wrong?" I ask, swimming closer.

She wipes her eyes. "I'm not crying because something is wrong," she exhales. "I'm crying because I'm happy."

The water is warm, yet chills cover my body. I pull her closer to the shore where we can stand—close enough so I can feel her breath against my own. I take her in with my eyes until I can no longer keep myself from her touch. I wrap her legs around my waist, the two of us becoming one with the current.

I don't know if this is love.

I've never known love.

Whatever this is, I don't care to live without it.

CHAPTER TWENTY

HARLOW

Days are flying by faster now that I'm finally doing what I love. I never would have thought that chasing passions over a paycheck would have this sort of impact on me. I'm immersing myself in the songs I write with Eren, and life becomes more exciting by the second.

The beauty of it all is that each day feels new. There's no plan to stick to. There are no expectations besides writing about whatever makes its way into my heart, which is Eren more and more each day.

I fall asleep and wake up in his arms, which has become more of a home than mine ever was. Eren has shown me that home isn't a place. Home is wherever your heart is, and my heart is with him.

I haven't thought about work once. I didn't tell Father how long I would be gone because I don't know how long I'll be gone. We've written well over eight songs, in addition to old songs we found deep in our notebooks. The past couple of days have been all about tweaking bits and pieces to perfection before the final part of the process... recording Fai's vocals.

With Eren and I working extensively on the lyrics, Fai has taken on more of a paternal role. He spends his time teaching us how to write better by day and then cooks for us by night. He even agreed to let me cook breakfasts, which Eren loves because it reminds him of Montana.

"I think I want a tattoo," I say as Eren kisses my neck.

He props himself up on his pillow. "A tattoo, huh?" He smirks. "You know you already took the leap, right?"

I raise a brow. "Yes, I know. What are you trying to say?!"

"Nothing! I just mean tattoos are permanent. You should put some thought into what you want to get tattooed on you before you get one. That's all I'm saying."

"Hmm." I rest the back of my head on my pillow. "What was your first tattoo?"

"My mom's angel wings on the back of my neck," Eren says while placing my hand on the back of his neck. "I was 18 when I got it, but I knew the moment she died that it would be my first tattoo."

My thumb traces the outline of the wings. "So, the moment inspired the art."

"That's usually how it goes, right?" Eren brings my hand to his lips. "So, my advice to you would be to think of a moment that inspired you and then find a place on your body for that moment to live forever."

I put some serious thought into Eren's advice, running through moments in my mind.

There was the night we met in the alley.

Running into each other at RAW.

The night I rode on his motorcycle for the first time.

And so many more.

"I have too many moments to choose from," I sigh. "Help me choose."

Eren bites his lip, studying my naked face, neck, and body.

He drags his eyes up and down, deep in thought. I've never been more willing to let a man look at me the way I've let Eren. He gently tucks my hair behind my ear, and I see the answer appear in his eyes.

"Music notes," he says. "Behind your left ear."

I tilt my head, envisioning the symbols outlining the skin behind my ear. "That's so specific. Why behind the left ear?"

Eren smirks. "It's inspired by the first moment you let your hair down back in Montana. It was the moment you discovered the side of you I'm falling for. If you get the tattoo behind your ear, then whenever you tie your hair up again, the tattoo will be there to remind people of that newly discovered side of you. The side you set free."

Warmth fills my body, starting with my cheeks. "I love it," I whisper.

"And I say the left ear because…" Eren taps behind his left ear. "It's one of the only spots I haven't covered in ink yet."

"Wait," I cover my mouth in shock. "We're getting matching tattoos?!"

Eren laughs. "If you're okay with that."

"I love that idea," I say.

I pull his lips to mine, feeling the excitement behind every kiss. At this rate, if I get a tattoo for every inspirational moment I share with Eren, I'll be covered from head to toe in no time.

♫ ♫ ♫

"So, let me get this straight," Fai whispers. "Your brother is Blake, Eren's manager?"

"That's right," I reply as the two of us board his boat.

Fai pinches his eyebrows together. "And you and Eren are…" He slowly twiddles his fingers. "You and Eren are a thing?"

"That's also right."

Fai loads a bin with towels. "That has to get weird at some point, no?"

"It's not as weird as you might think," I say, holding back a laugh.

Fai raises his hands. "Hey, I'm not judging. You two obviously bring out the best in each other, so run with it."

I turn toward Fai's house to see Eren, Blake, and Charlie approaching Fai's dock. After making some serious progress on the album the past few days, Fai offered to take us out on his boat for the afternoon. I don't know much about boats, but I can spot a nice one when I see it. And Fai has a nice one.

White booths line the back and front sections of the boat. The sections are divided by the cockpit, a shaded structure covering an array of buttons, levers, and switches Fai begins adjusting.

"Thanks for having us, Fai!" Blake says while carrying Charlie onto the back of the boat. "I can't remember the last time I've been on a boat." Seconds after finishing his sentence, he almost trips over a step.

Fai chuckles at Blake's inexperience. "My pleasure! And who is this little guy?"

"This is Charlie," Blake says.

"Doobo," Charlie says from Blake's arms. He reaches his chubby little arms toward Fai's face.

Fai takes off his tinted glasses and puts them on Charlie. "Lookin' good, Charlie," Fai says. "Now, let's hit the water!"

The boat glides through the bay, skidding across the clear blue water. The warm breeze sweeps through my hair as I stand at the front of the boat, adrenaline coursing through my veins as we catch air between rises and dips.

Charlie laughs hysterically from Fai's lap as Fai steers the boat. The boat turns right, circling a yacht full of women waving in our direction.

"I think I need to move to Miami!" Blake shouts over the roaring wind.

"Miami women are a different breed, my friend!" Fai teases from the cockpit. "Tread carefully!"

Blake smirks while adjusting his sunglasses. Since Blake lost Miranda, I was beginning to think that he was blind to other women. It's nice to see him coming out of his shell.

I cuddle up next to Eren on the booth across from Blake.

"You think you're ready to get back into the dating scene?" Eren asks.

Blake shrugs. "Maybe. It's been years." He looks back at Charlie and Fai. "Things are a bit different now. I'm not just dating for me. The woman I end up with would also be Charlie's stepmother."

"You'll figure it out," Eren says. "Maybe you'll bump into her in an alley." His hand tightens around my shoulder. "If you're as lucky as me."

Blake's eyes bounce between Eren and me. "I can't get over you two. I've known Harlow my whole life and Eren for 10 years. Not once did I see you two together until that morning in Montana."

"Which morning?" I ask.

"The morning you came in with your hair down," Blake replies. "And Eren spit coffee all over my son."

Blake and I let out a laugh. Eren covers his face, then mutters, "It was a natural response. I don't know what else to say."

"It was a response that made me realize you have feelings for Harlow. I think the best part is, you two are bringing out the better sides of each other. You're like day and night. Order and chaos. You're opposites that perfectly cancel each other out. And…" Blake's eyes lock onto Eren's. "If one day I'm able to love somebody again, I hope to look at that somebody the same way you look at my sister."

It becomes a surreal moment, seeing Eren and Blake connect. The boat slows down as if picking up on the intensity of the moment.

"Blake, I want to apologize." Eren lets go of me and leans forward. "All this time, I kept you at arm's length, even when Miranda passed. It wasn't because I didn't care about you. It's because I was *scared* to care about you. Losing my mom as a kid shattered me. I made a promise to myself to never get attached to anybody ever again. I made it a rule, one I followed to protect myself from getting hurt again. It kept me from being there for you when *you* were hurt, and I'm sorry for that."

Blake extends his hand, and Eren clasps it with his palm.

"You were protecting yourself. I get it," Blake exhales. "I know we work together, but you really are the brother I never had."

Eren's lip quivers. Blake grins as he spreads his arms. "Gimme a hug, man."

Eren leaps forward, embracing Blake. To think that the man I'm falling for is also becoming a best friend to my brother, I simply can't believe it. It's too good to be true. It's fiction. It's anything but real.

Eren sprawls himself beside Blake, his arm remaining wrapped around Blake's shoulder. I pull out my phone, taking a picture to commemorate the moment. Eren is becoming a part of our family. My eyes pan from Eren and Blake to Charlie and Fai driving the boat. *Or maybe I'm becoming a part of Eren's family.*

"So, when do I get to meet the future in-laws?" Eren teases.

He gives Blake a playful nudge, then straightens his leg, his foot now pressed against my thigh. The sunlight glistens off his tattooed body, illuminating the art he literally embodies. I wish the world would stop spinning, so I can live in this moment forever.

"Careful what you ask for." I raise a brow. "Blake's birthday is this weekend."

"That's right!" Eren shouts. "Are you excited?"

"I'm nervous," Blake mutters.

"It'll be fun, man. Don't worry."

Blake flashes a hollow grin in response to Eren's optimism. There is nothing I look forward to more than spending time with Eren. But the thought of spending time with Eren around my parents makes me nervous, too. I'm the worst version of myself when I'm around my parents and the best when I'm around Eren. *What will happen when I'm around both?*

Eren's face goes blank for a moment before he asks, "So, when do I get to meet the future in-laws?"

Blake laughs. "You just asked that." He tilts his head. "Are you alright?"

"Yeah!" Eren replies dismissively while pressing his palm to the side of his head. "I think the Florida heat is really starting to get to me."

"I can literally feel the sun on my skin," I say, suddenly aware of the sweat between my back and the booth.

Blake turns to Fai and Charlie. Fai is teaching Charlie what each button does, and Charlie nods like he understands what Fai is saying. The boat suddenly jolts forward, and the three of us grip whatever we can to keep from flying backwards.

"Whoops!" Fai chuckles. "You can thank Captain Charlie for that one!"

We give Charlie a thumbs-up.

"What do you guys think of me inviting Fai to my birthday?" Blake asks without looking away from Charlie. "He's been super nice, and Charlie loves him."

"Would Mother and Father be okay with that?" I ask.

Blake rolls his eyes. "I was okay with them inviting all of *their* friends. Plus, it's my birthday. I'm gonna invite him."

"I'm with it." Eren shrugs. "Sounds like a good time."

I cringe at the thought of Blake's birthday weekend being a couple of days away when I'll be introducing Eren and Fai to my parents. Managing the collision of two worlds, Eren's and my own.

"It'll be a *great* time," I lie.

It's going to be a disaster.

CHAPTER TWENTY-ONE

EREN

"Just a little farther!" I shout, helping Fai dock the boat.

When I step onto the boat to help unload everything, I notice Harlow and Charlie lying peacefully asleep on the booth. The setting sun casts an orange hue across their faces as their chests rise and fall to the rhythm of sleep.

"Should I wake her up?" Blake whispers.

I shake my head. "I'll carry her to the room."

Blake, Fai, and I finish unloading the towels and remaining snacks. I carefully lift Harlow, making it my mission to carry her to the guest house without waking her. Her body is warm against my arms, her auburn hair falling gracefully toward the ground. She places her palm on my chest, expressing her gratitude without fully waking. She is the most exhausted I've ever seen her, and still, her presence gives me energy.

I gently place Harlow on the bed and kiss her forehead.

"Hi, rockstar," she whispers without opening her eyes.

She knows my lips.

"Sweet dreams, love," I whisper back.

Harlow smiles and makes a light moaning sound. After tucking her in, I make my way to Fai's kitchen. I've got more energy than I thought I would, and I'm assuming it's from the amazing day I just had.

Being in good company after spending all these years alone feels surreal. The more I open up to Harlow, Blake, and Fai, the more ridiculous my once-golden rule seems.

"Blake and Charlie are taking naps," Fai says as he enters the kitchen.

I sigh. "So the day is over?"

Fai puts his hands on his hips. "It doesn't have to be." He smirks. "I'm gonna make a few quick phone calls. Grab your boots and meet me outside of the garage in five!"

I put on an oversized button-up, a pair of distressed jeans, and my combat boots. When I walk out of Fai's front door, I see him wearing almost the exact same outfit.

"Good taste, kid!" he teases. "So, hear me out…" Fai raises his palms, putting careful consideration into his pitch, although there's no need for him to. We become more alike the more time we spend with each other, so I have no doubt that I'll be interested in whatever he wants to do.

Fai clears his throat before saying, "I'm gonna take you somewhere very special to me, but first, I've got a surprise for you."

He gestures for me to follow him to the garage. After pressing a button on his phone, one of the doors opens. As Fai opens up his stance, my eyes are pulled to the brand-new motorcycle standing under the fluorescent lights. The bike's bodywork is painted matte black, the coating so fresh that it reflects the garage lights. The aluminum frame shines like it was made with white gold, in perfect contrast with the black tires.

"It's yours," Fai says. "You mentioned you were gonna get a new motorcycle, and Harlow described your last one to me. I bought the motorcycle closest to her description. Hope this is okay."

I take a few steps past Fai, but I can't touch the bike. I don't believe it's mine. It can't be mine.

Fai itches his goatee, then shrugs. "It's a gift, I guess. For writing the album."

"You're already overpaying me to write the album."

He steps up beside me. I have a lump in my throat, feeling both grateful and confused.

"I'm paying you the right amount," Fai says. "You deserve it, kid."

I don't deserve this.

It becomes difficult for me to look at the motorcycle. I haven't put much thought into riding since I crashed my last bike in Montana.

"Fai, I can't," I whisper.

"You can." He places a hand on my shoulder. "It's yours, Eren. Forget about the album. This is my gift to you for keeping me company. You and Harlow are doing a lot for me, more than you know."

I reach forward and place my hand on the bike—*my* bike. My fingers glide over the matte-black body, then across the leather seat. I notice a second seat has been added to the back of the bike.

Fai notices my eyes are fixated on the second seat. "It's for her," he says softly.

Without saying a word, I turn and wrap my arms around him. I'm overwhelmed by the light that Fai has brought into my life.

He's giving me a place to stay.

He's keeping me company.

He's supporting me.

I don't know what it's like to have a father or a family.

But it doesn't matter. This will do. This is more than enough.

Fai pats me on the back. "Okay, so that's the gift. Now, it's time to take you to a special place—one I think you're really gonna like."

"Which car are we taking?" I ask.

"*Which car*?" Fai laughs. "I'm taking my motorcycle, and you're taking yours."

♫ ♫ ♫

If you would've told me I'd be riding a motorcycle side by side with one of my favorite artists, I would've called you crazy. Because even as the moment unravels before me, it still seems too good to be true. When I first got the offer to write Fai's album, I thought there was a catch. But maybe Harlow is right. Maybe there isn't always a catch. The same way there are bad times, there are good. And these are good times.

The neon lights shining over the road we ride over. Swerving through South Beach traffic like we own the night. The warm breeze splitting my button-up down the middle.

This

can't

be

real.

I pan from the moonlit ocean on my right to the wall of nightclubs to my left. People are dressed to impress in vibrant colors, waiting to get into the clubs. My eyes land on a neon-pink and blue nightclub sign that reads, "PRIME." The name is reflected off of Fai's helmet visor as he rides next to me. He nods his head for me to make a left. I do so, following him down a series of back roads. As we weave through the roads, the colorful lights turn to towering warehouses. I follow Fai into a wide alley, separating rows of warehouses.

The warehouses are different shades of gray, each with a rolling door large enough to fit a semi-truck. I flip my visor up so

I can read the numbers spray-painted next to each door. Up ahead, three sports cars are parked carelessly in front of a closed rolling door. Fai parks his bike next to them and pulls off his helmet.

"What is this place?" I take off my helmet.

Fai smirks. "Just wait."

He bangs on the metal rolling door, and after a few seconds, it rolls open. A broad man in his mid-fifties appears from the shadows.

"It's about fuckin' time!" the man shouts. The two hug until he catches sight of me. His broad frame is covered in dark-blue denim, and his boots click against the cement as he approaches me wide-eyed. "I'll be damned. Y-you're… you're him?" he whispers.

My eyes flick to Fai, who attentively watches me shake the man's hand.

"I'm Eren."

"I know who you are," the man exhales. "You're–"

"Writing my album," Fai interjects.

The man shakes his head. "Right!" he clears his throat, his calloused hand still wrapped around mine. "You gonna make this old geezer a star again or what?!"

"Doing the best I can," I reply with a smirk.

"Well, I hope your best is enough!"

"Where are the rest of you?" Fai asks, turning into the warehouse.

"They're setting up," the man says.

He joins Fai, and the two of them begin walking into the darkness.

"Wait!" I catch up to them. "I didn't get your name."

"Danny Walker!" the man shouts from the darkness.

I pause. Chills run down my arms at the sound of his name. *Danny Walker*. One of the greatest Rock & Roll drummers to play in the 90's. Even the artists running the top charts today use his drum samples.

"W-wait, like… you're *the* Danny Walker?!"

I itch the side of my head while catching up to Fai and Danny. The warehouse is so dark, I can't see how deep it goes. In the distance, two flashlights hover over music equipment. Danny's boots echo throughout the warehouse, the sound lingering as it becomes one with the void.

As we approach the two floating flashlights, it becomes apparent that they belong to two more men. One of the flashlights points in my direction.

"So, this is him?!" a voice asks.

"You did alright, Fai," another voice says. "Are we gonna go in raw?"

Go in raw?! What the hell did he mean by that?

My palms begin to sweat. I'm in a pitch-black warehouse with a group of strangers who somehow already know me and plan to "*go in raw*." I've seen enough crime documentaries to assume that the next one may be about me. I turn toward the rolling door. Before I can make a run for it, it rolls shut.

Everything goes dark.

"Yeah, we're going in raw," I hear Fai's voice say. "Keep it dark, too. I want Eren to feel it without seeing a thing."

I brace myself, preparing to be groped, stabbed, or both.

BOOM!

An overwhelming thud suddenly fills the warehouse as a narrow spotlight shines from the ceiling just 10 feet away. Shining under the spotlight is a standing microphone and acoustic guitar. The spotlight has an orange hue, providing warmth in the midst of the chilling darkness. A hand makes itself known on my shoulder.

Fai's voice is smooth as he says, "Do you remember when I told you, '*The best way to get over your fear of performing is to forget you're even performing at all?*'"

"Yeah," I whisper, eyes fixated on the guitar and microphone.

"Eren, it's just going to be you singing in this big empty warehouse. Don't worry about what's outside of that spotlight
because it doesn't matter. Focus on the rawness of your voice and
the sound of each note you play on that guitar." Fai gives me a light
push. "Go on."

With every step I take in the direction of the microphone, my
head grows lighter. I can hear my heartbeat in my head. My legs are
growing weaker by the second.

I step under the spotlight, which is becoming too much to
bear. I try to catch my breath, but it escapes me.

I slowly spin in a full circle, seeing nothing but darkness. I
look up, immediately blinded by the orange light. I pull the guitar
strap over my head, my hands now caressing the neck and body of
the guitar.

My own breath sends me into a panic as I hear it from every
angle, and I realize the microphone is hooked up to surround-sound
speakers. I pluck at a guitar string, and I'm enveloped in the sound
as it bounces off the warehouse walls. I hum a note into the microphone, my hum now joining the sound of the guitar.

I look out. I see nothing. Yet, I feel everything.

I don't hear my guitar. I feel it.

With my eyes closed, I think through the songs I've written
with Harlow. I'm brought back to the night we met in the alley. The
first time I laid eyes on her, and how her presence alone made me
feel something I had never felt before.

I begin with that thought, my hands strumming through
chords that fill the room. Though my fingers lightly graze the guitar
strings, the sound is amplified tenfold. I open my eyes again and see
nothing but darkness—an endless void.

After one last exhale, I close my eyes, ready to commit myself to the words I wrote for Harlow that night. My lips mold to the top of the microphone, my voice overpowering the darkness around me.

I strum like it's all my arms know how to do.

I sing my lyrics like they're an extension of my heart: "*I'M AFRAID TO FLY, I'M AFRAID TO FALL, I'M AFRAID OF LOVE, BUT FOR YOU, I THINK I MIGHT TRY THIS…*"

All that exists is everything the spotlight touches–me, my guitar, my voice. The roundness of my vocals is captured by the microphone as I sing the verse.

I envision myself speaking to Harlow when I sing the lyrics aloud, and as I approach the middle of the verse, I hear a light drum pattern start playing from somewhere in the darkness. The snares are sharp, the bangs thumping just enough to elevate the sound of my voice and guitar.

When I strum harder, the drums hit harder.

When I sing softer, the drums cease to play at all.

It's Danny Walker. Only a musician of his talent can ride my rhythm with such pristine accuracy.

My strums become a palm mute, bringing attention to my voice as I build up to the chorus. I get chills when the sound of a piano fills the darkness, taking the song to a whole new level.

It's Fai.

I erupt when I reach the chorus, singing and strumming like never before. I can feel my voice hitting the walls, then flying right back at me. My guitar strums, Fai's piano keys, and Danny's drums provide depth to my lyrics: "*I CAN'T FAKE IT, LOVE'S CALLING, WHEN I FACE YOU, I'M ALL IN, NOW I'M FRIGHTENED, I'M FALLING…*"

We continue to play through the song, and I just can't stop smiling. I never thought it was possible to connect with others on a musical level. Not like this. Not in the darkness of a warehouse somewhere in Miami. It gets me higher than any drug I've ever done.

I strum the final chord, letting the sound disappear in the void that surrounds me. The warehouse is still for a moment, and I take it as a sign to play the next song Harlow and I wrote for the album. I begin plucking individual strings, something I had envisioned for the first song Harlow and I wrote in Montana. The guys join in with their instruments, and together, it sounds like we've played together for years–maybe decades.

I didn't know talent until I heard these guys play with me now.

The way I don't have to tell them how I think the song should sound. *They already know.*

The way I don't have to tell them what will happen next. *They already know.*

As we play through each song, I find myself getting more comfortable with my voice, more comfortable with my guitar and the lyrics, more comfortable performing. Nothing around me matters because the words are coming from within. The songs aren't perfect because they sound perfect. The songs are perfect because they're true to Harlow and me. The songs tell a story—one of love, hardships, and taking leaps.

The songs are inspired by my life, the life I've shared and will continue to share with Harlow. And I have Fai to thank for that. Without him, I wouldn't have found the inspiration to write something true to who I am.

When I finish playing the eighth song, there is a moment of silence. I keep my head down, my fingers trailing the neck of the guitar where a tear lands, then another, until I no longer hold them back. I undo the guitar strap and drop to my knees.

I look above me, directly into the spotlight. My teardrops settle at the corner of my lips as I smile toward the heavens–toward Mom.

"Mom, did you hear that?" I whisper in a quivering voice. "I'm doing it. I'm making it happen. I'm righting my wrongs, Mom. I'm changing the road I'm on."

A narrow pair of legs appear under the spotlight. I look up to see Fai, the orange light revealing a halo around his head. He takes a knee and removes his glasses.

"That was beautiful, kid," he whispers. "That was beautiful."

I throw my arms around him. Words could never express my gratitude for Fai. He taught me that life isn't about the road. It's about the people you share the road with.

Harlow.

Blake.

Charlie.

Fai.

The two of us stand as the warehouse lights turn on. I shield my eyes until they adjust to the fluorescents. I'm surprised to see it's just a typical warehouse stripped down to the bare minimum. Massive speakers are scattered around the perimeter of it, some stacked on others, and the floor is littered with propped-up instruments.

"That…" Danny sighs from behind his drum set. "That was one of the most intense sessions I've ever been a part of."

Danny and two other men approach Fai and me with smiles across their faces. They all appear to be roughly the same age, some with tattoos and others with piercings. I see a bit of myself in them, each withered by the road, but they still managed to find their home.

I wipe the remaining tears from my cheeks before addressing the group. "I don't think you guys realize how much this means to me."

One of the men places a hand on Fai's shoulder. "Anybody special to Fai is special to us."

"You're welcome here anytime," Danny says, handing me a

key. He pats Fai on the back and smirks. "Dinner is on Fai tonight."

CHAPTER TWENTY-TWO

HARLOW

I wake up to a trail of kisses making their way up my naked back. I know these kisses. I crave these kisses. I'll take waking up to kisses over an alarm clock every day of the week and twice on Sunday.

"Morning, love," Eren whispers against my ear.

"Good morning, rockstar," I say. "More kisses, please."

I hear Eren laugh as he pulls the sheets down past my waist. He makes a trail of kisses down my back this time, my body becoming so relaxed I could melt right into this bed.

I roll onto my back, rubbing my sleepy eyes. Tomorrow is Friday, which means we're flying up to the Hamptons for the start of Blake's birthday weekend. I can feel the pressure starting to make itself known. Introducing Eren and Fai to my parents, being surrounded by their toxic friends, the possibility of my parents inviting Jordan.

How will Jordan react when he sees me with Eren? There is this lingering fear I feel growing inside of me, the one where Jordan loses his temper and hurts me or someone I care about. Jealousy can convince people to do nasty things, and I can only hope it doesn't get to Jordan.

"Can we just fast-forward through this weekend?" I groan. "Or better yet, can we freeze this moment? If we can stop the world from spinning, maybe we can stay in this bed forever. A moment that lasts forever. A *forever-moment*."

"A forever-moment." Eren props himself up on his elbow.

"Let's do it!" I prop myself up. "We just stop time. Sounds simple enough."

"But then I wouldn't be able to show you what I recorded last night."

I blink at him. "What you recorded?"

"I want to show you something," Eren says with a gleam in his eye. "But first, I'm gonna give you the greatest massage of your life."

"Mmm, okay. What'd I do to deserve this?" I ask, turning onto my stomach.

He lays my hair to my right, then kisses the left side of my neck. "Over the past few weeks, you've brought out the best of me, so I plan to give it to you."

♫ ♫ ♫

After a morning of bacon, waffles, and Blake explaining why he thinks Guitar Hero is the greatest game of all time, the five of us funnel into the studio. Fai, Charlie, and Blake sit shoulder to shoulder on the couch as I sit in one of the swivel chairs, watching Eren nervously pace around the room.

Eren clears his throat, unable to stand still. "So, Fai and I stayed up all night recording eight songs all the way through. It's not entirely finished. It's more of a rough draft. Like a starting point, I don't know. Just think of it like–"

"I think we get it," Blake says.

"Right. Yeah, no, yeah." Eren nods as he continues pacing nervously around the studio. "But just know that even though Fai had me sing the album all the way through, Fai will be the one singing it. Remember, it's a rough draft, s–"

"Press *Play*, Eren," Fai interrupts, holding back a laugh. "I think they get the picture. You stole my album for yourself, and it's completely finished and perfect with not one thing to fix," he teases.

"Alright, you get it," Eren sighs. "Here goes nothing." Eren leans over me, presses *Play*, and backs himself into the corner of the studio. He turns the lights off, the studio now pitch-black. "Lights off for the full effect," he adds.

The room goes utterly still until the faint sound of a guitar brings light to the darkness. I close my eyes.

I haven't heard this song yet.

Heat flows under my skin when I hear Eren's voice through the speaker. A slight reverb effect has been added to his vocals, making it sound like he's singing in an empty room. It encompasses me–holds me tight, making me forget about the world around me.

I slowly nod my head to the melody, his voice so alluring I could make love to it. I suck in a quick breath when I focus on the lyrics… "*When you walked my way, when I saw your face, then I felt a change, now for you, I think I might try this.*"

I'm immediately taken back to the night we met in the alley. The way we stood there, fixated on each other for the first time. *This song is about Eren and me.*

I love this song. I love this song with everything in me, with everything I am. I don't want it to end, and I know that when it does end, I'll continue to replay it. It marks the beginning of something that I pray will continue to blossom for as long as I live. It's the beginning of us, making it the perfect first song for our first album.

When the song ends, I turn to Eren. A faint light highlights his face as he leans against the wall in the back corner of the studio.

He's appreciating the way I'm appreciating the song. He smirks, his eyes fixated on mine.

The rest of the group remains silent as the next song plays. We let the album play all the way through. I spent my entire life writing songs in my notebook, believing they would remain ink on a page. It's as if my words are living. No… they've surpassed living. The words are eternal–divine.

Eren didn't just pick from the songs we wrote together. He picked from songs I wrote on my own, piecing together the perfect portrayal of how we came together.

As I listen, our story plays in my mind like a movie. I can see it…

The night we met in the alley.

The night at RAW.

Our first time writing together.

Our first time riding together.

Every moment we've shared up until now, poured into our music.

It's our debut. The perfect debut.

When the eighth song comes to a close, Eren flicks the lights back on. I open my eyes to Fai, Charlie, and Blake staring blankly at the album tracklist on the computer screen. Fai is smiling, well-aware of the beauty we just witnessed firsthand.

"Why didn't you tell me?" Blake silently stands to his feet. The group exchanges looks of confusion. Blake rephrases the question for Eren. "Why didn't you tell me you could sing like that?"

Eren slides his hands into his pockets, looking at the ground between us. "I've always been a songwriter. I didn't know how you would feel about me getting into the performing side of the business. I figured you'd just have me stick to what I know, which is writing for artists instead of becoming one myself."

Blake lets out a sigh, his hands now on his hips. "Eren, you should know by now that I want the best for you. I always have. You're gifted in more ways than one. As your manager, I want to make sure you become the artist you want to become. And as your friend, I'll make sure you're happy doing it. I support you."

I cherish my relationship with Eren, but it's Eren's relationship with the people around him that makes me cherish him even more. When the man you're falling for wins over the people who mean the most to you, it takes the relationship to new heights.

I'm falling for Eren.

And I'm falling hard.

"It's amazing," I say aloud. "I always thought the songs were great. But I didn't realize *how great* until now."

"We have something really special here," Fai states from the couch. "The album is special, too," he teases.

♫ ♫ ♫

"I have a surprise for you!" Eren shouts before I get in the shower. "Don't come back into the house until I say so!"

"You're not coming in?!"

He smirks from the bathroom door. "I have to go set up."

"Okay, okay. Text me when to come inside!"

All afternoon, Eren has been raving about a surprise that he and Fai have for me. I've never been spoiled the way Eren spoils me, from writing albums to the morning kisses. I'm starting to think I will never be able to repay him for introducing me to this new life. When my world was falling apart, he offered me his. And I have never been happier.

Nearly an hour has passed when Eren finally texts me.

EREN: We're ready for you:)

I take one last look at my reflection. My hair is frizzier from the humidity, giving it more volume than I can handle. I scrunch it at the sides, then let it fall past my shoulders over my cream-colored knitted bandeau. I adjust my floral skirt, having no idea if I picked an appropriate outfit to receive whatever this surprise is.

When I open the front door of the guest house, I notice a candle at my feet. My gaze follows the trail of candles decorating the walkway to Fai's house. My bare feet are warm against the cobblestone walkway, fingers grazing the lush wildlife reaching over the edges.

The tropical plants open up at the end of the walkway, where Blake is standing in a suit. He's standing at the foot of the stone staircase, smiling cheek to cheek. His jacket and pants are several sizes too big, most likely belonging to Fai.

"Good evening, Ms. Loser," he says, offering his arm.

I giggle. "Hello, winner," I reply, locking arms with him.

Blake guides me up the stairs and through the back door. Charlie is sitting on the edge of the kitchen counter, feet dangling.

"Gogo," he mumbles, holding up a tiny booklet.

I glance at Blake, who nods for me to take it.

"Whatcha got there, Charlie?" I whisper, taking the booklet.

I open the booklet to a page that reads, "*Whichever one you want. Love, Eren.*"

Three designs are stenciled into the next page, each design a string of music notes unique in their own way. The designs are made up of quarter, eighth, and beam music notes. My attention is immediately pulled to the design in the middle, the one meticulously drawn in an elegant fashion. The notes are chaotic on their own but orderly aligned in a crescent shape.

My finger lands on the design. "This is the one."

"Blahbo," Charlie says.

"I agree with Charlie," Blake adds. "Great choice."

He guides me left, and we follow a path made of dark-red rose petals into the living room. The first person I see is Fai, smiling in my direction from the corner of the room. He's sitting in a chair, wearing a black dress shirt and slacks, guitar in hand. He looks toward the center of the living room, and I follow his gaze to see Eren and a man standing behind two chairs.

My heartbeat doubles in tempo when I see how much effort Eren put into his appearance. Brown hair curls over the shaved sides of his head, his jaw defined by his trimmed beard. His ear piercings reflect the dim lighting and his tattoos are more pronounced than ever, showing between the opening of his white dress shirt. His shirt sleeves are rolled up, ink-covered hands locked in front of his waist as he stands straight. He even put on dress pants. It blows my mind how someone can consider tattoos to be "dirty" because Eren is far from it.

The man standing to Eren's left is in a similar outfit, but his dress shirt is dark red, similar to the rose petals covering the floor between us. Every centimeter of the man's skin is covered in tattoos, some even covering parts of his face.

Fai starts strumming, the sound as peaceful as the ambience. I feel Blake's arm loosen around mine, and when I turn to him, he nods for me to join Eren. I just can't stop smiling, even though I have no idea what happens next. My eyes remain fixated on Eren's until I'm a few feet away.

Eren takes my hand and places his other on one of the two chairs facing each other. I can't help but notice his hand shaking as he nervously guides me into the chair. He sits across from me and releases a deep breath, his deep-brown eyes flicking between mine as he smirks.

"Hi, love," he says.

"Hi, rockstar," I whisper.

Fai stops playing, the room now silent. Blake hands the man the booklet and points to the center of it. The man nods before addressing Eren and me.

"We are gathered here today to give Eren Gratis and Harlow Beck their first tattoo together," the man says. "A tattoo is a symbol of commitment. A portrayal of passion." He turns the booklet toward us and points to the design in the middle. "Do you… Eren Gratis… take this symbol to be tattooed behind your left ear? From this day forward, to feel and to see, for better, for worse, to love and to cherish?"

With his eyes locked on mine, Eren whispers, "I do."

"Do you… Harlow Beck… take this symbol to be tattooed behind your left ear? From this day forward, to feel and to see, for better, for worse, to love and to cherish?"

"I do," I say.

My first tattoo. One to share with the man I've fallen for.

I do. I do. I do.

The world can stop spinning now.

Because I want this moment to last forever.

My forever-moment.

"I will now place the stencil exactly where the tattoo will be," the man says softly.

Eren pulls my hair tie off his wrist and gives it to me. In one swift motion, I tie my hair into a top bun. The man steps behind me, and I feel a warm sensation against the skin behind my ear. My eyes don't leave Eren's. Not for a second.

When the man removes the stencil, he hands Eren a mirror.

"What do you think?" Eren asks, holding the mirror up to me.

I pull my left ear forward, turning my head to the right. Music notes form a crescent shape, outlining the back of my ear. The design immediately feels like a part of me, as if it's an eye color or a birthmark, something interchangeable. Something that lasts for as long as I will.

"It's perfect," I say.

The corner of Eren's lips curls up. He nods to the man standing over my shoulder. I take one last look across the room at Fai, Blake, and Charlie. Blake is sitting on the couch with Charlie on his lap while Fai begins strumming again. Eren holds my hands in his.

I flinch at the sound of the tattoo machine turning on. "Harlow, I'll need you to keep still as I tattoo over the stencil," the man says.

Eren tightens his grip. "Just keep your eyes on me."

Our eyes lock. I immerse myself in this moment. Fai's voice over the guitar. Eren's gaze. The feeling of Eren's hands fitting perfectly around mine. Before I know it, the tattoo machine goes silent. The skin behind my ear is tingling, which is all it was from beginning to end–a tingle. I always thought getting a tattoo would be painful. Maybe it is, but Eren's presence overpowered that pain.

The man makes his way behind Eren and pulls up a chair. Eren lowers his chin, his eyes still on mine. After placing the stencil behind his ear, the man turns on the tattoo machine. Eren doesn't flinch. If there is one thing Eren knows well, it's how to get a tattoo.

Eren remains still as he asks, "Did you have any idea this was gonna happen?"

"No idea," I reply. "But isn't that the point?"

"The unknown."

"Promise me something," I say.

"Anything."

"Promise me every day will be different. No plans. No rules. We just follow life's current wherever it takes us."

Eren smiles. "I promise."

When the man finishes, he hands us each a mirror. We hold them up for each other, admiring the art we just engraved into ourselves for as long as we live.

"You may now…" The man looks around the room. "Kiss, I guess. I don't know. I didn't really write up to this point. I'm a tattoo artist, not a wedding planner."

Eren stands, and I let out a laugh before leaping into his arms. My lips caress his, and when we pull apart, the group claps. Fai remains silent, thumbing tears under his glasses.

"Are you crying, Fai?" I ask.

Fai turns away. "Me? Crying? No, no."

I run across the room to give him a hug.

Eren follows and places a hand on Fai's shoulder. "I owe you the world, Fai. None of this could have happened without you."

Fai pulls a handkerchief from his pocket with a shaky hand. "You don't owe me anything, kid." He wipes at his tears. "You're doing much more for me than I am for you. Trust me."

CHAPTER TWENTY-THREE

EREN

"Text me when you land," I tell Harlow and Blake before they get in the S.U.V.

"We will," Harlow replies. "What time are you and Fai flying up?"

"We'll be up there around seven. Fai said he has one more surprise for me, so I guess we'll fly up after."

"So many surprises," Harlow says. "Is life on the road always full of surprises?"

"Something new every day, that's for sure."

"In that case, I can't wait to get back to it. I'll see you soon, rockstar."

I smile. "See you soon."

I shut her door and take a step back. Charlie and Blake wave through the window as they turn out the driveway. I cross my arms, contemplating what this next surprise could be.

Is it related to the album?

Is it another motorcycle?

What more is there for me to receive?

I walk back into the house. One of our songs is playing

from down the hall, and I follow the sound to the studio. Fai's back is to me, his head slowly bobbing to the rhythm of the song. I catch his eye in the rearview mirror attached to the computer. He presses *Pause* and rotates his chair to face me.

"You should be really proud of yourself," he says.

I sprawl myself on the couch. "It's just a rough take. When we get your vocals on it and add layers, the album will really start sounding good."

Fai twiddles his thumbs. I haven't known the man for long, but it's been long enough to notice that he's nervous. I clear my throat and lean forward, resting my elbows on my knees. "Fai, listen. I really don't need another surprise. You've given me more than enough."

"It's not a surprise," Fai mutters. "It's–um… well, it's news." He adjusts his glasses. "I think it'll make sense after writing one more song."

I tilt my head. "Another song?"

"One more." He turns his back to me and opens a blank document on the screen. His breathing becomes less steady by the second. "I'll pay you for it, don't worry."

I stand to my feet. "No, you won't pay me for it. I won't let you." I take a few steps toward Fai and notice his fingers trembling against the keyboard. "Is everything alright?"

Fai's hands become fists as he lowers his head, hair hanging over the sides of his face. "I'm fine," he whispers. "Sorry. Yeah, I'm fine."

"What's on your mind?" I ask, sitting in the chair next to him. "Or what is it you want to write about?"

"An apology," Fai says, staring blankly at the keyboard.

I tap my finger against my bottom lip. "An apology? Okay."

Judging from Fai's restlessness, I keep from asking any follow-up questions. I just pull out my notebook and begin writing a verse.

I hand Fai my notebook. He quietly reads each line.

"It's a great start," he mumbles without looking up. "Can you hand me a pen?"

I give him my pen, and he carefully starts writing and rearranging my lyrics. He turns the notebook to me, and I read over what he wrote.

Our words are coming to life, the song now possessing its own heartbeat–a trace of truth.

I squint at the lyrics. "If this is the chorus, it should be something catchier," I mutter, grabbing the notebook and pen from Fai's hands. "Repetition could help with the flow of it."

Fai attentively watches me jot down my thoughts and add a second verse.

"Something like this," I say, placing the notebook in front of Fai.

He runs his hand over his goatee, quietly reading over my lyrics. Without saying a word, he offers me his palm. I place the pen in it and wait for him to finish writing the second verse. The pen shakes against the page, making writing seem difficult. Or maybe it's difficult because the words don't want to meet the page.

These words are difficult for Fai to bring to life. I've written songs before about some really tough topics, but I never found them difficult to write about because the lyrics were never my truth. They were always somebody else's. It's evident that whatever Fai is writing is his truth.

When he finally manages to finish the verse, he slides the notebook in front of me. There is a thin layer of fog under his tinted lenses, and I notice a tear slide out from under.

My eyes flick from Fai to the page as I read the verse he wrote.

My world collapses on itself when I see it–when I finally read the lines–when I find Fai's truth: *"Knowing you were my son."*

"No," I exhale. "Tell me these are just words."

I clench my jaw to keep from crying. I'm pulled back to the page as I read another line out loud this time. *"Many nights, I needed time, to show you why."*

The truth hits me like the hardest bass drop known to man. It rocks my world.

Fai is my father.

It all makes sense…

Fai overpaying me to get my attention.

How easy it was for him to take me in.

The motorcycle.

The way he gets emotional when I do something he taught me.

Fai is my fucking father.

I stand so fast, the chair falls from under me. "Fai, tell me these lyrics are just words." I suck in a quick breath. "Don't you tell me you're my father. Don't you tell me you've waited 28 fucking years." I feel my face turning red. I clench my fists as my blood boils. "Don't you tell me that Mom killed herself because she couldn't make her dream a reality… a reality that's been yours this whole goddamn time!"

Fai slams his elbows on the table and drags his hands over his face. "Eren, this is more complicated than you think."

I pace from one end of the studio to the other. With each second that passes, my head is consumed by a constant pounding. My vision blurs, and I feel my sweat seeping through my undershirt. I cling my palm to my forehead, assuming my emotional pain is so severe that I'm feeling it physically.

My eyes dart around the studio, one of the thirty rooms in

this mansion big enough for Mom and me. "For the longest time, I blamed myself," I state. "I thought she killed herself because I kept her from becoming the singer she dreamed of becoming. But in reality, it was *you* keeping her from that!"

Fai slides his glasses to the top of his head, rivers of tears running down his cheeks. He doesn't say anything because he can't. How can he, after everything he's done and also failed to do?

"I never had a home, and here you were… in a fucking mansion?! Performing in stadiums?!" I scream, leaning toward Fai. "You didn't just rob me of my own mother. You robbed me of a life. You robbed me of my childhood."

Fai slowly lifts his head from the table. I've never seen a grown man cry like this before, and though I think he deserves it, a part of me wants to hear the bullshit-excuse he has for waiting 28 years to find me.

"Why, Fai?" I ask. "Why would you walk out on us?"

Fai wipes his eyes with the back of his hand, attempting to regain his composure. "I loved your mother more than anybody in this world, and I still do," he says, his voice cracking. "We were on the road, on tour. She was one of my backup singers. We fell in love. She told me she was pregnant with you and–"

"You chose fame," I snap, my tone sharp. "You chose life on the road over your own family."

"I was 20," Fai sighs. "I was raised on a stage since I can remember. I sang when people told me to sing. I performed when people told me to perform. Fame was all I knew, and when the record label found out about your mom, they told me the media would twist the story in a way that would ruin me. A rockstar knocking up the women working for him. I had my whole life ahead of me. I was selfish and stupid for thinking I was making the right decision by choosing my career over you two."

I feel the pounding in my head finally subside, my muscles

relaxing as I unclench my fists. It sounds like Fai's childhood might not have been much better than mine.

"When I met you, you said something about wanting to trade in your music success to start your own family."

"I meant every word," Fai states. "Success and money aren't worth anything when you end up alone. The only thing real to me is you. My son. And I realized that when you first showed up here."

I lower my head, letting his explanation sink in. I take a deep breath. I'm fuming, but I can keep from losing control.

"You know she loved you, right?" I lift my chin. "You know the entire 10 years I spent with her, I wanted to hate you for walking out on us, but she still defended you. She even hid your identity from me."

"For good reason." Fai slouches. "I wasn't a good man back then. All the drugs, sex, and money. She was protecting you from the monster I was becoming."

"Why did you wait to come find me?" I shake my head. "Why now? Why after 28 years?"

Fai's chest rises, and he holds in a breath for so long, I'm almost afraid he might suffocate.

"I'm dying," he exhales.

"What?"

"I'm dying, Eren," Fai states, his eyes locked on mine. "Liver cancer. Stage 4. I only found out a couple months ago. For years, I wanted to reach out to you, but I dreaded the thought of you hating me for leaving, for choosing music over you. The thought of you hating me caused me more pain than the cancer itself." He slowly stands and his gaze softens. "When I found out about the cancer, I considered it a sign from God that this is the time. This is the time to right my wrongs by giving you the best of me now, for whatever that's worth."

I suddenly remember seeing the machine in Fai's room, the

table topped with tons of pill bottles.

My initial instinct is to turn toward the door. To run. To ride to any place far from here. But I stop myself, not because I don't want to leave, but because that isn't me anymore.

I cleaned up my act.

I fell for Harlow.

I opened up to Blake.

The attachments I once avoided are now the reasons my life is worth living. And it's all thanks to Fai because I wouldn't be where I am now if he didn't ask me to write this album.

This album changed me.

I want to hate Fai for never being a father to me.

But I want to love Fai because he *is* my father.

"How much time do you have?" I ask softly.

Fai picks up on the softening of my tone, and I catch a glimpse of hope in his eyes.

"A couple months," Fai says. "But it's God's plan."

Of course, I finally meet my dad when he only has a couple months left to live.

"There's always a catch," I mutter under my breath.

Fai tilts his head to the side. "*A catch*?"

"Since I read your contract, I've had this thought that there would be some sort of 'catch…' some kind of hidden problem. I've lived long enough to know that good things never come easy, and this all came too easy."

"I'll never be able to rewrite the past, the wrongs, the regrets I live with till this day. I mean, look at me." He lets out a laugh. "The life I chose is what's literally killing me. It was only a matter of time, and now I don't have much left of it."

"And there is nothing you can do to cure it?" I cross my arms, eyes darting around the room, looking for an answer. "You have to be able to afford some kind of treatment or surgery. There has to be a way."

Fai shakes his head. "Some problems are too expensive for money." He gently taps his fist against the tabletop, thinking of what to say next. Or maybe there's too much to say after spending 28 years apart. "This problem is gonna cost me my life."

My gaze is pulled to the computer screen, the eight files, each file a song making up the album.

"It's yours," he states.

"What's mine?"

Fai adjusts his glasses. "The album. You and Harlow wrote it."

"Fai, you don't have to do that."

"It's your debut album. It's been yours from the beginning. When I'm gone, you will get my estate, music royalties, and everything else under my name." My jaw drops as Fai continues. "You'll have enough cash to live life on the road the right way with the woman you love. It wasn't the life I had with your mom, but it's the life you can have with Harlow."

I feel behind my left ear for the tattoo Harlow and I now share. It's becoming difficult for me to hate Fai when he is the reason for both my pain and *joy*.

Fai exhales, continuing to tap his fist against the tabletop. "I don't expect you to love me as a father. I don't deserve your love. I'm just happy that I got to be a father for the short time we were together."

As much as I want to think he doesn't deserve my love, I can't. I can't help but think about how I'll regret not making amends with my father when I had the chance. And here I am, with that chance. Here I am, standing in the same room as my father, the man I didn't expect to meet in this lifetime, the next, or any after.

For 18 years, I considered myself the reason for my mom taking her own life. I constantly looked for ways to right my wrongs.

I even thought the right way was living out her dream, but it's not. The right way is putting love before my dream… before my own desires.

Fai put his dream before loving my mom.

My mom put her dream before loving me.

I refuse to put my dream before loving Harlow.

I embrace Fai, tightly wrapping my arms around him. He's taken by surprise, and a second passes before I feel him hug me back.

"It's not too late to change the road you're on," I say. "We'll make the most of what we have, even if we don't have a lot."

CHAPTER TWENTY-FOUR

HARLOW

"Welcome back to New York, Ms. Harlow and Mr. Blake." Francis opens the car door for us. "And good afternoon to you, Mr. Charlie. I hope you all had a smooth flight."

Blake and I greet Francis before climbing into the back of the S.U.V. The weather in New York is far cooler than it was in Miami. It's as if I left Eren's world to return back to my mine, where Eren will soon be for the first time.

I don't know if Eren is ready to be a part of the world I came from. Eren has always been open to new experiences, but the Hamptons may be as foreign as it gets for a guy like Eren.

Blake nervously traces the rim of his cup holder with his finger, his mind elsewhere. This weekend will be a weekend of two worlds colliding, and there is a lot of pressure that comes with being stuck between the two.

To be in Blake's position…

Overseeing an album for an artist as big as Fai.

Battling the negative opinions of your own parents.

Setting up your sister with your best friend.

Coping with the loss of your wife.

And raising Charlie while doing all of that.

How does Blake manage all of that pressure?

I remember Jameson telling me that pressure makes diamonds. If that's the case, Blake will be shining brighter than any diamond money can buy.

"Birthdays are supposed to be enjoyable, right?" Blake asks dryly.

"I would say so."

He sighs. "I don't think I'm gonna enjoy this one."

"You mean you're *not* gonna enjoy an entire weekend spent with our judgmental parents and their friends?" I flash a smirk.

Blake rolls his eyes. "Well, when you put it that way–"

"Baba," Charlie blurts out while jamming an action figure against his seat cushion.

I nod. "You're right, Charlie. It's gonna be a *long* weekend."

When we turn into the estate, the driveway is littered with trucks of all sizes. Men and women are unloading equipment for the party, which is starting to look like more of a gala. From tables and chairs to flower fixtures, the front of the estate is a madhouse.

Blake and I peek our heads between the front seats.

"This is no party for me," Blake mutters. "This is for them."

Francis nods. "For what my opinion is worth, Mr. Blake… I agree."

"Your opinion means the world, Francis." Blake pats Francis's shoulder. "Especially when you agree with me."

Francis chuckles as we pull up to the stone staircase at the front of the house. Blake, Charlie, and I hop out of the car with our bags. Jameson is at the top of the stairs in a freshly-pressed suit, tending to the vendors and staff. He catches sight of us walking up the steps.

"Good afternoon, children," Jameson greets with a smile.

"Mr. and Mrs. Beck have asked that I inform you of this weekend's itinerary. Guests will begin arriving this evening. During that time, champagne and hors d'oeuvres will be served in the living room and backyard terrace. Tomorrow, Blake's birthday celebration begins at noon."

"Thank you, Jameson."

"Thanks, Jameson."

"My pleasure, children. If you will allow me to escort you to your rooms..." Jameson smiles and opens his stance.

We enter the house where people are bustling in every which way, making final arrangements. Jameson leads us up the wooden staircase and I feel the nostalgia kick in. The dark wood and lavish rugs I've stepped over a million times as a child. The smell of the rare antique furniture lining the wide halls. Unlike the halls on the first floor, there is actual evidence of a family living in this home upstairs. Family portraits line the walls, each professionally painted by artists around the world.

I've been coming to our weekly brunches since I moved out around five years ago, but I haven't stepped foot in my old bedroom until today.

Jameson comes to a halt and raises an arm toward Blake's room. "Mr. Blake and Mr. Charlie," he says softly.

"Thanks," Blake says before turning into his room.

Jameson continues up the hall. After a few steps, he raises his arm again. "Ms. Harlow."

My eyes lock onto my bedroom door, but I don't move. Jameson folds his lips between his teeth, sensing my reluctance. A part of me is afraid to go inside. I'm afraid that when I walk into my old room, I'll become the old version of myself. A weak, passive, shell of a child who let her parents live their lives through her. Over the past few weeks, I've fought to rid myself of that inner-child. And I don't think I want to see her ever again.

"Oh, Ms. Harlow." I'm pulled from my trance when I hear Jameson's voice. "Do you remember when I told you that you grow a little more every time you walk through that front door?"

I force a smile.

"Well," he continues. "You've walked through that front door hundreds of times. That is a lot of growth if you ask me. You are no longer the little girl you once were." His eyes focus on my hair falling gracefully past my shoulders. "You're changing, Ms. Harlow. Changing in the best way." He lightly pushes the door open. "Now, don't let the world you came from change you. Change the world you're in now."

I take a deep breath and step through the door Jameson closes behind me. The room hasn't changed in the slightest. The same glass chandelier hangs from the center of the white ceiling. Sunlight seeps in through the window directly ahead, shining over my cream-colored furniture. I slide out of my slippers, feeling the warm wood under my bare feet. *It's warmer than I remember.*

I walk up the two wooden steps my bed is elevated on. My parents haven't changed the rose-gold-colored sheets. I run my palms over the fabric. *It's more comfortable than I remember.*

The white bookshelf across the room is still filled with novels I read to escape my reality. I brush a finger across the spines of books, starting from the highest shelf to the lowest, where I find my songbooks.

I drop to my knees and open one after another, reading through songs about anything and everything a little girl thinks about. From middle school crushes to angsty teenage ballads, I flip through the ink-covered pages–lyrics written, erased, crossed out, and rearranged. All come together to form a portrayal of my teenage heart.

Nothing in my room has been touched since I left, as if prepared for me to come back at any time. I've heard stories about people coming home to their rooms being turned into home theaters or hobby rooms. But not my room, and I appreciate that.

The lights automatically turn on when I step into my bathroom. White marble wraps the walls, bathtub, and floor I stand on. My feet are cold against the marble as I walk an entire 10 steps to my closet. The closet lights turn on for me, an impressionable chandelier hanging from the ceiling and a light illuminating each shelf.

Ever since Eren showed me how amazing life on the road can be with nothing but the clothes on our backs, this lifestyle seems extra. I hate that the clothes and jewelry in my closet are worth more than the average house, and I hate that my closet alone is bigger than the average bedroom. But it's just the world I came from.

My eyes are pulled to the two cocktail dresses laid out for me by my mother.

Some things never change.

The dress on the left is a plunge neck split-thigh dress designed to show off the middle of my chest and my left leg. I feel the velvet material between my fingertips, admiring its grayish-blue color.

The dress on the right is a two-piece champagne-colored maxi dress, the sleeveless crop top with a halter neckline. The matching skirt has a high banded waist designed to flow down to my ankles.

While I usually roll my eyes at Mother picking my outfits for me, I won't deny she has good taste. I hold the blue dress over my chest, looking at my reflection.

"I thought I would let you pick out the heels for once," a familiar voice says from behind.

Mother steps into the bathroom behind me. Her heels click against the marble, her silver dress shimmering over her fair skin. Her hair is pulled back into a top bun and the cheekbones under her piercing blue eyes are pronounced. The corner of her lips curls up as she says, "I've always liked blue on you. It works so well with your eyes."

Our eyes.

When I look back at my reflection, my mother steps up behind me, placing her soft hands on my shoulders. For once, I feel a sense of compassion behind her touch. It's a sensation similar to the one I felt when she hugged me the last time I was here.

My gaze meets hers through the reflection. "I don't expect you to know this yet, but being a mother gives you life and also kills you at the same time." She feels my hair in her fingertips, her tone softening as she continues. "It gives you life, putting your child entirely before yourself. But it kills you to watch them no longer depend on you."

Her bottom lip protrudes and she tilts her head. "I know that I'm selfish when I say that it kills me to watch you grow into a woman who no longer needs me. But I'm learning that dying is a part of life. And I need to come to terms with letting you live your life while I return to mine."

"Mother…" I lower my dress and look down at it, the velvet smooth between my fingertips.

"The truth is you don't need me," Mother exhales. "And there is nothing wrong with that. For the longest time, I thought there was something wrong with it, but it's the opposite. I should be proud of you for it." I feel her hands run along the sides of my head as she pulls my hair up into a top bun that matches her own. "I'm here for you–your father and I both–and we always will be. There's a first for everything, especially when it comes to being parents. We're still figuring it out."

I lift my chin, letting tears fall. It's as if this mere conversation serves as an apology. Her words carry so much weight in this moment, I find myself willing to let go of everything leading up to it.

When she finishes tying my hair up, Mother's eyes widen at

the sight of the tattoo behind my ear. She lets out a gasp, placing an open palm over her mouth. I instinctively lower my head, bracing myself for her harsh judgment.

She hates it.

"I love it."

She loves it?

I look up over my shoulder at her. "You love it?"

Mother closes her eyes, letting out a laugh. She slowly reaches up and pulls the tie out of her hair. "You think you got your spontaneity from your father?" With an elegant shake of her head, her wavy hair falls well-past her shoulders. "You came from me, you know."

I can hardly recognize my mother at first. She doesn't look anything like the Claire Beck who raised me. If anything, she looks more like the version of me I discovered in Montana. The version I set free.

"All these years, you made me tie it up," I say.

Mother undoes my hair tie. After my hair falls, she turns me so that we're both looking into our reflection. "I thought being a mother was about turning the chaos into order." She hugs me from behind. "But you taught me that you need a *balance* between the order and the chaos."

I spin around and hug Mother tighter than I ever could have fathomed. I found her. I finally found the mother I'd been looking for. And little did I know, she was here the whole time, the same way my wild side was with me the whole time.

The two of us become one, the way a mother and daughter should. I'm a reflection of her, and I'm proud. I found the real me, the version yearning for adventure and discovering the unknown. I see the yearning in my mother. Maybe my father was her unknown, the same way Eren is mine.

With my cheek resting against the warmth of her chest, I

hear her whisper, "Your father will come around. He loves you and Blake more than anything. He just doesn't know how to show it." She pulls back and gives me a reassuring smile. "I'll see you down there."

"I love you, Mother." The words leave my mouth before I think to say them. Maybe because the words don't come from the mind. They come from the heart.

Mother smiles. "Love you, Harlow."

♫ ♫ ♫

When I finish getting ready, I unlock my phone to see texts from Blake.

> **BLAKE:** Meet me in my room
> **BLAKE:** Loser
> **HARLOW:** Coming now
> **HARLOW:** Winner

I take one last look in the mirror. The woman in front of me is more ready than she will ever be to confront the storm brewing downstairs. The woman in the reflection is nervous, but excited. She is polished, but imperfect. She is domesticated, but wild. Above all, she is ready for the unknown.

My phone vibrates, and I look down to see a text from Eren.

> **EREN:** Heading to the airport in a few hours… ready to meet the future in-laws;)
> **HARLOW:** You better be ready, rockstar;)

With my eyes closed, I nervously place the phone over my chest, hoping it'll slow my heartbeat down. A sense of peace comes over me as I run a gentle finger over my tattoo. I can feel a bit of Eren's excitement through the phone. I took my leap. In a way, he's about to take his own, immersing himself in my world.

After Mother opened up to me a little over an hour ago, it helps to know that she's on my side. She may be willing to accept Eren with open arms, unlike Father.

I'm hesitant to tell Blake about my conversation with Mother. She might not have talked to him yet. I would hate to mention that Mother and I made amends before she attempts to do the same with Blake.

When I reach Blake's bedroom, he opens the door seconds after I knock. "We've been expecting you," he says with a devilish smirk.

Charlie mumbles something from Blake's bed.

"You boys are up to no good." I narrow my eyes at each of them. "I can sense it."

Charlie giggles, slamming his tiny hands against his toy piano. Blake gestures for me to come in. When he steps aside, the GameCube catches my eye. It's been a long time since we played, which means this face-off has been a long time coming.

"You did *not* set up the GameCube!" I shout, running into the room to pick up my controller.

"Prepare to meet thy doom." Blake picks up his controller, and the two of us sit against the foot of the bed.

Mario Kart lights up the screen, the video game that sparked our sibling rivalry.

Before pressing the *Start* button, Blake says, "Have you talked to Mother?"

"Yeah. She just came to my room."

"I talked to her, too," he replies. With his eyes fixed on his controller, he murmurs, "Maybe there's hope… for us to be an actual family." He lets out an exhale. "Just waiting on Father."

"He'll come around."

"We'll see." Blake shrugs, dismissing the idea that Father would ever make amends like Mother just did. "Are you ready to lose again, loser?" he teases, pressing *Start*.

"This is the last time I'll refer to you as 'winner,' winner."

"Whatever you say."

We anxiously wait for the game to load. I rub my sweaty palms against my dress so that my hands don't slip when the race begins. Charlie mumbles something from above, and I look up to see him sitting at the edge of the bed between Blake and me. His feet are dangling between us, his googly eyes fixated on the T.V. screen.

The game counts us down.

3

2

1

GO.

We play the full Grand Prix. 16 races on 16 different tracks. Blake starts off at the top of the rankings, coming in first place. But I quickly gain momentum, coming in first for a few consecutive races.

"Have you been practicing?!" Blake asks, his thumbs pressing an array of buttons on his controller.

"Nope," I snap back with a smirk. "If I had been practicing, I'd be destroying you right now instead of just beating you."

"It's not over till it's over."

By the time we get to the final race, I'm only one point behind Blake. For a year, I've been called "loser," which is a year too long.

It's time to flip the script.

To come out on top.

To win.

"You've gotten better, loser," Blake admits as the final race loads. "But I'll always be the best."

I give him a playful nudge. "It's not over till it's over," I tease in my best Blake-voice.

"May the best Beck win," he whispers.

"Oh, she will."

The game music plays as the character on the screen counts us down.

3

2

1

GO.

We're off, our two karts weaving through the other karts. Blake boosts forward, keeping a steady lead until I manage to pull ahead. We create obstacles for each other and do our best to keep from cursing in front of Charlie.

We round the final corner, and I hold my breath, refusing to exhale until I cross the finish line in first place. Our karts are neck and neck, the finish line in sight. Our eyes are glued to the screen as we slowly stand to our feet.

"Come on, come on," Blake whispers, his kart centimeters ahead of mine.

"Go, go, go," I mutter, grinding my teeth together.

Our karts hit the final ramp, our characters now flying through the air. The room goes still.

"NO!" Blake shouts when he sees my kart is about to land on a speed-boost pad.

Our karts land at the same time, but mine zooms ahead upon landing on the pad… across the finish line first.

"YES!" I scream, jumping up and down in front of the T.V. "YES! YES! YES!"

Blake throws himself onto his bed face-first. He screams into his pillow as Charlie jumps up and down on the bed, matching my level of excitement.

"I can't believe it," Blake groans, turning onto his back. "You beat me on my birthday weekend."

"Don't worry," I say. "You'll get the next one, *loser*."

"You win this round," Blake sits up and offers me his hand. "*Winner*."

Blake picks up Charlie, and the three of us head down the hall in high spirits. With Eren and Fai on their way and a new winning title under my belt, I think I have the boost I need to get through the weekend.

The farther we walk down the hall, the easier it is to hear the music being played downstairs. When I reach the top of the staircase, I look down to see Jameson greeting guests as they walk through the front door. He smiles up at us.

"You look lovely, children." His deep voice fills the entryway, causing heads to turn as we reach the foot of the staircase. "I suppose I shouldn't be referring to you as children anymore," he adds.

"Babafaffi," Charlie replies.

Blake looks down at Charlie, then back up at Jameson. "Charlie says, 'we'll always be your children.'"

Jameson blushes. "Enjoy your birthday, Mr. Blake."

The three of us follow a group of guests into the living room, where a crowd is gathered. Waiters weave through the crowd, offering platters of champagne and hors d'oeuvres.

"Do you know any of these people?" I whisper to Blake.

"Nope."

"Well, it's nice of them to show up to your birthday party," I tease.

We move around the perimeter of the room until we find an open cocktail table near the violinists. My eyes pan around the room of strangers, my ears picking up on conversations about all things Wall Street. The group is well-dressed, not a single person looking younger than 50.

The sight of the polished crowd begins to make me nervous. There is no doubt Eren and Fai are going to stick out like a sore thumb. The two of them will be taller than everyone else, their tattoos bringing even more attention to themselves.

My phone vibrates, and I get butterflies when I see Eren's text.

EREN: Taking off sooon!

The music suddenly cuts out, and people turn their heads to the front of the living room. Standing under the grand archway is my father wearing a white suit with a baby blue pocket square. His piercing blue eyes hold the gaze of each and every guest as the great William Beck greets the crowd with Mother at his side.

Blake subtly fixes his tie, waiting to be recognized by Father. "Can you hold Charlie for a second?" he whispers to me. "I think Father might ask for me."

"Sure," I reply, picking up Charlie.

"Good evening, and welcome to our home!" Father exclaims. "Claire and I are delighted to be hosting all of our friends… and *Tom*."

The crowd laughs at Father's joke, and a man raises his glass toward Father. *That's probably Tom.*

Father continues. "Jameson should have shown you all your designated rooms. We are delighted for you to join us and look forward to catching up with you at some point throughout the weekend."

Father's chilling eyes hover over the crowd from left to right until they land on the three of us. He raises a hand, and Blake straightens his posture, ready to be recognized. Suddenly, the violinists continue playing music from right behind us. Blake's smile dissolves when he realizes Father was cuing the band, not acknowledging his son.

My jaw drops.

Not a single mention of Blake's birthday being tomorrow.

"And the weekend has begun," Blake mutters as he snatches a champagne glass from a waiter's platter.

Mother and Father make their rounds as Blake and I hold empty conversations with people we have no desire to speak to. Time seems to go by faster as I drink more champagne, so I remain as close as I can to the cocktail waiters.

Father hasn't even acknowledged our existence, and I hope that remains the case when Eren and Fai get here. That way, we can keep to ourselves without worrying about all this noise.

"You look amazing," a smooth voice whispers from behind.

I pause the champagne glass just centimeters from my lips. I slowly look over my shoulder to see Jordan standing over me. Leave it to my father to invite my ex into our home for an entire fucking weekend.

"You haven't been answering my calls or texts." Jordan's eyes narrow. "I thought we were gonna give this another go."

I fold my lips between my teeth, realizing now is probably the best time to tell Jordan that my heart is with Eren. Either way, he'll find out before the end of the weekend.

"I can't do this again."

"What do you mean you can't?" Jordan raises a brow and tugs at his turtleneck collar. "What changed since we last talked?"

Here goes nothing.

"I'm with Eren now."

"*Eren.*" Jordan mutters Eren's name with disgust. He looks over the crowd. "Is he here?"

"That shouldn't matter." I turn my back to him and take a long sip of champagne.

He steps into my line of sight, his tone frustrated as he says, "So, you start seeing a guy for a week, and all of a sudden, I don't exist?"

I swallow the rest of my glass, then glare at Jordan. "Did I exist when you were fucking Penny in our bed?"

Jordan grabs my arm, yanking me closer. It's just subtle enough for no one to pick up on his aggression. "I already fucking told you. I fired the bitch right after it happened." He pulls me even closer, his lips now pressed against my ear. "You might be through with me, but I'm not through with you."

He lets go of my arm, and I stutter-step backwards, noticing a vein appear along the side of his forehead. It's the first time he's ever snapped at me. My eyes drop to his hand, the same hand that I'm sure just left a bruise on my arm. My state of shock keeps me from speaking.

With his hand now on the small of my back, Jordan whispers, "I'm staying in the room at the end of your hall. The last door on the right." He scans the party, but his voice is directed toward me when he says, "I'll pay you a little visit tonight, and we'll talk."

"You stay away from me, or my parents will–"

"Will what?" he snaps. "Your father loves me, and he runs this family. He rules your world, which means I do, too, babe." His breath brushes my ear when he finally whispers, "I look forward to meeting Eren." He lets go of my back, snatches a glass of champagne from a waiter, and disappears into the crowd like a snake slithering into the brush.

Being here was a horrible idea, Blake's birthday or not. My heavy-tempered ex-boyfriend is staying in the room a few doors down from me, there is already tension between Blake and Father, and I'm about to loop Eren and Fai into all of this mayhem.

Blake was right.

The weekend has begun.

My phone pings, and I unlock it to see a text from Eren.

EREN: Here:)

CHAPTER TWENTY-FIVE

EREN

I've been to more places than I can count.

I've met thousands of strangers.

I've done my time in juvie.

I've written for world-renowned artists.

I've thrown myself into the depths of the unknown, and yet... *I've never been this nervous.*

Fai and I approach the stone steps in front of Harlow's childhood home. I remind myself to breathe as my anxiety creeps in. My stage fright can't hold a candle to the thought of diving into Harlow's world. But I've worked through my stage fright for my mom, and now I'll work through this weekend for Harlow.

The things we do for the women we love.

I'm standing shoulder to shoulder with Fai, our necks cranked all the way back just to see the second floor as we grip our duffle bags.

"Don't be nervous," Fai whispers.

"Do I look nervous?"

"Just a bit."

I adjust the collar of my black dress shirt. This is the first time I've ever tucked in my shirt. I feel like an imposter. It baffles me that people feel the need to dress up for stuff like this. Dressing up is like wearing a mask. It's as if who you are isn't good enough, so you need to compensate with fabric. I don't know how people do this every day when they go to work.

"Hey." Fai grips my shoulders, turning me to face him. "You got this, kid. Your girl is in there waiting for you."

"It's not Harlow making me nervous. It's her parents."

I like to think I've done a decent job playing down meeting Harlow's parents. I've shrugged and made light of this weekend while the thought of it has been stirring somewhere inside of me, making me uneasy.

Fai smirks and raises his palms. "If it's any consolation, Harlow didn't seem too nervous meeting *your* dad."

I roll my eyes. "Too soon, Fai. Too soon."

It's crazy to think that I went from 18 years of no attachments to falling in love with Harlow and meeting my dying dad in the same week. For somebody who is a master in the art of apathy like myself, juggling these emotions makes me feel like I'm fighting for my life.

I feel a sharp pain in the right side of my head, causing me to drop my bag and sway backwards.

"Woah, woah." Fai holds me still with a firm grip. "You alright?"

I press my palm against my forehead, the sharp pain becoming a constant pounding. It dawns on me that these headaches have come and gone since I arrived in Miami. I assumed it was the humidity, but at this point, I'm starting to think it's the emotional rollercoaster I've been on.

"I'm good," I exhale.

"Take a deep breath." Fai looks at me from over his glasses. "I think your nerves are getting the best of you."

The headache subsides. "You're probably right."

I take a deep breath, then exhale.

"Let's do it."

The two of us head up the stone staircase. The balustrade is decorated with white ribbon and floral decor, candles lining the sides of each stair. When we reach the top, my eyes are pulled to a towering wooden door. My–I mean, Fai's loafers I'm borrowing–click against the stone until we reach the door.

Fai knocks a few times, then runs his hands over his goatee and slicked hair. He's wearing a gray dress shirt with black suspenders holding up his cropped slacks. His tanned ankles show between the bottom of his slacks and the top of his loafers. It's the most put-together a rockstar can look.

I keep my sleeves rolled down and my shirt buttoned all the way up to hide most of my tattoos. The ink on my neck and hands is exposed, but I plan to keep my hands in my pockets most of the weekend to keep from being judged by Harlow's parents.

"Remember to keep the news about us a secret until the end of the weekend," I whisper. "This weekend is about Blake."

Fai nods. "My lips are sealed."

A loud click comes from behind the door. It slowly opens, and our eyes drop to a surprised man in a tuxedo. He's an older man. The sides of his eyes wrinkle as he masks his confusion with a smile. "Good evening, gentlemen," he greets with a slight bow.

I clear my throat. "W-we're here for…" I look at Fai, then back at the man. "We're here for Blake's birthday…?"

"But, of course," the man replies. "May I please have your names?"

"Eren and Fai."

He smiles. "Just a moment for me to review the guest list, please."

The door closes. Fai and I glance at each other before the

man opens the door again. "Welcome, gentlemen!" He pulls the door wide open, gesturing for us to enter. "My name is Jameson. First, I will show you to your rooms where you will leave your things. Then, I will escort you to the 'Welcome Soiree.'"

"A '*Welcome Soiree*.'" Fai raises a brow at me. "Sounds ravishing."

I give him a playful nudge.

I may not have a home, but if I did, this place would be far from anything like it.

Fai and I step into the dim entryway. The ceiling is so high, it might as well be the sky. Dark wood lines the walls, and I'm captivated by the massive family portrait staring at me from above. In the portrait, a man is sitting in a plush leather chair, his wife with her hand on his left shoulder, a boy with his hand on the man's right shoulder, and a girl with auburn hair sitting on his lap. Their eyes are piercing blue and their faces appear to be made of stone.

This family portrait is all I need to see for me to understand where Harlow and Blake came from. Just one look and I understand why Harlow waited so long to chase her dream. I understand why Blake rolls his eyes every time their parents are mentioned. This portrait says it all.

We follow Jameson up the wooden steps and down a hall that seems to stretch on for forever. When we're about halfway to the end, Jameson points to a door on our left. "Fai, this will be your room."

"Thank you, Jameson." Fai flashes Jameson a smile and enters the room with his bag. "Eren, come grab me before you head downstairs. Otherwise, I'll get lost."

"Right this way, Eren."

Jameson slowly continues down the hall. I remain a few steps behind, appreciating each family portrait I walk past.

Without turning back, Jameson says, "Eren, I hope you don't

mind my asking. How do you know Blake and Harlow?"

I straighten my posture. "I'm a songwriter, represented by Blake. And I'm co-writing Fai's album with Harlow," I explain to Jameson's back.

Jameson stops in his tracks, and I nearly bump into him. He slowly turns over his shoulder, eyes glossy as he looks up at me.

His voice nearly cracks when he asks, "Harlow is writing an album? An album of songs?"

"Y-yeah," I stutter. His emotional response catches me by surprise. "She's an amazing songwriter. We actually just finished the eight songs."

Jameson's eyebrows draw apart. "She's writing songs?"

"*She's writing songs*," I reply, growing more confused when his eyes well up with tears. "Is everything alright?"

Jameson pulls out a handkerchief, lightly dabbing it over his eyes and cheeks. "My apologies. Right this way."

He continues down the hall again, and I come to the conclusion that this weekend is already off to a bizarre start. We reach the second-to-last door, and he points to the right. "And here is your room."

He opens the door to a spacious bedroom. The dim lights reflect off of the dark leather couch I toss my bag onto. Behind the couch is a large bed with thick red sheets.

When Jameson leaves, I walk into the bathroom to see a man looking at me from inside the bathroom mirror. His dark hair curls over the shaved sides of his head. Tattoos cover his skin, from the top of his neck to his fingertips. The bathroom lights illuminate his deep-brown eyes–eyes longing for the motivation to do what he's about to do.

The man was but is no longer broken. His tattoos tell his story. It's a story of repeated mistakes and self-destructive patterns that have ended to make room for a new beginning.

I reach a hand toward the man, but I can't touch him. My hand is stopped by the mirror between us. The man in the mirror is me, and I'm finally glad that he is.

"You can do this," I say to the man in front of me. "You can fucking do this."

"Hey, rockstar," a gentle but raspy voice says from behind me. The voice belongs to the girl I fall harder for every day. "You ready for the shit show?"

I turn to face Harlow, my back now pressed against the sink. She effortlessly holds my gaze, her wild hair falling over her blue dress.

I've never seen a girl more stunning.

I've never heard a voice more alluring.

I never knew love.

Until I knew Harlow.

"I love you," I state with every ounce of my being. I take a step toward her. "I love you." I take another step. "It's okay if you don't love me back. I love you regardless. And I'm gonna keep loving you." Harlow opens her mouth to speak, but I don't let her. "I know it hasn't been long at all. I know you just got out of a relationship. But I also know that I love you… that you saved my life… that you make me want to be a better version of myself. I love you for that and so much more."

"Eren, I–"

"Like I said, Harlow–it's okay if you don't love me back. I just want you to know–"

"Eren!" Harlow grabs the sides of my face and pulls me even closer. "I love you," she exhales. "I love you, I love you, I love you."

I close the gap between us, my lips now caressing hers. I take her in, feeling her do the same. I kiss her lips, her cheeks, her forehead. I shower her in kisses, making her laugh.

I love this laugh.

I love this face.

I love this girl.

With my arms locked around her back, I smirk and say, "I'm ready to meet my future in-laws."

Harlow smiles. "They aren't ready to meet you." She kisses me once more. "But they're going to meet you anyway."

She laces her hand in mine and leads me out of the room, where we join Jameson and Fai.

"It's spelled J-A-M-E-S-O-N," Jameson whispers to Fai with his back to us.

Fai finishes autographing Jameson's handkerchief, then hands it back to Jameson. "There you go." He looks at us over Jameson's shoulder. "You kids ready?"

Jameson's eyes widen at the sight of Harlow and me. He quickly slides the handkerchief into his pocket. "Oh, I–hello! Yes, right this way!"

As we near the living room, sounds of laughter and conversations grow louder. The hallway opens up to a luxurious living room with cream-colored furniture. Tall glass doors lining the back wall are open, allowing the crowd to pour out onto a backyard terrace. People sit, stand, and make their rounds. They spew out facts about business and finance, most terms going right over my head.

"It was a pleasure meeting you both," Jameson says before turning back to the entryway.

Harlow tightens her grip on my hand, picking up on my nerves. "Blake and Charlie are out on the terrace," she whispers.

Fai, Harlow, and I weave through the crowd that grows quieter the deeper we get. Smiles toward Harlow become skeptical stares when they catch sight of Fai and me. I glance back at Fai to see if he picks up on the tension, but it's hard to tell based on the calm smile under his tinted glasses.

"You guys made it!" Blake shouts when we reach the terrace.

I embrace him. "I know it's a day early, but Happy Birthday."

"I appreciate it," Bake slurs. "Let me grab you something from the bar. Whiskey?"

"A sparkling water, please," Fai says.

"Make that two, sir," I add with a smile.

"You got it!"

Charlie giggles as Fai picks him up to say hello. A girl fills the space Blake creates when he leaves, her eyes darting between Harlow and me. I recognize her from the night I met Harlow for the first time.

She sticks out her hand. "Wow. Okay, hi."

"Talia, right?"

Talia pinches her eyebrows together until she sees the tattoos on my neck and hands. "Oh… my… God." She covers her mouth in shock. "You're him! You're the guy who was on that stage at the restaurant!"

I smirk while shaking her hand. "Hi, I'm him. I'm the guy who was on that stage at the restaurant."

"This is Eren," Harlow says, her hand grazing my shoulder.

Talia flashes Harlow a cheeky grin. "Okay, Harlow. I see you," she whispers with a wink. "Eren, it is a pleasure to meet you, and you are still hot. Don't tell my boyfriend I told you that, wherever the hell he is right now."

Blake returns to the group, handing us our drinks.

"To the birthday boy!" Fai shouts.

The group holds up their glasses, all shouting, "To the birthday boy!"

We form a half-circle at the edge of the backyard terrace, facing the crowd of people. Wealth is in the air, and it's so potent, I can taste it. These are not my people, but if they're Harlow's, I'm more than happy to stick around.

Harlow doesn't leave my side as we share stories and crack jokes. Cocktail waiters stop by from time to time to make sure we never see the bottom of our glasses. While I was nervous at first, I finally relax by immersing myself in Harlow's world, listening to her, Talia, and Blake ramble on about their childhood in the Hamptons.

I find it hard to picture Harlow as the little girl in the family portrait, the same Harlow tightening her hold on me every couple of minutes to remind herself that I'm here and I'm hers. When I'm handed my fourth sparkling water, my bladder makes it known that it's time for me to relieve myself of the first three.

I kiss the top of Harlow's head, then whisper, "I'm gonna use the bathroom real quick."

"Do you want me to show you where it is?"

"I got it. Make sure Fai doesn't feel left out. I'll be quick."

Harlow lets go of my arm, and the second I walk away, I hear Talia pressing her for details about us. I maneuver through the crowd, feeling dozens of chilling stares drawn to me. I keep my head down, avoiding eye contact.

"Excuse me!" a lady hisses from behind.

Please don't be talking to me.

"Excuse me!"

I reach the end of the living room and spot Jameson. If anyone knows where the bathroom is, it's him. Before I take another step, a hand latches itself to my arm.

"EXCUSE ME! Staff should not be wandering throughout the estate," the lady snarls.

"Staff?" I turn to see a blonde woman, her piercing blue eyes freezing me where I stand.

She glares at me, then at my neck and hands. "The caterers are to use the portable restroom across the driveway. You shouldn't be in here!"

The people around us grow silent, picking up on the tension

between this random lady and me.

I pinch my eyebrows together. "I'm not a caterer, ma'am."

Her eyes flick to the tattoos on my neck and hands again. "Oh? So, I suppose you think you're a guest," she hisses.

When her face flattens, I recognize her as the woman in the family portrait. *Harlow's mother.*

My jaw drops. Before I introduce myself, Jameson comes to my rescue. "Ms. Beck, this is Eren," he says. "He is a friend of Blake and Harlow's."

Ms. Beck doesn't move a muscle. This is the coldest I've ever felt. I can't imagine this woman being a mother to anyone, let alone to the one I love. In an attempt to shake her hand, I slowly lift my hand between us. Ms. Beck looks down at it, then up at me.

"It's n-nice to meet you, Ms. Beck," I stutter.

She keeps her hands at her sides. "A pleasure, Eren." She turns and disappears into the crowd.

Jameson pats my shoulder.

"That went about as bad as I thought it would," I admit.

"I've seen much worse, Eren. Believe me," Jameson says. "Are you looking for the restroom?"

"I was, but I think I just pissed myself."

We laugh as he escorts me down the hall. When I'm done using the bathroom, I wash my hands and take a moment to freshen up.

"So much for a good first impression," I mutter to my reflection. "Keep it together, man. You're only a couple hours in."

I open the door just as a man is about to enter. We bump into each other, and the man scoffs at me. "Hey, buddy. Watch where you're going." His green eyes widen at the sight of my tattoos.

I apologize and move around him, catching a whiff of tequila on his breath. I'm halfway down the hall when I realize who he is. I look back over my shoulder to see the man, Jordan, still looking at me. I clench a fist at my side, fighting the urge to tell him to leave Harlow alone. He glares at me with his jaw flexed.

He remembers me, and I'm glad he does.

A few guests step around me, making their way to the bathroom. Jordan slowly shuts the door, his eyes not leaving mine until it's completely closed.

It's gonna be a long weekend.

But I'm ready for it.

CHAPTER TWENTY-SIX

HARLOW

It isn't hard to spot Eren making his way back through the crowd. His good looks are one thing, but his height and tattoos make him impossible to miss. Talia and I watch him from the back of the terrace.

"You *love* this guy," Talia whispers, locking her arm in mine. "I don't care how long you've been with Jordan. You never looked at him the way you look at Eren."

"I know." I bite my lip to keep from blushing. "Crazy, right?"

"Nope." She shrugs. "You've always been quieter around Jordan and your dad, always particular about your routine and the way you look. But you have this other side of you I've caught glimpses of. I feel like that side of you is the real you. It shows in the way you simply stand next to Eren. It's like he's bringing out the good in you."

"You have no idea, Talia," I sigh. "Eren is changing my life."

We watch Eren awkwardly weave through the crowd, looking back over his shoulder every couple of steps.

"Hold on to him," Talia replies. "It's nice to see that there are good men outside of our little world. He's also hot, which I'm sure you're well-aware of."

"Trust me. I'm well-aware."

Eren lets out a sigh of relief when he makes it back to me. "That was a journey."

Talia wipes a pretend-tear when she sees Eren wrap an arm around me. "Please excuse me. I'm gonna go look for *my* love." She finishes her champagne and trudges into the house.

I smile at Eren. My hand grazes over his arm, and I notice how tense he is.

"You seem tense," I whisper. "Everything okay?"

"Huh? Yeah, I'm fine." Eren sucks in a quick breath, his eyes panning from the terrace to the living room. "I sort of met your mother."

"You what?! When?!"

"On the way to the bathroom," he says. "Where I ran into your ex."

"My goodness."

Eren bites his lip, then smirks. "Your mom thought I was one of the caterers."

I lower my head, embarrassed. "She did *not*. Eren, I'm so sorry."

"Don't be sorry." He squeezes my arm. "I'm here for you and Blake." He lifts a hand toward the crowd. "This is all just a bonus."

"Aren't bonuses supposed to be a good thing?"

"This *is* a good thing. All of it." Eren turns me so that we're leaning over the balustrade, looking over the rest of the backyard. "Nobody has ever brought me around their family. So, it's an honor to be around your family, regardless of how I'm received by them."

I rest my head on his shoulder as we become one in the moment. White candles float over the pool's surface below. Beyond the pool is the grass lawn that's been covered by a towering gala tent. Its white surfaces are smooth as silk with several points that rise at different heights. The moonlight reflects off the ocean surface in the distance, creating a white strip that stretches out to the horizon.

The moment is peaceful.

The moment is pure.

"You must be Eren."

The moment is *ruined*.

Eren and I turn to see Father standing just a few feet away. He stands straight as an arrow, one hand gripping his champagne glass and the other at his side. His white suit shimmers, making his crowd of corporate minions look dull and unimportant, the way he wants them to.

Eren extends his hand to my father, and I brace myself for some sort of catastrophe. Father looks at Eren like he is gum on the bottom of a shoe–unanticipated, disgusting, an inconvenience. But Eren doesn't budge. Instead, he smiles and introduces himself.

"Good evening, sir. I'm Eren Gratis."

Father narrows his eyes at Eren's hand.

But then…

To my surprise…

Father shakes it.

"I'm William Beck," Father says, puffing out his chest.

"Ah, yes. I recognize you…"

Father lifts his chin smugly, inviting the typical Wall Street praise.

"... From the family portrait," Eren continues. "The one at the front of the house. You're Harlow's father."

Father blinks at Eren, then releases his hand. It's the first time someone has recognized Father in a way that isn't associated with Wall Street. It's also the first time Father has been explicitly labeled as *"Harlow's father."*

"Y-yes," Father stutters. "Harlow's father." Father pinches his eyebrows together, wallowing in a state of confusion until Mother appears at his side. "This… this is Claire."

Eren extends his hand toward Mother. "Right! Yes, we've met." The two shake hands. "Good evening, Ms. Beck. I'm Eren, the caterer," he teases while shaking her hand.

Mother opens her mouth, but nothing comes out. Both of my parents are stuck in a state of shock, and I don't think I've ever been more entertained. Just when I think it can't get any better, Fai steps up.

"Mr. and Mrs. Beck." Fai's tone is warm as he politely greets them. "You have a very lovely home. Or should I say, you have a very lovely *resort*."

The group flinches as Mother gasps. She places her hand over her heart. "You're… Fai. The… the… singer!"

Father's head swivels between Mother and Fai. "Singer?"

Mother tugs at Father's sleeve, whispering the names of Fai's most popular songs.

"Harlow and Eren just finished writing my album," Fai says softly.

My parents' eyes flick to mine. Father tilts his head. "Harlow, is that what you've been doing instead of working? You've been writing songs for a *has-been*?"

"He's not a *has-been*." Eren takes an aggressive step toward Father, but I subtly hold him back.

Fai lifts his sparkling water. "I'll be whatever William says I am while in his home," he says with a smirk. "But William will be whatever I say he is while in *my* home."

"And what would I be in your home?" Father hisses.

"You'd be a pompous jerk," Fai says coolly.

Father purses his lips, his face turning red. He takes a small step forward, but Mother pulls him back. I feel Eren's muscles tighten under my grip and the tension rises until a cocktail waiter holds up a tray of champagne glasses between the group. "Champagne, anyone?" he offers with an innocent smile.

I grab a glass and raise a brow at Mother and Father. "It's Blake's birthday tomorrow, in case you forgot."

"We are aware of our own son's birthday, Harlow," Father snaps. "Come, Claire. We have a few more rounds to make before the evening comes to a close."

Father turns back into the living room. Mother flashes an apologetic look at us before following him inside. The second they're gone, I want to drop to my knees and beg for Fai's forgiveness.

"Fai, I'm so sorry. I knew this was gonna happen, and I feel like an idiot for not stepping in."

"Don't be sorry. I'm the one sorry for calling your dad a pompous jerk."

I let out a laugh. "He needed to hear it. No one has ever stood up to him like that."

"Where's Blake?" Eren asks.

The three of us look in different directions. Even as people begin to clear the living room for the night, there's no sight of him.

Fai, Eren, and I scan the near-empty living room and halls– still no Blake. It's been a long night for me, which means it's been an even longer night for Blake. I wouldn't blame him if he left and never came back. After tonight, I don't see a reason for either of us to stay in a place like this, especially on his birthday.

I hurry up the stairs, praying we find him in his bedroom. It's the last place he could be. I slowly open Blake's bedroom door and let out a sigh of relief when I see him cuddling with Charlie, both of them sound asleep. The room is dark, despite the light emitted from the T.V. screen. I tiptoe inside to turn off the T.V., then tiptoe back out.

"Was he in there?" Eren whispers as I shut the door behind

me.

"They're asleep."

"When do you think he came up?" Fai asks.

I shrug. "Not sure, but I don't blame him. My parents didn't say a single word to him all night when this weekend is supposed to be about him."

"Well, we'll make sure tomorrow is his day," Eren says.

"Alright, kids. It's past my bedtime," Fai sighs while checking his watch. "I'm gonna hit the hay. Don't party too hard." He winks and struts across the hall into his room.

Eren and I glance at each other and immediately start laughing. I cover my mouth, but there's no point in trying to hide it.

"This is insane," I whisper, shaking my head.

Eren raises a brow. "Which part? Your mom thinking I'm a caterer? Or our dads almost getting into a fistfight?"

Wait.

"Did you just say... '*our dads*?'"

Eren's face goes pale.

I let out a laugh. "Did you just refer to Fai as your dad?"

"Did I?" Eren itches the side of his head, avoiding eye contact. "I think I had too much to drink."

"You've been drinking sparkling water all night."

Eren nervously looks around the hall. His discomfort leads me to realize that Eren is a terrible liar.

My eyes widen. "Eren…"

"I can explain. Well, kind of. I'm sort of still processing everything myself."

Before he can say another word, I pull him into my room and slam the door. "Fai is your *dad*?!"

"Shh!" Eren shushes me before realizing we're in my room. "Wow. So, this is the room you grew up in?"

"Eren!" I snap. "Focus!"

Eren untucks his shirt and rolls up his sleeves. "It's a little hard for me to focus right now, Harlow." He paces to one side of my room, then the other. "Your parents think I'm one of the party caterers. I'm walking around with my shirt tucked in. I just found out Fai is my dad. Not to mention, he's dying of cancer–"

"FAI HAS CANCER?!" I whisper-shout.

Eren stops pacing and slouches. "I was gonna tell you after this weekend," he admits. "I didn't want to take away from Blake's birthday."

"When…? How…? Why…? I don't even know what to say." I cross my arms. "Are you okay?"

"I don't know." Eren sits on the edge of my bed. He rests his elbows on his knees and looks at the floor. "The craziest part of it all is that I think *I am* okay." He looks up at me. "I can hate him for waiting 28 years to meet me, but I also don't have a lot of time to spend with him. I can't spend the little time we have together hating the man."

I press my back against the bedroom door and slide myself to the ground. "Fai knew all along?"

Eren nods. "That's why he wanted me to write the album. It was so we could finally meet."

"And you're not mad about him walking out on you and your mom?"

"How can I be? Without the album, there would be no you and me." Eren walks across the room and sits on the ground next to me. "In a weird way, it sort of all worked out. I'm not alone anymore." Eren gently dips his forehead to mine. "I just want to be done with all the shit I put myself through. I want to pack it all in and drop it. I want to start new with you."

I caress the side of his face with my palm. "I get it."

"Fai is a good man," Eren whispers. "He messed up, and he's suffered enough because of it. A son to him is the least I can be.

Otherwise, I may regret not taking this chance to make things right between us."

I pull away from Eren, not because I want to. It's because I need to see that this man sitting before me is real. This selfless, loving, gentle man. A man who knows how to forgive. A man who knows how to *live*.

I press my lips to his, then I pull him against me like I have no self-control. I thought I looked good in my dress, but Eren shows me it looks even better on the floor. Within seconds, his shirt joins my dress, then his pants.

I've known love to be many things.

Love is consistent.

Love is sacrifice.

Love is unconditional.

And love is *heavy*, which is why our kisses carry more weight than before. There's more on the line when love is involved, and Eren and I are willing to risk it all.

He makes me feel lighter than air when he picks me up and gently lays me back on my bed. My chest rises and falls with every breath I breathe for this man… the man who introduced me to the unknown.

While standing at the foot of the bed, Eren's eyes fixate on mine. "Don't move," he says softly.

I prop myself up on my elbows. "Why?"

"I just want to take a moment." His eyebrows draw apart. "To look at you."

"I don't think I've ever told you this, but I love the way you look at me."

He crawls over me, his smile inches from mine. "It might be my favorite thing to do besides love you."

Our bodies mold together as I feel his love in every which way.

Physically.

Mentally.

Emotionally.

Eren meets my desires by simply breathing the same air as me.

Eren feeds my addiction by simply lending me his touch.

Eren gives my life meaning by simply saying…

"I love you."

They're the only words I need to hear.

Like a song on repeat.

A song I'll replay for eternity.

♫ ♫ ♫

I wake up to a knock on my bedroom door. The room is pitch-black. I hear nothing but the sound of Eren's light snore. I rub my eyes awake, wondering if the knocking was something I dreamt. Until I hear it again.

KNOCK! KNOCK! KNOCK!

Shit.

The first thought that comes to mind is Eren lying asleep with me in my parents' home. The person at the door could be Mother or Father or both. I gently move out from under Eren's arm, then grab my robe and tiptoe to the door.

I slowly open the door to a drunk Jordan. A cold sweat comes over me. He reeks of tequila, his hair hanging messily over the sides of his face. His green eyes are bloodshot and he can hardly keep them open. His dress shirt is unbuttoned all the way down, a thin layer of sweat coating his forehead.

"I want to talk," he slurs.

I look back over my shoulder. Eren's silhouette is peacefully lying under the sheets.

"Go to bed," I command Jordan in a whisper.

When I push the door closed, Jordan stops it with his hand. His red eyes narrow. He clenches his jaw and drunkenly mutters, "Dream Team."

I try to force the door shut. He's already stepping into the room. I feel his hand against the back of my neck, forcing me toward his sweaty lips. I let out a whimper as Jordan yanks at my robe while forcing me against him.

"Jordan, stop."

The robe starts to tear until a shadow consumes the two of us. Jordan's hand releases me. I blink, and when I open my eyes, Eren is pinning Jordan's head against the wall with his forearm. He drives his fist across Jordan's cheek once, then a second time.

"You motherfucker," Eren growls, ready to throw a third punch.

Jordan suddenly dodges the third punch and wraps his arms around Eren, lifting him before forcing them both to the ground.

"Stop!" I whisper-shout. As much as I want to call for help, I'm afraid Mother and Father would be quick to assume Eren started the fight.

"You think she likes you?" Jordan hisses, pinning Eren to the ground. "You're a rebound, you fucking hobo. Harlow's only with you to get her parents' attention." He lifts his arm, but before he can punch Eren, I latch onto his fist. Jordan turns to me and shoves me against the foot of my bed. "You wait your turn, baby."

"You're a dead man," I hear Eren snarl.

I look up to see Eren palm the side of Jordan's face just before he drives it into my bedroom floor. With Eren now pinning Jordan to the ground, he shouts, "If you ever touch Harlow again, I'll—"

The bedroom lights flick on, and our attention is pulled to the man standing at the doorway.

"Get up." Father's voice sweeps the room. "Both of you, get the fuck up."

Chills run down my spine when I look back to see Eren on top of Jordan. One of Jordan's eyes is already swelling shut, his lips and teeth covered in blood as he flashes me a smirk before calling out to my Father.

"Mr. Beck! Is that you?" Jordan blurts out from under Eren. "This man just came in and attacked us."

Eren…? Attacked us…?

Eren lifts himself off of Jordan, attempting to wipe Jordan's blood onto his own sweatpants.

"That's not what happened at all!" I stand from the foot of the bed, my head swiveling between Father, Jordan, and Eren. "Jordan came in and tried to–"

Father lifts a finger, pointing it directly at Eren. "You come into my home, into my daughter's room, and resort to violence?!"

There is panic in Eren's eyes as if he's mortified by his own actions, though he shouldn't be.

"Eren was protecting me," I state, glaring at Father.

He examines the blood coating Eren's knuckles and Jordan's face. "It looks to me like *Jordan* is the one in need of protection."

My voice cracks as I plead, "Father, please let me explain. Jordan is the one who attacked us."

Father doesn't acknowledge a single word I say. I lower my head in sheer disappointment. Mother made it sound like there was hope for us. But in reality, Father has always been against me, and he always will be.

"I should have known something like this would happen if I allowed a criminal to stay in my home." Father takes out his phone, his eyes locked on Eren. "I'll let the police deal with you."

"*You're* the criminal," I whisper loud enough for my father to hear.

Father blinks at me. "Excuse me?"

"You're a bitter, hollow shell of a man." My voice rises with every word I spew out at him. "You're no father. A father would listen to his daughter. A father would want the best for his kids, but you don't! You can't even take your daughter's word for something that just happened in front of her own fucking eyes!"

Father's brows draw apart, and he lowers his phone to his side. Jameson appears in the doorway at the sound of my shouting. I don't stop. I hope I wake everybody up. I hope the entire house hears what I have to say to William Beck, the puppy dog who claims to be a wolf.

"How can you be okay with the way Jordan treated me?! How can you take his side and invite him into our home without asking me?! I'll tell you why. It's because you don't give a fuck about how I feel. You don't care about me. You don't care about Blake. You only care about what *you* want, and you just want us to be your puppets like everyone else in your world!"

"Harlow…" Eren tries to calm me down, but there's no stopping at this point.

"You're pushing us away," I continue, my words infused with resentment. "And we're gonna go far, far away. This is no family. We'll start our own family, Blake and Charlie included. We're gonna keep your grandkids away from you and this toxic place. And we'll be happier without you!"

There's a shift in Father's eyes, and he's no longer the wolf he claims to be. I finally see him for who he is. A man blinded by his own ego. A man who masks his insecurities with wealth and power.

There comes a time in every child's life when the godly form their parents have taken on is shattered. The child realizes that their parents are not perfect, but rather flawed. They're human. And it's in this realization that the child begins to see eye to eye with their parents, rather than relying on their parents' lens to see.

It's time to let go of the resentment I hold for my father. It's time to accept him for who he is because I can no longer live like this.

Jameson clears his throat before whispering, "Mr. Beck?"

Father doesn't take his defeated eyes off of me. "What is it, Jameson?"

Jameson takes two steps into the room, now standing at Father's side with an iPad. "I think you should take a look at this. It's footage from the surveillance camera at the end of the hall."

Father's eyes finally leave mine so that he can watch the footage. Jordan slowly stands to his feet, realizing Father is about to witness what actually happened. The room is silent. Eren gives me a reassuring nod. I finally feel myself relax.

After about 30 seconds, Father's eyes flick up to Jordan.

"Mr. Beck…" Jordan raises his palms. "I can explain."

Father takes a step forward. Naturally, everyone else takes a step back. "Jameson, notify the authorities of Jordan's actions."

Jameson immediately steps out of the room.

Father's face turns red as he closes the distance between Jordan and himself. He's fuming as he whispers, "You're fucking finished. After everything we've done for you, you dare disrespect my daughter–my own family–in my home."

Jordan's jaw drops, his bottom lip quivering in fear as Father continues. "I'll have you know that as a father, I want you dead. But I wouldn't be a good example to my family if I killed you here and now."

There's an audible gulping sound that comes from Jordan's throat. Eren and I shrink as Father's anger grows. "Get the fuck out," Father snarls. "Jameson! See to it that Jordan doesn't leave unless it's in the back of a police car. Do it before my anger gets the best of me."

Jordan slouches forward and wipes blood from his lip as he

steps around my father, then out of the room.

Father lowers his chin, and a shaky breath escapes him. He's not standing as tall as he usually does. He's wounded. And while I never thought this day would come, I actually feel bad for him.

He silently looks up, eyes flicking between Eren and me. For the first time, I notice the bags under his eyes and the wrinkles on his face. I see him for who he is, and he is *trying*. Maybe he's always tried, while Blake and I just never noticed.

"Are you okay?" he asks me softly.

I nod.

Father turns to Eren, then glances back at me without saying a word. The silence in the room is interrupted by the sound of his slippers against the wood floor as he slowly walks out. He places his hand on the door, and before closing it, he takes one last look at us.

He pinches his lips together and forces a smile. It reminds me of the moment I had with my mother in our backyard a week ago, when she gave me that awkward hug. It was difficult for her to be vulnerable with me, which means it must be infinitely harder for my father to do the same.

Regardless of what Father says or how he expresses his love, he was there for me tonight.

Mother was right when she said, *"There's a first for every-thing, especially when it comes to being parents."*

My parents are figuring it out.

And after what I just witnessed, I have hope that…

Father is on my side.

CHAPTER TWENTY-SEVEN

EREN

I wake up with Harlow in my arms.

In her room.

The room she grew up in.

And I can't help but wonder how I got here.

I don't understand how a guy like me can end up with a girl like her. I haven't done anything to deserve her besides suffer for most of my life. I suppose, in a weird way, suffering pays off. After all, all that suffering got me here.

I wish I could say that what happened last night was a dream. I feel bittersweet about it. Bitter, because I hate that I lost control of myself in front of Harlow. Sweet, because Jordan is now gone, and it seems like Harlow finally got through to her dad.

I haven't resorted to violence since I was a teenager. I can only pray that Harlow doesn't think I'm a violent man because I'm not. I guess I'm just a violent man when someone threatens Harlow. Either way, I don't regret doing what I did to Jordan last night.

Harlow makes a moaning sound, and I feel her stretching beneath the sheets. I smell the perfume on her neck, lingering from the night before. The silver flakes in her blue eyes reflect the morning sun as she looks up at me. "Good morning, rockstar," she whispers, rubbing her sleepy eyes.

"Morning, love."

She grazes my shoulder with her nails, gently running them down my arm. After a few blinks, her eyes widen at the sight of my pillow. "Is that blood?!"

I look down at the pillow to see a few drops of dried blood. I feel my neck and head for open cuts but find nothing.

Harlow sits up and reaches for my left ear. "It's in your ear, too. Are you hurt?"

I feel my ear and look down at my hand to see more dried blood. "That's weird. I feel fine."

After Harlow's dad left the room last night, I took a shower to get Jordan's blood off of me. I could've sworn I got it all.

"Jordan's blood," I say. "I must have still had it on my hand when I fell asleep without realizing it."

"I guess that makes sense."

"Do you think your dad is upset with me for what he walked in on?" I ask.

Harlow pecks me on the lips before saying, "If he were upset, he wouldn't have let you stay in my room."

I shrug. "Good point. What time do we need to head down?"

Harlow checks the time. "We should start getting ready. It's almost noon."

I give her one last kiss on the forehead before standing beside the bed. The room suddenly begins to sway. I feel a sharp pain on the side of my head, sharper than any pain I've ever felt. I press my hand against the pain and stutter a few steps before Harlow appears in front of me.

"Eren?"

How did she get here so fast?

"Eren, are you okay?"

The sharp pain becomes a throbbing, one more pronounced than the other headaches I've been getting. Harlow sits me on the edge of the bed. My headache becomes so severe, I need to shut my eyes.

"Eren, answer me." Harlow hands me a glass of water. "Do I need to call somebody?!"

I chug the water. "No, no. Don't."

Today is Blake's day. The last thing I need is for anything to be about me.

I take deep breaths, forcing myself to tolerate the pain. The throbbing finally lessens, and I'm able to open my eyes again.

"I think the pressure is getting to me," I admit. "Being here, meeting your parents, my fight with Jordan. I think I'm just processing it all."

I keep calm, but in reality, I have this gut feeling I need to see a doctor. I can't deny that these headaches have been getting worse. Ever since Montana, the sharp pains have grown more severe. Then again, I've gotten this far. I can get through one more day for Blake and Harlow.

Harlow rests her head on my shoulder. "We should just leave."

"We can't leave Blake. Especially on his birthday." I face her. "He's done so much for me. The *least* I can do is be there for him on his birthday." I press my forehead to hers. "It's just one more day. Then we ride west, wherever life's current takes us."

She pulls back, then nods. The hope in her eyes is all I need to get through today.

Just one more day.

We shower and get ready while blasting music on Harlow's speaker. I tuck my white dress shirt into my khaki pants, and before putting my jacket on, Harlow asks me to zip the back of her dress.

She holds her hair up, looking at me through the reflection.

"Should I tie it up?" she asks.

I zip up the back of her dress. "Either you let it down or show off your new tattoo." I smirk. "It's a win-win."

Harlow smiles and lets her hair down. When we finish getting ready, Fai meets us in the hallway.

"I had this weird dream William and I got into a fistfight," Fai whispers to me as Harlow knocks on Blake's door.

"Funny," I whisper back. "I did more fistfighting than I did dreaming last night."

Fai blinks at me just as Blake opens his door.

"HAPPY BIRTHDAY!" we shout.

"Thanks, guys," Blake groans as he walks out with Charlie. "I'm so hungover."

Blake and Charlie lead the way in their matching suits. Fai is in a gray suit, bringing out the gray in his tinted frames, while Harlow's champagne dress ties in perfectly with the suit I borrowed from Fai.

Jameson is the first to greet us at the bottom of the staircase. "Good morning, all! And happiest of birthdays to you, Mr. Blake."

"Thanks, Jameson." Blake's smile fades. "Do you think Mother and Father remembered?"

Jameson chuckles. "I would certainly hope so, Mr. Blake."

The group continues through the house while I stay a few steps behind with Jameson.

"Listen, Jameson. I want to thank you for coming to my rescue last night."

"For over 20 years, I've seen everything that happens in this house, Eren. From helping raise the children to taking out the trash. Don't thank me for rescuing you. Thank you for rescuing Ms. Harlow." He grins appreciatively, then gestures for me to catch up with the group.

We're guided through the kitchen, across the backyard terrace, and down to the white gala tent. The sky is a pure blue, and a cool breeze sweeps the spacious yard.

I'm nervous, which is probably why my head feels heavier than ever, as if my mind is carrying the weight of both Harlow's world and my own.

One more day, I remind myself.

There is nothing I want more than to be back in Miami with Fai, Harlow, Blake, and Charlie. Back on my motorcycle. Back to writing songs and picking the next town we'll ride to together this time.

We follow the various guests across the grass lawn. Blake suddenly pauses at the sight of portraits leading up to the tent's entrance. Each portrait is mounted on an easel, propped up for guests to see on their way into the tent structure. Guests gather around the portraits, all pictures of Blake as a kid.

We stop in front of a portrait. Blake must be a little over a year old in this one, his big blue googly eyes buried behind his chubby cheeks.

Harlow laughs. "It's scary how much you look like Charlie here."

Blake picks up Charlie and points at the portrait. "You see, Charlie? I had a big head, just like you."

The white tent stretches over a dance floor surrounded by round tables and a rectangular table just below a stage where a band is playing. The tables are decorated with white cloth, flowers, and scattered polaroid photos of Blake.

"They definitely remembered," Blake whispers, his eyes fixated on a colossal birthday banner hanging across the stage.

I catch Harlow getting teary-eyed watching Blake take in his surroundings. The amount of effort that has gone into this setup is surprising, given the history between Harlow, Blake, and their parents. I subtly urge Harlow to stand with Blake. She wraps her arms around him, and the two of them admire the setup together.

"A *Taylor 214c.e. Deluxe*," Fai whispers, pointing at one of the acoustic guitars on the stage. "One of my favorite guitars right there."

"You gonna get up there and play a song for Blake?" I tease.

"We should."

"*We*?!" My eyes widen. "I was kidding."

"I was, too. But I don't know." Fai lowers his head, eyeing me from over his glasses. "The thought is growing on me."

Fai and I wander to the seating chart near the stage. Names of guests are neatly written over the seating arrangements, and my eyes are pulled to our names written over the rectangular table by the stage.

"We're sitting with the Becks?"

Fai nods. "This should be fun."

I let out a nervous exhale as people make their way to their seats. The tent is now bustling with guests, most of them stopping to wish Blake a happy birthday.

"You ready, rockstar?" Harlow asks, taking my hand.

"Did you put Fai and me at your family's table?"

She peeks at our names on the display. "My parents must have done it."

Fai follows as Harlow pulls me in the direction of the table. My feet become blocks of cement when I see Mr. and Mrs. Beck standing behind the table, talking to Spud and Talia.

As we cross the dance floor, Blake and Charlie join us. The world slows down as I make eye contact with Mr. Beck. His hands are behind his back, chin held high, as he stares at my hand inter-twined with Harlow's.

Does last night need to be addressed?

Is there still tension between him and Fai?

How is this all going to play out?

I feel the sudden pressure building up in my skull again. I replace the pain with the courage to show Harlow's parents how much their daughter means to me. We finally reach the table, the silence between us louder than the surrounding conversations.

Fai suddenly steps forward. "William, I'm gonna come right out and say it." My body stiffens as he clears his throat. "I'm sorry for calling you a pompous jerk. I think you've raised two incredible kids, and I'm honored to be hosted by you and Claire."

Our heads all turn to Mr. Beck. We anxiously await his response to Fai's peace offering.

After a silent beat, Mr. Beck says, "Calling you a '*has-been*' was a pompous thing for a jerk like me to do." His piercing blue eyes pan from Fai to Harlow and Blake. "It's among the many other things I'm sorry for."

Mr. Beck averts his eyes from the group, acting as though saying what he just said was easy for him to do. But it couldn't be more obvious how difficult it was for him. It also couldn't be more obvious who his apology is really for.

Blake sits at the head of the table, while Charlie, Fai, Harlow, and I are to sit directly across from Mr. Beck, Mrs. Beck, Talia, and Spud. At the opposite end of the table, there is an open seat, one I assume was for Jordan.

Mr. Beck remains standing as the group sits. "Eren, may I have a word?"

I'm reluctant to stand, my nerves getting the best of me. With his hands still behind his back, Mr. Beck turns out of the tent and begins walking across the grass. I look down at Harlow and Blake, who seem to be just as confused as me.

"Are you coming?" Mr. Beck calls from a distance.

I adjust my jacket and join him out on the grass. His linen suit is a pastel-blue, tying into the colors of the ocean beyond the edge of the lawn. I take as many deep breaths as I can, considering they could be my last if this conversation goes south.

Mr. Beck doesn't look my way when I step up to his right. He remains fixated on the shore. We stand shoulder to shoulder. Silent. Still.

"Has she been with you?" he asks, his tone tough to read.

"*Been with me?*"

"The past few weeks. Has she been staying with you?" Mr. Beck lifts his chin and takes a deep breath, bracing himself for my answer.

I keep my answer short, afraid that he could get me to over-share. "Yes."

"Is she… happy?" he asks.

I turn to face him with my lips pressed together. His question seems complex but also simple. So, I simply answer, "Yes."

Mr. Beck nods, his eyes now glossy. I look over my shoulder to see guests eating their food as the band plays, unaware of the intensity of this moment.

"I've always known that there is a side of my children I can't relate to–the 'music' side," he says disheartedly. "I was afraid to let them embrace it because I know nothing about it. And if they pursue something I know nothing about, then I'll lose them."

"Forgive me for offering an opinion here." I jam my hands in my pockets, my eyes hovering over the shore. "But I think that you trying to keep them close is actually what's pushing them away." I brace myself for his interjection. He nods for me to continue. "You don't have to know music to support them. I think you just have to be *present*."

Mr. Beck wipes his eyes. "Present?"

I picture Fai and what his presence in my life has led to. It doesn't matter how long he's been in my life. It doesn't matter how much money he gives me or how well this album does. All that matters is that he showed up. Fai is *present*.

"Yeah, be present. Instead of putting down their passion for music, maybe find out *why* they're passionate about music. You don't have to be interested in it, but it might help to know why your kids are interested."

Mr. Beck turns to face me, his eyes meeting mine. "Do you have a good relationship with your father?"

"I didn't have a relationship with him at all." I look back at the tent to see Fai making the group laugh. "But I do now because he's present in my life." I pause for a moment, then give Mr. Beck a half-glance. "If you don't mind me asking, sir. Why are you talking to me and not your kids?"

Mr. Beck laughs under his breath. "Being a father is the most difficult job I've ever had, Eren. It makes working on Wall Street seem like a hobby. When you're in my position, people don't give you advice, so I'm forced to make decisions for myself. And I've made some shitty decisions. I suppose I'm talking to you first to gauge how I should go about talking to them."

Seeing how hard it is for Mr. Beck to open up to his kids is actually helping me better understand my relationship with Fai. Like Fai, Mr. Beck has everything on the outside—the house, money, and successful career. But on the inside, they have no idea how to be fathers. But they're both trying. And that might be all that really matters at this point.

"I think they'll hear you out," I say. "If you're open and honest with them like you are with me."

"Thank you," Mr. Beck exhales, then places a warm hand on my shoulder. "I'll talk to them." He smiles. "I look forward to getting to know you, Eren. But I'll have to return you to my daughter now. I feel her burning a hole in my cheek for stealing you away."

The two of us face the tent, meeting eyes with Harlow. She quickly looks away, pretending to be involved in the group's conversation.

We return to the table, and when I sit, Harlow whispers, "How bad was that?"

I take off my jacket and hang it on my seat. "Surprisingly, not bad at all," I whisper, still processing what just happened. "But it's not really for me to talk about, out of respect for your dad."

Harlow glances across the table at Mr. Beck, who flashes a subtle smile. Harlow smiles back, and there is a shift in the air. It's not an obvious shift by any means, but it's there. The shift makes itself known when Mr. Beck says, "Blake, tell me about this album."

Mrs. Beck places a gentle hand over Mr. Beck's.

"Th-the album?" Blake glances at his dad for a moment before saying, "It's… uh… eight songs. Harlow and Eren wrote it for Fai to release."

Mr. Beck waits a beat before asking, "When will we get to hear?"

Blake pinches his eyebrows together. "Y-you want to hear the album?"

Mr. Beck's eyes flick to mine. I give a subtle nod.

"Yes," he says. "I want to hear it."

"Why don't we play a song for you now?" Fai asks. The mere sound of his voice lifts the mood.

Mr. Beck smirks before whispering something to Mrs. Beck. The two of them stand and make their way to the side of the stage.

"What the hell did you say to my father?!" Harlow whispers to me.

I shrug, flashing a smirk. "You'll find out sooner or later."

My eyes pan around the crowd of nearly a hundred people, all strangers. I lean toward Fai. "I've never performed in front of this many people."

He raises a brow. "What did I tell you?"

"Best way to get over my fear of performing is to forget I'm even performing at all."

"Thatta kid. And by now, you should know that performing is in your blood."

I suck in a quick breath.

You can do this, I think to myself. *You can fucking do this.*

As the band finishes their song, Mr. and Mrs. Beck take the stage.

"Good afternoon, all." Mr. Beck's voice is thunderous through the surround-sound speakers. "Claire and I are happy to have you here as we celebrate Blake's 30th birthday. As you all know, I can give speeches all day long, but today isn't about me. It's about my son." He smiles in our direction. "Now, some people are defined by their success, others by their looks or their passions. If there is one thing I've learned, it's that I wish to be defined by being a father. Claire and I are proud of you, Blake. And we're sorry for not being the best at showing it." Mr. Beck raises his champagne glass, eyes fixated on Blake and Harlow. "Here is to 30 years of *you*."

The crowd raises their glasses in Blake's direction. Blake smiles, raising his glass toward his parents and then the crowd.

After taking a sip, Mr. Beck continues. "For 10 years, Blake has worked in the music industry, which, as you can most likely predict, I know very little about, given the fact I'm tone-deaf and have two left feet."

The crowd chuckles.

"This may come as a shocker to you all, but I don't have a creative bone in my body. Thankfully, my children aren't like me. I'm a numbers-guy. I see the world in black and white. Blake and Harlow see it in all kinds of colors, which is a beautiful thing. It's recently come to my attention that my children are putting together an album for an artist you may know. An artist who goes by '*Fai*.'" The crowd whispers excitedly at the mention of Fai, who casually lifts his glass. "If you would do us the honor of playing a song…"

The crowd's eyes light up, and an applause fills the massive tent. A hand lifts me from my chair, and I turn to Harlow and Blake. "Go! Go! Go!" they shout over clapping hands.

Fai and I stand and make our way to the stage.

Mr. Beck raises a hand to introduce us. My eyes meet his one last time. "Thank you," I say softly before addressing Fai. "Which guitar do you want?"

"I'll take the Taylor," he says with a smirk.

I pick up another guitar. "How are we supposed to play without having rehearsed?"

"Just play like you did in the warehouse, kid. I'll fill in where I need to."

I wrap the guitar strap over my shoulder, thinking once I hold the guitar, my stage fright will subside. And for once, it does. My fingers graze the gloss-coated wooden neck and the guitar pick molds to my fingertips. When I turn to face the microphone, I become one with it.

This finally feels right.

I grab the mic and bring it close to my lips. The crowd anxiously waits for us to start. It's nearly impossible for me to envision myself in Fai's pitch-black warehouse, considering I'm standing on a stage in broad daylight. Before I can let it get to me, my eyes land on Harlow. She gives me the strength I need, the same way she did at the bar back in Montana.

I close my eyes and strum, the sound of my guitar becoming one with the moment. I get chills when I hear Fai's–my *father's*–guitar making itself known behind mine.

I start where the album starts. From the very beginning.

The righting of Fai's wrongs…

Written by Harlow and me.

The crowd erupts when I finish singing the final note. Tears well up in my eyes as Fai throws his arm around me. "Your mother would be proud."

The moment I walk off the stage, my head feels like it's on the verge of imploding, the pressure becoming too much to bear. I try to suppress the throbbing as Blake and Harlow embrace me.

I sit, and Harlow kisses me, but I don't feel it. She says, "We wrote that," but I hardly hear it. I'm reading her lips, the heartbeat in my head consuming me whole. I force a smirk, trying to downplay my pain like the other times before. As much as I want to enjoy this moment, it quickly becomes impossible to.

The smile on Harlow's face fades as she pulls her right palm from my left ear.

Blood.

Harlow's face flushes.

I blink, and suddenly Harlow is standing over me.

I blink again, and a man is telling me to stay awake.

I want to stay awake. I want to enjoy this moment with the love of my life, my father, and my best friend. But I can't. Because my world goes black.

CHAPTER TWENTY-EIGHT

HARLOW

My world collapses when I see Eren collapse in front of me. Within seconds, a man from a nearby table came running, calmly stating he's a doctor.

"What's happening?!" I ask the doctor crouching over an unconscious Eren.

Fai drops to his knees next to the doctor. "Eren?" his voice cracks. "Stay with me, kid."

Guests silently stand over each other to stare at Eren, and it makes me angry to see them just stare. All they've ever done is stare at him.

I'm ready to demand that they look away, but a hand grabs mine. The hand belongs to my mother, who whispers, "Calm, Harlow. Be calm."

"JAMESON!" Father shouts. "CALL–"

"An air ambulance is on the way!" Jameson shouts back. He carries Charlie out of the tent.

The doctor crouching over Eren lowers his head. "Seems to be a hemorrhage," he states. "Did he hit his head recently?"

My body goes numb.

Hit his head? Recently? How recent?

"Harlow, answer him," Blake says.

I run through memories of the past couple of weeks in Montana and Miami, trying to remember when Eren could have hit his head.

Montana.

There was the night in Montana.

We rode into town together on the motorcycle.

The motorcycle.

THE ACCIDENT.

I try to gather my thoughts, remembering what Eren told me back in Montana. "Th-there was a motorcycle accident that Eren mentioned," my voice trembles. "He said that he ruined his motorcycle. That he hit a log." I shake my head. "But he was fine! He said he was fine."

"When was this accident?" the doctor asks, his voice sharp.

Panic brews within me as I try to think straight. "A couple weeks ago? I don't know exactly."

Fai flashes me a half-glance over his shoulder. "She's right," he says. "Last week, Eren said something about wanting a new motorcycle. He must have totaled his last one in the accident."

"The brain can hemorrhage weeks after a traumatic head injury," the doctor says, keeping his palm pressed along the side of Eren's head. "It's possible that Eren was in a severe state of shock that allowed him to overlook his injury."

Blake lowers his head, his lip quivering. "How the fuck did we miss it?"

How did I miss it?

Tears fall when I look back down at Eren. His eyes are shut, his lips parted. You would think he's peacefully asleep if there wasn't a trail of blood dripping from his ear.

Open your eyes, Eren. Just open your eyes and look at me

the way you always do.

I begin to hate myself for missing the signs. For being so close to him the past weeks and not realizing. For failing to see that his brain was slowly giving way this entire time, a ticking time-bomb counting down what might be his final moments.

Father steps around us, facing the crowd. "EVERYONE, PLEASE." He lifts a hand toward the house. "PLEASE GO BACK INTO THE HOUSE."

"You should go," I tell Talia.

"We're staying here with you," she snaps.

Spud nods. "We both are."

Fai shakes his head, removing his glasses to wipe his tears. "Eren's been complaining about these headaches he's been getting." He lowers himself over Eren and whispers, "Dammit, son. Don't you dare beat me to your mother. You've got so much ahead of you. Please."

Napkins and party decor fly across the gala tent as Father waves up to the sky. A helicopter lowers itself onto the lawn, and two medics hop down from the aircraft. We make room for them to kneel over Eren. After exchanging a few words with the doctor, they lift Eren onto a gurney and wheel him to the helicopter.

I stand frozen, watching Eren's body wheeled across the lawn. I feel myself becoming detached from the present moment. The roaring propellers become muffled, the panicked voices around me completely muted. I'm watching my world be lifted into the back of a medical helicopter.

Eren's voice plays in my mind, clear as day… *"There's always a catch."*

Maybe Eren was right. Minutes ago, I had it all.

My family.

My music.

My love.

Is losing Eren my "catch?"

Blake steps into my line of sight, the vein in his neck pulsing as he shouts something at me. The muffled noises gradually become understandable again as I reattach myself to the present.

"Francis has a car ready for us, Harlow! Let's go!" Blake shouts over the roaring propellers.

He turns me, and we run to the front of the house. Before reaching the inside, I look back one last time to see the helicopter lifting itself into the sky.

"Eren," Father says sternly into his phone as we run down the front steps. "E-R-E-N. He is on his way now. Give him the best of whatever the fuck he needs. By order of William Beck."

Francis is patiently standing next to an S.U.V. with all of the doors already open. Father sits in the passenger's seat as Fai, Blake, Mother, and I funnel into the back. Mother and I sit with our backs to the front seats while Blake and Fai sit facing us.

"A police escort to N.Y.U. Langone Hospital has been arranged, per Jameson's request," Francis says as he climbs into the driver's seat.

The group remains silent as Francis starts down the gravel driveway. I watch the dust rise between us and the house as we drive onto the road, where four motor officers are waiting. Their sirens flood the streets as two officers pull ahead of our S.U.V. and two ride closely behind.

When our car pulls onto the highway, Francis asks, "Was it a guest that has been sent to the hospital?"

With my head pressed against my headrest, I mutter, "It's Eren."

I notice Francis straighten his posture in my peripherals, remembering Eren. "Seat belts, please," he says sternly. The car suddenly jolts forward, picking up speed.

The road is entirely ours as cars pull over on both sides. I watch people turn their heads, curiously watching our procession make its way into the city.

The silence forces me to think about what I could've done to save Eren–to keep him from getting into that accident.

Maybe if I never left Montana the first time...

If I would've kissed him the night we rode into town...

If I would've chosen him over Jordan like my heart was telling me to...

Then Eren wouldn't be fighting for his life right now.

"Harlow, stop," Blake says as if reading my mind. His fingers are laced in his lap, his leg shaking up and down. "He's gonna be alright."

My palm muffles my words as I whisper, "I shouldn't have left. If I would've stayed in Montana with Eren, he never would've crashed."

"You don't know that." Blake's eyes narrow at me. "You can't blame yourself for something that's out of your control."

"How can I not be to blame?" I hiss. Blake closes his eyes, wincing at every word that comes out of my mouth. "It's *my* fault that I left him alone out there. It's *my* fault that I didn't think much of the blood on his pillow this morning. It's *my* fault–"

"Shut up!" Blake leans forward. "I blamed myself for not catching the cancer that killed Miranda soon enough, and it's that blame that has been slowly killing me since. I would think that you spent enough time with Eren to learn that life can be real fucking cruel and unfair. He can't control that he has a deadbeat father, his mother killed herself, and he was abused as a teenager."

Fai lowers his head as Blake continues. "Eren still found the good in a world that was cruel to him because he would let go of what he couldn't control. This is all out of your control. So, stop blaming yourself. Let go."

I lower my head.

Life really is cruel and unfair.

It feels like just yesterday I was standing next to Eren in Fai's backyard. We were watching the current pull at the water when he said it's time for me to trust life, to trust that whatever happens will happen, to trust the current.

My eyes meet Blake's once more, and despite the tears falling from our eyes and the injustices unraveling before us… I accept that this is all out of my control.

♫ ♫ ♫

The waiting room is cold, judging by both the look and feel of it. The fluorescent lights and the gray walls, chairs, and floor. It grows colder by the hour. It's been an entire afternoon of Father pacing around the room, calling for second, third, and fourth opinions from surgeons… Mother giving me her shoulder to cry on… and Blake and Fai staring blankly at the ground between us.

We all stand as a surgeon steps into the room wearing his scrubs. The surgeon takes one last look over the clipboard, then addresses the group. "A few hours ago, we performed an emergency procedure on the bleeding in Eren's brain. We were able to relieve some of that pressure in the skull."

Eren? Emergency procedure? Bleeding in his brain?

I feel my consciousness begin to remove itself from the moment as I process the severity of the situation. But I'm pulled from my trance when I hear the doctor say, "He is stable for now. But we're not sure how much longer he'll be in this state before we need to go back in to operate."

I shutter at the doctor's words. "*Not sure how much longer.*"

Father gets in the surgeon's face, drilling him with questions. "So, what's your plan of action? Who's looking after him right now?"

The surgeon raises a hand. "Sir, please. If we're going to let you see your son before the next surgery, you'll need to be as calm as possible."

Father cocks his head back. "I'm not his father."

"I am," Fai says.

Blake pinches his eyebrows together as he watches Fai step forward. Fai places a hand on my father's shoulder, prompting Father to take a step back.

"Word it simply, Doc. How's he looking?" Fai asks. He removes his glasses and hardens his jaw.

The surgeon's eyes pan around the room. They meet Fai's again as he says, "The next procedure will be a very extensive, very dangerous surgery. Had we caught the bleeding sooner–"

"How's… he… looking?" Fai asks again, remaining calm somehow.

The surgeon lowers his head and sighs. "I would make the most of the remaining time you have with him. And I would do it now."

I always thought the term "heartbreak" was a mere expression. Hearts don't actually break. Or at least, that's what I thought since I was a kid. But I feel it here and now. I feel my heart not just break, but I feel it shatter into a million pieces. I feel what's inside my chest pour onto the floor. It stains our clothes and shoes. It stains everything that ceases to matter when the world is ending.

Father catches a glimpse of the brokenness behind my eyes. He turns to the surgeon. "Aren't you a fucking doctor?! There has to be a way. We have the money. We'll pay for anything. We'll fly in the best surgeon, or we'll fly Eren to the best hospital."

"Eren won't make it to the next hospital before this next procedure," the surgeon says sternly. "You can come in one at a time to speak to him before we operate," he adds. "We don't want to overwhelm him while he's in this fragile state."

There's a moment of silence until Fai turns back to me. "You go first, kid. He'll be excited to see you."

I nod, then follow the surgeon through the double doors and up the hall. The bottoms of our feet click against the tile floor among the sounds of beeping machines and whispering nurses.

I've never been in a hospital, and it dawns on me how cushioned my life has been until now. My heart has never been broken. I've never lost a loved one. Loss itself is foreign to me, and I wish I had more time before I'm forced to get to know it.

The surgeon comes to a stop in front of a door, and upon opening it, he gestures for me to enter the room. I take a deep breath as if it will prepare me for what I'm about to see. Deep down, I know that it won't.

There is a man lying in a hospital bed. His head is heavily bandaged. Tattoos cover his skin, from the top of his neck to his fingertips that rest over the hospital bed's blanket. The dim fluorescent lights illuminate his deep-brown eyes–eyes happy to see me.

The man is full of life, despite his life-threatening condition. He smiles up at me and slowly lifts a hand.

"Hey, rockstar," I whisper to the man in front of me.

"New place, new look," Eren says, forcing a smirk. His voice is so fragile that it dissolves the moment it reaches the air between us.

I pull up a chair and set it next to his bed. I hold his hand, my eyes fixating on his with the same intensity as every time before.

"How are you feeling?" I whisper. It's the most my voice will give.

"Believe it or not, I've felt better," he teases.

He squeezes my hand, somehow getting me to smile amidst our suffering.

"How can you joke right now?" I ask, forcing back tears.

Eren's eyes flick up to the ceiling as he ponders an answer.

"Do you know what death is?" he asks.

I shake my head. "No, I don't."

"Exactly. It's the unknown. The greatest unknown. I would be a fool to get you to take leaps while being too afraid to take my own." He tightens his grip around my hand. "I've lived a wild life, and for most of it, I didn't understand how I just kept living." He lowers his head and lets out a deep breath. "I was trying to outrun my vices, and they just caught up to me, like they did my Mom. But they caught up to me after you gave me the chance to right my wrongs. And I love you for that."

I avert my eyes from him because I don't know how to respond or how to feel. It almost feels inhuman for Eren to be so okay with potentially dying, for leaving me behind while he goes on his next adventure. I've never known pain like this.

"You're gonna be alright," I assure him out of sheer hope. "Say that you're gonna be alright."

Eren's gaze softens, and he pinches his lips together.

"Say it," my voice trembles and rises at the same time. "I need to hear you say that you're gonna come out of this okay. It's just too sudden. And you're too good of a person for this to happen to. It's not fair."

"Life's never been fair to me. If anything, it's been cruel until it gave me you. Life doesn't owe me anything, Harlow. Which is why every day I've lived has been a blessing."

I release a defeated sigh. Eren thumbs a tear from my cheek as he continues. "I realized that since the moment I met you, my life was no longer about me. I wanted you to chase your dream. I wanted to make you the best version of yourself. It's what you did for me, and as time went on, it's all I wanted for you. I wanted to give you my best."

"But what about the album?"

Eren smiles. "Have Blake represent you as a songwriter. Use

this album to get the next project and the next one after that. This is your dream. I got you the farthest I could. Blake and Fai will help with the rest."

I let out a shaky breath, feeling the reality of it all set in. "The album needs a name," I say softly.

Eren looks around the room. He suddenly smiles, and there is a gleam in his eye when he says, "*Write My Wrongs.*" He sits up. "Like writing our wrongs. It's our story written through our lyrics. You overcame your fear of taking on the unknown. I overcame living a life without attachments. And Fai made up for time lost by bringing us together."

Write My Wrongs.

I get chills when I hear it.

It's catchy.

It's witty.

It's true.

We corrected the way we were living our lives. And we have eight songs to show for that.

"Write My Wrongs," I whisper. "I love it."

There's a knock at the door, and I turn to see Fai. "Sorry to interrupt. Doc said we're short on time. Do you mind if I…?" His voice cuts out.

I force a smile and nod. As much as I want Eren all to myself, I'll have to accept that there are other people who love him almost as much as I do. My hand tightens around Eren's. I stand to my feet, and my lips meet his once more, a kiss that may very well be our last, though I hope with everything in me that it isn't.

"I love you," Eren says. "Thank you for making my life one worth living."

I let out a quivering breath. It takes all my strength to stand, but I somehow manage.

I speak the words I feel with every ounce of my being…

"I love you, rockstar."

CHAPTER TWENTY-NINE

EREN

When Harlow walks out of the room, I can no longer suppress my tears. I'm angry at myself for literally driving myself to my breaking point. And I'm angry at Death for being impatient with me.

I want to ask Death…

Why now?

Why when I'm the happiest?

Why when I finally have it all?

Fai exhales a deep breath as he sits where Harlow sat. He crosses one leg over the other and tilts his head toward me. I can hardly see his eyes behind his fogged-up lenses. His bottom lip trembles, and we both break into tears.

"I'm scared, Fai," I say softly. "I think I kept it together well enough for Harlow, but I'm scared as shit."

Fai wipes at his tears. "It's okay to be scared, kid. I was scared when I first got diagnosed."

"How did you deal with it?"

"I prayed for strength," he says sternly.

"Strength to fight cancer?"

"I thought that's what I was praying for. Instead, God gave

me something better. He gave me the strength to meet *you*."

A pressure makes itself known in my head, making it difficult for me to keep my eyes open.

"I would always see you praying before we eat," I murmur. "You think you can pray with me before my surgery?"

Fai places a shaky hand over his mouth. Tears fall below his glasses as I hold his gaze. "Of course," he whispers.

I've never actually prayed, and I didn't see myself praying anytime soon. But your perspective changes a bit when you're practically lying on your deathbed. I've submitted myself to life's current for as long as I can remember. I suppose submitting myself to God can't be much different.

Fai places his hand on mine, and we bow our heads.

"Hey, God." Fai's voice is shaky until he takes a deep breath and exhales. "S-so, I… I want to thank you… for the wild ride it's been. I'm here with my boy, the gift you gave me 28 years ago. The gift I never knew until you gave me the strength to receive it. That's what we're here looking for right now, God. Strength. A while back, I came to you looking for strength. You helped me find it, but not in the way I expected. So, now, I come to you with my son, Eren. And I ask that you give him the strength to submit himself to whatever it is you have planned for him. It's up to y–" Fai's voice gives out like his words don't want to leave his lips. He clears his throat and continues. "It's up to *you*, not us. Selfishly, we want Eren here with us. Look, regardless of what should come of this, please be good to my boy." His eyes meet mine. "Amen."

"Amen. Thank you, Fai." I tighten my grip on his hand, feeling slightly more prepared for whatever is coming my way. "I need a favor."

"Anything."

"Harlow wrote the album. Make sure she gets credit for it. We want to call it '*Write My Wrongs*.' It's inspired by the three of us coming together through the songs we wrote and how we fixed the way we've lived our lives."

"I love it." Fai smirks. "Consider it done." I feel a sudden reluctance in the way he holds my hand. "I know Blake wants to get in here before your next surgery. I'll see you soon, kid. I want you to know that you and your mom are all I've looked forward to."

"Wait." I wince at a sudden pinch in my skull. My eyes meet his one last time. "Love you."

"Love you, kid."

Fai slowly backs out of the room. Within seconds, Blake throws the door open. He takes a few steps in with his hands in his pockets.

"You're on my shit-list, Eren," he says, forcing a grin below his tear-filled eyes. He sits at the edge of the bed, giving me a half-glance. "New place, new look?"

I laugh under my breath. "Listen, man. I'm sorry that I was so distant for so long. I–"

"Shh," Blake shushes me with a finger raised. "You can apologize to me after the surgery."

"Blake…" My smile slowly fades. "Make sure Harlow keeps writing. I told her you would represent her and that this album is hers."

"Eren, come on. You're gonna be fine."

"Promise me you'll make sure she keeps writing."

"You can make sure yourself when you–"

"Blake!" I shut my eyes at the sudden pain in my head. "Promise me, dammit."

Blake purses his lips before muttering, "I promise."

"And promise me that you'll sign her, and she'll use this album to get her next project."

"I promise."

I smile between sniffles. "Your kid is gonna be a star, you

know."

"Why? Because he has a big head?"

We laugh.

"Well, there's that. Most importantly, he has it. The charisma. Charlie is always brightening everybody's day. Whatever it is that stars have, he has it."

Blake sniffles. "I love you, man."

I offer him my hand, which he takes in an instant.

"Love you."

The moment Blake leaves, doctors and nurses begin prepping me for surgery. I hear them mumbling medical phrases that might as well be a foreign language. I never thought I would end up here, but I suppose that's the point. We never truly have life figured out. We don't know where we're going or where we'll end up.

We're just following the current.

The pressure in my head builds as my bed reclines so that I'm now facing the ceiling. I hear mumbling amongst the nurses and there's a slight pinch in my forearm. The ceiling gets brighter and brighter until it's so bright that it blinds me.

When the light fades, I'm no longer in the hospital.

I see my mom sitting in the front seat of her car, the windows rolled down. I see her dark-brown hair blowing in the wind. She sings to the music. It blasts in and around the car as we claim the open road ahead. I look at the trees stretching over us as I sing the words with her. She looks in the rearview mirror and shouts, "Sing it, baby! Sing it!" I sing like Mom said to, and I could see her loving me for it.

I stick my hand out the window, feeling the breeze force it back as we drive forward. The roaring sound of a motorcycle builds until it's blaring right outside my window. I look up, and at the edge of my fingertips, I see a girl riding my motorcycle, her wavy auburn hair blowing in the wind. She looks right at me, her piercing blue eyes meeting mine.

Harlow.

With one hand on the grip, she offers me the other, *but I can't reach it.*

"Eren?" Mom calls from the front seat. My eyes lock onto Mom's eyes through the rearview mirror. She's concerned. "Sing it, baby!" she shouts, turning up the music.

My eyes are pulled to the road ahead, soon to split in two. Harlow will go one way while Mom goes the other. There's a sense of urgency in both Mom and Harlow's eyes as we near the fork in the road.

Choose.

My head grows light, heart now racing.

Mom's eyebrows draw apart. She sees where my heart lies.

I look left once more.

Harlow rides closer to the car, *her hand now in reach.*

CHAPTER THIRTY

HARLOW

"Take my hand," I tell Blake as he paces around the waiting room. "You should sit."

"How can you sit still right now?" he asks, avoiding eye contact.

"Like you said on the way here, '*it's out of our control.*'"

Blake stops pacing and sits down next to me. "The last time I was at this hospital was with Miranda."

I take his hand, now holding it in my lap. For the first time in the hour we've been waiting here, Father is sitting. Mother rests her shoulder against his as he stares at Blake's hand in my lap.

I ran out of tears to cry within minutes of leaving Eren. I'm clinging on to remnants of hope in my heart... hope that somebody in scrubs will walk back into the waiting room to tell us Eren made it.

"I always thought I was doing the right thing," Father says, breaking the silence. With his fingers laced in his lap, his eyes bounce between Blake and me. "Everything I did as a father. I meant for it to be in the best interest of you two. But in reality, I think it was only in the best interest of myself."

Blake silently stares at Father for a few beats. "You never

supported me, you know," he finally says, removing his hand from my lap. "You laughed when I told you I wanted to be in the music industry. Even after Miranda died, I never heard from you or Mother. I was grieving, and you two acted like she meant nothing to me. Be honest. You never liked her. You never wanted her around to begin with."

"We thought she was taking you from us." Father's jaw tightens. "And we weren't ready to lose you. Your mother and I wanted you two to be secure, and we always thought that meant keeping you close. The truth is, we don't know what's best for you. *You* know what's best for you. I buried myself in my work because I was too afraid of failing at being a father. Little did I know, burying myself in my work was one of the reasons I failed you. And I'm sorry."

Fai sniffles from the corner of the room, making his presence known. His dress shirt is half-open and untucked as he sprawls himself on his seat. With his tinted lenses, it's tough to tell where he's looking as he chimes in. "I chose work over Eren. Took me 28 years to finally try to make up for it. As parents, we can only hope that our kids forgive us for having wronged them."

Father's eyes fall from Fai to his own lap.

I never viewed my relationship with Father through his perspective. I never understood how difficult it is to be a parent and how every little thing you do can have a make-or-break impact on your child.

In my case, built-up resentment all these years.

In Eren's case, distancing himself from relationships and responsibilities.

Both cases are consequences of our broken relationships with our parents.

"I forgive you," Blake says to Mother and Father. "I'm tired of resenting you both. I'm tired of holding on to this anger and bitterness. And I'm ready to be a family. A real family."

"*We* forgive you," I add. "And I'm ready for the same."

It takes a lot to be as successful as William Beck, but it takes even more for William Beck to admit that seeking out success wasn't in the best interest of his family.

Fai slowly stands and places a gentle hand on Father's shoulder. "William, you have a lot of nice things, but the one thing I'm envious of is your family still being together."

"Fai, I had no idea you're Eren's dad," Blake says as Fai takes a seat next to Father. "Did you know when you reached out to us?"

"I've known for Eren's entire life." Fai sighs. "I was on a country-wide tour when I met and fell in love with his mom, Addison… Addison Adkins. She had the most beautiful voice you ever heard."

He strokes his goatee, looking up toward the ceiling as if he sees the memory of her playing before him. "Addy had this fire burning within her, and you could see it. Hell, you could feel it when she was on stage with me. She was one of my backup singers, but I knew she would be so much more. She knew it, too.

"We lived this life on the road, traveling by day, then performing and partying by night. I was young at the time, in my early twenties and so was she. One night, right before a show, she fell ill. I had known something was off about her and she knew it, too. She was pregnant with Eren. I told her to take time away from the tour to decide whether or not to have him."

"You didn't want her to have him," Blake interjects, his words coming across as more of a statement rather than a question.

"I was a kid. I didn't know what I wanted other than being a rockstar," Fai continues. "I spent my entire life on a stage, always rehearsing, always practicing. It all turned into fame before I was even old enough to drive. That takes a toll on a kid who never had a childhood. Regardless, I was madly in love with Eren's mom. I just wasn't in a good place with my addictions–my vices.

"Addy took time off the tour. Word got out, and my manager came to me one day, telling me that raising a child would ruin my image and my entire career, which was all I had. My love for Addy wasn't enough to get me to clean up my act and even she knew that. Which is why I'm convinced she went through with having Eren."

Fai releases a quivering breath, preparing himself for the following words. "Addy had Eren because she knew he would save me from myself. My career was taking off at the time, which made it easier for me to bury the responsibility with fame, drugs, and alcohol, while my manager cut checks to Addy that she refused to take.

"She would write to me. She told me when Eren took his first steps, that he was singing my songs, that he has my voice. But my addictions only got worse, so I kept my distance. I became this clout-chasing narcissist. I didn't think I could ever be the father Eren deserved. It wasn't until months ago that I was diagnosed with stage four. As terrible as it sounds, I'm grateful I was diagnosed because that gave me the courage to reach out to my boy."

The room falls more silent than silence itself. When you look at Fai, you see a charismatic man with a successful past. But after hearing him speak, you only see a man longing for forgiveness from his son, who is fighting for his life at the end of the hall.

Eren was right when he told me that there is so much more out there than just the world I came from, each person dealing with the phenomenon that is life.

There are people out there who are falling in love.

There are people out there who are hurting.

There are people out there living their best lives.

And there are people in here dying.

Who was I to think that I was in complete control of life itself?

Who was I to think that I was in control of something so harsh, yet delicate?

So unfair, yet just.

So complicated, yet simple.

This "*life*."

It comes at us in waves, and we can only hope to stay afloat.

It shakes us like an earthquake, and we can only hope to be strong enough to hold on.

Regardless of how life gives, takes, tosses, turns, ebbs, and flows… we go where it takes us. We do what it commands.

And while I can't control what happens next, I can pray for the strength to take it on… for the strength to submit myself to life's constant current... to the *unknown*.

CHAPTER THIRTY-ONE

EREN
(6 MONTHS LATER)

"You ready, rockstar?!" Harlow shouts from the driveway.

"Almost," I reply, making my way down the front steps with Mr. Beck. "I'm telling you, sir. Charlie is bound to be a guitar player. Just look at his little fingers!"

"Nonsense," Mr. Beck scoffs. "My grandson was born to play the drums. Look at how beefy his little arms are."

"Please stop looking at my kid," Blake says, tossing his bags into the car trunk. "I think Charlie should be the one deciding what instrument he's gonna learn to play."

"Blake has a point," Harlow chimes in, placing our bags in the trunk next to Blake's. "Also, Charlie doesn't need three dads. Blake is already more than enough of one."

"Thanks, winner," Blake says to Harlow before strapping Charlie into his car seat.

Harlow smirks. "You're welcome, loser."

Mr. Beck lifts his hands in surrender as I lunge forward and sweep Harlow off her feet. I twirl her in a circle, melting at the gleam in her ocean eyes when they fixate on mine. Today marks six months since my surgery, which means I'm finally clear to travel. I should know because I've had this day marked on my calendar since my recovery began.

Facing death like I did six months ago will teach you a whole lot, one of the most important lessons being cherishing every day like it's your last. It's one thing to say it, and it's another to feel it. I feel it now more than ever.

"Please be responsible while on the road!" Mrs. Beck calls out from the top of the stairs.

"You got it," I reply.

"I know *you'll* be responsible, Eren. I was referring to Harlow." Mrs. Beck winks.

"No promises," Harlow teases as I set her down.

She tucks her hair behind her ear, and I catch a glimpse of her–*our* tattoo. Seeing it takes me right back to Fai's living room that night. It's among the many other memories we had the chance to make before he passed away a few months back.

After my surgery, Harlow, Fai, and I released "*Write My Wrongs*," my debut album written by Harlow, Fai, and myself. It gained traction quickly, getting tons of radio spots and streams.

Shortly after the album's release, Fai passed away peacefully in his sleep… with a smile on his face. Harlow and I would make music with him in his studio, spending late nights cooking dinners. Fai would talk endlessly about how grateful he was to see me love Harlow the way he wasn't able to love Mom. He grew happier the closer he got to his final days, ready to be reunited with her.

"*I can hear her voice, kid,*" he told me one night. "*I can hear her beautiful voice calling for me. I'm ready to respond.*"

Having to let Fai go was hard, but it was something I could take on with Harlow and Blake by my side. Given Blake's experience losing Miranda, he made sure I dealt with loss the healthiest way I could. He showed me that *gratitude for what we have* will always triumph over *missing what's no longer with us*.

Since we released the album, Blake has received a plethora

of emails from artists asking us to write for them. So, now, here we are… leaving Sunday brunch at the Beck's to head west for the next project. We have no idea where we're going, but I guess you could say that's the point. *We're just following the current.*

The afternoon sky is painted in shades of orange and red as we claim the road ahead. I gently graze the top of my finger over my tattoo, turning over my shoulder to catch a glimpse of Harlow singing with Charlie in the back, her auburn hair blowing in the wind.

I've been through hell and back to find the peace I have now, and I'll never take this peace for granted. After all, it's not about the road, and it's never been about the road. It's about the moments shared with the ones willing to ride with you.

"Dada," Charlie blurts out from the back seat.

Blake suddenly pulls the car over and slams the brakes. Harlow covers her mouth, eyes wide open. We turn to Charlie.

"What did he just say?!" Blake shouts. The three of us stare at Charlie. He smiles up at us from his car seat, googly eyes bouncing between us. "Charlie, say that again. Say, '*Dada.*'"

"Dada," Charlie says again.

"Yes!" Blake shouts, pounding on the steering wheel. "My boy is gonna be a damn star!"

The four of us clap and laugh while pulling back onto the road.

"RA BA WONGS!" Charlie adds.

"Alright, alright," I reply. "I'll play '*Write My Wrongs,*' only because you asked nicely."

I change the song to "*Love is Calling,*" the first song on our album.

We start playing the album from the beginning because that's what we've been given.

A new beginning.

A chance to change the road we're on.

I reach my hand toward Harlow. She holds it as we close our eyes and listen to the music. There's no telling what tomorrow will bring, and I find peace in knowing that regardless of what happens next... I was able to right my wrongs.

FOLLOW THE MUSIC

To stream "*Love Is Calling*" and other songs written by Eren and Harlow, scan the Q.R. code below

or search "*Eren Gratis*" on any music streaming platform.

ACKNOWLEDGMENTS

I want to start off by thanking Eren and Harlow. To most readers, these two may be fictional characters. To me, they are so much more. They are symbols of my own personal hardships and struggles, so I am forever grateful for being able to pour my heart into these two.

This book tested me beyond belief, and I thank God for giving me the strength to push through. From the tight deadlines to discovering how lonely this writing journey can be, I rode some serious highs and lows. I broke down more than once. I put relationships on hold. I questioned whether or not I had what it took to see this through, and by the grace of God, this book has been written exactly the way I intended for it to be written.

Thank you, Mom, for not only being the first to read my drafts, but for always checking in. You saw the many different routes I considered taking this book, and it's safe to say that your guidance made *Write My Wrongs* a story worth telling.

I want to thank Taylor, Sammy, Austin, and Makayla. These amazing people offered me very valuable feedback that took this novel to a whole new level.

A big shout out and thank you to The Bookish Girls Team! Your notes and feedback really opened my eyes to new possibilities with my characters, settings, and the overall story. I'm forever grateful!

Lastly, I'm thankful for *you*… the person who read this far. When I write, I like to think that I have it all figured out, but I don't. The truth is, I'm learning as I go, and to have you alongside me means the world.

So, I thank you for reading. I thank you for diving into this world I've created. And I thank you for giving me a reason to keep telling stories.